ULVERSTON

ULVERSTON

12/96		- 3 JUL 1997
	-9	
	2 8 MAY 1997	- 6 NOV 1997
2 0 JAN 1997	2 0 JUN 1997	2 0 NOV 1997
		99
- 8 FEB 1997		1 8 DEC 1997
	1 0 JUL 1997	19
1 0 FEB 1997	- 2 JAN 1998	99
2 1 FEB 1997		
	- 7 AUG 1997	- 3 JAN 1998
1 1 MAR	1 1 AUG 1997	
		1 7 JAN 1998
2 7 MAR 1997	- 9 SEP 1997	3 0 JAN 1998 99
1 7 APR 1997	1 2 SEP 1997	KENDAL
2 4 APR 1997		2 0 FEB 1998
		2 8 FEB 1998
		1 4 MAR 1998

Heritage Services
LIBRARIES

This book is due for return on or before the last date above.
It may be renewed by personal application, post or
telephone, if not in demand.   3 0 MAR 1998
C.L. 18F

FLIGHT FROM HONOUR

FLIGHT FROM HONOUR

Gavin Lyall

Hodder & Stoughton

First published in Great Britain in 1996
by Hodder and Stoughton
A division of Hodder Headline PLC

British Library Cataloguing in Publication Data

Lyall, Gavin, 1932–
    Flight from honour
    1. English fiction – 20th century
    I. Title
    823.9'14 [F]

ISBN 0 340 68189 6

Typeset by Palimpsest Book Production Limited,
Polmont, Stirlingshire
Printed and bound in Great Britain by
Mackays of Chatham PLC, Chatham, Kent

Hodder and Stoughton
A division of Hodder Headline PLC
338 Euston Road
London NW1 3BH

1

The little fishing boat didn't take shape in the dawn mist until long after the creak of its oars and the irregular slap of water had reached the shore. Then it gradually grew detail and colour as it scraped its way past bigger boats into Muggia's inner harbour. Any watcher might have wondered why it was back so much later than other boats in the local fleet. However, nobody was bothering to watch, since everyone in the village knew it had paused to take on a Mysterious Stranger from an Italian ship in the Gulf. But the Stranger himself was city-bred and still believed he was on a Secret Mission as he stepped on to the fish-scaled and slippery quayside.

Although he was shivering with cold and damp, he still saw the huddled village as having the charm of a stage set. And indeed, if anybody had written an opera about fishermen of the North Adriatic, he could have taken the whole inner harbour, with its boats and cluttered quays, and fitted it onto the stage of La Scala. Only the tiny castle in the background and the narrow alleys leading off in all directions, and already beflagged with damp washing, would have needed to be painted on the backdrop.

One of the two fishermen led him through an arch and into a raucous café in the corner of the town hall. Five centuries of Austrian rule hadn't much changed the Venetian buildings – there was still a carved Lion of St Mark set into the stonework above the café – nor the straight-nosed faces and brown hair of the inhabitants.

The Stranger was small, with dark lank hair, a thin sharp face and spectacles which he had continually to wipe clear in the steamy indoors warmth. Being Parisian, he asked for a large coffee and a cognac, which surprised the fisherman. On the other hand, the brandy he was given surprised the Stranger. Then everybody else politely didn't notice as he surreptitiously paid the fisherman for the voyage and was taken out to the road that ran around the bay and the shipbuilding yards into Trieste.

The Café San Marco was far larger but, in contrast with the deliberate Italian dignity of other big cafés in Trieste, had a comfortable Mittel-Europa sprawl. It could have been in any one of a dozen cities of the Austrian empire: Prague, Budapest, Salzburg or Sarajevo. Indeed, in that summer of 1913, many would have said that the rule of the Viennese café was stronger than that of the aged Emperor in Vienna. And they would have said it in just such a place, with its darkened gilt frescoes, marble and mirrors, among the old men playing chess, students doing their homework, writers writing, artists arguing and journalists reading themselves in the newspapers on cane frames handed round by the waiters. And two men who might have called themselves middle-aged doing nothing but talk as quietly as they could in a busy café at mid-morning.

The one with the bony, ascetic face and deep-set eyes was a count, a Venetian title equal to a marquis from anywhere else, or so Venetian counts said. He was dressed with dignified raffishness in a wide hat, floppy maroon bow-tie and a short light cape, whilst his delicate fingers with their jewelled rings constantly fondled a silver-topped cane.

Senator Giancarlo Falcone – who was using neither his rank nor his real name in Trieste – was shorter but strong and bulky in comparison with the Count's apparent fragility. He had a large and hooked but very thin nose that could have looked sinister if it hadn't been set in a reassuringly meaty face with prominent dark eyes and an easy smile. His crinkled hair was now white and thinning out, and while you would remember him as well dressed and groomed, you wouldn't remember just how because it seemed impersonal. In the same way, he looked successful but not at anything that touched him deeply.

He looked at his wristwatch but all he said was: "I heard that they invented these for Santos-Dumont, the aviator."

"Is that why you wear one?" The Count's Italian was Triestine, Falcone's Piedmontese, but they had no problem understanding each other.

"No." Falcone gestured at his jacket, buttoned so high that it showed only a brief triangle of shirt behind his necktie. "How can I reach a proper watch under this?"

2

"You are a slave of fashion," the Count observed.

"Perhaps," Falcone said comfortably.

The Count sipped at the tiny coffee cup. Small delicate things seemed right for him; you couldn't imagine him lifting a pint of beer. "I regret the passing of frock coats. Does anybody wear them nowadays?"

"In Italy, only royalty, diplomatists and the more corrupt of my colleagues. I regret them, too. But they need skilled cutting to hang properly at the back and should not be worn by anyone who hurries. Of course, in London you still see many."

"Are you going there?"

Falcone nodded slowly. "Probably. Brussels first, but most likely I will find what we need in London. I could be there about the middle of September – do you yet know the date of the relief?"

"October the second."

Falcone nodded. "Time enough. And your new friends – they will accept such gifts from you without suspicion?"

"I was talking only the other day with the Commandante, preparing the ground, arousing his interest . . . Ah, I believe this is the lad now."

Falcone didn't turn, he just watched the Count's eyes watching over his shoulder. "He looks young," the Count said. "Now he has seen Aldo's magazine and carnation. He is going across . . . he introduces himself . . . he sits down . . . Aldo is summoning a waiter; how imperiously he does it. Servants are much better at grandeur than we poor aristocrats."

"Is anybody following him?"

"As I said, they needn't follow him in here: the waiters are all spies for the police or somebody."

"Then why are we meeting here – like café conspirators?"

"Because the waiters in every other respectable café are spies, too. You can't expect a good waiter to live on the sort of tips I give. And I am known to have been conspiring in here for twenty years: it would seem most suspicious if I were seen conspiring elsewhere." He leant back and blew a delicate cloud of smoke that was immediately swirled away by the passing rush of a waiter. "Believe me, this is the only way; you've forgotten just what a small world Trieste is. But I'm not being flippant about the dangers. Not only from the Austrians, but now the Slovenes."

"Slovenes? Those farmers from the Carso?"

"A little more, in these days. Now the Slovenes are given money to develop what they call their 'folk arts', and are favoured in recruiting for the police. So they hope to keep us Italians in our place and the Slovenes too busy to concoct their own plots. The Austrians can find a lazy way of doing anything, even govern an empire. But sometimes it works, so I beg you, take great care, particularly when you leave Trieste."

"I shall be leaving this afternoon for Venice," Falcone muttered, his unease back in full spate. "Now, can we get this settled . . . ?"

"You can look round now. He's busy talking to Aldo."

Falcone turned as if searching for a waiter and gave the Parisian a swift raking stare. "His clothes are a disgrace. Just looking at him, you'd know he crept ashore in a basket of fish."

"You judge men too much by their clothes."

"But the police judge men by the way they enter a country."

"The boy knows nothing of our proposals, he's merely to tell us if, and when, the Poet will be . . . available. And dealing with the Poet one has to accept a little flamboyant secrecy." The Count lit a cigarette and fitted it into a long amber holder. "Did you hear the charade of his fleeing Paris, the first time he went to Arcachon? All midnight meetings and smuggling his trunks from hotel to hotel. It's a wonder all Paris didn't turn out to watch."

Still looking irritated, Falcone asked: "From whom was he fleeing that time? – debtors or a woman?"

"Both, I imagine. He doesn't do things by halves. Which is what we're counting on, are we not? We need his name, his reputation."

"Yes, yes of course." Falcone spoke abstractedly. He was staring down at the table-top, at the empty cups, the coffee stains and cigarette ash on the cloth, then he glanced slowly around at the scurrying, weaving waiters and heard the continual clatter of crockery and conversation. He shook his head.

The Count did a good job of reading his thoughts and said dryly but sympathetically: "Yes, life all seems so mundane and unalterable. And sometimes one looks at a woman and knows what she's expecting and wonders how in the world one can ever . . . But you rise to the occasion when the time comes. I imagine it's much the same for soldiers in battle. But perhaps some men, like the Poet, don't suffer such doubts. They live on a grander scale. And set us an example so that, occasionally, we can achieve grandeur, too. We Italians are particularly susceptible to that. And that's also what we're counting on, is it not? Now, I told you nobody would follow the messenger in here, so should I signal Aldo to bring him over?"

Despite his anxiety, Falcone smiled wryly. "Your cynicism doesn't lack grandeur, old friend."

"Cynicism is my daily bread," the Count said simply. "I do not live for bread; it enables me to live. Now, shall we hear the news from Arcachon?"

2

The room was damp. It had been damp in high summer and would go on being damp the year round until the whole tenement around it fell down, probably because of the damp. But the stones would survive, as they had outlived being part of the Roman amphitheatre buried below, then in the walls of a Venetian warehouse, and would probably outlive whatever was built next. Yet still the damp would come trickling down from the Castello on the hill behind and rise up through them like sap through a tree – although it would help if the cats were fewer and with better manners. Less than a hundred yards from the city's Chamber of Commerce and its fanciest shopping street, Triestines would go on living in such tenements.

But not the two men sitting at a scarred table in a ground-floor room; they only rented it by the hour for irregular meetings. And for the elder of them, a slight, bespectacled and grey-bearded man in an academic jumble of clothes, no meeting yet had been more irregular. He was nervously recounting little stacks of gold coins – English sovereigns, Napoleons, German 20-mark and Austrian 20-crown pieces – a deliberately random collection. They had just finished an anxious argument about how it was to be spent.

"Fourteen hundred crowns – as near as possible," he said miserably. "Is that high or low, for a man's life?"

"Distinctly high. But it includes the cost of travel, and for Jankovic as well. And these are supposed to be men of skill and experience." The second man was squat and muscular, with a moustache that was neither too individual nor too humble, but trimmed to place him precisely in the hierarchy of his trade or profession. However, his clothes gave no clue to what that was, since he had taken most of them off and was preparing to put on a long thick black cloak. He wasn't hurrying, because the room was greasy-warm as well as damp.

"And I hope you understand that, with all the hurry, most of this had to come from the Governor's fund to promote our folk arts." They were both speaking the local Slav dialect.

"The Governor doesn't care what we do with the money. He certainly doesn't give a fart for our arts, he just wants to play us off against the Italians. And that's fine with me: I'm going to have an important Italian played right off the field."

"But how do I explain what's happened to the money?"

"You're the Treasurer, what do you usually say? Claim an Italian embezzled it. The rush isn't my fault, it's that unburied corpse of a Count suddenly coming up with a real plot for once."

"You aren't going to do anything to him?" The Treasurer became even more worried.

"No. For him, I need real proof. He's too much of an ancient monument." He sounded regretful, all the same. "*And* he's been sucking up to the Governor lately. But he can't be the ring-leader of whatever they're plotting, not from a table in the San Marco."

"So you're no closer to finding out what that is?"

"I *haven't* found out, anyway. The French boy was just carrying messages he didn't understand. I had to pretend to be on their side, and he'd have got suspicious if I'd started stubbing out cigars on his balls." He squinted at his watch, lying on the table, and began buttoning the black cape.

The Treasurer took a deep breath and said: "Then we – you – are going to have a man done to death without even knowing what he's guilty of?"

"I know he's guilty of trying to start a war between Austria and Italy. What else? – it's the only way they can ever own Trieste. They may *think* they can steal the foundations without the house falling down, that the Austrians won't fight for their only real port, but . . . whoever wins such a war, it won't be us."

He shook his cape fiercely. "This is too damned hot to get angry in. I'm going to boil inside it." He shook it again to let more air in. "And if sending an interfering Italian by express train to Hell prevents a war, it's cheap at the price . . . They'll be here in a few minutes: Jankovic will show them up. You and the money just stay out of sight until we come down again."

*   *   *

The small room at the top of the tenement was also damp, but at least the broken shutters leaked in a little air that didn't smell as if a mule had just belched it. It was lit only by a single candle, its flame wavering in the draught. On the table beside it, spread on a black cloth like religious relics, were an ornate dagger, a little wooden cross, a pistol and a small blue bottle.

The man in the black cape, now wearing an executioner's hood as well, said in sonorous Italian: "The bottle contains a deadly poison."

The other two men looked at it. Both were dark, wearing tightly buttoned black suits and broad-brimmed, high-crowned hats. It was helpful in that light that one was a head taller than the other; his name was Silvio (he said) and he was the one with some brains; now he was looking at the bottle sceptically. In fact it was filled with tap water – but from a tap in the tiny courtyard behind the building, so the masked man reckoned he might have been telling the truth.

"You will swear," he said, still keeping his voice low and ponderous. He indicated the smaller man, Bozan. "You will swear first. Repeat after me: I swear by the sun that warms me . . ."

"I swear by the sun that warms me." Bozan had no problem in sounding toneless. He spoke seldom, and usually as if his voice and what it was saying were quite separate from anything he might think or feel – if indeed he did either. The fashionable mind-doctors in Vienna would have a banquet with this one, but it was policemen who knew the type and the only cure: on the next train or under it. Then call the doctor.

"By the earth that nourishes me . . ."

"By the earth that nourishes me."

"Before God, by the blood of my ancestors . . . On my honour and on my life . . . That I will from this moment until my death . . . Be faithful to the laws of this society—"

Silvio suddenly burst out: "We didn't come here to join any fornicating society and promise a load of pigshit! You hired us to do a job. The only thing we'll swear is that if you don't come up with the money we'll stuff you and your society both up the arsehole of your ancestors! Isn't that right?"

"Quite right," Bozan said, just as solemnly as he'd been swearing selfless loyalty a moment before. I was right about him, the masked man thought. In fact I was right about both. He tried to restrain a satisfied smile, then remembered the hood concealed it anyway.

"But we must be assured of your true dedication to our cause," he protested.

"You show us gold and we'll show you dedication," Silvio assured him.

"But the other Committee members of the Ujedinjenje—"

"Piss on the other Committee members. If they want a load of oath-swearing, let them pick a couple of students who can't wipe their own arses or recognise a police detective if they fell over him. We're professional men."

The man with the shovel who walks behind the Emperor's horse has a more prickly pride than the Emperor himself, the hooded man reflected. But he persisted. "I have the first instalment downstairs. In various gold pieces, as you requested. But I must insist that you remember you are working for the Ujedinjenje ili Smrt." He was determined to get that name into their heads. Into Silvio's, anyway. "And the vengeance of the Ujedinjenje ili Smrt has a long arm—"

"And a black hand at the end of it – if you read the newspapers. Is that why it has to turn to us when it needs a proper job done?"

"Very well. If you will follow me downstairs . . ." Even for that short time he felt uneasy having them behind him.

*   *   *

The vibrations of the Treasurer's nerves were almost audible as Silvio counted the coins and moved his lips in currency exchanges. In the grey light his face seemed an unfinished sculpture, all the features too prominent and the skin rough and pocked. At last he seemed satisfied with his own arithmetic and pushed the coins over to Bozan, who began to play with them, stacking, shuffling, mixing them, and tipping them to watch the glints. He seemed happy, inasmuch as he seemed anything; his face was round, smooth and frighteningly innocent and untouched.

The man in the hood and cape had kept them on and was stifling, but he went doggedly on. "His name is Senator Giancarlo Falcone. He used a different name here – Vascotti – perhaps you'd remember that, he may always use it again. But we're quite sure of who he is. His father was Triestine. Now comes the difficult part – which is

9

why we need men of your great experience." He paused for either man to show he'd taken in the flattery, but got nothing. Silvio's tetchiness seemed assuaged by the sight of gold and he sat calmly waiting; Bozan was still playing with the coins like pretty beach pebbles.

"He has a villa near Venice and another in Turin. We believe he's there now. But we don't want him killed in Italy if possible. The Italian police will invent their own motives and play politics with it. So I want you to go to Turin – do you know it?"

"Like my mother's purse." Silvio had relaxed enough to smile, showing uneven teeth, probably broken in the early days when he was making a reputation on victims who fought back.

"Good. Find lodgings and send the address to Jankovic, care of the Poste Restante there. He will make arrangements for you, he knows languages, other countries, you can rely on him. But we rely on you for the real work." This was delicate ground; honour was involved. "And that will come when Falcone leaves Italy."

"Is he suspicious?"

The hooded man paused, trying to think as well as stifle. "In Trieste he was jumping at his own footsteps. But he isn't used to being suspicious, so it probably comes and goes. He's important, so he thinks he's clever, which should make it easier for you."

Silvio might have agreed, but wasn't going to show it. He just grunted.

"If you have no questions . . . ? The Committee has one other request, but it's no more than that." He groped under his cape and laid an automatic pistol on the table, politely keeping the muzzle pointed towards himself. "We'd be grateful for your opinion on this if you care to use it in the execution. You may already know it: the new English Webley .455-inch."

Bozan had stopped playing with the coins and was staring at the gun with glistening eyes. Then his pudgy little hands stabbed like biting snakes, seized the pistol and flickered over it like snakes' tongues, finding the magazine catch, snapping the empty magazine out and in again, cocking the action, sighting it . . . in a moment he seemed to have a lifetime's experience of it. The Treasurer stared with horrified fascination.

The hooded man laid two handfuls of short, heavy cartridges on the table and watched them snatched up and slipped expertly into the magazine. He glanced at Silvio, ignoring the theory that you

10

watched the eyes of the man with the gun. He was relieved to see that the other, more normal, eyes seemed quite calm.

So he continued: "You note that it fires an exceptionally heavy bullet for an automatic pistol. This may or may not be to your taste. There might also – for us – be the advantage that, if the bullet is recovered and identified, the English Secret Service could get the blame. But that's a small matter."

Silvio smiled and stood up. "We'll think about it. Now put it away and come along, Bozan."

Bozan unbuttoned the bottom of his jacket and swiftly tucked the pistol out of sight. Silvio then made the mistake of reaching for the gold; Bozan's hands slapped down on the pile and he made a whining sound like a disappointed dog. Silvio sighed. "All right. You can play with them later, but bring them along now." His look challenged the other two to comment, but they said nothing. In fact, the Treasurer was holding his breath, and went on holding it until they heard the front door crash shut. Then he let out an enormous gasp.

The man in the hood ripped it off and gulped for air, red-faced and streaming sweat. "Sweet Jesus forgive me for ever having eaten lobster." He took a half-smoked cigar from a saucer and relit it, breathing the smoke as if it were all the scents of Paradise. "And where in God's name did you find that hood? It smelled as if a dog had died in it. Also I must have swallowed a kilo of fluff." He spat to prove it.

The Treasurer was staring at his own hands on the table-top. "I'm still shaking. Just look. Where do you find people like that?"

"It's my job to find people like that. And their job depends on being found." He stood up and began unbuttoning the cloak. "And what do you expect mercenary assassins to be like? – it isn't a job you drift into because the baker doesn't need an apprentice."

The Treasurer nodded gloomily. "That Bozan . . . is he the one who does the killing?"

"I'd imagine so."

"I don't want to imagine any more than I've seen." Then, immediately contradicting himself: "Imagine having him after you . . ."

"It's all they exist for – but Jankovic will keep them in order. Without him, they'd be lost north of the Alps." He had stripped off the cloak and the shabby old trousers that might have showed beneath it. He bundled them into an old travelling bag. "And don't forget all the junk upstairs."

"Was all that business with the oath really necessary? And did you have to give them a gun? Seeing the way that Bozan . . ." He shivered.

"Men like that want to know who they're working for. They don't care, they just like to know. So now they think they're working for Colonel Apis and his regicides in Belgrade. And that's all they can tell anybody if they get caught. Nothing to do with Austria or us, just the Serbs. Nobody looks for motives from them."

"Are they likely to get caught? And all that money going to waste?"

The other paused in his dressing to give the Treasurer a twisted smile. "Now I hear the ring of true concern. No, of course not, not before they kill Falcone. They won't have done anything to be caught for. But afterwards . . ." he shrugged and smiled; "there's always the chance of Jankovic dropping a hint that they had a gun like that. It's still quite rare."

"So if they use that gun, it betrays them?"

"Betrayal? You talk of *betraying* that trash? Do you really want them wandering free?"

"No, of course not," the Treasurer said hastily. "Just . . ." Then he changed the subject. "So all that about the English Secret Service was nonsense, too? Thank God. We certainly don't want them involved. Aren't they supposed to be the best in the world?"

"One hears things." He had buttoned up his working clothes and picked most of the fluff out of his scalp. "But they're only men." He put on his cap and looked around, but there wasn't a mirror in the room. Quite likely not in the whole building. "How do I look?"

The Treasurer hardly glanced at him. "Like what our *masters* pay you to be: an upright and honourable Captain of Police."

3

Brussel's civilian aerodrome lay in the south-eastern suburb of Etterbeek, only a few minutes by train from the Quartier-Leopold station. It didn't look impressive, but aerodromes never did: just a few stark wooden sheds floating on the last of the early morning mist. But to O'Gilroy it could have been the new Jerusalem.

He headed for a group of men standing back from a single monoplane which was being fussed over by a couple of mechanics. Most of them were clearly Belgian; that is, wearing gloomy dark suits or sombre, sturdy overcoats. One man stood out in his light fawn suit, light hat and a bronze-coloured overcoat draped dashingly around his shoulders. O'Gilroy decided this must be his man, and shook his head disapprovingly at his prominence.

"Excuse me, sir, but would ye be Senator Fal-con-e?" He pronounced the name as if reading it, badly.

"Yes?" Falcone looked at him critically. The new man was tall and loose-limbed inside a rather stiff tweed suit of the sort Continental cartoonists used, accurately, to denote Britons travelling abroad. He had a lean, bony face, dark hair under a tweed cap, and a wry, almost sneering expression.

Now he nodded. "The Embassy said ye wanted someone to watch yer back. I'm it. Conall O'Gilroy."

They shook hands. O'Gilroy went on: "I asked for ye at the hotel and they said I'd be finding ye out here. No trouble at all, they jest told me."

He sighed when Falcone didn't see the import of that, just saying: "Very good. Are you armed?"

"I am." O'Gilroy made no move to prove it.

"Very good," Falcone said again. "So now . . . ah, you will guard me, no?"

"Ye think someone's trying to kill ye?"

13

The blunt question disconcerted Falcone. "Ah, I am not . . . How can I be sure?"

"Ye'd best make up yer mind. I like to know if I'm saving yer life or jest standing around looking pretty."

Falcone glared; this was *not* the way a bravo should act. As a senior senator, his demand for help from the British embassy had been instinctive. But the shadowy figures glimpsed in the streets of a strange city seemed mere fancies on this bright morning in the familiar – to him – atmosphere of an aerodrome. He felt annoyed at himself and transferred it easily to O'Gilroy.

"I am a senator in Italy and I am to meet with your Foreign Office in London," he announced firmly. "I have been followed, I am sure of it. There are two men – one is tall, the other is short. And yesterday a man with a Slav accent asked at the hotel if I stayed there. He did not want to meet me, just to know if I am there."

"Is there a good reason they'd want to kill ye?" O'Gilroy asked calmly. That didn't help, because Falcone wasn't going to answer truthfully. He looked around, and saw that the little group around the aeroplane was dispersing and the pilot climbing in . . .

"I must go for a flight now. It is arranged a long time, but it will be quick. We will talk when I am back."

"Arranged a long time? – so plenty of people know about it?"

"What you think is not possible. I am worried about guns, knives—"

"They're not the only way to kill ye. Anything else happen?"

"No, no—" Then he seemed to remember something, and quietened into a puzzled frown.

A stout man with a moustache you could have hunted tigers in came up beside them, tipped his homburg hat to Falcone and spoke swiftly in French.

Glad of the distraction, Falcone explained: "The aeroplane is waiting. Now I must—"

"Now hold on," O'Gilroy persisted. "I'm not being buggered about like this. What yer life counts to yerself, I'd not be knowing. What it counts to me is a job done proper."

Falcone renewed his glare. "Your embassy told me—"

"Sod the embassy, yer dealing with *me*. What else happened?"

The stout man was looking at O'Gilroy with a good deal of distaste. Falcone smiled weakly and resumed the conversation in French. The stout man shrugged and walked away.

"The pilot will do a . . . a flying test first," Falcone said. "But *then*, most certainly I will go . . ."

"So what happ—"

"Today, as I leave the hotel, there is a box sent to me. I leave late, it should have come after I am gone . . . perhaps that is the plan. It says on it – in Italian – 'Good luck in the flight. Please give to Senator Falcone when he returns'."

"What was in it?"

"I was late, hurrying, I did not open it."

The engine of the aeroplane sputtered into life, briefly clouding the pilot in smoke, then settled to a steady buzz. A couple of mechanics took hold of the wingtips and swung the machine round, then guided it out across the worn and oil-stained grass.

To Falcone's relief, this fascinated O'Gilroy; at least it stopped his cross-examination.

"Do you know aeroplanes?"

O'Gilroy's sneer turned to a wry smile. "I've read all I can about them, but never been up in one."

"Ah. It is magnificent." Falcone grabbed the chance to reassert himself. "A new world. I am an aeronaut, in Italy I am one of the first ever to fly. But two years ago, I am in a crash and my back . . ." He patted himself around his kidneys.

O'Gilroy nodded, forced himself to look suspiciously around the little scatter of spectators, then concentrated on the aeroplane.

Having positioned it about fifty yards away, the mechanics stood aside. The engine buzzed more fiercely, the aeroplane rolled forward and its tail lifted. It did two long bounces and rose just above the ground. Standing a pace behind Falcone, O'Gilroy saw the Senator's shoulders lift, unconsciously urging the machine upwards. He smiled briefly.

The aeroplane climbed steadily, swaying a little, then tipped into a turn to the left. It kept climbing.

"Would it be a Blériot, then?" O'Gilroy asked.

"The design is of a Blériot but is made here with changes by a Belgian company."

"And what engine does it have?"

"A Gnome rotary. You know the rotary engine?"

"Read about it."

"It is imbecile, but it works. The whole engine turning round with the propeller, and the . . . the crankshaft staying still, fixed to the aeroplane. And oil – *poosh!*" He jerked his hands explosively. "Oil everywhere. But it is light of weight and has very little vibration."

The aeroplane levelled out, having circled until it was back over the aerodrome, then its nose dipped and a few seconds later, the puttering engine noise died.

"Ah, he cuts the . . . the ignition," Falcone said, enjoying being in charge again. "With the rotary engine, you do not use so much the air and petrol controls, it is more simple to stop the ignition."

The aeroplane was drifting down – vol-planing, they called it – to come in to land.

"I think he will need just a little more of the engine," Falcone predicted. "He does not want to—"

Then the aeroplane *writhed* and something big twisted off: the whole engine and propeller. Unbalanced, the aeroplane reared on its tail. "*Madre di Dio!*" Falcone whispered.

Then, delayed by distance, they heard the engine backfire, buzz for a moment, and cut out. The aeroplane flopped forward and immediately reared again, twisted, and the pilot fell out. The tiny figure fell, arms and legs flailing, with a horrible purposefulness that the fluttering, prancing aeroplane lacked. Then they heard his scream.

It went on long after he had hit the ground in a puff of dust. It ended as the aeroplane struck, turning from a shape into a heap in a bigger cloud of dust. They heard that crash, and then it was over. No fire, just the drifting dust and running men.

"I don't think me pistol'd have saved ye from that," O'Gilroy observed.

Back at the Grand Hotel, O'Gilroy watched as Falcone undid the wrapped box. Inside, resting on crumpled newspaper, lay a single white lily. And a crudely drawn picture of a gun, a dagger and a bottle marked *veleno*.

Falcone had gone stiff and pale, but also perplexed.

"What's it mean?" O'Gilroy asked.

"The Ujedinjenje ili Smrt . . . It is a secret society of Serbia . . . But I not understand Serbia . . . Why do they want to kill me?"

O'Gilroy didn't know, either, but was content that Falcone now believed somebody really did. It made it easier to keep him alive. "So what's yer plans now?"

Falcone came to a firm decision. "I want to go to England. Will you come also?"

"Sure, I'm due back. I'll—"

"The hotel will get us tickets on the boat for tonight."

"No. Give me some money and *I'll* get the tickets. Ye stick here and pack. Have ye got a gun of yer own?"

Falcone found it in his overcoat pocket: it was identical to O'Gilroy's own, a Belgian-made Browning automatic.

"Fine. Shoot anyone who comes in. Except me."

4

Perhaps quite unintentionally, the September sun stared brightly in through the southern windows of the Secret Service Bureau. However, it was only half past ten in the morning and the Bureau was, after all, a Government office, so as yet there was hardly anyone there to notice the indiscretion. Captain Matthew Ranklin, Royal Artillery, was one of the few, but he was shuffling papers in an office on the far side of their set of attic-shaped rooms and his window faced west to the roof of the new War Office building.

Major Dagner came in. It was only his second day in the office and he still wore uniform, which Ranklin had hinted wasn't strictly necessary in the Secret Service. Dagner had thanked him politely but pointed out that, living so near the War Office, it virtually counted as a disguise. The uniform was Indian Army, a Gurkha regiment, and had the DSO heading a row of campaign ribbons. He put his cap and stick on a table and tossed his gloves into the cap. "Is the Chief in?"

Ranklin nodded towards the sound-proofed inner door. "He's still saying his goodbyes to the stenographers."

The Commander (Ranklin flatly refused to call him 'Chief', that was a stoker's rank) was going on holiday, much delayed whilst he waited for Dagner's arrival. At least, he called it a 'holiday' but what it involved was letting his moustache grow, kitting himself out with a high-buttoned green hunting jacket, Tyrolean hat, a swordstick, and booking a ticket for Bavaria. Most of the Bureau seemed to think this was absolutely wonderful, particularly since the old boy spoke so little German. Ranklin thought it was monumentally childish.

But there was a lot of the child left in the Commander. And Ranklin had begun to see the value of his stubbornness and

18

wilfulness when it came to protecting the young Bureau from more carnivorous Government departments.

Anyway, once the Commander had gone, there might be a chance to get the place organised. Right now, he was browsing through the annual Confidential Reports of the four young officers who had just joined them. He opened a new one and lit his pipe.

"Nice day again," Dagner said, staring down into the street. "I still can't grasp how much London's changed. All these new buildings; Whitehall's being completely taken over by Government offices – and motor-cars. London used to smell like a stable-yard; now it stinks like an engine-room. All in ten years."

Ranklin raised his eyebrows. "You must have been home on leave at some time in that long?"

"I'm afraid I haven't got a home in England," Dagner corrected gently. "And not even any close relatives here by now."

Ranklin scowled inwardly at having forgotten that the Indian Army officers did tend to belong in India. Or thought they did. Dagner had made his name (secretly, that is) playing the "Great Game", probably disguised as a tribesman on the North-West Frontier, and he looked very much the part. As, of course, he would have had to: lean, dark-haired, a hawk face still bronzed by the sun or the last coating of walnut juice or whatever they used. Now he had come to be the Commander's deputy and pass on his expertise to the new Bureau and its crew of enthusiastic but as yet mostly amateur agents. Or, as Ranklin preferred to put it, spies.

Dagner turned from the window. "The Chief was saying yesterday that, in the interests of secrecy, he felt I should be known as Major X." He might have been slightly embarrassed, but it was difficult to tell with that controlled face. He hurried on: "And, by the same token, you should be Captain Y."

Ranklin frowned. "I'm not sure that I want to be Captain Why?"

"Ah. Yes indeed. Then I suggest you take to signing papers Captain R and present him with a *fait accompli* when he gets back. Is that the training programme?"

"No, just the new chaps' CR's. I'll get down to the programme once he's gone."

Dagner smiled as sympathetically as his face allowed. "We must have a chat about our new boys . . . How did you get landed with the training?"

"I complained once too often about how little I'd been taught myself, and the Commander said Fine, you're in charge of drawing up a programme, then."

"The old Army game. Have you done this sort of thing before?"

"I did my three years as adjutant."

"Splendid," Dagner murmured. "May I ask what the programme will comprise?"

Ranklin tried not to look rueful. "I don't think we can give them more than a light dusting of practical skills: following people and spotting if you're being followed, lock-picking and so forth."

"And its real aim?"

Ranklin acknowledged this with a nod; a proper training programme should have an ulterior purpose. "To teach them *not* to be Army officers – which they've been learning to be ever since they left school." And seeing the frown starting on Dagner's face, added quickly: "Europe's a civilian society."

"Yes. Yes, of course. I must get used to that. And nothing we teach them can be as valuable as experience, but ..." Then, as if wanting to get something off his chest but unsure about whether or not it was a Shameful Episode: "I dined with Sir Aylmer Corbin of the Foreign Office last night. Do you know him?"

"Met him." Ranklin quietly began to fill his pipe, watching Dagner's face. Behind its control, he thought he recognised the look on the faces of men coming out of their first battle: sheer disbelief that the world could be like that.

"I just can't accept that I heard what I think I was told. That while I'm in command here, I'm expected to do nothing. *Nothing.* That the Chief's great failing was that he would send people to places and do things, and that I was expected to redress the balance ... Just whose side are those people on?"

Ranklin tried to radiate sympathy and had a good face for that. In many ways he was the physical opposite of Dagner: fair-haired, shortish but not too tubby, at least not to his own mind, and with a round schoolboy face on which he usually wore a small hopeful smile that adjusted easily to the sympathetic. In any case, the hopefulness was entirely deceptive, belonging with his current "disguise" as a middle-ranking civil servant dedicated to the future of his pension and the Empire. And nobody could now force him back into uniform since he had thankfully shaved the regulation moustache which, even at the age of thirty-eight, had grown only as a juvenile fluff.

"Some do say," he said, sucking experimentally on his pipe, "that, being the Foreign Office, they represent foreigners. Myself, I think that's too simple, because whatever the FO is, it isn't simple."

Dagner's smile was cold and brief. "But we're an official Government department – or Bureau – as well. What do they expect of us?"

"Oh, I think Sir Aylmer was quite straight with you there: they want nothing. Or, at most, to take us over themselves and disband us. But I fancy that the sub-committee which thought us up foresaw that; that's why they put us under the protection of the big, bold Admiralty and with a Naval man in charge.

"I suppose—" he put a match to his pipe and began puffing up a smokescreen; "—that they see our very existence as a standing reproof: that they can't learn everything by their own methods. And to be fair, we may occasionally tread on their toes. Perhaps the problem with Europe is that, if we're caught, we *don't* usually get quietly tortured to death and dumped in a ditch. It can happen, of course, but we're more likely to get a well-publicised trial producing a Diplomatic Incident, which means our ambassador there gets a roasting, the FO here gets a wigging from the Cabinet *and* His Majesty – and we sit in the shadows saying smugly: 'But we don't exist, you can't blame us.' That's the way the FO sees it, anyway."

A true, slow smile broke across Dagner's stern face. "Thank you, Captain . . . R," he said formally. "I can see I've got a lot to learn. But the Chief said that I could rely on you, as the senior agent present, for an uncompromising view of our work and its problems."

That startled Ranklin. Senior agent? – he had only been with the Bureau for nine months, only "home" in London – which had never been his home – for the past two weeks. Granted they had been busy months, and he was probably the oldest in the office bar the Commander and Dagner himself, but *senior?* Of course, Dagner had said "present", so it might be that the Continent was crawling with the Bureau's more experienced and skilled spies, too valuable to keep in London. But Ranklin doubted it.

"Nice of him to say so," he mumbled.

"So I hope you'll forgive me if I rely rather heavily on you until I find my feet."

"Oh, quite, yes, of course."

Then the Commander came out of his inner office to shake hands with Dagner while still patting the shoulder of a rather tearful stenographer who was telling him to be sure not to get into trouble with the nasty Germans, and calling for someone to find a taxi.

Finally he shook Ranklin's hand, said: "Get everything organised so that I can ruin it when I get back, Captain," and chuckled loudly. "And don't forget that Sir Caspar Alerion's coming to lecture you all on Friday. Give him my regards and apologies. Don't come down to see me off." Then he drew and flourished his swordstick, nearly emasculating a hanging light, and was gone in a swirl of green cloak.

Nobody wanted to be the first to speak after that exit. Ranklin began cleaning out his pipe, gradually others began a gentle bustle, and then Dagner said: "Very well, then. I suppose I'd better say a few words to set the pace for the coming weeks. Captain, would you make sure everybody's here in, say, five minutes?" He went through into the Commander's sound-proofed inner room.

Ranklin directed the rearrangement of chairs into a rough line. Three of the new recruits were Army officers, one a Marine, and all around thirty years old. They had trickled in over the past week and he knew very little about them apart from their reports. And CR's were tricky things, supposedly frank assessments by former CO's, but seen by the reportee himself. It helped if you knew the CO's – which he didn't – and could read between the lines, which he had been trying to do.

He gave a mental shrug; whatever the CR's said, these were the people he had to try and train. And it wasn't your seniors who forced you into believing in what you were doing, it was having damned juniors whom you mustn't disillusion.

After precisely five minutes, Dagner reappeared. He stood looking at them for a moment, cautiously tested a table for its solidity, then sat on the corner of it, swinging one long leg. "Smoke if you want to," he invited them, then began: "We – you and I – are all new boys in this Bureau. Although I've played the Game out in India for a few years, already I've realised that I've got a great deal to *unlearn* in the very different climate of Europe. So we're starting at the bottom of the ladder together."

He had an easy confidence, Ranklin conceded. It took that to admit ignorance to subordinates yet be sure you wouldn't lose their respect.

"But one thing I think I shall find is the same: that there comes a time when all the scaffolding of authority falls away and you have to stand alone. And it is not how you cope with that loneliness that will make you an effective agent but how you do more than cope, how you decide and act." He paused, then went on thoughtfully, almost diffidently: "It can help to remember that at such moments you are working *directly* for your country. The link is simple and unimpeded. I suggest you let that be your guide.

"Now —" he relaxed and let a small, friendly smile show; "—we aren't going to send you out equipped with only a few noble thoughts. Captain . . . R is laying on a training programme to give you some basic knowledge and skills that you'll find useful in the field. That will begin—" A telephone rang and Ranklin almost knocked over his chair in reaching it.

"I thought I asked you not to put any calls through here," he whispered huskily.

The telephone girl was unimpressed. "It's Mr O'Gilroy, sir."

"All right, I'll come out there. Don't lose him." He hung up, nodded apologetically at Dagner and tiptoed out.

The outermost room of the suite was both spartan and had the Feminine Touch, being staffed by girls, and one widow, of good naval and military families. All wore a semi-uniform of dark skirt and demure high-necked white blouse fixed with a bow-tie or cameo brooch. Somebody – perhaps they had organised a rota – brought in fresh flowers for each desk every day, and there were cheerfully dull prints of Scottish landscapes on the walls.

The telephonist indicated a spare instrument, then did something brisk and technical with her wires and plugs. Ranklin picked up the earpiece and said: "Hello?"

O'Gilroy sounded very stilted and exaggeratedly Irish. "Matt? Matt? Is it yeself, Matt?"

"It's me." He settled himself for an obscure and roundabout conversation; O'Gilroy wisely didn't trust telephone operators. "Where are you speaking from?"

"The hotel. Jest got into town. Seems like nobody was meeting us."

Blast Scotland Yard. They'd promised to have someone ready to take over from O'Gilroy the moment he came ashore at Harwich. Arranging that had been a courtesy on the Bureau's part, to demonstrate that their people were not "active" on British soil.

"Sorry about that. I'll remind them. Did you have a good crossing?"

"Wasn't exactly a storm." That probably meant a flat calm; O'Gilroy was a dedicatedly bad sailor.

"Any trouble in Brussels?"

"The feller was right about having problems. Near had a nasty accident with an aeroplane."

"An aeroplane?" How on earth . . . But the telephone system wasn't private enough for explanations. "Was anybody hurt?"

"Nobody we know. I thought it was mebbe in the papers." Come to think of it, Ranklin had noticed a small item about a fatal aeroplane crash in Brussels. But he hadn't read more – it was a common enough headline – and certainly hadn't connected it with O'Gilroy's work.

"Anyway, you're back. Which hotel are you at?"

"The Ritz."

"The Ritz? Good Lord, with dinner, that could cost him a pound a night."

"I'm thinking he'd never notice."

"Then I don't suppose you're in any hurry to leave, but I'll get on to the Yard anyway. Come back here when you're relieved."

"Thanks, Matt. I'll say goodbye, then. Goodbye."

Ranklin hung up, thinking: It's unfamiliarity with telephones that makes O'Gilroy sound so stilted, but can it be the electricity that somehow emphasises his accent? If so, and you had somebody whose English was good but you suspected he was foreign, then perhaps . . . Then he shook his head and asked the girl to get him through to Scotland Yard.

He got back to the agents' office just as the meeting was breaking up and went up to apologise to Dagner, who waved it aside. "You didn't miss anything. Was it important?"

"It was O'Gilroy—"

"Ah, our wild Fenian boy."

"— and Scotland Yard losing its notebook. I wouldn't call him a Fenian."

"I'm looking forward to meeting him. I heard you captured and tamed him yourself single-handed, on a mission to the Irish jungle.

Come in and tell me a little about him – and yourself." He led the way and sat at the Commander's table, which briefly startled Ranklin. Yet in the Army, when the CO moved out, his number two moved in; logical and sensible. Perhaps it was that the room was so personal to the Commander, cluttered with gadgets, maps and his display case of pistols – everything except paperwork.

Dagner clearly didn't believe in paperwork either, because he didn't consult any before saying: "I understand that, a year ago, you joined the Greek Army's artillery and fought in the Salonika campaign. How did that come about? – and was it why the Chief recruited you?"

By now, Ranklin could recite his recent past in the flat tone of someone reading an engineering manual. "I had to resign my commission here because I was about to go bankrupt. Nothing dramatic, just that my brother made a mistake in the stock market and I'd guaranteed him. And the only thing I know about is the Guns, so I looked around for the nearest war. I went to Greece because – the English always side with the Greeks, don't they? Byron and so on. It's probably the classical education. The Commander had me brought back and made an arrangement with my creditors and had me reinstated here."

He was curious to see if Dagner acknowledged that recruitment as pure blackmail and what it said about the finest secret service in the world. But he made no comment. Presumably the Commander would have told him most of it anyway, so perhaps he just wanted to know how it looked from Ranklin's side. He nodded. "You must tell me more about that campaign one day. Now, how about O'Gilroy?"

"He was in the infantry for ten years, took his discharge as a corporal. I first met him in South Africa, when we were bunged up in Ladysmith – in the siege. Then I ran into him again in Ireland when he was certainly working for the Fenians or something like them. That ended with him killing one of them, his own nephew, actually, and he became rather *non grata* over there. I think the Commander took him on because he thought his experience – of outwitting us, I suppose – would be useful."

It did no harm to emphasise that it had been the Commander's decision. And there was more to the story than that, but that was for O'Gilroy to tell, if he chose.

Dagner nodded again. "There's nothing like secret service work for breeding myths and legends. I wonder if it's that we're the last place that isn't swamped with paperwork? If they'd had paper and typewriting machines in Ancient Greece we'd never have heard of their gods and heroes, just their orders of the day and ration returns. D'you trust him?"

"I do."

When Ranklin didn't say any more, Dagner asked: "Could he tell our counter-intelligence people anything useful about his erstwhile colleagues in Ireland?"

"'Could' I don't know. Certainly he didn't."

Dagner raised his eyebrows gently. "And you trust him."

"I do tend to trust a man who refuses to betray his friends."

"Yes." But it was another meaningless sound and Ranklin sensed that Dagner was shelving rather than concluding the topic. "Now, to the rest of our flock: what do you make of the new boys?"

"So far, no more than what their CR's tell us. If there's a common denominator, it's that they all started off as go-getters—" He saw Dagner's puzzlement at the American slang and made a hasty revision; "—recommended for accelerated promotion, then something got lost along the way. Two of them were down to 'delayed promotion' by the end. Collectively, I'd say their last CO's were only too glad to be rid of them."

"Quite," Dagner agreed. "Not exactly the cream of the crop."

"In the British Army – I don't know about the Indian – you won't get the best regimental officers volunteering for Intelligence work. No promotion, no medals."

"We certainly don't want glory-hunters . . . But at least they volunteered."

Ranklin said nothing. Army interpretations of the word "volunteer" would fill a lexicon. Technically, he himself had volunteered. Dagner continued: "The trouble is, I haven't your experience of command, of bringing up young officers. I was working so much by myself. So I may be no judge . . . But they seem bright enough."

Ranklin nodded. "And they're what we've got."

"Quite. Now – I'd better know what's going on. What was O'Gilroy doing in Belgium?"

"He was in Brussels looking at some documents – technical drawings – a commercial firm of spies had offered for sale. And some Italian senator who was coming to a meeting at our Foreign Office had gone to our embassy there and said he thought his life was in danger and could he have an armed escort? They asked us, and O'Gilroy was free, so he took it on. I gather that there *was* an incident, but this was on the telephone . . ."

"So the Foreign Office can occasionally find a use for us . . . May I assume they'll be told the job was properly carried out? Good. But did you say a firm of *commercial* spies?"

Yes, Ranklin realised, that must sound a bit odd. I accept them because they were there when I came into this business and everything seemed odd. "You find such people, particularly in Brussels and Vienna, buying and selling secrets. Really, it's no more than a formal version of the informers you probably had in the bazaars at Peshawar and Lhandi Kotal. Some are better than others, of course, but they are useful on the technical side, now we seem to be living in an age of Secret Weapons. What with submarines and torpedoes and mines and all sorts of flying machines, it's risky to disbelieve anything."

"Or, of course, believe too much of it," Dagner said thoughtfully.

5

"How very nice to see you back in town, Mrs Finn," said one of the sub-managers or floor-walkers or whatever Debenham's called the people it dressed as diplomatists. Corinna flashed him a dazzling smile while privately thinking it extraordinary presumption to assume that just because she hadn't been in his damned shop for a few weeks she couldn't have been in London. But that was English shopkeepers for you; maybe Gordon Selfridge with his Chicago background would shake them up a bit.

But not go so far as banishing such places as Debenham's Ladies' Club Room. This was just what it sounded like except without the *deliberateness* of a men's club. You just drifted in when you got exhausted with choosing new curtains for the ball room, sipped a coffee, skimmed a magazine – and picked up any mail addressed to you there. Corinna guessed that this last was what appealed to Adelina, Lady Hovedene; at any rate, she was already seated at a delicate little writing-table scribbling a reply to a letter that (Corinna assumed) she wouldn't have liked her husband to see.

She waved her pen at Corinna, who dropped into the most comfortable chair she could find, asked the maid for coffee and picked up a newspaper, turning to the finance and shipping page and becoming instantly engrossed. Stuck for a word, Adelina glanced back at her and thought *Really* . . . There was quite a lot to be *Really* about with Corinna. She couldn't help being young – thirty or so, which was young for a widow – nor her height, but did she have to sprawl like that? English girls at least had the self-respect to carry themselves as if they already had rheumatic necks, but Americans seemed to be all education and no deportment. And that wraparound skirt in royal blue might suit a Paris boulevard, but it wasn't due to be fashionable in London for another year at least. *And* reading the finance page, probably even understanding it . . . *Really*.

She finished her letter and sealed it in an unaddressed envelope. Then, of normal height and slightly cottage-loaf of figure, hobbled – because she was wearing a proper hobble skirt in acceptable pastels – across to sit by Corinna.

"Oh Lord, how can one sound *passionate* in a draper's shop at twelve o'clock in the morning? And do put that paper away, you've got far too much money already."

"It's not money, it's finance. Two quite different things." But Corinna put the newspaper aside, then noticed and picked up a Tauschnitz edition of a novel that had been banned in Britain. Adelina had obviously had it sent from Germany by post. "Have you read this yet?"

"No. Will I learn anything?"

"I very much doubt it."

"Oh, *bother*. And it doesn't even have any pictures."

"Pictures? – in a Tauschnitz edition? They're supposed to be literature."

"It was *supposed* to be unspeakably corrupting," Adelina said wistfully.

Corinna laughed. "If it's pictures you want, I'm sure they have such things in Paris. I'll send you some."

"Would you really? Not for myself, you understand, but some of my . . . friends seem to need a little *inspiration*. And don't actually send them. People can be so dreadfully helpful at undoing parcels."

"And you don't want to corrupt the servants' morals."

"Their morals be damned, it's their time I'm concerned about. If they get the idea that there's more to life than a quick wham-bang in the airing cupboard then I'll never get any work out of them."

In truth, Corinna suspected it wasn't really bedroom athletics that drew Adelina into *affaires*. She might enjoy believing she was falling in love – Lord Ronnie was a pillar of society and indeed a pillar in his own right, but hardly romantic – but Corinna guessed that what she really sought was friendship and involvement. But while English society accepted clandestine adultery, it was suspicious of overt friendship between men and women, so Adelina had little choice.

However, at least she had found involvement. The list of

Adelina's lovers (as far as Corinna had been able to compile one) suggested that she believed a woman's place was in the know. Her hospitality was precisely aimed to give her an unmatched insight into Cabinet, Court and diplomatic circles. If Adelina told you something was going to happen – *if*, because she didn't retain her position by being a blabber – then you could bet money on it. Corinna had.

But, of course, you were expected to pay your way by gossip of your own.

"And how," Adelina went on, "is your gadabout life?"

Correctly interpreting the question, Corinna said carefully: "He's an officer in your Army."

"My dear, I would certainly assume he's an officer, but what regiment?"

Corinna hesitated; she wasn't going to mention Ranklin's name, but this much could hardly hurt. "He's in the Artillery. Do they have regiments?"

"They're one big regiment, almost as bad as a Corps. And I do think Guardees or the Cavalry are safer: less chance of their being fortune hunters."

Corinna just gave an unladylike grunt, since she didn't think any man's regiment would stop him hunting her prospective fortune. Moreover, she didn't care whether Ranklin were in the Guns (as he called them) or the Loyal Snowballers since he wasn't really in either but – though he stubbornly never admitted it aloud – in the Secret Service.

"But perhaps he's got money of his own?" Adelina suggested.

"Not by my standards." In fact, she believed that Ranklin was, technically if not legally, bankrupt.

"Your standards, in that regard if no other, are commendably high. But Gunners sound terribly mechanical – is he? Mind you, there's nothing like a Guardee for doing things by numbers. One ends up feeling trooped like a colour."

"He's well travelled and I don't think he's always kept his pants on."

"Corinna, you really are the most dreadful trollop, and if you want to keep on being one, you're going to have to get another husband."

"So useful about the house and to take for walks? Isn't being a widow enough?"

"It wears off. A husband will define your place in society."

Corinna's eyebrows went up. "I think people know who I am."

"Reynard Sherring's daughter. Quite. But it isn't the same thing. A single lady can suddenly be dropped by society – women never quite trust her, anyway – but it's a much more difficult thing to drop a man who's got a proper position. And a husband can be the most useful protection for . . . for behaviour quite as interesting as anything you want to get up to."

This time, Corinna's smile was a wry one. "It seems a pity to marry some poor guy just to cuckold him."

"My dear, he certainly won't be poor once you marry him, and if it disturbs your conscience, you can rest assured he'll certainly be doing the same to you."

"I'm not so certain I'd be reassured. I might even get mad and shoot the bastard."

"Oh, you Americans are such romantics." Adelina frowned thoughtfully. "I know some American influences have been welcomed in society, but I'm not sure that shooting husbands is one." She thought a moment longer, then changed tack. "Now, dear, what I really wanted to ask you about is your brother. Andrew, isn't it? I hear he's in town."

"More or less."

"And single? Now, do I invite him? – single men aren't thick on the ground at this time of year."

"You could invite him, but I couldn't promise he'll remember to come."

"Oh *dear*."

Corinna laughed outright. "And if you want to say 'What a family', go right ahead. The thing about Andrew is, he's an engineer – an inventor. And right now he's crazy about airplanes."

"Flying machines?"

"I think he'd regard that as a little passé, but sure, flying machines."

"What is it about aeroplanes? – if that's what I must call them. Men can break their necks far more respectably falling off horses."

Corinna smiled politely. "According to Andrew, Britain's the place for airplanes this year, where the real progress is. That's the only reason he's here."

"I thought it was an American invention."

"Sure it was – though I think the French dispute that; they would. But it seems you've taken to it like a duck to . . . well, flying, I guess. And unless you can promise him he'll meet some famous aviator at your house, I don't think you'll get him to wash the oil off his hands."

"I *will* say it: what a family. Not even if I asked you to bring him yourself?"

"Oh no, you don't make me my brother's keeper." It suddenly occurred to Corinna that, by the rules of English society, Adelina shouldn't be in London at all, but settling into her country home to enjoy its draughts at their winter best. "Anyhow, invite him to what?"

"The *Wedding*, my dear girl. Where *have* you been?"

"Off-hand, I'd say New York, Paris, Budapest, Kiel—"

"Well, in a month's time, Prince Arthur's marrying the Duchess of Fife. But if you didn't know, you can't have accepted any invitations for that time. So I can count on you."

"Oh sure – provided I'm still in London. But you know how Pop is . . ." The half-truth that her father, long divorced, had called her to act as hostess in some far city had saved Corinna from many dull dinner parties.

"And I'll be sure and invite some suitable husbands for you."

"Suppose I want to marry my Gunner?" Corinna said provocatively.

"Not *marry*, dear; keep him for afterwards. No, with your looks and money you should get quite a tolerable house."

"House? I thought I'd be marrying a man."

"Go for the house, you'll see far more of it. The town house can usually be changed, but hardly the family seat . . . And don't get tempted by a castle. They're all on the edge of nowhere and the *plumbing* . . ."

Corinna only half-listened. She had her own views on marriage, the main one being that it was a lousy alternative to life as Reynard Sherring's daughter. When she had said that money and finance were different things, she had meant it. She had always had money and, like good health, valued it but seldom thought of it. But she was fascinated by finance – money you could neither touch nor see yet which could build and bring down empires.

It had begun when her father had tried to explain his world to her brother Andrew, who was expected to take up the rich man's burden. But when Andrew had gone back to pulling Sherring's new automobile to pieces (he was a practical, if spoiled, child) Corinna had kept asking questions, for the skittish dragons and dark forests of international finance enchanted her as no fairy story ever had. Sherring philosophically accepted that it was all his wife's fault, told the chauffeur to put the automobile back together again, and began training his daughter instead of his son. After all, he figured, it would outrage his friends on Wall Street.

It did far more. Now, when people spoke to her, they knew they spoke to the House of Sherring and its power to move millions – a power which she had come to share. And knowing – or better still, deducing – where the dragons were heading next was something Corinna loved, really *loved*. As a woman, it was the best she could achieve, whereas marriage would be about the worst. It would define her. Legally, socially, in every way she would just be A Wife, living happily ever after. As a child she had watched, not understanding then, as her mother turned sour trying to do that, and no thank you.

Perhaps if Adelina had spent more time studying her own sex, she would have understood most of this, because they were both doing much the same thing. Men might have a near-monopoly of action, but nobody could stop women *knowing*.

All this, however, brought Corinna a problem with her private life. She had been still a girl at a Swiss finishing-school when she realised that, in Europe, misbehaviour was reserved for married women and widows. And since it would be a pity to reach death without trying out the fates worse than it, she sat down to some careful thinking.

She neither flouted nor tried to change society. She vaguely admired the women who tried, and paid the penalty, but for her life seemed too short. So she just made the minimum changes to herself to get what she wanted. The first was to marry Mr Finn, the second to have him die in the San Francisco fire of '06 that also destroyed the public records of such things as marriages. This hurt nobody, not even Mr Finn, who was pure fiction, and actually benefited the Chicago forger who had done a near-perfect marriage certificate for her.

Hardly anybody knew her secret except her father, brother

Andrew and now Matt Ranklin. She wasn't quite sure why she'd told him, but not others before him. But if you can't trust the Secret Service to keep a secret . . .

6

The Bureau's rooms were right up under the eaves of the building, with sloping walls and odd little turret windows in corners, and even in September a sunny afternoon gave them the atmosphere of an Egyptian tomb. To make it worse, the Commander had forbidden the opening of windows. At first Ranklin had assumed this was an ineradicable naval fear of the sea getting in; he had been crisply informed that, here on the eighth floor, it was a more sensible fear of secret documents blowing out. Not that they were encouraged to put much in writing.

But with the Commander away, it was a treat to clarify his thoughts by getting them on paper, and the only alternative was hovering near the inner door for O'Gilroy to finish his interview with Dagner. But he put down his pen the moment O'Gilroy rambled out. And *rambled* was the word for his loose, long-legged movement that gave no hint of his Army years. Now he began rambling around the low-ceilinged room, glancing out of the window, picking up a newspaper and dropping it . . .

"For the Lord's sake, sit down," Ranklin said. He pushed his cigarette case across the table; he himself hadn't felt settled enough to light a pipe. "How did it go?"

O'Gilroy collapsed onto an upright chair and reached for a cigarette. "Well enough."

Ranklin waited. With his lean face and dark untidy hair, O'Gilroy was a schoolgirl's vision of the thinking pirate, and whose thoughts were now rather sombre. "He was terrible polite, but I wouldn't say he'd hire me if he hadn't got me. Asked how I felt, working for you English." He lit the cigarette.

"And you said?"

"'Twas a job, though I hadn't heard of any pension to it."

Ranklin winced. You might say O'Gilroy had fought for the

Empire in South Africa, but O'Gilroy himself wouldn't say it. He more likely saw it as fighting for his pals alongside him and because fighting was his chosen trade. Wisely, the Army skipped quickly over King and Country to preach loyalty to the regiment – your pals. It knew what it was doing; surely Dagner must remember that.

"What else did you talk about with Major Dag— X?"

"Falcone."

"I beg your pardon?"

"The Italian feller from Brussels."

"Ah. Did you gather what he's up to, and why someone wants to kill him?"

O'Gilroy took a long drag on his cigarette and said, as if he were working it out: "He *says* he's looking at armaments – and aeroplanes – for the Italian Army. The fellers wanting him dead . . . there was a note from some Serbian secret society—"

"The Ujedinjenje ili Smrt?"

"Sounds like. But Falcone wasn't believing that so much. And me being just a bodyguard . . ."

Ranklin took the point: O'Gilroy had done right to play the part of a simple 'bravo'. "Have you any idea how someone contrived to make the aeroplane crash?"

"We was talking about that on the boat. Falcone reckoned they'd got at it in the night – 'twas only in a wooden shed – and loosened the bolts holding the engine on. Ye could do that and pack the gaps with something, scraps of wood or metal, so it'd hold firm a while but gradual-like the scraps'd fall out. Then, when ye give the engine a jolt, like sudden switching on again, the turning weight of it'd tear it right off. Anyhow, the bolts *did* give way," he added sombrely. "I saw it."

"It certainly sounds a bit technical for that Serbian gang. They're usually simple bomb-and-bullet people."

O'Gilroy nodded. "What Falcone said. Puzzled, he was. But he asked something else: did I have any idea how he'd get in touch with our Secret Service." O'Gilroy had a sly smile waiting for Ranklin's astonishment.

"He—? So what did you say?"

"Said I'd ask around."

"You told the Major that, of course?"

"Surely. He said he'd talk to yourself about it. And Falcone wants to go to Brooklands aerodrome this weekend so I thought mebbe

36

I'd go down with him. The Major said Fine to that, stay in touch with him."

Ranklin found himself nodding absently. It was lucky that O'Gilroy had become a recent convert to aeronautics – although entirely predictable. Anything new and mechanical seemed to O'Gilroy a sunbeam from some bright future; perhaps Irish back streets left you with little longing for the past. In the last few weeks he had wallowed in technical magazines about flying and even, Ranklin suspected, made surreptitious enquiries about learning to fly.

Ranklin took out his watch. "Then if you've nothing else to do, take a couple of our new boys out and teach 'em how to shadow each other. Try not to lose them permanently."

O'Gilroy stubbed out his cigarette, glanced at his own watch – he had, of course, one of the new and unreliable (Ranklin thought) wristwatches – then collected his legs and arms and rambled out. Ranklin stared down at, the paper on which he had written *Most important to* . . . and tried to recall what had been so important ten minutes ago.

He was still trying when the buzzer from the Commander's room rang. It was a rather peremptory arrangement, but inevitable once the sound-proof door had been fitted. He tucked the paper into an inside pocket – another newly acquired habit – and went in.

Dagner had several Naval log-books, presumably the ones the Commander seemed to use as his personal records system, spread across the table. Desks were rare in Army life; they suggested bankers, civil servants, a permanent commitment to shuffling papers.

"Firstly, do you know anything about this Sir Caspar Alerion who's coming to give us a talk next Monday? – should I have heard of him?"

"I think he's just some crony of the Commander's. He's a retired dip. I mean diplomatist," Ranklin added quickly, "not dipsomaniac. At least, I *think* it means that in his case. From what the Commander said, his career was a bit . . . well, it lasted as long as it did because he comes of a good family. They didn't mind the drink and women so much, but he dabbled in espionage and that upset his ambassadors. His last posting was Rome, then he exchanged to the Foreign Office in London, and resigned six or eight years ago."

"It sounds as if he could be interesting, then. If there's any

37

arrangements needed, could you . . . ? Thank you. Now—" he glanced down at the log-books again; "—just remind me of how many agents the Bureau actually has, will you?"

Ranklin stood there, nodding gently. "Ah. He didn't tell you, either."

By now, Ranklin had begun to recognise degrees and variations in Dagner's lack of expression. This time, he might – just might – be struggling to retain control. And, of course, winning. After a time, he pushed his chair back and said quietly: "Then that's one secret we can't give away. D'you think it's written down anywhere?" He looked around the cluttered office – but the clutter all seemed to be telephones, models of futuristic warships, naval gadgetry and the Commander's collection of pistols.

"Not unless it's in those log-books," Ranklin said. "Frankly, I think he keeps it all in his head."

"Which, by tonight, will be in Germany." Dagner stared at the table-top for a few moments more, then reached for his uniform jacket. "I've breathed all the air in here a dozen times already. I'm going for a walk. And you're coming with me."

*   *   *

They crossed the endless belt of honking traffic in Whitehall, went through the arch of the Horse Guards and on to the parade ground itself. This was the very heart of the Empire's military and naval bureaucracy and Dagner's uniform meant he was saluting in all directions, majors being mere groundlings in this theatre.

The uniforms thinned out as they reached the edge of St James's Park, its trees still green but now dulled with dust and rustling dryly as they waited for the collapse of autumn.

"How many agents," Dagner said abruptly, "do you know we have abroad at this moment?"

Ranklin sorted his experience. "From the reports I've seen, we have one, I think permanently, in St Petersburg. And somebody in Cairo, and I think Germany, but I don't know where."

"And that's all?"

"All I know of." He felt he ought to say more. "Actually getting people on to our establishment, like O'Gilroy and myself and now the new boys, seems to be quite recent. Until now, I think what happened was that the Commander ran into a chap who's interested in Intelligence and had some money of his own, gave him dinner at one of his clubs – and sent him off somewhere to look at something. He wasn't paid or reimbursed from our funds, we didn't see him in the office, we *may* see his report – if he doesn't wind up in jail somewhere. Is he one of ours or not?"

"I see. And that's how the world-famous British Secret Service works." Ranklin wasn't imagining the bitterness any more than Dagner was hiding it. "Did it surprise you, too, when you joined?"

"It did, rather."

Dagner stopped and looked back through the trees at the jumbled skyline of the Horse Guards and Whitehall. "There must be a dozen departments in those buildings, all with budgets and staffs bigger than us, and all doing damn-all but churn out paperwork for each other to file in the wrong place. And I learn that K at MO5 only got his majority last month – forgive me, Captain." But Ranklin was just as gloomy that the head of the nation's spy-catching service, currently codenamed MO5, was only one recent rank above himself.

Dagner went on: "I grew up on legends of the British Secret. Invincible, all-pervasive . . . Well, I've learnt not to trust legends like that, but to find the whole *thing* was a myth until three years ago . . . In India we've been organised for decades. What happened before the Bureau was founded?"

"The Army and Navy had – and still have – their own specialised Intelligence departments. The Navy looks at harbours and fleets, the Army at other armies. And the Foreign Office decides who are heroes and villains. I *think*," Ranklin said tentatively, "the idea was that we needed a more catholic approach, someone to look at potential enemies' industry and economy and financial strength, as well as just counting uniformed heads."

"That sounds sensible enough."

"Yes, only that's where we come into direct conflict with the Foreign Office."

They had reached the Mall, wide and serene with no motor-buses and only a few of the more elegant cars among the horse-drawn cabs and carriages. Perhaps the view overlayed memories of the Foreign Office, because Dagner smiled and said: "Ah, this is more the London I remember . . . Wouldn't it be more sensible if we came directly under the Prime Minister or Cabinet?"

Ranklin wagged his head vaguely. "They probably think spying belongs in a cheap novel – as the FO does. After all, they *could* have started the Bureau ages ago if they'd wanted to."

Dagner's frown was as brief as his smiles. "Yet in India, the Game was well respected – accepted as a part of policy. Our civil servants were as petty-minded as any, of course, but nobody denied our value."

"But you were only spying on natives. We spy on gentlemen."

Dagner stopped dead in the middle of the pavement. "Is that a serious remark, Captain?"

A bit surprised, Ranklin said: "Certainly it is. At the top levels, all European society's intertwined. It isn't just royalty marrying royalty, the aristocracy does it, too."

"Yes, I know all that. So—?" Dagner started walking again.

"But also our politicians and diplomatists and top civil servants mostly spent a year at Heidelberg or the Sorbonne, and *their* top dogs were at Oxford or Cambridge for a while, and even if they don't intermarry, they're still in and out of each others' houses for holidays and shooting-parties and the like. And they don't like us spying on their cousins and old college chums."

He realised Dagner was giving him a steady and thorough stare. "And do you share that viewpoint, Captain?" he asked gently.

Ranklin sighed. "It bothered me to start with. But as a Gunner I'm prepared to kill those people. Why should I jib at spying on them?"

Perhaps that didn't sound quite enthusiastic enough, because Dagner said gently: "*I* believe we belong to an honourable profession, Captain."

"We belong to a necessary one. I don't know that honour comes into it."

Dagner might have been about to say more, but didn't. Instead: "I had a chat with O'Gilroy . . . It seems that this Italian senator wants to meet someone from the Bureau. What's your feeling?"

"I'd say Yes, he sounds intriguing. Would you like me to . . . ?"

Dagner shook his head slowly. "No, I think I'll call on him myself – he's staying at the Ritz, I think? It'll do me good to start meeting people in European politics . . . shan't belong to the Bureau, of course, just be a civil servant in touch with them . . . D'you think a rumpled, tweedy academic sort? – no, an Italian probably wouldn't get the point. Old-fashioned, frock-coat and topper? No, that wouldn't be right for an Italian industrialist either. I think he'd talk most freely to someone brisk in a business suit. D'you agree?"

Ranklin just mumbled, taken aback by the confident way Dagner had run through the parts he might play. It was a reminder that the man was a true professional, and that his 'attitude' might span both creeping up the Khyber Pass in a turban and calling at the Ritz in a business suit.

With that decided, Dagner's mind took a new turn. "About O'Gilroy . . . clearly you have no problem relying on a man with his . . . ah, background and connections."

Ranklin took a deep breath. "If you're asking about his attitude, he believes in a free Ireland and isn't going to stop. But the House of Commons believes that, too. It's the Lords that's blocking Home Rule. I'm not pretending O'Gilroy hasn't done anything illegal in the past; I know damn well he has. But I'd guess it was mostly for the fun of it – and that's really why he's working for us now. And my only worry about his old friends, Fenians or whatever, is that they'll kill him on sight. That's why I'd rather we were sent to Europe again as soon as possible."

Dagner pondered this. "You don't make his commitment to our cause sound very deep-rooted."

Ranklin shrugged. "If you asked O'Gilroy to stand up for the King and Empire I think he'd more likely fall off his chair laughing." Dagner almost lost control of his expression; his face froze for a moment. Ranklin went on: "On the other hand, if I wanted somebody to guard my back in a dark alley I'd choose O'Gilroy any time. He's . . . I'd say he's loyal to the day," he summed up. "Probably, by your standards, we're both pretty incompetent. He doesn't know foreign countries or languages, I don't know how to survive in dark alleys. Together we may add up to one passable spy."

Despite himself, Dagner smiled faintly at that concept. "Hm. Being, as it were, Siamese twins among our agents could be seen as rather inflexible, I fear."

But we're what you've got, Ranklin thought grimly. Us and the four new boys and an unknown, uncontactable number of agents abroad. What else do you expect in a Bureau so new and with so many powerful enemies among its friends?

However, he said nothing because Dagner was what *he'd* got, and was very glad of it. For a grim week, it had seemed that he

41

himself, with experience as an adjutant and a willingness to make himself unpopular by organising people, might be deputising for the Commander. And while it was one thing to take over a battery or even a brigade that had the impetus of regulations and traditions to keep it rolling along, even with a nincompoop in charge, it was quite another to take over the Bureau from the man who had invented it only three years ago.

No, Ranklin was very glad that Dagner was here.

*   *   *

The little triangle of Clerkenwell enclosed by Rosebery Avenue and the Clerkenwell and Farringdon Roads was an odd patch of short steep hills in an otherwise generally flat area. Perhaps because of that, the recent tide of rebuilding had flowed around it, leaving it as it had been for the past half-century, London's Little Italy.

There was nothing Italianate about the architecture; in fact, there wasn't much architecture about Eyre Street Hill, Back Hill, Little Bath Street and the rest. But dingy houses, cracked paving and uneven cobbles are international, and the shop signs, the bright headscarves, the cooking smells and the chatter around the shopfronts were comfortingly Italian.

Relaxing as the familiar sounds and smells were, the scene wasn't exactly the Corso Umberto Primo. Bozan said nothing, but his expression said it all, and Silvio nodded. "Naples without the weather."

"Why didn't we stay with Janko?" Bozan whined. "I'm sure *he's* at a proper hotel." Tiredness made him fractious, and it had been a long, complicated day.

"Because we don't want to be seen together. This way, we'll be with our own people. And perhaps they'll be more help than he was."

"You should have let me kill the Senator in the street at . . . where was it?"

"Brussels. I agree, but we had to let Jankovic try his clever bit first. *Now* we'll do it our way."

He stopped by an old man sitting on a doorstep smoking a reed pipe and asked politely for directions to an address in Back Hill Street.

The old man's eyes wrinkled warily; it was obvious that he knew the address, and just as obvious that he knew it wasn't an address to be doled out to strangers. But strangers to what? These two, with their expensive Italian shoes, could well belong to what the Back Hill Street house belonged to, and it was politic to help such men. And then forget all about it.

Anyway, no names had been mentioned, and an address is just an address; they'd find it in the end anyway. He directed them, and when they had gone, knocked out his pipe and faded back into the tenement building.

Ten minutes later they were sitting in a surprisingly and floridly luxurious first-floor room with tiny cups of real Italian coffee by their chairs. Their host, whom Silvio tactfully addressed as just "Padrone", was dressed in severe black like a village elder from the South, with a white moustache and olive skin. But the face, while heavily lined and thin, was still blunt, not sharp. He might never have worked in the stony fields, but it took generations to breed out the farm.

He was being elaborately welcoming, but also probing. "And if there is anything I can help with . . ."

"We need to find a man, a senator from Turin, who is visiting London . . ."

"That may be difficult for strangers in a big city. He is rich, this . . . ?"

"Giancarlo Falcone. Yes, he is rich. In Brussels he stayed at the Palace Hotel . . ."

Bozan said: "You should have let me kill him there."

It was a swipe with a club to the delicate cobweb of unfinished sentences and non-commitment. Silvio smiled wanly. "Bozan is somewhat impetuous."

The Padrone nodded gently, his own dark eyes quite as blank in their way as the innocent ones of the young assassin. "I understand. It is no matter. If the senator likes the best hotels, it becomes easier, but London still has many such places. And this is a private matter . . . ?"

"Only a small matter of business, you understand . . ."

"Then anything you wish, you have only to ask." In other words, the Padrone would have been wary of interfering in a feud, but from a business killing he felt free to grab as much profit as he could reach.

"You are most kind. But even in business there is still a question

43

of honour." Or: we'll pay for help, but we promised to do the job and it's ours.

"That is understood. But first, you wish a place to stay, safe and comfortable?"

"We would be most grateful for your advice."

The old man stared at the far wall. "There is the house of my son, but he has many children . . . perhaps that of my brother-in-law, only my sister is sick . . . I think the house of my daughter's husband . . ."

Silvio smiled outside gritted teeth. They would end up where they were put; the recital had been a warning that the Padrone's family was all around them. He waited.

Bored with the silence, or perhaps because he'd forgotten he'd said it before, Bozan asked: "Why didn't you let me kill him there?"

The Padrone was listening anyway, so Silvio explained: "We had another man, some Slav, with fancy ideas about arranging an aeroplane to crash, and we had to let him try his way first."

"And the aeroplane did not crash?"

"Oh yes, it crashed and the driver died – but the Senator was not in it. So clever. And the Senator ran to here and now he has, perhaps, a bravo with him."

"I can kill them both," Bozan said indifferently.

Silvio wasn't too sure of that. What he said was: "Perhaps now he is in England he will feel safe . . ."

The Padrone asked: "He has bravoes, this Senator?"

"In Brussels, there was a man . . ." Silvio was inwardly furious at Bozan for betraying more of their problems. But oddly, it didn't quite work that way.

The Padrone had been thinking. "London is a city made of many villages . . . This is . . . *our* village." He had almost said 'mine'. "If an important Italian is killed, and it seems it is done by other Italians . . . the police may come first to look here . . ."

Ah-*hah*, Silvio thought: you're worried that the police will come and shake your pisspot little kingdom until it spills on your shoes. *I* understand.

"You can be sure we will do nothing to cause you difficulties," he said, to show he now knew they could.

The Padrone smiled and inclined his head graciously. "Good. Now, the matter of finding the Senator . . ."

And some people thought killing a man was simple.

7

Apart from the Bureau, Whitehall Court was mainly expensive service flats and small exclusive clubs, ideal neighbours for not poking their noses into each other's affairs. One of the flats had been leased by the Bureau after the tenant had died suddenly, possibly from a surfeit of William Morris floral wallpaper. It was intended for agents 'passing through', but now used by Ranklin and O'Gilroy, who were normally abroad but in any case couldn't afford anywhere of their own. They also acted as informal night-watchmen to the office upstairs, fielding out-of-hours telephone calls and cablegrams, without making any fetish of staying in to wait for them. The Bureau was serious, but not oppressively so.

O'Gilroy was still out on the shadowing exercise, so Ranklin made a pot of tea – which just about exhausted his cooking skills but was all the flat was equipped to do anyway – and sat down with an evening paper to read about the peace conference between Turkey and Bulgaria that had just begun in Constantinople. So that, he reflected, was probably the War Season over for the year. Nobody wanted another winter campaign, while the memory of last year was still strong. But come next summer, in 1914, when the roads had dried out for artillery and supply wagons, and the sun brought delusions of immortality and everybody knew that *this* time it would be quick and almost bloodless . . .

O'Gilroy came in, took one look at his expression and said: "Jayzus, ye've been reading the newspapers again." He reached for the decanters on a side table. "Whyn't ye try dying of drink? – might even be slower."

Sipping his sherry, Ranklin gloomily agreed that solitary newspaper reading was indeed a destructive vice. You needed someone with O'Gilroy's buoyant cynicism to put things in perspective. "So, how did our new boys do at shadowing?"

"An omnibus'd do it more invisible. But mebbe I got something into their heads. They get the idea of it quick enough – keeping a pocket of change for buses and cabs, and paying for yer tea when ye get it so yer away fast, stuff like that, but are they thinking ahead on what a man might be doing next? The devil they are, and them close up when they should be far back and t'other way besides."

"We all have to learn," Ranklin said complacently, remembering that a year ago he wouldn't have known what O'Gilroy was talking about.

O'Gilroy gave him a look sharp enough to puncture even a Gunner's condescension, but said only: "Other ways, though, they're sharp fellers – for officers."

"Well, if they volunteered for the Bureau, they're hardly likely to be average regimental types." And certainly not above-average, he added silently. Intelligence work was reckoned, correctly, to be a promotional dead end.

O'Gilroy looked at him curiously, but asked: "And where'll we be eating? I hear there's some good places around London."

There were indeed, and in happier times he'd have enjoyed taking O'Gilroy out to rediscover some old haunts, particularly if the Bureau would foot the bill. But London's big Irish population made any unnecessary venture out of doors an extra risk for O'Gilroy – the key word being unnecessary. Ranklin drew a clear distinction between risk in the line of duty, like that shadowing exercise, and risk just in finding a meal.

He sighed; why the devil couldn't they be posted back to Paris, where there was no problem and they were perhaps a day closer to any European trouble that might brew up? And where you could actually make money on your subsistence allowance because the pettifogging accountants didn't know how cheaply you could eat well in the little bistros, even in the tourist season. Then he stopped, a bit ashamed of his own thoughts.

"We can eat downstairs," he said gruffly, "or have something sent up. We'd better not be far from the office. The Commander might telephone or cable just to see if anybody's minding the shop."

O'Gilroy, who knew perfectly well the true reason, shrugged. "Things go on like this, whyn't we buy a cooking book?" But that was a joke: the idea of men knowing how to cook (except badly, over a camp-fire) was as alien to Irish back streets as it was to English drawing-rooms. "All right, have 'em send it up – but ye

47

don't read newspapers over yer food. Ye can tell me something about Italian affairs instead."

This surprised Ranklin as much as it pleased him. O'Gilroy's usual question about a new country – after asking about the food and drink – was whether it was friendly or (potentially) enemy, disregarding subtler shadings. Ranklin had tried to develop his interest in Europe by pinning up a large map – which also hid several square feet of wallpaper – and chattering about foreign news over breakfast. But he hadn't thought it had taken hold.

"I can try, anyway," Ranklin agreed. "First let's order dinner."

*   *   *

The deceased tenant had left behind a mahogany Victorian dining table so large that if it fell through the floor (which seemed quite possible) it wouldn't stop before the basement. The size had amused O'Gilroy so much that at first he had insisted they ate at opposite ends and called for each other to walk along and pass the salt. Luckily that had palled and they now sat sensibly around one corner, and O'Gilroy got his amusement from Ranklin putting on a velvet smoking jacket so the waiter wouldn't think they had gone completely native.

"I don't know any detail about current Italian politics," Ranklin began, "but I can give you the general position. The first thing is that although Italy *looks* very much like one country—" he nodded at the map; "—with all that coastline and the Alps sealing off the top, it's only actually been united as one for fifty years.

"And I'd guess that's the key to Italian policy. It's trying a bit of everything because it just isn't *used* to being one country with a single policy yet. One faction pushed the government into grabbing some bits of Africa off the Turks, and others want Nice and Corsica back from the French, and Trent and Trieste from the Austrians. And your Senator Falcone feels he can go swanning round Europe buying aeroplanes for the Italian Army on his own initiative. Everybody's pushing their own policies and the Government isn't used to resisting the pressures yet. It's unstable and that could be dangerous."

He paused to disentangle a fishbone from the back of his tongue.

No matter how carefully he, or the waiter, filleted a Dover sole or any other fish, Ranklin always got at least one bone. But who was he to question God's ways?

O'Gilroy watched admiringly. "Ye do that real polite, Matt. Jest what does being a senator mean? Is it like a lord?"

Ranklin trawled his memory. "I think it means a lord-for-life. The King appoints successful public men, industrialists and so on, to the Senate. That sounds like your man, doesn't it?"

O'Gilroy nodded. "So whose side's Italy on?"

Ranklin sighed. Why did everyone assume a country had to be on one "side" or another? It was like a form-room feud among eleven-year-olds. Or, he concluded gloomily, like modern Europe. "Theoretically, she's allied with Germany and Austro-Hungary, but I doubt Italy's worked out where her self-interest really lies, and meanwhile Austria's her traditional enemy."

He got up and tracked his finger down the long Adriatic, in places less than a hundred miles wide, that separated Italy from the Dalmatian coast and the witches' cauldron of the Balkans behind it. "You can see why Italy has to worry about who owns that coastline. And Austria owns both Pola and Trieste – which is mostly Italian inhabitants, I think – right opposite Venice and only four hours' steaming time away."

"An hour by aeroplane."

"If that matters." Ranklin was getting fed up with aeroplanes creeping into every conversation. He sat down again.

O'Gilroy went on gazing at the map. "And ye said Italy was into Africa?"

"A couple of years ago they invaded Libya, which was sort-of-Turkish. The Turks pulled out, but the local Arabs went on fighting back. Still are, I believe."

"Now—" O'Gilroy waved his fork to halt Ranklin whilst he finished a mouthful of his steak-and-kidney pie; "—now was that where they used aeroplanes in war the first time?"

Ranklin was about to declare a total ban on aeronautics, then recalled reading something about that. "Ye-es, I think so. I don't think they contributed much . . . But," he admitted, "the desert would be a good place for aerial scouting."

"Falcone was telling about it. Him and other fellers with money got together with some aviators and made up a squadron – called it a 'flotilla' – to send to Africa."

49

"Very patriotic of him," Ranklin said, thinking it the sort of romantic but useless gesture Italians did so well.

"They was shooting from the aeroplanes as well as scouting."

"A great help that must have been," Ranklin said, imagining aiming a rifle from a moving aeroplane.

"Ye'd be needing a machine-gun to be much use, sure, but—"

"What about the weight? The Maxim gun runs to around a hundred pounds – and one thing I do know about aeroplanes is that they can't carry much weight."

"They'll get better," O'Gilroy said defensively. "And machine-guns're getting lighter. There was talk in Brussels about one invented by an American. Lewis, his name was. Weighs jest twenty-five pounds with a magazine, not a belt, so it should fit an aeroplane jest right."

"Really?" Ranklin was affronted, since he prided himself on keeping up with weaponry gossip; it was his bedrock of knowledge in the shifting sands of Intelligence.

O'Gilroy's voice took on an infuriating tinge of superiority. "Been around some time, I'm thinking. Anyways, they're making it in Belgium, same as Browning pistols, but it's not going so well, I heard, so BSA here's making 'em, too."

"Birmingham Small Arms?" Now Ranklin really was annoyed: it had got as far as *Birmingham* without him noticing.

"That's right," O'Gilroy smiled. "I was talking about it on the boat, and Falcone made out he'd never heard of it, but he was carrying a catalogue of 'em in his baggage."

Ranklin frowned, but no longer in annoyance. "So the Senator's looking for aeroplanes and hiding the fact that he's heard of a lightweight machine-gun. D'you think he wants Italy to have a secret armada of armed aeroplanes?"

O'Gilroy shrugged but was obviously taken by the idea. "And other fellers' secrets being our business . . ."

"Quite. Mind," Ranklin remembered, "Major Dagner's seeing the Senator for himself, so he may come back with the whole story. Still, it's something to watch out for if you're still taking the Senator to Brooklands this weekend."

O'Gilroy got up to find his cigarettes and an ashtray, asking over his shoulder: "What d'ye make of the Major?" The hand-crafted casualness of his tone suggested that Ranklin would have no qualms about discussing a senior with a junior.

"I fancy he knows the game inside out; he's been at it far longer than either of us."

"In India."

"Espionage is adjusting successfully to circumstances. And in India the consequence of failure to adjust can be more prolonged and painful than in most parts of Europe."

"Ye know some lovely long words, Matt." O'Gilroy sighed. "I'll give ye some short ones: he don't trust me."

"In India," Ranklin said thoughtfully, "the Intelligence wallahs may have had more choice of volunteers. He'll have to learn that here, he uses who he's got. Like you. And me."

O'Gilroy breathed smoke slowly. "And why d'ye all call it a 'game'?"

"To try and get the English to take it seriously."

8

Looking back on that Thursday, Ranklin came to the self-pitying conclusion that the only person who enjoyed it less than himself might have been Princess Sophia of Saxe-Weimar, because she committed suicide that day. On the other hand, she thereby let herself off part of the day. He got it all.

It began innocuously with Dagner giving the new recruits a brief, chatty but pointed talk based on his own experience – in this instance, with journalists.

"Resist your immediate instinct to despise them. Some are pretty good at their job, and all of them have been doing that job longer than you have yours, at the moment. But remember that journalists have opinions, even if they may try not to let them show in print. And more: after years of listening to the policy-makers, they want – perhaps secretly, even unconsciously – to make policy themselves. One way, of course, is to publish a demand for such-and-such a policy. But that's open, nailing your colours to the mast – and their editors may not let them do it anyway. The other way is *not* to publish: To support the policy-makers they believe in by withholding unpleasant facts about them, facts that might ruin their careers and place in society. And those, gentlemen, are the stories you want to hear. They may be well worth the price of a drink."

He paused, swinging one long leg from his perch on the edge of a table. "Only – don't fall into the same trap. Don't conceal, in your own reports, the nastier side of people you have come to like or believe in. Show you are more reliable than journalists by reporting without fear or favour, and leave policy to your country's policy-makers."

He left them to clip or précis a pile of learned foreign-affairs journals, and Ranklin to get on with drafting the training programme.

Lock-picking, he wrote. Probably safe-breaking was an art that

52

took years to acquire, but it would be useful if they could open ordinary doors, drawers and luggage without leaving traces. Perhaps Scotland Yard could recommend a reliable criminal to give a demonstration . . .

Forgery: The Commander presumably had access to the Government printers for elaborate and official-looking documents, but a spy in the field might need to alter a name on a passport or write his own letter of introduction. Again, the Yard should be of help, but British forgers might be a little insular. They really needed to study the slanting French script, the upright and rather childish Italian styles, the angular German . . .

Personal weapons . . . But then Dagner came out of the inner room with a letter from someone in the War Office. "I've got a chap here asking us to explore the suitability of the terrain in Schleswig for cavalry operations. He says we're the experts on invasion by sea – are we? And is somebody proposing to invade North Germany?"

Ranklin pushed back his chair and relit his pipe. "As I understand it, an important argument for setting up the Bureau was to explore the threat of being invaded *from* North Germany—"

"We heard about that scare even in India. What did we conclude?"

"Oh, it's rubbish, of course. But our elders and betters have a vested interest in keeping any sort of war scare going, realistic or not, to justify increased spending on new ships and things – even on us I suppose. So it isn't in their or our interest to *conclude* that it's rubbish. We just report – provisionally – from time to time that it's unlikely to happen this week."

"I see." Dagner glanced at the letter again. "So that makes us the acknowledged experts at something we don't believe in. It sounds positively theological. But do we believe in ourselves invading Germany?"

"I doubt it. But when a general gets a bee in his bonnet it can fly both ways. I'll handle it if you like."

Dagner passed the letter over but also asked: "How?"

"Sit on it for a week or so in case we need to send someone to Schleswig for a good reason as well. Otherwise, get someone – like Lieutenant P, he reads German well – to see what he can dig out of libraries. There was probably some cavalry action there in 1848 or '64. Finally, send in a report that's coy about its sources."

Dagner looked uncertain, so Ranklin added: "It helps the cause: shows willing but doesn't waste too much of our time."

Dagner sighed. "I suppose so." He went back into the inner office.

Personal weapons – then it was the telephone girl with a call from a manufacturer of phonographs wanting to speak to the Commander. Ranklin got the call routed to himself and discovered, by roundabout questions, that the Commander was thinking of buying such equipment – presumably for mechanical eavesdropping. On the instant, he became the Commander's assistant, hinted that it was to do with wireless training in the Navy, swore the manufacturer to secrecy, and said the Commander would be in touch when he returned.

Personal weapons – only now he had to support Dagner at a meeting with an Admiralty accountant over a proposal to set up a bank account in Amsterdam. It turned out that the accountant couldn't authorise this himself, merely recommend it if they convinced him it was necessary. The argument quickly dwindled to whether "necessity" was an absolute concept like having a rudder on a ship or a sensible precaution like having a lifeboat. It was unlikely that the Admiralty accountant had ever seen a ship, but it seemed polite to use nautical analogies. Such tact meant the proposal was at least still breathing when it was shelved indefinitely due to the pressures of lunch.

"I hate to say this," Ranklin observed as they walked back across Whitehall, "but the simplest solution would be to produce a document – code or technical drawing or order of battle – and swear we paid five hundred pounds for it in Brussels. And start the account with that."

After a moment, Dagner said: "But don't you think that, in our situation where nobody can really check on whether we've been strictly honest in our claimed expenditure, it behoves us to *be* strictly honest?"

"Perhaps," Ranklin said, who no longer thought so.

Personal weapons, Ranklin resumed after lunch, and waited for the next interruption. It didn't come, so he moved on cautiously. Carry a pistol only if your (adopted) persona would carry one in those particular circumstances. And then avoid anything exotic that suggests you care about pistols. Don't carry a knife, but know how to use one. It's not an Anglo-Saxon weapon, but it's usually easy to come by. You only need a four-inch blade to reach a man's heart, thrusting slightly upwards through his ribs—

How the *hell* do I know that? he wondered, staring at the page as if it had spat at him. I certainly didn't know it a year ago. Did someone in the Greek Army tell me? Or O'Gilroy? Or was it one of those odd scraps of knowledge that seem to settle and cling to me now I have the stickiness of a spy?

He shrugged mentally and tried to think of other personal weaponry that was both effective and unsuspicious – but then Lieutenant M got back from lunch having learnt from an old friend of his father's that the Japanese were trying to stir up the Finns to revolt against their Russian masters—

"Really?" Ranklin put on an impressed expression. "What instances did he cite? And names?"

The point, Lieutenant M bubbled on, was that the Japs wanted to keep the Russians busy in the West while they machinated in the East. Surely the Cabinet should know about this *immediately*. Others could supply instances and names.

"The point," Ranklin corrected gently, "is that those others are us. The Government can usually come by its own rumours. When it does, it should turn to us to verify or deny them by supplying the details. So can you go back to this chap and see if he knows any hard facts?"

"He's rather a tetchy old boy." Lieutenant M looked dubious. "I don't how he'll like some whipper-snapper like me cross-examining him . . ."

"But isn't that our job?" Ranklin smiled sweetly. "We're sp . . . secret agents, remember? We use tact, flattery, bare-faced lies – whatever's appropriate – and we come back with the details, don't we?"

Sometimes, Ranklin told himself when Lieutenant M had gone, I seem quite good at this job. Now: *Personal weapons*—

So then it was O'Gilroy with an aeronautical magazine and eager to explain the arguments for and against the Dunne 'inherently stable' biplane. Ranklin, who privately felt that anyone who got into an aeroplane was inherently unstable to start with, sent him out with any recruits he could find to practise shadowing again.

Personal weap— and now Dagner again, leaving the office in Ranklin's charge while he went off first to meet Senator Falcone at the Ritz, then change into mess kit for a dinner at the officers' mess in the Tower of London. Ranklin politely wished him joy of it and turned back to his notepad.

He hadn't even got his mind into gear when the senior secretary came in, looking for Dagner and waving an official buff envelope that had just been forwarded from the War Office. The handwritten addressee was *The Officer Commanding the unit to which Lieut. P—* (their own Lieutenant P, in fact) *is currently attached*. And marked both *Urgent* and *Private and Confidential*.

Ranklin made chewing expressions as he looked at it. The secretary said: "Shall I keep it for Major Dagner in the morning, sir?"

Ranklin certainly wasn't P's CO, but strictly speaking, neither was Dagner. And he was getting bored with *Personal weapons*. He stuck a finger under the gummed flap and raised his arm at the secretary. "Jog my elbow, will you?"

She smiled frostily and gave him a nudge that wouldn't have shifted a fly. He tore the envelope open. "Oops, look what I've done now. Oh well, I suppose I may as well see what it's all about . . ."

But if the secretary thought she had earned a look, too, she was disappointed, and hobbled away with a distinct sniff.

What the letter and its enclosures boiled down to was that when Lieutenant P had left his last posting he had also left (a) an unpaid mess bill and (b) a young lady who claimed he had promised marriage, but taken (c) a motor-car of which he was only part-owner. Ranklin sat still until he had worn through surprise, indignation, amusement and arrived at exasperation, then went to look for P.

He had just got in, having failed to shadow O'Gilroy through the Piccadilly traffic. "Simply not your day, is it?" Ranklin said, handing him the letters. P skimmed them, smiled ruefully, and began: "About the motor—"

"Don't tell me," Ranklin said. "Just sort it out. You can't marry without your colonel's permission, and with any luck he'll refuse it if you pay your mess bill promptly. If that doesn't work, write to the girl's father asking will he lend you a thousand quid to pay your gaming debts. Now about the motor-car: where is it?"

"Here in London."

"And who else part-owns it?"

"Two chaps from my battalion who—"

"Fine. It's about time the Bureau had the use of a car. Tell them it's being repaired in Scotland. Any questions?"

A bit dazed, P asked: "Are you going to show these letters to Major Dagner, sir?"

"What letters? I haven't seen any letters. *But . . .* you won't be much use to us until you learn not to get into trouble that's going to catch up with you."

In other words, solve life's greatest problem by teatime tomorrow. Oh well . . . he had a feeling that Dagner might take the whole thing too seriously. And the Commander? He just couldn't tell.

But it all added up to a long day and when he finally got down to the flat, he ignored the sherry and poured himself a serious whisky. He hadn't even finished *Personal weapons*. But that was something he should consult O'Gilroy about, anyway.

*   *   *

O'Gilroy hadn't meant to lose his followers. Not quite – just make it difficult for them. But they had obeyed only half his order to "stay back and think ahead" and missed the gap in the Piccadilly traffic that let him cross safely and unsuspiciously. So now . . . But it wasn't, he told himself, something he could be absolutely sure about. *Maybe* they had suddenly got the hang of it, become invisible and were still shadowing him. So he had to play the game out. He kept going, but headed north from Piccadilly Circus to explore some Soho streets he didn't know himself.

He was used to cities and their abrupt boundaries that let you go from high fashion to crumbling poverty in the length of a breath. The few steps that took him into Soho were like that, but different. Entering Soho, he seemed to have gone from England to Europe: here he was being jostled by French-speakers, Germans, Italians and politely avoided by Chinese. But no student spies. Past episodes of being a wanted man had given O'Gilroy an acute sense of when he was being followed, and there was no sign of . . .

But there was somebody.

A slightly shorter man in a wide cloth cap, hands thrust deep into the pockets of a donkey jacket. Turning a corner confirmed that he was following, and glancing both ways before crossing the street gave a glimpse of his face. O'Gilroy knew him: Patrick, Patrick something, from down Broad Lane way in Cork. And definitely one

57

of the 'boyos' whom Ranklin had feared. Moreover, making no attempt at subtlety, but grimly plodding along behind.

O'Gilroy still had choices: he could run. Or just just hurry back to Piccadilly and hail a taxi. But perhaps it was best to try and bluff it out, settle the matter with a lie, and if that didn't work, well, it was just one man and smaller than himself. But one choice he didn't have was killing Patrick. He couldn't have explained why, but would have thought anyone who asked for an explanation very odd indeed.

A few yards further was a narrow alleyway leading to a courtyard behind the buildings. O'Gilroy turned in, and waited in the deepest shadow, so Patrick would be outlined against the bright street behind.

Patrick stumped around the corner, stopped and said: "Good day to ye, Conall O'Gilroy – or did ye change yer name along wid the colour av yer soul?"

This, O'Gilroy realised, is going to need one hell of a lie. "Have ye got a message for me?" he demanded.

He couldn't see if Patrick was surprised, since his face was shadowed, but he paused. Then he said: "We have that," and glanced back as another, larger, figure turned into the alley behind him. "Me and Eamon. Right here in our pockets."

How in hell did I miss the second one? But he knew just how: over-confident once he'd spotted Patrick's open following, he hadn't thought of Eamon moving less conspicuously, well back and on the other side of the street. Yet it was a trick he'd been teaching the two recruits half an hour ago. Now he longed for a miracle in which they found him again in the nick of time – but an angel swooping down to carry him off was more likely. Far more likely, if you believed the priests.

Patrick took out a short knife. "Mebbe ye'll take a message yerself—" Behind him, Eamon made the same movement.

His only luck seemed to be that they weren't carrying guns, but neither was he. Legally he could have done so, particularly since he was now a 'gentleman' at least by trade, but London had seemed safe enough, and a gun in the pocket was suspicious. All he had was his walking-stick.

"To yer dead nephew Michael—"

To Ranklin a stick was just a gentleman's accountrement like a pair of gloves; he had never even thought of including it

58

among 'personal weapons'. But at least O'Gilroy had. His wasn't a sword-stick or loaded in any way; like a pistol, such things could arouse suspicion. So it was just an ordinary silver-knobbed stick except that where the brass ferrule had worn and split he hadn't closed the jagged break.

"—yez can tell him rest easy. He's been revenged."

Now O'Gilroy gripped the stick across his body, one hand at each end. It almost touched the walls at either side, leaving no room for sideways swipes. But that was why he hadn't run for the unknown but certainly more open courtyard behind. Here there was no room for the two to come at him together; one had to lead and it was Eamon, the big one. He probably wasn't a knife-fighter, just a knife-killer, but there was no stagey overhead stuff, either: he held the blade properly flat and underhand as he edged forward.

O'Gilroy let go with his left hand and jabbed towards Eamon's midriff. Eamon didn't bother with his knife, just tried to grab the stick with his free hand, and almost got it. He moved fast for a big man.

O'Gilroy took a step back and resumed his two-handed grip. Eamon feinted a lunge to test O'Gilroy's response: he just pushed the stick forward to block. Eamon lunged further, expecting to hit the stick and slash sideways along it to cut O'Gilroy's left hand. But O'Gilroy let go with his right, flipped the knife further aside, then stepped in and banged his right palm into Eamon's face.

The big man bounced against the wall, blinking angrily – but didn't drop the knife. And seeing an opening, Pat scurried past him, ducked as O'Gilroy threw his back to the wall and slashed with the stick, and went right on past.

Now O'Gilroy was surrounded.

He jabbed with the stick to keep Eamon unbalanced, and charged at Pat before he got into his stance, holding the stick like a lunging sword. It missed, he felt the knife slash and catch in his jacket, then he sprawled over Pat, flattening him.

Maybe Pat was winded, certainly he was slowed. O'Gilroy twisted onto his knees, slashed the jagged ferrule across Pat's forehead, then grabbed for his knife arm. Pat screeched and let go the knife. O'Gilroy fumbled for it as he looked up for Eamon, cut his hand but had it before the bigger man reached them.

"Move an inch and I cut his fucking head off!" He tried to snarl it, but it came out panting.

Eamon stopped. "And yer own wid it."

By now O'Gilroy had his left forearm across Pat's throat from behind, soaking his sleeve in the man's dripping blood. "Mebbe. But I'm done fighting the both of yez. If yer still want to kill me, it's with him dead, and that's plain sense."

Pat wriggled, O'Gilroy tightened his grip and jabbed the knife right on the edge of Pat's cheekbone, an inch from his eye. One push, two inches deep, and . . . Pat went very still, breathing fast and very shallow.

Eamon took a heavy breath himself. "Let him loose and I swear on me mother's grave—"

"Shut up." O'Gilroy eased from a crouch to a bend and began slowly dragging Pat backwards. "And stand yer ground," he added as Eamon followed.

After perhaps three yards, the alley opened into a long cobbled yard, overlooked by the backs of two dozen small buildings, but with nobody in sight. Just a stack of old timber and a couple of hand-carts.

O'Gilroy got his back to a wall, the knife back at Pat's eye, and told Eamon: "Walk past me and as far as ye can go. Move yeself!"

The big man moved, slowly and perhaps uncertain of what he was actually going to do. O'Gilroy said nothing, just held the knife very steady.

As Eamon passed out of reach, his movements became more sure; he had decided to obey.

Then Pat went limp. Assuming it was a ruse, O'Gilroy shook him, but his head just flapped, spraying blood; he was out . . . dead? Not when he was still bleeding freely. Half choked, shocked and losing blood, he had fainted. Then Eamon looked back and saw Pat's lolling head.

"I *didn't*, he's not dead!" O'Gilroy screamed. But Eamon was past hearing, was roaring with rage as he charged.

Oh Christ!

O'Gilroy threw the knife. It most likely wouldn't have stuck in, but was still a knife and Eamon swerved. O'Gilroy heaved Pat up by his scruff, toppled him at Eamon's feet, and ran, *ran* for the alley and street and his life. He didn't waste time looking back. He'd know if Eamon caught him.

He came into the flat with one jacket pocket ripped loose and the sleeve soaked with blood. He had a bloody handkerchief around his right hand and the rest of him looked as if he'd been rolling in a filthy alleyway. He'd lost his hat and stick.

Ranklin gaped. "What the devil happened to you?"

"Coupla boyos from Cork, they found me. Like ye was worried about." It was almost as much a relief to tell the truth as reach the sideboard decanters. O'Gilroy felt he had given a lying explanation for his condition at every step from Piccadilly.

Ranklin was about to ask for details, but then didn't. He'd be told if O'Gilroy felt like it; more likely, he'd never know. But before he went to fetch the travelling medicine kit, he had to ask: "Did you kill them?"

Without turning from the drinks, O'Gilroy shook his head. And for once Ranklin was sorry about that. It left unfinished business.

9

The Guards battalions took it in turns to be billeted in the Tower of London, and only when a kilted soldier challenged the taxi did Ranklin know it was the turn of the Scots Guards to keep an eye on the Crown jewels and any fresh-caught traitors housed there. But thereafter, any sense of history had gone with the daytime sight-seers, leaving only black cutouts of battlements against the stars. At ground level there was just the mundane military domesticity of any barracks square. Lamps glowed through the plane trees, turning their leaves back to spring green, and half-lit the gossiping groups of soldiers and wives below. Children darted from group to group, and somebody still on fatigues staggered by slopping a filled bucket.

Ranklin paused at the foot of the officers' mess steps, expecting to feel nostalgia for its comfortable comradeship, but instead felt quite alien. This really wasn't his world any longer. However, his manner immediately convinced the mess corporal when he introduced himself and his mission. A minute or two later Dagner's host, a Major Lawther, appeared.

"Were you asking for Major Dagner?"

"Yes, sir. Captain Ranklin, RA. I, er, work for Major Dagner."

"Ah." There was a knowingness about that 'ah'. "With you chaps I imagine everything's Most Urgent. I'm afraid he hasn't got here, yet. Come in and have a spot."

It was tempting but, again, no longer his world. "Very kind of you, sir, but I think it would be less disruptive if I got a quick word with him out here."

"As you please . . . Did you know Dagner before . . . before he came home?"

"I'm afraid not."

"We met in India, of course." That surprised Ranklin; it was difficult enough to move a Guards battalion out of London, let alone Britain. Seeing his expression, Lawther smiled. "When I was attached to the Viceroy's staff. And they brought him back from . . . whatever he was doing, when his wife fell ill. Sad business, that, he was very cut up when she went."

"His wife died?"

"You didn't know? – the usual typhoid, I believe."

Ranklin nodded. "He hadn't mentioned it. But we only met a few days ago."

"Ah. This was, oh, must be seven years ago now. Ah, I think I hear a cab."

It was really a motor-taxi, but Major Lawther belonged to a generation and class that would for ever hear them as cabs.

Dagner appeared in his Gurkha mess dress of rifle-green and glittering black wellingtons. "Good evening, Major. And Captain Ranklin – I suppose this means a little hiccup in our affairs?"

"Evening, Dagner," Major Lawther said hastily. "His Lordship ain't here yet, so I'll leave you to it." He went back inside.

"It's O'Gilroy," Ranklin said. "He ran into a couple of what he calls the 'boyos', the ones he knew in Ireland. I didn't get the full story, but they tried to knife him and he fought them off, but didn't kill them. So I'm afraid we have to assume the word, that O'Gilroy's to be found in London, will get around. I thought you'd better know immediately. Oh – and I took it on myself to tip off Major Kell, since it touches on his field. He said he'd be along as soon as he could." He paused, then added: "And when he comes, could we refer to O'Gilroy as Gorman? – it's his normal alias."

"Quite. Thank you." Dagner thought this over. "Then, also before he comes, d'you have any solution to suggest?"

"Only to send O'Gilroy and myself abroad. It's where we belong. And Paris is a good half-day closer to most places."

"Hm. But I don't like letting you go until the training pro-gramme's really under way."

Ranklin had expected that. "Then I had one rather wild idea for O'Gilroy himself—" They had heard neither taxi nor cab, but there was Major Kell stomping up the cobbled slope, wearing plain evening clothes (as Ranklin was: he had changed, assuming that anything less would get him redirected to the Traitors' Gate). Kell headed the counter-intelligence service and didn't bother to call himself anything like "Chief". That apart, he was a year or so older than Ranklin, with an oval face, smallish moustache, smoothed-down hair and a bland pop-eyed expression that suggested that he'd like to believe you, but . . .

They each knew other already and Ranklin's by-hand-of-bearer-for-your-eyes-only message had given Kell the bones of the story, so Dagner opened by asking bluntly: "Do you regard these Irish thuggees as being in your province?"

"Not if I can bloody well help it," Kell said quite as bluntly. "I try to leave them to Special Branch at the Yard – that's what they were originally set up for – and keep my tiny band for dealing with real espionage. And, if I may say so, I never approved of your Chief mixing the two up. But—" he sighed dramatically; "—I suppose your Bureau's requirements are different from mine. What's the worst that can happen now?"

Ranklin said: "They try to kill him again."

"That being the case," Kell said, "is your chap ready to say who this pair was? Names, descriptions?"

"No," Ranklin said quickly. "And I don't think he can be persuaded."

Kell said: "Assuming they didn't come to London looking for your man, they came for some other purpose – such as planting a bomb that will kill a dozen people."

"I doubt if they'll be up to it; Gorman came back covered in blood that wasn't his own. And if they think he'll report them, they've probably left London already."

Kell nodded without commitment. "Perhaps. But if there is what the press calls 'a Fenian outrage' we can hardly keep this from the Branch. And then they'd probably arrest your own man on some pretext and sweat the names out of him."

Ranklin glanced at Dagner, but was left to answer himself. "We try to select men who don't babble just because a policeman gives them a nasty look. And having worked with Gorman in the field, I can say confidently that he doesn't. All we could do is turn him into an enemy."

They had instinctively begun to pace up and down in the pool of light by the steps, just as instinctively falling into step and about-turning when Dagner, the senior, did. The soldiers had given them one superior glance of those off duty for those still on, then ignored them.

Kell said: "All that may well be so, but let me put *my* position.

None of us really cares about a dozen Londoners getting blown to bits; we've got bigger things to worry about. But in order to do my work, I need the complete confidence of Special Branch, in effect Scotland Yard itself. As much as anything, just to save my men from getting arrested. Like you, we don't officially exist, so all our eavesdropping and opening mail and general Peeping-Tomism is strictly illegal.

"So if I denounce your man to the Branch it *won't* be because I think he'll tell them something. Frankly, I don't care if he does or not. It'll be because I just can't risk having Sir Basil think I'm covering up for Irish brigands and withdraw his co-operation. My work would stop dead."

The lamplight occasionally reflected off his glasses, alternating his intense pop-eyed stare with complete blankness. "I am prepared to wait," he went on, "and see if there is a bomb or whatever – and pray that it isn't the assassination of an important man. If it happens, then for my own protection I shall go straight to Sir Basil and tell him what you've told me. The best I can offer is to pretend you've only just told me."

"Quite." Dagner looked at Ranklin. But Ranklin couldn't find anything to say.

Kell said: "I'm sorry to be so blunt, Major, but you don't depend on police co-operation. Of course, if they came looking for your . . . Gorman? – and he was, say, abroad and out of touch . . . well, that's up to you."

"Quite," Dagner said again. "And thank you for delaying your dinner. May I try and arrange a taxi-cab for you?"

But Kell apparently had a friend waiting outside in a car. When he had gone, Dagner said: "I do see his point of view. But before he came, you were about to suggest something."

"It's a bit fantastical, but at least it gets O'Gilroy out of London: send him to Brooklands to learn to fly."

Ranklin had been braced for Dagner to react with astonishment, so was startled when he said: "Yes, that's rather a good idea. Aeroplanes do seem to be the coming thing. It could help if the Bureau had some expertise there. Only – d'you think O'Gilroy's up to it? And doesn't it cost rather a lot?"

Still recovering from his surprise, Ranklin said: "He's certainly very keen, and his strength's on the practical, mechanical side.

65

Anyway, I don't think it can be all that difficult: I believe there's even some women pilots by now. As to cost, I believe it takes seventy-five to a hundred pounds to get your certificate of competence."

Assuming that Dagner never expressed anything except deliberately, he now deliberately winced. "That's quite a serious sum."

It was indeed. A hundred pounds was almost exactly half Ranklin's yearly pay as a Gunner captain. "But I could contribute something towards it. Half, say." Ranklin's expression – guileless innocence – was also under control as he waited for Dagner to ask how a man so deeply in debt could raise such a sum – and counting on an officer and gentleman not to ask any such thing.

Probably Dagner wouldn't have asked such a thing anyway, but right then a closed Rolls-Royce trundled gently up the slope towards them. Dagner finished off quickly but smoothly: "That's most generous of you. And in that case, I feel bound to authorise the other half. Can you get this under way immediately? – tomorrow?"

"Certainly. I'll start by getting O'Gilroy down to Brooklands first thing. Then find who the best people are to teach him. I have a connection with someone there."

"So I understand." So the Commander had told Dagner about Corinna.

10

Ranklin was up early next morning, first telegraphing to the only hotel he could find near Brooklands – the Hound and Spear at Weybridge – to book a room, then sending O'Gilroy off without waiting for a reply. For the first time, he had seen the Irishman really taken aback by good fortune. Tailored clothes, grand meals and travelling by the Orient Express were things O'Gilroy had not so much shrugged off as on. As some men feared their name was on a bullet, he accepted that his was on a pot of gold at the rainbow's end. That was how he passed unquestioned in his new life since the world, lazy as ever, accepted him at his own valuation.

But being sent to learn to fly was an entirely new rainbow.

Even if he was, in part, paying for it himself. Dagner had been right in thinking that – at least legally – Ranklin no longer had any money of his own. However, he and O'Gilroy jointly shared some £600 tucked away in a Versailles bank, acquired by selling a false codebook to the Austrian embassy in Paris. Ranklin had tried to persuade himself that cheating a potential enemy was pure patriotism, and been alarmed at how easily he had succeeded. Not telling the Bureau about it had been . . . well, it was O'Gilroy's secret, too.

Anyway, the Bureau *expected* its agents to have some money of their own. Its blinkered attitude to their expenses showed that.

Oddly, when they had discussed payment the night before, it had been O'Gilroy who had been the more concerned. "But if yer putting up money of yer own, won't he be knowing . . . I mean thinking . . . ?"

"I can't stop him thinking."

"But if'n he thinks ye . . ." The trouble was O'Gilroy wasn't supposed to know about the bankruptcy. But it was one of those secrets that, like Army-issue trousers, had worn until you could see right through it.

"What he believes is his business." Ruthless as Dagner might be, Ranklin didn't think he'd risk the shame of prying into a brother officer's financial affairs.

O'Gilroy didn't understand this. But then, he knew Ranklin didn't share his desire to fly – or many other things. Their partnership had never been based on the self-deception of mutual understanding.

*   *   *

Only when O'Gilroy had gone did Ranklin realise Dagner had got in even earlier and was sitting at a table in the Commander's room surrounded by books and newspaper cuttings. At first he assumed this was preparation for Sir Caspar Alerion's lecture – he was due at eleven – but then saw one of the books was *Jane's Fighting Ships*.

He apologised for barging in, but Dagner waved that aside. "I'm just checking on some rather disturbing naval news I picked up last night . . . Though strictly, naval affairs aren't really our business, are they?"

"Well, coming under the Admiralty and them with an Intelligence department of their own . . ."

"Hmm." Dagner shut the book with a snap. "You got O'Gilroy off, then? Then you probably want to talk about Sir Caspar, late of the Foreign Office . . ."

Looking at Sir Caspar, Ranklin rather hoped he'd led a life of indulgent wickedness; otherwise, nature and age had been cruelly unkind. He was short and very fat, had several chins, a bulbous mottled nose, watery eyes and a skin mapped with broken veins. Yet he carried himself with immense dignity, his waddle seemed an imperial strut – provided you ignored his wheezing – his frock-coat was perfectly cut and his waistcoat, if a trifle artistic, at least suggested a fashionable portraitist rather than a Bloomsbury daubster.

They met in the dining room of the Whitehall Court flat: Sir Caspar, flanked by Ranklin and Dagner at one end, the four recruits along the sides.

"Had to be awake rather early to get up from the country,"

Alerion said, unashamedly spiking his coffee from a hip flask. He drank, looked at the four young faces at the other end of the table and, slowly, beamed. "Gentlemen, you have no idea how glad I am to see you. You represent, to me, the end of a long road from the Battle of Fontenoy, nearly two hundred years ago. Where Lord Charles Hay of the Grenadiers invited his opponents: 'Gentlemen of the French Guard, fire first.'

"Luckily the French commander was just as much of a blithering idiot and he returned the invitation so the British ended up taking the first shot. That would have come too late for me if Lord Charles had been my commander, because I'd have been over the hills and far away instanter. But that attitude that it's *unfair* to take advantage of an opponent, even to the point of scouting out his strength and positions, has taken longer to die than the tens of thousands of men it got killed. We still have our Lord Charles's."

He gave a little grunt of pain and moved with fragile stiffness in his chair, then sighed and relaxed slightly. "Your business, gentlemen, is not secrets but the men who know the secrets. Every nation has a class entrusted with secrets and the power to create them. Such men are usually obvious, and often their weaknesses are, too – a love of drink, women, money, little boys – but let me point out another: their ideals.

"In the past century there's been a great rise in nationalism – call it patriotism, if you like – replacing the Continental outlook of the old aristocracy, family and class loyalties that didn't bother with frontiers. Lord Charles wasn't thinking of his men's lives or winning the battle for England, just upholding the honour of his own – and the French commander's – kind.

"You may find this patriotism quite splendid—" it was clear that he had reservations; "—but, like all things, it comes with a price. The more loyalty a man gives his country, the more he expects it to be worthy of his loyalty, and the more he can hate the way it's being governed. The monarchist in a republic, the republican in a monarchy – extreme examples of men who consider themselves the only *true* patriots. And by upholding their ideals, are already halfway down the road to treason. It may be your task to drag them the rest of the way. Patriots, gentlemen, are your *prey*."

This was strong stuff, and expecting a surge of distaste to cross the new boys' faces, Ranklin was surprised to see them looking either amused or curious. He quickly adjusted his own face.

"Since you're going to spend much of your working life lying to people," Alerion said pleasantly, "it's perhaps only fair that you'll also spend it listening to lies. Some told in all innocence because someone believes, *yearns*, for them to be true. This is dangerous. But far, far more dangerous if you also yearn for them to be true, because you will have joined him in his cosy, warm fantasy."

He smiled suddenly. "For instance, that story about Lord Charles Hay at Fontenoy is almost certainly untrue. We believe it because it makes us feel superior to Lord Charles – and because it comes from Voltaire, who's known to be a great writer. But he became one by shaping stories to fit his own ends. Truth is a lonely business, gentlemen."

Two more cups of coffee later – both improved from the hip flask – Alerion slumped back in his chair, exhausted. It wasn't the sort of occasion for clapping, but after a silent moment, an appreciative mumble came from the dazed and surfeited audience.

Dagner said gravely: "Thank you very much, Sir Caspar." Then he leant forward, hands clasped on the table-top, face hard and even more inscrutable than usual. "Gentlemen: Sir Caspar has given you some down-to-earth advice. I want you to think about it, and the change it marks in your lives. Some of us have been in battle. We know it's not like *The Boy's Own Paper*, that it's nasty, messy, muddled and brutal. I'm sure it was always so, that Caesar's wars were no different: *De Bello Gallico* was a political tract. His soldiers would have written a very different book. War *is* brutal – yet all of us here have found ways to avoid becoming brutalised by it.

"You can now forget these.

"Forget the idea that you'll just be following orders. In this game orders can't cover every eventuality and you'll be beyond reach of any extra help. Forget the comradeship of battle: from now on, you will be acting alone. Forget the duty you had to save your men and friends from danger: on this battlefield, you have no men, and your friends will have their own battles elsewhere. I cannot stress too strongly what Sir Caspar said about being *alone*. And alone not even with your conscience, because you have no conscience save that of your country. You will be acting outside the law, even the laws of war.

"Yet, just as we learn not to be brutalised by battle, we must practise deceit, dishonesty and dishonourable behaviour without ourselves taking on these qualities. Because to be of any value to our country we *must* remain loyal, trustworthy and honest. No easy task, gentlemen." He smiled thinly. "Yet, I believe that if we can learn to cope with battle we are already halfway there.

"And one more thing to forget: any hope of reward. But in that, I believe, lies our true strength. Because unlike self-seeking generals and bickering politicians, unlike civil servants chasing vapid honours and businessmen piling up money, *we* are working only for what we believe in. The simple knowledge that our country will not reward us makes us free to act for it without any thought of self. It is a great freedom. Cherish it."

It was a good, an appropriate, speech, Ranklin had to agree. So what was wrong with him that his own reaction was to think *Yes, but* . . . and be glad O'Gilroy wasn't here?

*　　*　　*

The new recruits were gone, out to lunch or back up to the office, but the three of them still sat there because Alerion didn't seem to want to move. He was staring vaguely at the disarranged and empty chairs at the far end of the long table. The room was as bright as it ever got with daylight, but it was indirect, that cool interior light that the Dutch painters understood so well.

"Can I get you some fresh coffee, Sir Caspar?" Ranklin offered.

"No, you can get me a damned great whisky and soda." He roused himself and lit a small cigar while Ranklin went to the sideboard. "So those are tomorrow's unsung heroes, off to secret battle armed with my ramblings and your clarion call of King and Country—"

"I don't think you're being quite fair," Dagner protested mildly. "If I'd become overtly patriotic, they'd have fidgeted and looked at their bootlaces. But an agent does have to have a clear idea of who he's working for, far clearer than a soldier. History's full of mercenaries who fought, and fought well, just for love of battle and a shilling a day. But espionage has to have a purpose that you can believe in when you're out there on your own, facing far worse than battle. And we, sitting safe here on

71

our backsides, have to know that they believe, or how can we trust them?"

Alerion let out a mouthful of smoke with a long humming noise. "I want to see this Bureau of yours survive – and prosper. It's come nearly a hundred years late, we threw away everything we learned in the eighteenth century and the French wars . . ."

He saw the glass Ranklin had quietly placed by him, nodded his thanks and then addressed him for the first time. "You haven't been in this game very long, have you, Captain?"

Ranklin, who had isolated himself in his 'Yes, but . . .' mood, was disconcerted by the prospect of being asked his opinion. But then Dagner said: "Captain R is one of our most senior agents."

That may have headed Alerion off. But while he was looking at his glass, and taking occasional sips, he didn't seem to be addressing Dagner. Indeed, he might even have been talking to himself, in short disjointed phrases: "I mentioned the fantasies you run into in this business . . . It takes another form, too . . . When you've uncovered so many secrets that you think that now you *know* . . . Like an actor who's played the king too long comes to think he can change the world . . . Dare say we all want our dreams to come true, but mostly there's someone looking over our shoulder, messing it up, making it just another day's work . . . Probably just as well, really . . . Soldiering does destroy soldiers. How can we expect spying not to destroy spies? . . . Only how can you tell if you can't see any blood . . . ?" He shook his head impatiently. "I'm starting to ramble."

By now Ranklin was feeling thoroughly uneasy, and it was a relief when Dagner brought the conversation smoothly down to matters of fact. "I believe you know Italy well, Sir Caspar."

"Knew it, knew it . . . Always been a good place for the English to go to seed. I suppose I shouldn't ask if you've got a ploy going on there?"

"Do you feel we should have anything going on there?" Dagner turned the question deftly.

"Hm. You won't find much competition from our embassy, not under Rennell Rodd." He chuckled, then frowned. "But looking for secrets of Italian policy is looking for a haystack under a needle. In my day there was a policy on every café table and a couple of secrets underneath it and I doubt much has changed. Bismarck said it all, thirty years ago: 'Italy has a large appetite and very poor teeth'."

"Something I learned only last night," Dagner said casually, "and that rather surprised me. It probably shouldn't have done, but most of my soldiering's been done a thousand miles from the sea . . . That the Navy's pretty well pulled out of the Mediterranean."

This surprised Ranklin, too, but Sir Caspar just nodded. "Ah yes, that. You're thinking of the route to Suez."

"And India beyond."

"Of course. And you aren't the only one who's concerned about us passing that responsibility to the French."

Still befogged, Ranklin remembered that the only stupid question is the one you're ashamed to ask. "Was this something official, sir? – and when?"

"Not officially *announced*, good Lord no. But it happened about a year ago. One fine day the Royal Navy virtually vanished from the Med, and the French fleet vanished from the Channel and the Atlantic. The Kaiser didn't need any informers to tell him a deal had been struck on who guarded what for the other."

Ranklin nodded. A year ago, he hadn't been in this business, and his own problems were blotting out any interest in naval doings anyway.

Alerion went on: "The thinking goes that now Russia's our ally, she's no threat to India so there'll be no need for quick reinforcement out there. Meanwhile, von Tirpitz is certainly building a damn great fleet on our own doorstep and that has to be the Navy's greatest concern."

Dagner said thoughtfully: "But it does seem to mean that the Italian and Austrian navies, if they combined, would control the eastern end of the Med. And the route to Suez."

"Technically, Italy's already allied with both Austria and Germany in the Triple Alliance, but I doubt that means much. Italy's bound to join in a major war, out of sheer pride at becoming a new European Power – but who's going to pay the bill? *That*'s Giolitti's problem; he's been their Prime Minister, on and off, for twenty years and it looks as if he'll get back at the November elections. And he's a rogue but no fool, and knows his best policy is to wait and see who'll pay Italy the biggest bribe to take sides. And his worst fear is his own fanatics pushing him into a war with France or Austria – or even us – out of nationalist pride and without bribes."

"But meanwhile," Dagner reminded him, "the route to India . . ."

"I think we're realising that we can't be powerful everywhere. We have to leave some things to diplomacy – and your Bureau, of course," Alerion added politely.

11

While Dagner escorted Sir Caspar out, Ranklin checked the room over for any papers that might have got left behind, and called down by voicepipe for someone to clear away the coffee tray. Then went upstairs.

Dagner was back at the littered work-table; he looked up with a thin smile. "What did you make of Sir Caspar?"

"Can't say I followed everything he said," Ranklin said tactfully. "But most seemed to be sound, if cynical, sense."

"Quite. And he confirmed what I heard last night about the naval situation in the Med. Perhaps you gathered that it was a sort of reunion of old India hands? – we even got Lord Curzon to drop in . . ." Of course: Curzon had been Viceroy of India when Dagner had won his DSO, had probably pinned it on him. It must have been Curzon's Rolls-Royce Ranklin had seen at the Tower last night. "They were quite cut up about it all."

"Understandably," Ranklin felt he should say.

"And it ties up with something Senator Falcone was telling me yesterday afternoon." He pulled out his watch. "Would you care to hear about it over lunch downstairs?"

"Of course." Ranklin hadn't been sure he was going to hear what the Senator had said – nor that he really wanted to. The less he was involved in office strategies, apart from the training programme, the more free he'd be to get abroad again. Hiding O'Gilroy away down at Brooklands could only be a temporary measure.

The tables in the dark-panelled restaurant on the ground floor were widely spaced, and the lunchtime crowd had thinned out, so they were safe from being overheard. Even so, Dagner switched to Indian reminiscences whenever a waiter came near.

"How *au fait* are you with naval matters?" he began.

"A pure landlubber," Ranklin said promptly. "As I say, we don't usually touch on such things."

"It all seems to begin seven years ago when we launched HMS *Dreadnought*, which made every other battleship in the world – our own included – out of date. Since then, everybody's been building their own versions." He shot his cuff and consulted some figures he'd pencilled on it. "We've now got eighteen, plus eight battle-cruisers which are faster but thinner-skinned. And of those, according to *Whitaker's* – something anybody can look up – only three are in the Mediterranean. And the French, who are supposed to be guarding the Med, have only *two* dreadnoughts anywhere. Against that, the Italians already have four and the Austrians two and are building two more. So, on paper, we and the French are already outnumbered down there and it could soon be worse. Why are we happy with that? – I thought the Navy was there to protect our Empire and trade."

Ranklin hadn't seen Dagner so positive, almost aggressive, before. He just had time to murmur: "The German fleet in the North Sea . . ." before their soup arrived.

When they were alone again, Dagner said: "Quite. But the matter might be a little more urgent that most people suppose . . . Because what Senator Falcone came to tell our Foreign Office people was that, three months ago, the Italian Foreign Minister signed a secret treaty with Austria putting the Italian fleet under Austrian command in the event of a war. So we *would* be facing a unified fleet."

Dagner's quiet tone seemed aimed at understating this news and, by implication, emphasising it. So Ranklin put down his soup spoon and frowned. Then asked: "Has he any proof of this treaty?"

"That's what the Foreign Office asked him – not too tactfully, I understand. No, he hasn't. But he hopes to get a copy of the treaty before too long. Or so he says. So the FO suggested he come back when he'd got that. He then – mistakenly, I think – offered them a deal."

Ranklin winced, imagining the sudden Ice Age that would have visited King Charles Street. One did not offer the British Foreign Office *deals*.

"Exactly," Dagner smiled. "That's why he turned to us."

"He'd turned to us before he saw the FO. Though perhaps he guessed what sort of reception he'd get there."

"I wouldn't be surprised. He's very much an Italian nationalist who hates the idea of subservience to Austria. I find that reassuring, that one can understand his motives." He saw Ranklin's dubious look and smiled. "No, Captain, I'm not making the mistake of thinking because we agree with the Senator on one thing, he must be really just an Englishman with a funny accent. I'm sure that, quite apart from his nationalism, his own political ambitions are mixed up in this. We'll have to watch out for that— Did you ever hear about Hodson, the chap who actually set up Hodson's Horse?" That was for the waiter taking away their soup plates. And he did it so quickly that Ranklin never got to hear about Hodson.

"Anyway," Dagner resumed, "what he's offering is to prompt a strike in the shipyard at Trieste that's building most of the Austrian dreadnoughts."

"Oh." Ranklin couldn't think how to react. "Er . . . just like that?"

"I didn't ask how." Dagner gave him a reproving look. "And I doubt I'd understand anyway: I know almost nothing about industry. But I think we must accept that he does; that's how he made his money. And he claims strong family connections with Trieste – where most of the shipyard workers are also Italian. Building warships for Austria that *could* be used against Italy – one can see an inflammatory argument there. He also mentioned Oberdan – have you heard of him?"

Ranklin just shook his head, since the waiter was delivering their main course. He couldn't remember what he'd ordered but it turned out to be the rump steak with oyster sauce. He felt he had to justify it by pointing out: "With one thing and another, I didn't get any real dinner last night."

Dagner nodded and consulted his cuff again. "I've verified Oberdan, at least. He was an Italian nationalist but citizen of Austria who got hanged by the authorities in Trieste back in 1882, at about this time of year. Apparently he's become a martyr, a useful name to shout at riots. And that's what the Senator hopes for: not just a strike but a riot with the workers destroying the shipyard machinery in an outburst of Luddism."

"Sabotage," Ranklin muttered, but not really listening to himself because he felt this was either an opium dream or very deep water.

"I beg your pardon?"

"Sorry. Sabotage. New slang from the French railway strike last year, when they tore up the sleepers, that the French call '*sabots*'. Wooden shoes."

"Sabotage." Dagner savoured the word. "Thank you. So, such things can happen." He ate quietly for a while. Then: "I find that rather terrifying – even that such a word has appeared in our language. We talked of Secret Weapons the other day, but this could trump the lot."

Ranklin had long believed that any talk of bloody-minded, bone-idle, money-grubbing civilian workers should be a banned in Army messes, so wasn't going to get involved. Instead: "You said the Senator was offering a deal: what does he want from us?"

"Help with armaments. He's not just interested in naval affairs, but in improving the Italian Army as well."

"Money?"

"Oh no, no."

"That's usually all it takes. I don't believe there are any restrictions on the export of arms." He had wondered if Dagner, fresh from the Khyber Pass where selling even a rifle to a tribesman was probably a hanging offence, realised how easy the rest of the world found it to buy British battleships, French aeroplanes, German cannon, no matter who you were. All you needed was hard cash.

But Dagner seemed to appreciate this already. "He's just one man, rich but still not the Italian Government, and he thinks we could help in cutting red tape, speeding things up. And one thing he's looking for is an aeroplane – to replace the one he thought he was going to buy in Brussels."

Ranklin pushed back his plate, feeling that this was more his size. No longer heady talk of secret treaties and shipyard riots, just buying an aeroplane. "We need O'Gilroy. He was going to take the Senator to Brooklands this weekend."

"I know. But since he's there already, I wonder if you felt like escorting the Senator down there tomorrow?"

Ranklin thought for a moment, then asked: "Who am I?"

Dagner smiled. "Somebody from the War Office who's just been posted to the Flying Corps staff and is trying to get his eye in – so you don't have to know anything, just seem eager to learn."

But even that, Ranklin reckoned, showed a remarkable trust in his acting skills. And it hadn't been how he'd planned this

Saturday, but— "Actually, Mrs Finn has a brother who's involved in aeronautics there. D'you mind if I . . . ?"

"By all means make it a day out. Other people are always the best disguise. And do light a cigarette, I'm not having any pudding."

Dagner himself didn't seem to have any habits: he didn't smoke, didn't fiddle with his knife and fork . . . Probably he saw such things as elements of disguise; Ranklin had no doubt he could appear a confirmed smoker or cutlery-fiddler at will, but kept his real self stripped of any compulsions. The Complete Professional. What was he like at home? – but then Ranklin remembered that with his wife dead, there was no home . . .

"Happy to go," he mumbled, feeling guilty about even knowing that about Dagner. He lit his cigarette. "Then are we going ahead on this . . . this 'deal'?"

"We can't change the Admiralty's – and presumably the Cabinet's – mind about withdrawing protection from the India route. But that matters less if Austria's new dreadnoughts are delayed."

"Or if," Ranklin said thoughtfully, "a shipyard riot gets out of hand, Austrian troops open fire on Italian workers . . ."

"And there's bad blood between Italy and Austria. Yes, I'd rest easy with that – particularly since our own part is so much in the background that it won't be suspected."

"You don't feel it comes a bit close to policy-making?"

Dagner began to look stern, then decided not to and spoke gently, almost as if explaining to a child. "But doesn't the policy already exist? It was to set up our Bureau to further Britain's interests by secret means. Sooner or later – clearly later, in Britain's case – every government realises it needs such a service to do things it cannot be caught doing itself. Politicians want to be able to say truthfully 'We didn't know, we didn't order this' while being glad it's been done. Whether that makes their business cleaner than ours, I won't presume to judge. It certainly makes ours dirty, and we have to face up to that. But we have been given a *mission*, Captain, a mission, not a sinecure."

Back upstairs, Ranklin tried to raise Corinna by telephone, first at her flat, then at Sherring's City office. He caught her there, sounding brisk and business-like.

"About tomorrow," he began hesitantly, "I'm afraid I've got to escort an Italian senator down to Brooklands. He's hoping to find an aeroplane—"

"Introduce him to Andrew, then," she said promptly.

"Thank you. Another thing, O'Gilroy's also down there, to learn to fly—"

Her laughter nearly fused the instrument to his ear. "Conall? Learning to *fly*? Has he gone crazy about airplanes, too?"

"You know him . . ."

"Who's teaching him?"

"That's my next question: can he ask Andrew who to go to?"

"Of course. I'm not having Conall's neck broken by anyone but the best. I'll telegraph Andrew right away." There was a crackling silence, then: "Who's this senator?"

"A Signor Falcone from Turin. Something big in textile machinery over there, big enough to be staying at the Ritz . . ." He held his breath, waiting to see if she'd take the bait.

"Is that so?" she said. "I wouldn't mind hearing something about the Italian textile business . . . and seeing Conall again. Would I be welcome? I could bring the automobile and save you having to introduce yourself to Andrew as the man who's wronging his sister."

Ranklin stared at the earpiece as if it had become a snake. The line from here to the City was probably loaded with eavesdropping telephone girls; certainly one in his own outer office.

Mind, it was quite possible that that was why Corinna had said such a thing.

"Most welcome," he said weakly. "Could we say ten o'clock at the Ritz?"

After he had hung up, he wondered if he shouldn't have said something about the Senator being the target for some assassin. But that certainly wasn't for the eavesdroppers. And the Senator was under Scotland Yard's protection, wasn't he?

12

Only, when he met Senator Falcone ten minutes before Corinna was due, it turned out that he wasn't.

"In England," the Senator said jovially, "I am sure there is no problem. After they were sure I get alive to the Foreign Office, they were not much interested, and though I am sure your policemen are as wonderful as everyone says, they are still policemen. It is being followed by a strange dog."

Which told Ranklin little more than that Falcone's English was at least adequate. That apart, he seemed a beefy, friendly man whose clothes were . . . well, a little natty. His suit was a shade too light, his necktie a bit too cheerful and the cloth cap didn't belong until Ranklin realised the Senator was hoping to be offered a flight and would then wear the cap backwards, as aviators in photographs always seemed to. He was wearing a cap himself, but only because it went with his tweed suit and he reckoned that an aerodrome equated to a country race-course. He certainly didn't plan to risk meeting his God with his headgear back to front.

Then Corinna appeared in the back of a chauffeur-driven Daimler. It was a sunny day, but the car had a very upright Pullman body and the most they could do was open all the windows. It was her father Reynard's car, and he obviously didn't think the English summer happened often enough to justify a folding hood. Ranklin sat on a pull-down seat opposite Corinna and Falcone, who was carrying a large sealed envelope he had picked up at the hotel desk but not bothered to open yet.

Corinna was talkative and smiley, as she instinctively was with strangers. "You know we're going to the wrong place?" she said as they rolled down Park Lane. "They're having a big aerial race up at Hendon so all the action's going to be there."

"That is why I wish to go to Brooklands," Falcone answered, doing some toothy smiling of his own. "It will be more quiet there without all the peasants who wish only to see somebody killed. There is more time to talk with true aeronauts."

"I'd guess most of them will be at Hendon, too, but at least you can meet my brother. I know he'll be at Brooklands."

"Yes, Captain Ranklin is telling me your brother – Andrew, I think? – is building his own aeroplane."

"It's finished and flying by now, but not built by himself. It was done by proper craftsmen, but to his own design. What else did *Captain* Ranklin tell you?"

The emphasis was to warn Ranklin that he'd forgotten to tell her what part he was playing that day, a basic mistake he should have grown out of.

This wasn't the first time he had been to Brooklands, a banked motor-racing track built by a rich landowner to promote British motoring and please his motor-mad young wife. Ranklin had gone once to watch a motor-race, and then with a brother officer who wanted to test his new motor-car on the banking. But it was only in the last few years that aviators had begun to use the space enclosed by the track as a flying field, sharing it with a sewage farm into which they apparently crashed so regularly that a special hosing-down hut had been added.

They drove in through a tunnel under the banking on the north side and then down beside the finishing straight to the 'aviation village' at the south end. This was a collection of wooden buildings and a long terrace of identical sheds backing onto the banking of the motor track. Nobody seemed to be flying, but there were half a dozen aeroplanes of various shapes being tinkered with in front of the sheds. Ranklin later learnt that by mid-morning the day was already nearly half over, the windless hours around dawn and dusk being the safest time for novice pilots and unproven aeroplanes.

Corinna seemed to know her way around and, inevitably, to be known by almost everybody. She replied cheerily to several men in shirt-sleeves and oil smudges (whose names, Ranklin guessed, she couldn't remember) as she led the way to the Blue Bird Restaurant, a glassed conservatory in front of one of the workshops. They sat down at an outside table and Ranklin ordered coffee.

Falcone sat itchily, obviously longing to get closer to the aeroplanes, but Corinna smiled reassuringly and said: "Andrew'll show you around and introduce you to people."

"He knows you are here?"

"He knows. He'll just be scraping off the top layer of grease." There was a firmness in her voice that suggested a past occasion when Andrew had turned up unfit for social consumption.

Ranklin held up his pipe. "D'you mind if I . . . ?" She smiled approval and he lit it. In truth, she didn't approve of smoking at all, but would have choked to death rather than give men yet another excuse to get away by themselves. In the same spirit, she looked grimly at two little groups of wives and girlfriends making the best of each other's company while the men got on with their latest craze. Without being a tomboy, Corinna would happily have ruined her long white gloves rather than be left to gossip on the sidelines.

Coffee and Andrew Sherring arrived simultaneously. He was clearly his father's son, towering over Ranklin and Falcone, but to anyone who had met Reynard this was a papier-mâché version of the granite original. He carried his height and broad shoulders in a self-conscious stoop.

He shook hands, obviously having put on gloves for that purpose, since he was in shirt-sleeves and a half-buttoned waistcoat. Then he kissed Corinna. "Hi, little sister. I'm afraid we haven't got much to show you today, most of the guys are—"

"At Hendon, we know. But Senator Falcone prefers a quiet word with the back-room boys. And did you get my telegram yesterday?"

"Oh sure. I got your pal O'Gilroy fixed up with the Bristol school here. He'll probably be around at lunchtime."

"Thank you. Now—" clearly handing out a reward; "—Senator Falcone was telling me he was one of the guys behind the volunteer flotilla that went to Africa a couple of years back."

From that moment, she and Ranklin became part of the landscape. Andrew swung round on Falcone and his craggy-soft face cracked into a grin. "That's really so, sir? Then you know Cagno and Manissero? And maybe Professor Panetti?"

"But of course, they are my friends." Falcone's smile was just as delighted.

Andrew gulped his coffee. "Let me introduce you to a couple of the boys before they get off for Hendon. Corrie, can you and . . . ?" He waved a hand at Ranklin, having forgotten his name already.

Corinna smiled indulgently. "You go right ahead, we'll trail along in your dust. But you'd better find the Senator some overalls if—"

Falcone made a sweeping gesture across his jacket, which was pale enough to show a fly's footprint, said: "Oh, poof," and hurried to match Andrew's lanky stride.

"Greater love of machinery hath no man than he who won't take off a twenty-dollar coat to get a closer look at it." She sipped her coffee. "You, my poor darling, are obviously an anachronism. I've never known you get excited by so much as a pencil sharpener."

"I have a secret vice: leave me alone with an artillery piece and I can't keep my hands to myself."

"Is that so? Remind me not to share a room with one: I might be offended if I forced you to choose. I suppose I shouldn't ask just why you and Conall are interested in the Senator."

"O'Gilroy's here quite genuinely—"

"But not you."

Ranklin shrugged casually. "He's interested in buying stuff for the Italian Army, like aeroplanes. We're interested in his interest. By the way, d'you know anything about BSA? – Birmingham Small Arms?"

"Never heard of it, but I'll listen now." What they both heard was a sudden clattering roar from across the tarmac. "Shall we join the grease monkeys?"

*　　*　　*

Like most people, Ranklin had spottted few differences between the various aeroplanes he had glimpsed in the recent skies. If pushed, he might have recalled that some appeared to be double-decked in the matter of wings whilst others were single-decked – but no more. Now, after half an hour wandering around in the wake of Andrew Sherring and Falcone, and overhearing their chatter, he was astonished by the variety which they saw in even the half-dozen aeroplanes on view.

Clearly they varied in size: from just over twenty feet from wing-tip to wing-tip to twice that. And the chassis that held the ground wheels ranged from what looked like an upended iron bedstead bound with rubber bands to simple V-shapes clutching the axle. Some had the engine and propeller (he was impressed by the propellers, which were beautifully carved wooden sculptures) at the front, others at the back, which meant that the body of the aeroplane had to detour around them in a forest of struts and wires. Wires! – he had never been close enough to realise that every aeroplane was held together by what looked like the offspring of a birdcage and a harp.

But there were as many common denominators as differences: the framework was always of carefully shaped wooden struts and spars (he wasn't surprised to learn that there were many ex-boatbuilders among the workers) covered with tight-stretched fabric, often patched, and varnished against the weather. He flicked a finger surreptitiously against one machine and it was taut as a drum. And gradually he began to appreciate a mechanical logic in what he saw.

In fact, Ranklin had a reasonably good grounding in simple science and engineering: the first of his two years at the Royal Military Academy had been shared with future Engineer officers. Now he tried to recall that teaching and see how machines which he could clearly put out of action with a penknife might charge through the air at speeds which, as wind, would uproot strong trees and flip roofs off houses.

Abruptly he realised they were now standing outside a workshop and by a quite simple-looking machine, sparkling with fresh varnish, which Andrew had been explaining, and he had just said: "Do you think this could make Farnborough drop their stupid ban on monoplanes, Captain?"

Oh God, Ranklin thought: this is Andrew's aeroplane and I haven't heard a word he's said about it. *And* he thinks I'm something to do with the Flying Corps and the Royal Aircraft Factory at Farnborough. Speaking very slowly in a self-deprecatory tone he said: "I'm brand new to flying, just getting my eye in," while he stared desperately at the aeroplane's lines and rummaged through his thoughts like a man searching his desk for a lost cheque.

It had the engine at the front and a single wing supported above the 'cockpit' on a tripod of struts, while longer struts reached out from the base of the tapered square body. Dull metal (aluminium?) covered it from engine to cockpit, but the rest was the usual fabric on wood, still mostly unstained with oil and smoke.

Straight lines was the only thought he had. At least mostly straight and right-angled compared with some of the curves on other machines they had seen. That was what gave this aeroplane its clean no-nonsense look.

"I'd say," he ventured, "that it should be relatively easy to manufacture."

And God had smiled on him. Andrew punched the air with a gloved fist. "*Right* – you got it in one, Captain. *That's* what I was shooting for: don't add curves and complications just because they look nice. If there's a good reason, sure. But always think of the guys on the shop floor who've got to put the thing together. Right down to the sizes of bolts: we've got just six sizes of bolts in her. Some of your fellows are using twenty. 'Part from anything else, that's twenty mistakes they can make. Isn't that right, Alec?"

Standing respectfully a step behind him was a squat man in a white craftsman's apron with the age, moustache and bearing of a foreman. "We don't make mistakes, Mr Sherring, sir. And my lads would have built her any shape you like and got it right."

"Sure you would, but what about when you're turning out twenty airplanes a day and using boys just out of school? *They* won't all be skilled craftsmen." He took a short leather coat from the edge of the cockpit and began wriggling into it. "Get a couple of lads to hold the tail and I'll take Mr . . . Senator Falcone up."

He ducked under the wing to fiddle at the engine and Corinna said: "Twenty a day? What's the boy talking about?"

"War," said Falcone.

Corinna's eyes widened and she looked to Ranklin for an opinion. He gave a small shrug, but Andrew had been right. If aeroplanes were any use in war, you would need them by the dozen, expendable as worker bees, not hoarded and protected like the queen. And there was something very American in Andrew's thinking: this particular aeroplane might be a mere hobby, a waste of time and money, but he had instinctively designed it for factory production. Most Englishmen simply wouldn't have thought of that.

Andrew came back, pulling a cap from his hip pocket and putting it on backwards whilst Falcone, dark eyes shining, reversed his own cap. It was so much a ceremony that when Ranklin caught Corinna's eye, they had to look away before they burst into undignified giggles.

Andrew helped Falcone into the cockpit and climbed in after him. The seats were almost side by side, with the passenger's set back about a foot so that Andrew's shoulders overlapped Falcone's.

Foreman Alec had taken off his apron and appeared to be injecting petrol into each cylinder of the engine – the whole of which turned as another man moved the propeller around. This must be the peculiar 'rotary' engine O'Gilroy had talked about.

Then Andrew, who had been peering into the cockpit, presumably checking his controls, looked out and said the terrible words: "Captain – I'll take you up when I've given Senator Falcone a flip round the block. About twenty minutes, okay?"

Ranklin didn't hear the quick dialogue between Andrew and the foreman, was barely aware of the propeller being swung, the sudden metallic chatter of the engine and the thin blue-grey smoke whipping away in the propeller blast. He watched dazedly as the two men moved to steady a wing-tip each, helping steer the aeroplane as it trundled, rocking stiffly, across the rough grass.

But when it jounced into the air it left all science and engineering behind and it was obvious that that *thing* was never meant to carry anything as sane and precious as Capt. M. Ranklin, RA.

As it turned unsteadily over the concrete banking and the sound faded, Corinna asked gravely: "Have you ever been up before?"

"No," Ranklin croaked.

"Hmm. This really wasn't my doing. I suppose Andrew thinks you were looking for a ride, coming from the War Office and all that. I'm sure you'll enjoy it. And you don't want Conall out-bragging you, do you?" She was being sympathetic and understanding and Ranklin could have killed her. A woman's job was to assume men were fearless and leave them alone with their fear.

"Have you ever flown?" he asked.

"A couple of times. Not with Andrew, though. Somehow, when you've seen your kid brother trying to learn to ride a bicycle, you don't . . . well, you can guess how it is. I loved it – after the first few minutes."

Was this supposed to make him feel better?

For want of something to say, he commented: "Odd smell the engines have. I suppose it's the oil burning off, and it seems familiar somehow, but—"

"Castor oil. They use it in all aeroplane engines, Andrew says. Don't know why. I believe it can have an effect, but only after a long flight."

I wouldn't bet on that, Ranklin thought grimly.

*　　*　　*

By the time the aeroplane came rocking and switchbacking down, propeller turning only in bursts, and bounced back on to the ground, Ranklin was as ready as he ever would be. He had convinced himself he *was* from the War Office, here to assess the machine for scouting purposes (he had borrowed a map from the car) and decide where a Lewis machine-gun might be mounted on it – if that really was what the future held. In short, something to concentrate on and a pretence to keep up.

Unfortunately, of course, none of this could stop the flimsy contraption dissolving in mid-air and splattering him into utter non-Matthew-Ranklinness on the Surrey landscape.

Foreman Alec escorted him around to the right-hand side where the propeller breeze whipped at his hair (*not* wearing his cap backwards seemed to be the last control over his life that he had left). Falcone climbed down, passed over a pair of oily goggles, slapped him on the shoulder – a jolt his stomach could have done without – then helped him up into the cockpit. Short as he was, Ranklin felt like an elephant tiptoeing along a shelf of china, and wasn't reassured by the way the structure bent or bulged wherever he touched it. Then he was wedged in behind Andrew's right shoulder on a thin basket seat, the wing above just clearing his head, and grinning falsely to show he was ready.

"All snug?" Andrew bellowed above the engine noise, ignored Ranklin's answer, and waved to the men back at the wing-tips. The aeroplane swayed around, the engine buzzed, wind swirled in Ranklin's face and they moved. Jerk, bump, *lurch* as the tail rose, rock, skid, the thing was obviously quite out of control – then the ground sagged away, the movements stopped being abrupt and became dreadfully soggy and this was flying.

Ranklin relaxed – slightly – his grip on either side of the seat and looked ahead, ready to be impressed. He could see clouds, and they looked like clouds; he looked at the distant horizon and it was a distant horizon. He looked at the ground below, and it was the mouth of Hell, bottomless and beckoning. He looked quickly at the dashboard.

Noticing his stare, Andrew tapped a finger on one instrument – there were only three – that looked like a thermometer and

Ranklin saw it registered 500. Miles an hour? He was almost willing to believe it, then realised it must be feet above the ground. They lurched again and he grabbed for his seat, terrified that touching anything else might rip the machine apart or hurl it out of control.

"Few rocks in the air, with this sun," Andrew yelled. "Get above it soon after a thousand." That must mean something, but Ranklin didn't feel like opening his mouth. The sun suddenly glared at him from above the wing and he realised they were turning, the horizon sliding across the nose.

Quite abruptly, like a boat slipping into harbour, it was calm. Almost as if they had stopped. It was still noisy and windy, but a steady noise and wind. The lurching, the 'rocks in the air' (irregular air currents?) had gone, and when Andrew turned again it was a smooth inevitable movement as on the racetrack banking below.

Ranklin risked a deep breath and began to take in impressions. The way the fabric on the wing above quivered continuously, and a dribble of oil, flattened by the wind, crawled back along the metal skin ahead. Then, daring to look further, the way the landscape towards the sun was a bright haze but seemed crystal clear in the opposite direction. The vivid smear of white steam or smoke that must be a train – he'd never thought it would show up like that – and the obvious curve of the railway, far more distinct than the tangled, jinking roads.

But all oddly blotched, as if someone had spilled huge oil-stains over the landscape . . . which he suddenly realised must be cloud shadows. He had never thought of clouds as having *size* before, and stared at the evidence until their turn brought the sun sparkling off a bright snake that must be a stretch of river.

That reminded him of the map and he dragged it from a side pocket and cautiously unfolded it in the eddying wind around his lap. Andrew looked down, grinned and shouted: "We're not lost yet!"

Ranklin shook his head, grinned back and called: "Just experimenting." He had folded the map to show the immediate area, and taking the sun to be roughly south, tried to pinpoint himself. Andrew tipped the aeroplane towards Ranklin's side and pointed past him. "Byfleet."

Ranklin forced himself to look, but the bottomless pit had become toys: houses, trees, cars and carts. And dots with shadows that must be people except that none of them seemed to be moving. Then he realised they must have stopped to stare up at him, or at least the aeroplane wheeling and buzzing in the bright blue. He felt embarrassed, a poseur because he didn't belong in this aeroplane any more than they did, then grinned at his absurdity.

Andrew was pointing at his own mouth. "Lunch?" Ranklin nodded and swivelled the map to match their turn towards the obvious oval of Brooklands that suddenly appeared from under the nose. It was odd how things below did seem to appear and disappear, how much depended on the angle of the light and one's own angle, which ranged from the vertical to the horizontal. Map-reading from the air was obviously a new art.

Then he remembered BSA and the lightweight machine-gun. Pointing it straight ahead was one obvious solution, then you could aim the whole aeroplane and – oh dear: he'd forgotten the propeller spinning in the line of fire. And pointing it elsewhere gave a very small arc of fire and obvious aiming-off problems. He was trying to count the variables involved when the rocks in the air, and his stomach, came back. But salvation was in sight and he felt better diving towards it, the engine burping irregularly (but, he hoped, intentionally) than climbing into the unknown.

Then the ground was coming up faster and he was sure Andrew had misjudged it, or maybe was fainting, and braced himself just as the nose lifted and they were down with a thump and rattle which dwindled away to silence except for Andrew saying: "Damn, lost it," and he realised the engine had stopped.

They rumbled to a stop and Andrew began clambering out. "That's the one trouble with these engines, they will cut out on landing. We'll walk it from here."

He came around to guide Ranklin down, then went to the tail, lifted it to waist height and simply pushed. After an initial grunt, the machine rolled easily, helped by a couple of mechanics attaching themselves to the wing spars. Ranklin walked beside Andrew.

"Tell me," he asked, "how would you mount a machine-gun on an aeroplane like this?"

"With a hell of a lot of difficulty," Andrew said. "She's got a good view downwards, you saw that—"

Ranklin had. It had been quite good enough, thank you.

"—but any other direction, you'd be shooting off struts and wires and probably the prop. Vickers is building one with a pusher prop specially for their machine-gun; your War Office must know about it."

Ranklin mumbled something about how departments never talked to each other.

Corinna was waiting by the shed, head slightly on one side and wearing a very broad grin. Ranklin could feel himself grinning back like a schoolboy; it was lucky that everybody else was concentrating on the aeroplane.

"Well?" she asked.

"I did enjoy it. After the first few minutes. It's . . . it's different," he said lamely.

"There's some, like brother Andrew, would say it's a whole new world."

Ranklin turned to look back at the sky, realising that until only minutes ago it had always seemed to him a flat, painted backcloth to life. And that to most of the people who had stopped to stare up at him it would never be anything else. "Yes," he said, "I can see how it could be."

Corinna was looking at him gravely. "I'm glad you enjoyed it. And came back safely."

13

They found O'Gilroy waiting at the Blue Bird. Ranklin had anticipated Falcone's surprise at seeing his former bodyguard reappear as student aeronaut and old acquaintance of Reynard Sherring's daughter, but decided to let it happen. If O'Gilroy began to seem a Man of Mystery, and worth confiding in, it might not hurt.

They even managed to keep straight faces when Falcone introduced them to each other, O'Gilroy being "a friend I met in Belgium who also works for your Government".

"Really?" Ranklin said coolly. "It's a big government."

They managed to drift aside while Andrew and Falcone went back to the higher levels of aviation.

"Got me first flight this morning," O'Gilroy said chirpily.

"What a coincidence."

O'Gilroy stared. "Ye sneaky bastard. In Sherring's machine? How did ye like it?"

Ranklin already regretted spoiling O'Gilroy's triumph. "Terrified the whole time."

That repaired most of the damage. "I was pretty scared meself – but ye get over it."

"I'm not so sure. If God had meant me to fly he'd have had me hatched, not born. Do you know the menu here? – what should we order?"

Andrew and Falcone managed to cram in a few mouthfuls between chatter. But this time Ranklin listened carefully. He now felt like a day-tripper hearing two experienced travellers swap reminiscences of a new continent, largely unexplored but with some agreed and well-trodden trails – and already its heroes and martyrs.

One of the heroes was Adolphe Pégoud and Ranklin hadn't heard of him – but neither, to Andrew's surprise, had Falcone.

"But you must have done," Andrew protested. "The Frenchman who flies upside down."

Falcone's suspicious look showed he thought this was some Anglo-Saxon leg-pull. But Andrew persisted: "No, honestly, I'm not fooling. It's been in all the aviation magazines the last two weeks. He's giving a display here next Thursday."

"You say it is written about for two weeks? I have been travelling, not reading . . . But, upside down?" He revolved his hands for emphasis.

"Sure. He dives into it . . ." Andrew's hands joined in. "He's using a strengthened Blériot, and he's tied in, of course. He flies, I don't know, less than a minute upside down, but it's for real. Him and Blériot are both coming here. I want to get hold of Blériot himself, find out how he's stressed that machine. Hell, it's a *monoplane*, same as mine." He turned on Ranklin. "If your people can go on saying monoplanes aren't strong enough after they've seen *that* . . ."

Ranklin wanted to say "Sorry, old boy, but that isn't my department" but it was so exactly what a real War Office desk-hussar would say that it sounded a parody. So he said: "God and generals both have mysterious ways, but only God actually moves."

Andrew snorted. Falcone smiled and said: "So, I must be here on Thursday."

"After lunch. Only I'd get here before – you'll find me around here. Are you coming, Corrie?"

"Maybe."

"Captain?"

"It's a working day. Depends what my superiors want me working at."

They ate for a few minutes, then Falcone asked: "Your machine – what happens to it now?"

Andrew shrugged, a large, slow movement. "Don't know. Farnborough's at least agreed to test it, to see if the British Army could use it. I've got to deliver it there next week. But they're very old-maidish about monoplanes after just a few accidents . . ."

"You do not think of flying it in the Gordon Bennett race in France next week? That would be good advertising."

Andrew smiled wryly. "Coming in last? No, they'll be going forty miles an hour faster'n the Oriole. She's a *working* airplane, not a racer. No, when Farnborough's turned it down, I'll probably

tinker with it some more, then ship it back to the States and see
if anybody's interested."

Falcone chewed thoughtfully for a while, then said: "I believe
someone in Italy would like to show it to our army."

Andrew brightened up. "No fooling?"

"I will send a cable today . . . But you say it must go to
Farnborough next week?"

"Yes, that's official now. I'm sure they'll turn it down, but it's
got to go."

Falcone nodded. "I understand. We can talk some more – you are
always here? – but if you would please write for me the performance
figure, speed and distance . . ."

"Right away." Andrew began searching his pockets for pen
and paper.

"I do wish," Corinna said frowning, "you'd built a *peaceful*
airplane."

"Who for?" Andrew demanded without looking up from his
scribbling. "Airplanes cost money. And who's got money? –
governments. And what do governments spend money on? –
weapons. Not flying omnibuses and taxi-cabs, I'd be building
those if anybody asked, but the way things are . . ." He shrugged
and went on writing.

* * *

After lunch, the party split up. Ranklin would have liked to have
had a long quiet word with O'Gilroy, but that might make Falcone
suspicious of him. It was one thing for the Senator to be in touch
with the Bureau, but a mistake to let him know he was quite so
much in touch. So he stuck to Corinna.

"Were you planning to invite me to dinner?" she asked casually.

"I was. I thought—"

"In that case why don't we have it at my apartment?" This was an
annex to her father's flat in Clarges Street, which she had insisted
be self-contained except for sharing a kitchen and servants – only
two when Sherring himself wasn't there. "I kind of think the staff
have run up a cold supper and then taken the evening off."

Ranklin suppressed the warm surge of anticipation as they
strolled towards the car. The chauffeur was waiting, holding the
big envelope Falcone had picked up at the hotel and then forgotten.

"I took the liberty of looking after this, sir, rather nor leave it laying in the car. These days you can't trust—"

"Thank you, thank you." Falcone took it, wondered whether to tip the man, and properly decided not. "Will you permit it—?" He began opening the envelope. "I do not know what it is, I expected nothing . . ." And that was about what he'd got: a couple of rough-printed sheets of paper. He shrugged and looked around for somewhere to throw them away.

Suddenly Ranklin remembered his real job. "D'you mind if I see those?"

The papers gave the times of services and other information about the Italian church of St Peter in Back Hill, Clerkenwell – just the sort of thing to be handed out to a new immigrant or Italian visitor. At the *Ritz*? But there was no address on the envelope, just *Senatore G. Falcone*. The handwriting could have been Italian.

"Do they expect me to go to confession in Clerkenwell?" Falcone said jovially. "These priests, all they want is more money."

But an Italian priest would have anticipated that attitude and taken the trouble to write a personal note of welcome. Ranklin turned to Corinna: "Would you forgive us?" and he urged Falcone aside, annoyed that O'Gilroy wasn't here to handle this and leave his War Office character unbesmirched. But he had no choice. "I'm afraid it looks as if you *aren't* safe in England. I think you've been followed here."

Falcone was surprised, but Ranklin wouldn't have said scared. Nor was he used to this sort of thing, because he still looked puzzled.

"No address," Ranklin explained. "Somebody hawked the letter around the leading hotels until one accepted it. Now he knows where you're staying."

Falcone took this without argument, beyond: "It would be more quick to call by telephone."

"For you or me, yes. But probably these people don't have a private telephone, or don't speak English well enough . . . Do you have any idea of who they are?"

Falcone hesitated, looking at Ranklin carefully. "You say you are from your Ministry of War . . ."

"We're one big happy family and we try to be good hosts. *Do* you have any idea about these people? – this suggests they could be Italian."

"I may guess who sent them – but not who they sent."

"You could go to the police again. They'd have to take this seriously."

Falcone wasn't used to this sort of danger. The reality of it had taken time to sink in, but now his eyes flickered side to side and he wore a thoughtful frown. "Yes, that is possible . . . but it would be a trouble for them . . ."

He presumably didn't want to be murdered, but – Ranklin guessed – he didn't want British officialdom watching his every step, either. And Ranklin was in no position to insist on anything. But neither could he abandon Falcone now.

"Then I suggest you move out of the Ritz as soon as we get back – and leave no forwarding address. I don't know how easy it is to register under a false name in London hotels . . . You don't belong to a London club, or an Italian one with a reciprocal arrangement with one here? Or would your ambassador put you up?"

"No." Presumably Falcone was answering the last question first: he didn't want his embassy looking over his shoulder, either. "Perhaps I am going to a hotel by here?"

Why not? The Hound and Spear probably didn't meet the Senator's standards, but there must be others within easy motor-ride. Probably Corinna had a guide book in the car. Corinna! – Ranklin suddenly realised that if Falcone was in danger then so, until they got rid of him, was Corinna. His own eyes started flickering and he wished he were armed.

But, once they were in the car and with the window to the chauffeur firmly shut, he had to explain as much as he could. "It seems that somebody's stalking the Senator and they've pinpointed the Ritz. We have to assume they were watching, this morning, and saw him get into this car and they've pinpointed it, too."

She took it quite calmly. Which was useful but a little disturbing, as if she expected Ranklin to move in an aura of trouble like a permanent garlic breath. "Then," she suggested, "we could stop before the hotel and Senator Falcone could switch to a taxi. Or there must be some back way."

"No," Ranklin said firmly. "The other way around. We're going to try and unravel any association between him and this car, and you, by delivering him back to the main entrance in plain view. I am *not*," he went on, looking at Falcone, "having your problems spill over onto Mrs Finn. That is my first concern. We can start playing taxi-cab games after that."

Falcone was all gallant protestations that of *course* Mrs Finn's safety came first. Then he smiled and said: "You are most skilled in such . . . affairs. Like the Mr O'Gilroy who met me in Brussels."

"Oh, just my Army training," Ranklin said dismissively. "India, and all that," he added.

"Ah yes." Falcone seemed satisfied. And Corinna was watching the landscape as if it were the first time she'd ever seen a tree, a hedge or even the sky.

*　　*　　*

Ranklin went on being worried until he was holding in his pocket Falcone's own pistol, left uselessly in the Ritz suite, and watching as the Senator directed the packing of his luggage. He had taken a casual look around as they dismounted outside the hotel, but Piccadilly was far too busy for any watcher to show up at a glance. In such a situation without O'Gilroy he felt incomplete, like Lancelot fighting Sir Meliagrance with only half his armour on. But at least he could get Corinna out of the arena by sending her, disappointed but obedient, back to her flat in Clarges Street.

Falcone had picked on a country house hotel, Oatlands, just outside Weybridge itself. The Ritz hadn't been told the new address, merely asked to send letters to the Italian embassy. Now Ranklin was working out how to obscure the trail back to Weybridge and had decided to start by switching cabs at the relatively quiet Marylebone station.

There were several taxi-cabs waiting outside the hotel and Ranklin made Falcone show himself by going out to watch his luggage being loaded into one while he himself hung back in the doorway and watched. Particularly he watched the second cab on the rank, and when somebody came up to it, stepped forward himself.

Pretending not to notice it had been taken, he yanked open the door – it was a closed Unic – interrupting a cloud of Italian-flavoured explanations and getting a vicious glare.

He became Utterly English. "I say, I'm most *frightfully* sorry. Didn't notice you'd taken it, what?" But he was still holding the door open. "Perhaps I can help, what? I speak a couple of words of Italian and I couldn't help overhearing . . ."

"Can't make out what the gent wants, guv," the driver said.

"I ask him 'Where to?' and he just points straight ahead and gabbles."

"*Il autista demande dove . . .*" Ranklin began slowly. Ahead of them, Falcone's cab pulled away and was quickly lost in the jumble of Piccadilly traffic. Ranklin's passenger gave him another superheated glare, then banged out of the far side of the cab and stalked off down the street.

"Oh dear, I seem to have lost you a fare," Ranklin apologised, thinking *about five foot ten, longish dark hair with slight sideburns and down-turning moustache . . .*

"No matter, guv, he'd probly of tried to pay me in somefink foreign any'ow. Where can I take yer?"

"Marylebone station, please." . . . *age about thirty-five, long nose, broken uneven teeth* . . . If I hadn't given Falcone back his pistol, would I have tried to "arrest" him? But what for? – I'd have caused a rumpus, had to explain myself and probably learnt nothing but his name. And I certainly daren't have followed him, not after meeting him face to face. That's where O'Gilroy would have fitted in . . . *high-buttoned Continental style of black suit but looks as if he's bought a new English brown felt hat* . . . Lacks observation, too, he reflected, because *nobody* wears a brown hat in town.

But on balance, he felt quite pleased: he'd snapped the thread of Falcone's followers and probably not even revealed himself. He'd double-check at Marylebone, but if that was clear, they could take Falcone's cab on to Waterloo and put him on a Weybridge train. And then to Clarges Street . . .

14

Corinna had tea waiting, which showed remarkable confidence in Ranklin's ability to handle such affairs – or, more likely, she didn't care about wasting tea.

"Meet a Gunner and see the underworld," she said cheerfully. "Was that the Senator's past catching up with him?"

"It may be his future. He's up to something, so far up that somebody from back home wants to kill him for it, but he won't tell me what."

She got more sombre. "Is it anything to do with airplanes? That could involve Andrew?"

Ranklin hoped she didn't see his shiver as he remembered the fatal crash in Brussels. "I don't think it's *directly* connected . . . But I'd like to know if he approaches your brother again."

"I'll see what I can do." She reconsidered. "No, I'll damn well *do* it. Andrew just doesn't know Europe, the way things can happen over here. You could have told me the Senator was on someone's Wanted list."

Ranklin nodded gloomily, and not only at the way she seemed to lump Britain in with the Continent as "Europe". "I'm afraid we all assumed the danger was over once he'd reached London. The trouble is, he's an amateur at being someone's enemy. His caution comes in spasms. And unless he tells us what the danger really *is*, we can't do much . . ."

The sight of his gloom seemed to cheer her up. "It may never happen, whatever it is. And it's been a great day – and we've still got supper to come."

"Look, about that . . . With O'Gilroy away, there's nobody but me to mind the . . . shop." We must set up a weekend roster, he realised. One of the new boys to move into the flat whenever it's empty.

She solved that easily. "All right, I'll pack up the supper and we can have a picnic in your flat."

"I'd love that but . . . I mean, there's a doorman and he'll see you . . . what time you come out and . . . I'm thinking of your good name."

"That's very sweet of you. But I'll tell you a Very Dark Secret." Her voice became a conspiratorial whisper. "I've got a friend – I can't mention his name – who works for the *Secret Service*! Imagine that! And he's Frightfully Clever at being secret, so why don't I just leave the problem to him?"

After a while, the Frightfully Clever friend said feebly: "You could wear a motoring veil."

"There! – perfect. What did I tell you?"

*　　*　　*

The hall porter at that particular entrance to Whitehall Court – there were several – was an old sailor whose appointment might have been arranged by the Commander. He didn't – supposedly – know what went on in the top-floor offices, just that something did. And given the Commander's reputation, and that the top rooms had been his apartment before they became offices, secret servicing wasn't the only something that had gone on there nor Corinna the first veiled lady he'd let in.

She looked around the dark walls of the flat. "I hope this isn't your taste in decor."

"No. Just as we acquired it."

"Thank God for that." Her own taste ran to light plain colours and, in her bedroom, soft feminine fabrics. She wandered through to the dining room and saw The Table. "My Lord, my supper's going to look pretty meagre spread on *this*." She began spreading it nonetheless. You couldn't say it was enough to feed an army, because ordinary soldiers would probably have mutinied if served foie gras, plovers' eggs, lobster mayonnaise and quails in aspic. But the General Staff wouldn't have minded at all.

"And you and Conall manage by yourselves here?"

"Well, we have a little help from the restaurants and kitchens downstairs."

"I'll bet. But how are you on opening champagne?"

"That's one aspect of officer training I do remember."

*

100

Corinna interpreted 'picnic' as meaning a bite of this, then that, then back to the other and no nonsense about 'courses'. Currently alternating between curried prawn and foie gras, she asked: "How's Conall going to make out, learning to fly?"

"Pretty well, I'd say. He doesn't take chances . . . or rather, he does, but he knows what the chances are. I'd back him against the steeple-chasing young sprigs of nobility you seem to get in that world."

"Yes. Andrew's pretty sharp about those guys. He thinks the way they break their airplanes – and necks – gives aviation a bad name." She smiled thoughtfully around a mouthful of prawn. "I bet you never thought he'd wind up learning to fly when you rescued him from a life of crime in Irish back alleys."

"He didn't tell you that."

"He's kind of hinted at it."

"Well, he'll tell you the full story if he feels like it. But he wasn't any run-of-the-mill criminal. He might have deserved being in cells, but managing to dodge it, from our . . . from one point of view, that's a recommendation. And I don't think he was from any back alleys, either: he can read and write, for one thing, and knows how an Irish gentleman behaves. Anyway, the Army doesn't recruit from the slums, too many of them are wrecked before they're twenty by rickets and tuberculosis and God knows what – that's what those slums do for you. London's, too. We prefer country boys who don't panic at the smell of fresh air."

He refilled their glasses. "My guess is that he was born in the country – he can ride and he's been a servant in one of the Big Houses – and then his family moved to a town. Maybe his father took a job in one of the shipyards. I think O'Gilroy did, after the Army. Certainly some work with machines and metal."

"You say you're guessing: he doesn't confide in even you?"

"Why should he?"

She smiled and shook her head at the same time. Men. "But that doesn't explain how he got to . . . here."

Ranklin looked serious. "Perhaps we're starting at the wrong end. If you take an Irish country boy and reckon his chances at ending up as . . . in a job like this, of course it's a million to one against. But start with one in this job and look back, and all you can say is that he must have been exceptional. And he is. Lucky, if you like, as well. But you must meet exceptional people every day in your world. Perhaps they all had luck, too – at least not to get bogged down in routines of work and family and knowing their place . . ." He went on reflectively. "That's really what had happened to me, until a year ago. My life's been far more conventional, given my family and so on, than O'Gilroy's ever was."

She frowned at him. "Oh now . . ."

"No, I mean it. Joining the Army was pure convention for a younger son – I happened to choose the Guns, but I'd never have got into a fashionable regiment anyway, and then I drifted along, vaguely hoping for a war – not a big one – and a chance to make my name, but when I got a war, in South Africa, all I did was get locked up in a siege."

"Where you met Conall? He's talked about that, all right, the way you adopted him and taught him about artillery."

"I needed another gun number, that's all."

"Oh come on. I bet you *were* a better officer than you make out, saying you were only interested in guns and tactics." It exasperated her the way he dodged compliments. She knew the English well enough to recognise most self-deprecation as inverted boasting. But with Ranklin it seemed genuine. It suited the job, of course; he could hardly go around saying: "Really, I'm only a minor spy, quite unimportant" – but it went deeper than that.

But probably, she reminded herself, when he talks about his past he's remembering a man he once knew in a bygone world. Not his fault, except for that damned British gallantry which made him acknowledge the signature his elder brother had forged before his financial ruin and suicide. And financial ruin *was* terrible – but in her world, it was a familiar dragon. You knew you were fooling with it and if it bit you, then maybe, scarred but wiser, you recovered. But it had eaten Ranklin's world in one gulp. Almost overnight, he had gone from a predictable Army career to a mercenary soldier to a spy. Such things must change a man.

And from her point of view, very much for the better. If she had met that comfortable, doubtless worthy, Gunner officer, she wouldn't have given him a second glance.

She gazed around the walls, with the lowering wallpaper that pressed in on them like some Edgar Allan Poe story, at the inevitable picture of a dead hare nestling into a bunch of dewy fruit. Not, she thought coolly, very romantic.

"This isn't the . . . shop itself?"

"No, that's upstairs."

"And empty?"

"Yes," Ranklin said incautiously. "They put telephone calls through to here at night and weekends."

A slow grin spread across Corinna's face. "I suppose you wouldn't let me have a little peek?"

"No."

"You'd be with me. You could be Very Close to me, to make sure I didn't do anything I shouldn't."

Ranklin suddenly realised what she was proposing. "You are a bad, disgraceful, shocking little girl. Absolutely No."

"Oh *please*. Just once. In the headquarters of the British Secret Service . . . !"

"When you first join the . . . the shop, they tell you about shameless wicked women who try to uncover secrets by . . ."

"Tell me what the shameless wicked women *do*," she purred, stretching so that her blouse pulled taut over the swell of her breasts.

*   *   *

O'Gilroy flopped into bed alone but feeling as close to Heaven as he was ever likely to get in England, and content that there was no way he could have done or learned more in a single day. The Brooklands aviation village, he had found, had a cosmopolitan population with a class system of its own. If you were rich and well-born the flying schools would take your money as they would anybody's: in advance rather than argue with the executors of your will. But you were respected only for flying ability and knowledge, and if anybody asked politely about O'Gilroy's background, they forgot his answers immediately. That was part of Heaven, too.

But one where he was a very minor cherub. At first he had assumed he would have an advantage both because no other student could have studied aeronautical magazines as avidly as he, and because he was young and thus a quick learner. Instead, he had learnt quickly that everybody had read more than he, and that thirty was very old for a cherub. The one advantage his age gave him – if he survived to exploit it – was that he expected things to go wrong. He loved machinery, but knew it was mortal and that

103

he could only prolong that life by gentleness and mistrust. Mid-air was no place for thinking "I can always buy another one".

And he had two other advantages: that he had nothing else to do – no tailors or girlfriends in London needing his attention – and Andrew Sherring. When nothing was happening at the flying school, O'Gilroy haunted Andrew's shed or the Blue Bird, asking and listening. He saved his own opinions to impress Ranklin.

15

On Monday, Ranklin handed Dagner a brief report on Saturday's events and, ten minutes later, was called in to discuss it. For the first time, Dagner wore plain clothes, a dark grey lounge suit that was brand new. So probably he had worn uniform last week simply because, after years in India, he was waiting for his tailor to run him up some London clothes. Ranklin should have thought of that, and felt ashamed of his glib hints that Dagner abandon uniform.

"D'you think Mr Sherring's aeroplane fits Senator Falcone's needs?"

"He appeared to be talking seriously about it."

"Then let's hope . . . Now, about the Senator being followed. You obviously did the right thing in moving him to a hotel in the country—"

"I'm afraid he may now suspect who I really represent. He did comment."

Dagner smiled sympathetically. "Can't be helped. But the man trying to follow him from the Ritz: positively didn't speak English?"

"Quite sure."

"And dressed unsuitably . . . I know nothing about these organisations, but does that sound like, say, the Austrian KS to you?"

Ranklin noticed he knew enough to call the Austrian secret service by its initials, though. "No, they should be better than that. But if they wanted to keep their hands clean, they might have hired some assassin."

"Yes, there's always that. And if Falcone doesn't want a bodyguard, we can't insist. But I want to keep tabs on him . . . If he approaches Mr Sherring again, will we know through O'Gilroy?"

"Not necessarily. But I should hear from Mrs Finn."

"Ah yes." Dagner smiled, perhaps relieved that the lady's name had finally come into the open. "I must say I'd very much like to meet her myself . . ."

To see if she were suitable? But he still welcomed the idea. Once Corinna had met Dagner, Ranklin could at least mention him in conversation.

"I'm sure she'd be delighted. Should we say tea at one of the big hotels?"

"Excellent. I look forward to it."

*   *   *

It rained the next morning so perhaps, with October only a week away, autumn had finally arrived. Ranklin got out his winter overcoat and looked at it critically. It was made of tan broadcloth and only ten years old and so still perfectly wearable, but the cut was a bit full for today's fashion. He liked that shape – damn it, he *was* that shape – but suppose he had one day to look fashionable? . . . Well, he'd see. Meanwhile, perhaps he needed one of the new Burberry weatherproofs for a day like this. The trouble was, the advertisements always showed them on men as tall and thin as lances. On him, it would look like a tent. And Burberry never put prices in their advertisements . . . It could wait.

So, feeling better for having at least identified a problem, he put the overcoat away and walked upstairs to the office. Dagner didn't get in for half an hour, wearing a brand-new topcoat that fitted his slim figure perfectly. Ten minutes later he called Ranklin in to make a "morning report", a carry-over of Army procedure that hadn't happened when the Commander was in charge. For one thing, it would have implied that somebody apart from himself knew what was going on.

Ranklin summarised how the training was going, then added: "And I had a word with Mrs Finn yesterday evening. She suggests we meet for tea at the Carlton tomorrow, if that suits you."

"Certainly."

"And she's heard from her brother Andrew. Senator Falcone has made a firm offer to buy the aeroplane outright, provided he gets the right to make it in Italy and Andrew gets it out there and flies a demonstration. Andrew wants to agree, the price seems right, but there's a snag: he apparently offered it to the Royal Aircraft Factory at Farnborough to test for our Army, and since they agreed, it's become, as it were, *sub judice*. He can't take it out of the country until it's been tested. He's pretty sure they'll turn it down, there's a virtual ban on monoplanes for military use, but nevertheless . . . And Falcone seems in a bit of a hurry."

But Danger was just nodding contentedly. "That seems to be just the sort of problem the Senator anticipated, and that we agreed to sort out for him as our part of the deal. Do you know who I should speak to at the War House to get the tests cancelled or postponed?"

"No, but I can pop across there and find out."

"Splendid. You'd better get on with it. It's nearly half-past ten now and you'll need to catch them between getting in and going out for lunch." Dagner, it seemed, was not impressed by the hours worked at the War Office.

*   *   *

Ranklin himself saw the War Office as a cobweb. Most of it was immobile and just clinging on, but if you kept trudging and didn't get stuck, you ultimately found a spider who was ready to take a decision. By the time he got back with the name of the man to talk to, Dagner himself was out to lunch and there was a message to telephone Corinna at the Sherring City office.

"Good Lord, you don't care much if a girl doesn't get any lunch, do you?" her voice crackled. "I've been trying to reach you all morning. Listen: you asked me about Birmingham Small Arms, right? It turns out they're trying to raise cash so I asked them to come and talk and a Mr Viner will be here at three. He wanted to bring their new product to show me and for *your sake alone* I said Yes, so you'd better be here. Three o'clock, okay? As James Spencer, I think, devoted employee."

He had been in the Sherring office in Paris, a stately affair on the Boulevard des Capucines, but never the London one. Perhaps Sherring believed in local colour, because this was positively Dickensian, all rambling passageways and cock-eyed right angles. Corinna was waiting in a low-ceilinged room overfilled with leather chairs, bookshelves of ledgers, mahogany and green glass-shaded lamps that must shine all day. It looked a bit deliberate and made her, dressed in emerald green and gold, seem like a butterfly in a funeral parlour, but she sprawled unselfconsciously in one of the big chairs with papers strewn across the thick carpet.

The only decorations in the room were an old chart of the world, a portrait, and a ship model in a glass case. It was an ocean-going paddle-wheel steamer of maybe sixty years ago, still carrying two fully rigged masts, and beautifully crafted. Knowing he was behaving as any visitor would, Ranklin headed straight for it and stared in admiration. "Is this the ship that founded the family fortunes?"

"That's the story," she agreed. "Actually Pop says you English don't trust a bank that doesn't have a ship model in its partners' room, so he bought it when the shipping line went broke." She nodded at the portrait, of a large, ugly man with fully rigged white whiskers. "But that really is my grandfather, unless Grandma was way ahead of her time."

Ranklin smiled. "Before we get down to more sordid business, I've news about your brother's aeroplane: there may now not be any problem about Farnborough stopping it leaving the country. So if you're happy about Falcone's offer in other respects, it can probably go ahead."

Corinna slumped back, frowning. Then said carefully: "I'd like to see Andrew bring this off. He's tried so many things (probably not hard enough but he has *tried*) and nothing's ever quite . . ." Her voice trailed off, then renewed itself. "Pop never approved of Andrew going in for engineering, wanted him to come with him into the bank. And everything Andrew did, it seemed to Pop just like playing with toy trains – that's the impression he gave. But if this airplane really worked and people bought it, it would justify everything else Andrew's tried. The confidence it would give him, he'd really be out from under Pop's shadow . . .

"So I want to help, as much as I can. But not *too* much, not so it shows. Do you think Senator Falcone's really on the level?"

"As far as I can tell . . . Of course, I know nothing about the financial side—"

"No, I can take care of that. But if it's really any good, why hasn't your Army snapped it up? – because an Englishman didn't make it?"

"No. We can be that way, all right, but the aeronautical people aren't. The problem is that we've got a prejudice – virtually a ban – on monoplanes for military use. O'Gilroy told me something about this. They aren't supposed to be strong enough, and there's been crashes where aeroplanes fell apart in the air. I do see some of this: if you take a biplane with two layers of wing and join them with vertical struts and criss-cross wires, you've got a box structure, like a box girder in a bridge. But a monoplane's just a single plank. You can add all the slanting struts and wires you like – as Andrew has – but it still hasn't the inherent strength of the box shape of a biplane."

"You do sound as if you know something about it."

"I didn't spend my *entire* two years at Woolwich learning how to open champagne." Ranklin showed a flash of real annoyance.

"No, of course not." Corinna was so used to Ranklin seeming a little boy lost in this modern world that she forgot how much of it was a pose. Parts of the world, particularly the part where man's ingenuity could destroy other men miles away, he knew far better than most. She went on: "Do other countries have the same prejudice against monoplanes?"

"I doubt it, or nobody would make the things."

"So I could be worrying about nothing – except for your interest in Falcone. And whoever's trying to kill him, of course."

"I told you: we just like to know what arms Italy's buying. As to who's trying to kill him, d'you think we'd let them roam free if we knew who they were?"

"Um, I guess not . . . I just never know how sincere you are with your clothes on. All right. Mr BSA's due any minute." She looked Ranklin up and down critically. "You don't look exactly partnership rank. More like a bank teller. I'm sure it's an impenetrable disguise in Whitehall, but . . . Take your jacket off."

"What?"

"I'm not talking about your *pants*. Just get your jacket off. Look as if you owned the place. Or a few per cent of it."

A year ago Ranklin wouldn't just have refused, he would have denounced her to the Commissioners in Lunacy. Now he meekly took his jacket off.

"Better," she said, "but the necktie doesn't look expensive enough. Try one of Pop's." She found a couple in a drawer, chose one and watched Ranklin put it on. "Remember, it isn't *you*, it's James Spencer. And you won't see it when it's on."

But dressing a little oddly was a help in remembering he was playing a part. James Spencer was an alias he had used before, the name of a school friend who had gone to the bad thereafter. Fatally, he trusted.

She sat down again. "Now tell me more about BSA."

"Er, well, they make small arms—"

"And Daimler automobiles and motor-buses, too. How do they stand with the Government on the arms side? Are they going to buy this new machine-gun?"

It might seem inconsiderate of her to ask such questions, but neither of them had any shame about prying into each other's privileged knowledge, leaving the other to draw the line and not taking offence when they did. One of these days, Ranklin knew vaguely, it was going to go horribly wrong, but even without that, their relationship could have no tomorrow. Anyway, the arms trade had few secrets. Once you had a patent on something new, you shouted it from the highest rooftop you could find, and in as many languages as possible.

"They make a lot of the Army's rifles, but I haven't heard of any tests of this new gun. A decision'll be a long way off."

She made a note, then said: "It'll cost them to tool up for mass production of something like that. Perhaps that's what the new issue is about . . . I don't really understand this." She wrinkled her brow at a paper. "They're steadily profitable, and I'd guess their shareholders would snap up a new issue with no need for an underwriter."

"What does underwriting mean – in this context?"

"Underwriting share issues is pretty new, and Pop's still a bit leery about it. We guarantee them a price by buying whatever shares we can't sell in the market. So we take the risk and they pay us a commission for it. Only I can't see a risk here, and that bothers me."

"Are most of the other firms you deal with either London or foreign?"

"I guess so. Why?"

"Britain isn't just London and then bits with trees and cows on. This is *Birmingham* Small Arms, and probably Brummagem caution. They keep their cleverness for shaping bits of metal and play very safe with hard cash."

"A belt-and-suspenders town? Thanks, that helps." She glanced at her wristwatch and scooped up a handful of papers from the floor. "He should be here any moment. You'd best sit by the corner of the table and hand me these papers as I ask for them."

Ranklin sat as ordered, coughed drily, tapped the papers into a neat pile with his fingertips and tried to make his boyish face look dour.

"You'll do," Corinna smiled.

By contrast, Mr Viner of BSA looked cheerful. Even his moustache was cheerful, which Ranklin hadn't thought possible outside the music halls. It was also ginger and bristly like his hair, and he had light blue eyes and a frequent smile. Ranklin reckoned they were much of an age, but Viner was taller, slimmer and brisk in his movements.

Along with him came a uniformed chauffeur carrying a box about four and a half feet long, made of polished wood with brass fittings. Assuming that was the machine-gun, it was certainly far lighter than any Ranklin had met. Viner smiled and patted the box. "Our trump card, Mrs Finn. Thank you, Henry, that's all." He had an oddly flat voice, as if an accent – Brummie? – had been carefully washed out and nothing found to replace it.

The chauffeur withdrew, Viner sat down and let Ranklin pour him coffee, while Corinna apologised that her father was incommunicado on a train from Madrid. Viner just smiled boyishly and the conversation spiralled gently into business circles. Money, it seemed, was tight and interest rates up; the latest Hungarian loan had had to guarantee an extra half per cent and that in gold; the Paris market was, well, let's not talk about that; the Germans are buying gold in South America, I hear; fifty *million* working days lost to strikes in this country last year . . .

"But not at BSA." Viner grabbed the chance to become specific. "Our record is very good indeed – you only have to look at our dividends—"

"You've paid fifteen per cent for the last ten years bar one," Corinna said, without looking. "Most satisfactory . . . and now you're issuing three hundred thousand new cumulative B preference – James?" Ranklin passed her what he hoped was the relevant paper; "—thank you . . . paying six per cent, to expand the Daimler factory. But in fact you've already done that, so you're really seeking to replenish your working capital – have I got that right?"

"The times being what they are – alas—" the 'alas' was very perfunctory; "we expect new orders for rifles at any time now. The Army still hasn't fully re-equipped with the shorter model

Lee-Enfield . . ." Ranklin confirmed this with a slight nod, in case Corinna needed it. "But just let me show you what we're convinced is the true future . . ."

He unlocked the box and lifted out a fat-barrelled gun with a conventional rifle stock. Wood and metal gleamed dully in the lamplight and Corinna put on a look of false interest; Ranklin's was real.

"*This*," Viner said proudly, "is our Secret Weapon. The Lewis aerial machine-gun. Invented by Colonel Lewis, a countryman of yours, Mrs Finn, with – if I may say so – typical Yankee ingenuity. And on which we hold worldwide rights – except in the United States, of course. A real revolution in warfare, not least because of its lightness. A mere twenty-seven pounds fully loaded with a forty-seven-round magazine—" Ranklin had been wondering how you loaded it. Viner reached into the box and brought out what looked like a big cog-wheel and fitted it flat atop the gun; "—so it's ideal for use from aeroplanes."

"You're going to put that thing on *airplanes?*" Corinna said.

Viner seemed surprised, then tried to look apologetic. "That's progress, Mrs Finn – in this modern world. Actually, we say that just to advertise how light it is. We certainly won't be limited to the aeronautical market. We expect most of our sales to be for ordinary battlefield use. It can be carried and used by just one man – or woman, if you care to . . ."

"*No* thank you. But," she relented, "I'm sure James would."

So for the next few minutes she watched, with decreasing tolerance, as Viner and Ranklin reverted to being little boys. They put the magazine on and off, cocked the action, clicked the trigger; Viner, Ranklin noticed, was religiously careful about pointing the empty gun in a safe direction at all times. He also learned that the Lewis was air-cooled and fired from an open bolt: "An important safety feature," Viner explained, "since a round doesn't sit in the hot breech after the gun's been firing and perhaps 'cook off' as we say." It also meant you had to make sure both breech and magazine were empty if you wanted to uncock it by pulling the trigger, but as James Spencer, Ranklin didn't think he should realise that.

"I *think*, James," Corinna said at last, "that Mr Viner came here to talk finance."

Viner was immediately the perfect businessman, but Ranklin went on playing, at the risk of sunburn from Corinna's glare on the back of his neck. There was another, loaded, magazine in the box and he took it out to try its weight, then thumbed one of the cartridges loose. It was the normal .303 Army round. He re-examined the gun and found a Birmingham proof mark.

"Underwriting share issues is fairly new for us," Corinna was saying, "and I'm not sure we'd be ready to take the whole amount. But a hundred thousand of it—"

Viner looked boyishly sad. "We're very confident about this issue being taken up, and that we'll be able to place the entire amount through just one house – at four and a half per cent."

Ranklin said: "I see you made this particular gun: have you actually gone into production already?"

"No, we've just hand-built half a dozen to demonstrate to our – and other European – armies."

Corinna wore a puzzled frown. "Don't you have any problems selling to armies who . . . well, they could be your enemies next week?"

Viner misunderstood her concern. "Oh, no. Britain is devoted to Free Trade – in fact, there's no problem about shipping weapons anywhere in Europe, or further afield. We'll have no difficulty in fulfilling any export orders – which we confidently expect."

Corinna was ready to let the subject drop. Ranklin wasn't. "Are any particular European countries interested?"

Viner put on a deliberately wan smile. "I'm sure you understand we have to maintain a certain diplomatic silence."

"Of course," Ranklin said, thinking *Right, then, I'll have to find out in my own way.* He picked up the gun again, ignored Corinna's reignited glare, and resumed fiddling with it.

Viner was saying: "I'm afraid we're thinking of the whole three hundred thousand or noth—"

"And I think we'd be more interested at five per cent."

Viner got to his feet. "I don't think we'll need to go that high." He took the gun from Ranklin to put back into its box. "I'm sorry your father wasn't here, Mrs Finn. I think he'd have appreciated rather more—"

Ranklin said: "It's still cocked."

"Oh? – thank you. I find that men are more ready to—" and he pulled the trigger to uncock the gun.

The magazine was off, so it was only one shot, but in the partners' room of a private bank it was louder than Ranklin had expected.

But Viner had properly pointed the weapon down and away so only the panelling suffered, though Grandpa's portrait got a bit of a fright.

In the ear-ringing silence, somebody said: "Fucking hellsfire," and it sounded like a woman's voice, but that was impossible, so Ranklin put it down to his stunned hearing. Then the room was flooded with Sherring employees and he found himself taking charge. "See if there's any casualties on the far side of that wall. Where's a place for Mrs Finn to lie down? And I think some brandy would help. No need to call the police *just* yet. Meanwhile, *thank* you—" He took the weapon from Viner's trembling hands, uncocked it again, and laid it in the box.

"Thank you, James," Corinna said, her voice shaky. "No, I don't need to lie down, but brandy sounds a good idea." Somebody found a decanter and glasses. "The rest of you can go now, the show's over."

"I don't know what to say," Viner said, his smile long gone. "Somehow a round must have—" He looked at Ranklin, puzzled.

"Perhaps you'd best stick to percentages." She took a healthy swig at her glass and shuddered. "Ah, that's better. Now, where were we? I seem to remember something about us agreeing to underwrite a hundred thousand – at five per cent, wasn't it? A nice round shilling in the pound. I'm sure you can square that with whoever you find as principal."

"I say, five per cent seems a bit—"

"But with building repair costs the way they are in this modern world, surely that isn't too unreasonable?" Her voice had firmed up, though her smile was wide and friendly. "Now perhaps you'd get that thing out of here before it declares war again."

Ranklin helped Viner pack up the gun and its pieces, then insisted on carrying it downstairs for him. "Quite a change from the usual financial confab," he puffed cheerfully (it might be lightweight, but was still a machine-gun and the stairs were awkward). "Makes it an afternoon to remember."

Ahead of him, Viner was shaking his head. "I feel such a fool . . . And now I've got to tell another bank that we've already committed a third of the issue. It's really most awkward. Look, when you had the gun, did you—"

Ranklin didn't want to dwell on that. "Considering that you nearly shot the boss's daughter, I'd say you didn't do too badly. Silence, as they say, is also golden. Getting back to Continental interest, would that include Italy?"

Outside on the pavement they found a policeman staring solemnly up at the building. "Excuse me, gentlemen, but somebody reported hearing a gunshot. D'you know anything about that?"

Viner looked at Ranklin, who said: "In a private bank? I hardly think so, Constable. But these old buildings are very sound-proof and my friend was telling me such interesting things about Italy . . ."

A little surprised that the short, tubby man in shirt-sleeves who carried big boxes around seemed to be in charge, the policeman said: "It wasn't from this building, then, sir?"

"You could wait and see if they wheel out any casualties . . ." Ranklin shrugged as well as he could without dropping the box. "But probably just a motor-car backfiring."

The policeman nodded gravely. "Thank you, sir." But he only moved far enough to stare at the next building.

"Now," Ranklin said. "Were you going to tell me about a certain Italian senator?"

"Was I?" Viner was looking around for his motor-car, and escape.

"I'm pretty sure you were, but . . ." Ranklin glanced pointedly at the policeman a few yards away.

"No deals have been done at all, just . . . Look, can you assure me that this . . . accident isn't going to get talked about?"

"I feel on the brink of being sure."

Viner hesitated for one last moment, then muttered: "God knows how he managed it, but we had Lord Curzon asking if we could help out. The Italian ended up with *two* of the things, and we've only got half a dozen."

"Lord Curzon?"

"That's what I said. Ah, there's my motor."

"And ammunition?" But that was a silly question; you could pick up British Army ammunition anywhere. Ranklin watched the motor-car drive off, reflecting that Dagner had enlisted a very big gun to get Falcone his small guns. Strictly, Curzon was now just an ex-Viceroy and out-of-office politician, but he wasn't somebody a

115

government contractor said No to. He might be Prime Minister of the next Unionist administration.

So it was just part of the 'deal' they'd done with Falcone. Should he mention to Dagner that he'd uncovered it? Perhaps not: it might seem that he'd been prying. Ranklin suddenly became aware that he was standing on a London street without his jacket on. Only the financial district, of course, but even so . . . He hurried back indoors.

Up in the partners' room, Corinna was sitting and quite visibly shaking, her face pale even in the yellow lamplight. "I'm sorry . . . suddenly come on . . ." She gulped more brandy. "He could have *killed* me."

A dreadful sense of guilt was clouding Ranklin's judgment, and he almost said: "So could a passing motor-bus" but realised the light touch was wrong. So he put his arms around her and hugged her tightly. It was awkward, with her still sitting, but hardly less awkward than when she was standing, given her height. It was something they did best lying down.

Her shivering vibrated through his own body, then stopped, and he felt her take a deep breath. He said fiercely: "That idiotic bastard. I ought to have him jailed."

As he'd hoped, she became magnanimous. "No, it was just stupidity. And it ended well enough . . . I'm okay, now. Here, finish this." She gave him the brandy glass. "He wouldn't have agreed to split the issue if he wasn't feeling guilty. The trouble is, I can't okay anything more than a hundred thousand and I'd like to have taken the lot. But I'll take five thousand and a bullet-hole."

"Only five thousand? – isn't that rather small beer?"

"You've been reading the socialist newspapers again. Most of our earnings are from half a per cent here, a quarter there – steady stuff from clients who come back year after year. A big coup is rare, risky – and probably makes enemies, because if you suddenly make a pile, it's usually because somebody else has suddenly lost it." She found her purse and took out a small mirror. "Oh Lord, gunfire doesn't improve one's looks. Are you going back to your office?"

"Got to, I'm afraid."

"You'd better get along: this is going to take time. We're meeting at the Carlton tomorrow, then? And thank you. You're pretty good under fire."

Which made Ranklin feel even more guilty ... Still, he *had* helped her make £5,000.

16

The next morning, the weather had changed its mind about it being autumn. The sun rose into a near-cloudless and windless sky and before the dew had dried, O'Gilroy made his first solo flight.

For brief periods over the last five days he had sat beside an instructor as they floated soggily around the aerodrome in a training machine with the honest but unlovely name of 'Boxkite'. Set alongside the modern Sopwiths, Avros and Andrew Sherring's Oriole, it looked like the work of a Chinese scaffolding company, but it flew. And the cage of struts and wires protected the novice from his own mistakes or the ground – which amounted to the same thing. In this, he had notched up just over two hours of flight.

That might not seem much, but others had solo'd with less. And the truth, which O'Gilroy wasn't entirely ready to face, was that there wasn't much to learn because aeroplanes couldn't actually do much. They took off, turned, and landed; the rest was engine handling and navigation. It was only now that men like Pégoud were discovering what aeroplanes might really be made to do.

And now O'Gilroy was teetering on the edge of the nest. He could stop there, quit, walk away. But that thought lasted only long enough to remind him that he was here by choice. Then he checked the oil glass, which showed a proper one-drip-per-second, and eased the air lever forward a fraction, followed by the petrol lever. The engine – behind him in a Boxkite – whirred a little more urgently, the revs climbed past 1,100 and the machine ambled forward. There was no speedometer – 'airspeed indicator' they called it on more modern types – so he had to guess, to *feel*, when it wanted to fly. And nothing to tell if he was keeping straight, except an absurd thread of red wool tied to a strut and streaming back in the wind. Did that wind feel fast enough now? It felt quite different from when he had an instructor beside him. Perhaps a second or two more, like . . .

now. He pulled gently on the wheel and the Boxkite did nothing. And then flew.

It lasted – intentionally – only seconds, just a straight-line "hop" of maybe three hundred yards from start to stop. But it also lasted an age, in which he had time to think that if he left the engine levers as they were he could climb and fly on beyond sight until his petrol ran out. Time to feel utter loneliness because no way in the world could anyone reach out a hand to help if he forgot what to do next. And time for his perverse mind deliberately to forget, to feel a total stranger in a contraption from another world where there was no grass beneath his feet, no scent of pines in the breeze, nothing familiar at all . . .

And still time for his body to remember before his mind did, so that he had pushed the foot-bar to straighten the thread of wool, eased back the petrol, then air, then pressed the "blip" switch to interrupt the ignition, felt and heard the wheels rumble back onto the ground, his ground, his world. He wondered if he would ever experience a flight so long.

Half an hour and three more hops later, he climbed down and lit a cigarette. His hands shook a little, but they hadn't when it mattered, and that was as important as his instructor saying: "That was pretty good, you're getting the hang of it. Next time you can do a couple of turns. Just one or two points to bear in mind . . ."

O'Gilroy looked back at the clumsy, unlikely contrivance that had, nevertheless, flown. No – that *he* had made fly. There was grass underfoot and a pine scent in the air, but the sky was part of that world, too. His world, now his sky.

*   *   *

The temperature climbed towards the seventies, promising a bad-tempered day under the attic roof of Whitehall Court. The stenographers went about shaking at the necks of their blouses when they thought nobody was looking, and Lieutenant J turned up late and disguised, he said, as a plumber's mate. This involved a cool collarless shirt and no jacket. Dagner calmly sent him around the building knocking on doors and asking if they had reported a plumbing problem – then surprised Ranklin by erupting into laughter.

"That's more like it. I *want* them trying to put one over on us. If they can do that, perhaps they can do it to others."

119

"As long as we don't get one of them coming in saying he's disguised as an artist's model." But the others hadn't got J's flair. He came from a very aristocratic background and in him, that was an advantage. Being totally confident of who he was left him more time than most for studying others, and he had got the humble superiority of a skilled artisan exactly right.

* * *

Dagner insisted they arrive at the Carlton well ahead of the time Ranklin thought was politely early. But this was typical of Dagner's manner generally, and – Ranklin recalled – most Indian society. Out there, they clung to the manners and slang of twenty years ago, convinced that England had Gone To The Dogs and was gripped by fads and fashions that Ranklin had noticed, if at all, as mere ripples.

They ordered tea and Dagner insisted that a fresh pot be brought *the moment* Mrs Finn arrived. The tables were spaced for privacy even without the potted-palm jungle waving around them in the blast of fans that countered the unseasonable warmth.

Dagner said abruptly: "Am I right in thinking that the contract for Mr Sherring's aeroplane has been agreed?"

"I think it gets signed tomorrow. Mrs Finn's been handling the financial end."

"I believe she understands money." But Dagner said it without any implications; perhaps wives running an Indian household were also expected to understand money – though not in freight-car lots, as Corinna herself might have put it.

"And," Ranklin said sombrely, "I presume the Senator now goes home to start his sabotage strike in Trieste."

Dagner wore a smile of curiosity. "Are you concerned that he won't be able to do it – or that he will, and it'll get out of hand?"

"Getting out of hand."

"Oh, I think Europe can absorb a little local squabbling."

"Less than a year ago, I was tramping around the Greek mountains with a brigade of French 75's."

"But that *was* only a local war," Dagner pointed out. "Though I know no war seems local when you're fighting it. The Great Powers, led by ourselves, kept it so – and imposed a peace."

"It brewed up again within weeks."

"And *again* it was stopped from spreading. Perhaps you were too close to see how remarkable that was: after all these centuries, Europe realised it had the power to stop wars as well as start them. The *Pax Britannica* became a *Pax Europa*. I doubt we'll ever stop local wars any more than we'll stop crime. But a mature society can contain crime, not be destroyed by it."

Ranklin was hunched over his teacup, brooding back to the winter roads of Greece. But the memory was useless; the front line taught you nothing about diplomacy and Big Causes. You were too concerned about where the next shell would land.

He sighed. "Perhaps. I still feel there's a risk . . . Here she comes: we might ask her, she travels more than I do."

Corinna had felt untypically self-conscious about meeting Ranklin's new boss – of whom she'd only just heard anyway. She guessed that her suitability was on trial, which gave her the choice of being infuriated by their gall, or meekly going along with it for Ranklin's sake. So she got privately furious in a speech which almost melted her dressing-table mirror, then put on a demure tea gown of pastel silk (she liked stronger colours) and a stupid little flowerpot hat (with her height, she preferred wide hats). She already had such clothes because she sometimes had to be demure as the daughter of Reynard Sherring. But this wasn't helping any million-dollar deal, this was being demure as *herself*. Grrr.

At least the Carlton itself was familiar ground since she dropped in once or twice a week to see what other Americans were in town. The war scares of that summer had brought quite a turnover, sending some rushing home, bringing others rushing across to sniff the air for themselves. So she didn't feel out of place, only out of sorts. But having gone so far, she warned herself, for God's sake remember to behave as well. And as Ranklin and what must be Dagner rose to meet her, she switched on her smile.

The new man was tall – few men were much taller than herself – dark-eyed and with the hawk profile the English liked in their public men and heroes. His manner was somehow both shy and self-assured, as old-fashioned as his suit was brand new.

"Delighted to meet you, Major Dagner." And hastening to reassure him: "Matt's told me so *little* about you." She realised that was wrong, got flustered, and made it worse with: "And of course he hasn't told me what you *do*."

121

She looked longingly at her cup of tea but daren't touch it. It would rattle like dice.

Dagner's polite smile was undisturbed. "Just potter about the War Office shuffling papers, along with Captain Ranklin. He's been showing me the ropes."

"Oh, yes. You're, ah—" Was she even supposed to know he'd come from India? "—new to London. Are you settling down okay? I'm sorry – I don't even know if you're married?"

Damn, Ranklin thought, I should have warned her that his wife's dead. But Dagner said calmly: "Yes, but my wife's still on her way home. My posting was rather sudden: they shot me off on the first boat and left her to pack up our kit. The Army's a very primitive society: we still let the women do all the work."

Corinna laughed rather too loudly; Ranklin sat expressionless, but nobody seemed to notice. Then he thought: Of course, he must have married again, seven years is quite long enough. So he smiled too late, but luckily nobody noticed that, either. Corinna picked up her cup with a steady hand, sipped, and said: "So you've been with the Army in India. I remember now that Matt said."

"I hope he didn't say quite that. I belong to the Indian Army, the army raised there. The Army *in* India is just regular British units posted out there for a few years at a time. I believe Captain Ranklin – Matt – himself had a posting there."

"All those Indian soldiers look terribly grand in the pictures." She knew she was babbling, but now had to go on. "Was that what attracted you? – when you were younger, of course."

"I just joined *my* Army, Mrs Finn – as Captain Ranklin did his. My family's been in India for four generations. My great-grandfather fought at Mysore. But he reckoned Wellesley wouldn't need his help tackling Napoleon so stayed out there. And as for it being grand, I'm afraid the British Army looks on us as poor relations. We're even expected to live on our pay – the ultimate insult. So we don't get the young sprigs of aristocracy, not in garrisons six weeks' voyage from Piccadilly."

"Do you miss them that much?"

"Somehow," Dagner smiled, "we stumble on without. They're prepared to accept our hospitality on attachment when something's happening, as it usually is in India, but they aren't too keen on us cropping up in London to renew the acquaintance."

Feeling quite at home now, Corinna frowned at Ranklin. "Did *you* behave like that?"

Before he could answer, Dagner said: "No, I absolve Gunners: they despise everybody quite indiscriminately. They see themselves as an oblique aristocracy quite on their own."

"Not aristocracy," Ranklin said. "Gods."

She laughed freely, then said: "Yet for all that, you still talk of 'coming home'. Which *do* you think of as home? – England or India?"

Dagner sat back to think, throwing one long leg over the other. He still wears boots, she noted, well made and beautifully polished, but not shoes. And although he was nowhere near old enough, she placed him in her father's generation with its solid, dated manners and values. Of course, her father was really a buccaneer – but surely Dagner must also be one, in his own world.

He was saying: "D'you know? – it isn't easy to say. Perhaps it should be the same thing, but it isn't. When I'm here, I'm always startled at how seldom people think of India, compared with how much India thinks of England. And I confess that makes me feel a bit of a stranger. And, as it were, as one stranger to another, may I ask a question? Captain Ranklin and I were talking about war, a European war—"

"D'you ever talk about anything else?"

"Ah, that was almost the question. I understand that you travel widely: is it the same throughout Europe?"

"War talk? Yes."

"But do people really believe it could happen?"

"Sure they do."

Dagner shook his head in genuine puzzlement. "But with all the changes, new inventions—"

"Like the new battleships and submarines and Matt's guns *and* putting machine-guns on airplanes?"

"Quite, although I was thinking more of things like the telephone, faster travel, that are bringing the nations closer together. And must help trade. Europe's grown so rich. Yes, you still see poverty – but nothing like what you see in India. A Continental war – it seems almost a luxury, an absurd extravagance . . . if that doesn't sound too ridiculous."

She smiled sympathetically. "No, you may have hit on something there. Maybe these people think they can afford a war along with everything else. They could even feel they've already paid for it, with the new battleships and all, so now they're owed the glory. I don't know about that. But one thing's for sure, they don't think a war's going to be long and costly, so economic arguments just don't work a damn."

"But those can't be the opinions of political and industrial leaders."

"I don't talk to people on street corners," she said crisply.

"Of course not, I do apologise . . . but it seemed as if you were suggesting that some people might actually *want* such a war."

She glanced at Ranklin, who was no help, and then felt: he asked *me*, and this matters too much for tact. "Yes, I think some people do: they think it'll 'clear the air' somehow."

He clearly didn't believe her so, being Corinna, she doggedly went ahead and made it worse: "Europeans think we Americans don't know anything about war. But we did have one – before my time, but there're still survivors of it stumping around on one leg. D'you know how big the US Army – North and South together – was when it started? Just about fifteen thousand men. Four years later our war had killed six hundred thousand of them. So we think it's a little funny the Europeans think we don't know about war."

The figures startled Ranklin, but Corinna didn't get figures wrong. And his startlement proved her point: European armies *did* dismiss that war as "merely civil" and got on with studying the campaigns of the properly international Franco-Prussian one.

Dagner showed no reaction at all. An oyster doesn't slam shut. But although he was still smiling politely, it was clear to both of them that he was back in his shell, not at home to any more opinions.

"Alas, I hear the call of unshuffled papers – so will you forgive me if . . . ?" He stood up.

In perfect control, Corinna flashed her widest smile and extended her hand. "Delighted to have met you, Major."

When Dagner had gone, she let out her breath like – rather too much like – a surfacing whale, and said: "How'd I do? I felt so stupidly *nervous* . . ."

"That was my fault." He wasn't sure what was, but it seemed a safe thing to say.

"He didn't believe us, though." She mused. "Was that because I was a woman – or an American?"

"You did rather ram that in."

She grinned wickedly, then turned serious. "But in his job, he should be a better listener. And people living under a volcano ought to know it's there. You could have trouble with that man."

So Ranklin found himself defending Dagner out of loyalty. "He's been a long time out in India. It gives you a great impression that Britain, and Europe, are wonderfully efficient and sensible. Out there, believe me, you feel you're floating in a great river, no point in swimming against it and nothing you can do to speed it up or change anything. Give him time, he'll learn."

"If you've got time. Maybe his wife'll help, when she gets here. He needs someone to talk to. D'you know anything about her?"

"Er . . . no. Except she must be his second wife. His first died in India. So an old friend of his said."

"Was he doing the same sort of work in India?" Now Dagner was no longer a State Secret, Corinna wasn't holding back.

Ranklin tried a diversionary answer. "Out there, he's quite a hero – I mean an overt one. He was on Younghusband's expedition to Tibet and picked up a DSO."

"Whatever all that means."

"In 1904, they routed the whole Tibetan Army, fought their way through to Lhasa, the first white men to reach the Forbidden City."

"Yes? And what did that achieve?"

He tried to think back. According to Army gossip, policy had changed so that London's politicians censured Younghusband, disowned the expedition and ultimately forced Curzon to resign as Viceroy (Curzon again: had they refought the Younghusband campaign over dinner at the Tower?). You quickly learnt not to expect rewards – except medals, which cost nobody anything – and also that if you were to go on believing in Britain, you had to stop believing its politicians. And some, already with experience of the secret world, might conclude it was best to decide for yourself what was right for your country.

Was that, for one man, what Younghusband's expedition had achieved?

"Difficult to say," he mumbled.

17

On Thursday morning Corinna picked up Ranklin outside White-hall Court and they headed for Brooklands. They had planned on getting there in good time for lunch. But so had thousands of others, and nearly three hours before Pégoud was due to fly, the Sherring Daimler was in an ambling stream of motor-cars, pedestrians and cyclists wending up to the aerodrome gates. Hundreds more, reasoning that an aerial display could hardly be kept private so why pay the shilling entrance fee, had roosted on the high ground just outside the track with picnics seasoned by the dust from the road.

Corinna had had much the same idea, on her own scale. She ignored the overflowing Blue Bird restaurant and had the chauffeur lug a bulging picnic hamper over to Andrew's shed. A work-bench had been cleared and even laid with a tablecloth, albeit by somebody with oily hands. Andrew, Falcone and O'Gilroy had already started on bottled beer.

At Corinna's orders, the work-bench sprouted wine-bottles, cut-lery, pies, potted meats, bread, cheeses and fruit. Corinna, Falcone and Andrew loaded their plates and began a contractual discussion. Ranklin took the chance for a word with O'Gilroy, whom he still had to treat as a casual acquaintance in front of Falcone.

"How goes the flying?"

"Ah, it's . . ." For once, O'Gilroy couldn't find the words and his eyes were focused on some unimaginable vision. Unimaginable to me, anyway, Ranklin thought enviously. Is there any human endeavour that could still move me, that I could believe in, like this?

"Mind," O'Gilroy came down to earth, "there's a deal to be understood, with the engineering and physics of it. I wisht I had yer education."

Ranklin was damned if he was going to feel guilty about that, too, but changed the subject slightly. "Did you gather that Andrew's selling his machine to Senator Falcone? – if he can get it to Italy for a demonstration flight."

"Mr Sherring said things was going that way." There was no familiar "Andrew" for O'Gilroy. Mr Sherring was a proper pilot and aeroplane designer, resident of Valhalla. "Didn't know 'twas cut 'n' dried."

"Mrs Finn's been handling the financial side and the Senator should be giving her a bank draft today. Tell me, what's so special about this aeroplane?"

O'Gilroy took being consulted seriously. After a lot of thought, he said: "The seating, side by side. Ye don't get it on most aeroplanes with covered fuselages. Makes it a bit wider and slower but Mr Sherring says he'd rather lose a few miles an hour and have the two fellers able to talk – shout – to each other."

Ranklin saw that logic immediately. Most military débâcles were traceable to breakdowns in communication. "You remember telling me Falcone was also interested in the lightweight Lewis guns? – well, he's got hold of a couple. *Could* he be thinking of armed aeroplanes?"

O'Gilroy gave this proper thought, as well. "I'd think not this aeroplane. 'Twould be easier with seats one behind 'tother, so the feller at the back had the gun and a good field of fire. But I suppose ye can do anything, put yer mind to it."

Ranklin nodded absently. It was a perfectly reasonable, patriotic thing for a rich senator to be finding arms for his country (and buying the manufacturing rights to them, presumably with an eye to becoming richer). But there was neither law nor reason that said the senator had to be any good at judging those arms. God knew the British Army had been landed with some civilian-picked horrors in its time.

At the back of the shed, Falcone and Andrew were bending over a work-bench signing documents. They straightened up, grinned at each other, and shook hands. Corinna took Andrew's share of the paperwork and tucked it into her handbag.

"One thing, mind," O'Gilroy added thoughtfully. "When I met Falcone in Brussels, he was looking at a Blériot that a Belgian

feller had altered some ways by himself. I'm thinking why not go
to France for a proper Blériot? Or Farman or Deperdussin? Then
he comes here and still don't go to Sopwith or Avro or Bristol,
the big boys, he comes to Mr Sherring. Now he's good," he said
loyally, "but nobody's heard of him."

"Perhaps," Ranklin said, "Falcone's looking for a dark horse to
back. Or perhaps he can get the aeroplane and rights at cut price
compared with the big boys . . . The trouble is, we're just out of
our depth in these matters."

O'Gilroy smiled lopsidedly. "But we're good at being suspicious."

Ranklin nodded. Only – were they being suspicious for good
reason, or because, if Jesus Christ came back to Earth, they'd
demand to see his passport?

*   *   *

Shortly before four o'clock, there was a mechnical buzz from
the field, a human buzz from the crowd, and they wandered
out of the shed to watch the display. Ranklin moved alongside
Falcone and asked: "Have you seen any more signs of, ah,
followers?"

"Nothing, nothing." Falcone was in a cheerful mood.

"And did you ask the local police to—"

Falcone waved the idea away. "Your idea to move to a new
hotel was enough. I am sure I am safe here."

Certainly it was difficult to imagine danger among that sunny
crowd, but Ranklin gave the nearest spectators a glare nonetheless.
Watching the sky, they didn't notice.

A biplane – a Farman, O'Gilroy said – was already aloft,
apparently carrying a photographer to snap the Great Event. At
four o'clock Pégoud, with an upturned moustache, white sweater
and leather motoring helmet (the description was Corinna's: with
her height and a manner that melted those in front like a death-ray,
she had a better view), trundled out in his strengthened Blériot with
heightened king-post (the description was O'Gilroy's) and whirred
into the air.

As it spiralled upwards, Ranklin dared to ask: "What's actually
so marvellous about flying upside down?"

Andrew gave him a condescending smile. "Just it's never been done before – except by guys a few seconds before they got killed. If he can get into it – and hold it there *and* get out of it okay – it's one hell of a big step forward. I mean really historic. For airplanes as much as pilots."

Knowing Ranklin's range of knowledge better, O'Gilroy said: "How d'ye suppose a bridge would work if ye put it across a river upside down?"

Ranklin considered. Although he'd cited bridge-building to Corinna, he hadn't taken the thought far enough. Bridges, after all, stayed where they were put.

The now-distant monoplane seemed to level out – "At about three thousand feet," O'Gilroy reckoned, with a glance at Andrew – then began to spiral down. Abruptly its nose tipped down, tucked right under, and the machine levelled – more or less – upside down. There was a huge gasp from the crowd. The distant whirr of the engine stopped, but Ranklin's artillery experience of sound and distance told him Pégoud had probably stopped it before his inversion.

The crowd hushed as the aeroplane continued, gliding gently down. And then the nose toppled further, the machine curved down – and was flying upright and level again. The engine popped and whirred into life. The crowd roared, Andrew was cheering wildly, and around Ranklin the spectators bunched and swayed. Falcone leant on his shoulder, grunting something, then flopped forwards onto the concrete. Fantastically, the handle of a knife, thrust through a piece of paper, stuck from a dark red stain spread on his back.

"Get a doctor!" Ranklin screamed. "Ambulance!" Uncomprehending faces turned towards him, then looked down. The immediate crowd drew back, leaving him kneeling by Falcone and trying to rip the jacket and shirt from his back, and looking – instinctively, in an emergency – for O'Gilroy. He'd vanished.

O'Gilroy had taken a couple of steps away from Ranklin to get a clearer view of the aeroplane past a woman with a sunshade. He'd been half aware of a smaller man easing past towards Falcone's broad back, although he hadn't thought of it that way at the time, and then heard Ranklin's shout. Everybody around was looking down, except one woman staring open-mouthed away to the left. Following her look, O'Gilroy caught one glimpse of a short man, in a dark grey suit and wide-brimmed hat – slipping through the crowd. He took fast strides towards him.

He lost the man but kept to the direction, past the Aero Club and across the grass towards the cars parked along the motor track. The crowd, which had come to see a spectacle in the air, had had no need to bunch up as at a racetrack or stadium: it was scattered lumpily in groups, easy to zigzag through. He glimpsed a small man in a dark suit, but he was bare-headed, and dark suits were as common as the tweeds he wore himself.

Then he saw the wide-brimmed foreign-looking hat, abandoned on a picnic basket. And when he again saw a dark suit going in the right direction, it was topped by a more English flat cap.

The man was strolling now, and O'Gilroy thought *Right*, I move up, casual like, parallel to ye, then cut across, not catching yer eye – and I've got ye. He was unarmed, but had no intention of trying to grab the man or saying something stupid like: "I arrest you in the name of . . ." He would just hit him as hard as he could, one wallop out of the blue, and let things sort themselves out from there.

Then he realised the one man had become two, and that changed things. The second, also in a dark suit but with a brown felt hat, was taller and thicker. He wasn't going to attack two men, but two were easier to follow – unless they split up. But they were foreigners, likely to stick together and on main routes in a strange place. Staying off to one side rather than behind them, he matched their ambling, unsuspicious pace, and began to think ahead.

Probably they were heading for the exit, the railway station and London, as most of the crowd would eventually. He could call for help to the policemen at the gate, but O'Gilroy mistrusted policemen. They expected only the normally unexpected; he'd probably just get himself arrested.

He thought of his own appearance. The road outside would be crowded, but not many would be leaving at the height of the show, so he must assume he'd be noticed. The trick was not to be *seen*. He was respectably dressed – Ranklin would have taken it as a slight to Corinna if he'd worn his messing-about-with-aeroplanes clothes – and trying to vary his appearance by taking off his jacket or cap would just make him obvious. So forget looks, think of behaviour.

If they were indeed heading for the station, he could go ahead of them; people seldom think of being followed from in front. He decided to risk that and strode out, purposeful yet unhurried, to reach the gate first.

18

The spectators around the front of the hangar had taken up the shout for a doctor, and it always amazed Ranklin how many doctors you could find as long as you weren't waiting in their consulting-rooms, because they got two in as many minutes. The first was thin and elegant, a spectator taking the afternoon off from Harley Street.

He saw the knife, and the jerk of surprise almost dislodged his topper. "Good God, man, have you called the police?"

"I am the police – sort of," Ranklin said, kneeling to hold the bloody rags of Falcone's shirt around the knife that still stuck from his back.

"Then you haven't done a very good job."

"Set me an example, then," Ranklin snarled. But then what was probably the aerodrome doctor arrived, stout and busy, with a bulging bag ready to tackle crash victims. He said: "My God," but got straight down to work, muttering: "At least you didn't pull out the knife."

Ranklin had already ripped the piece of paper from the knife; he stood up and tried to read what it said under the dripping blood, but it was just a rough pencilled drawing.

The crowd had formed a circle trying to see, but not too much, around the group that still included Andrew, Corinna and now the Harley Street doctor, who had decided his duty lay in comforting the best-dressed woman in sight.

Ranklin snatched her away. "Did you see where O'Gilroy went?"

"No, I was look—"

"He must be following the man." He thought for a moment. "I need the car."

"I told Dixon we wouldn't want him until—"

"Can you drive it?"

"Of course."

"Then let's get moving." He grabbed her arm, but she needed no more urging. They left the doctor saying: "I *say* . . ." without having to decide just what.

A couple of policemen came trotting through the crowd as they reached the Daimler. "Head for the station first," Ranklin ordered. "They're probably on foot . . . Damn it! – how did they *know* Falcone would be here?"

The car had an electric starter, but either it disapproved of leaving early or Corinna hadn't mastered it, because Ranklin ended up hand-cranking the heavy engine. He climbed in beside her soggy with sweat, and found the closed interior like a furnace. His temperature wasn't lowered by the spectators along the track, who certainly disapproved of anybody leaving at this moment, and by the time they passed through the tunnel to the exit, he reckoned O'Gilroy was well over five minutes ahead.

And thanks to the unpaying crowd outside, they clawed nothing back on the road to the station. As they crossed the bridge that led to the London side, steam and smoke welled up from a train pulling out beneath them, on the up-line to London.

Ranklin tried to think where on earth this line ran – then realised he knew it like his own signature since it went on down to Aldershot, home of the British Army. Next stop would be Walton – no use – then: "Esher! Turn around!"

O'Gilroy had had an anxious few minutes waiting on Weybridge platform before the two men caught up, chatting and smiling so casually that they had to be professionals in their own line. Well, he thought, that makes three of us, and planned just where he must join the train. Assuming it was corridorless, he needed a compartment near but not next to them, and a window seat facing their way to see if they got off before Waterloo. Meanwhile, he stayed well back in the shadow of the station canopy, trying to keep his face hidden. He wished he had a newspaper – the shadower's best friend – but most of all, he wished he had a gun.

Corinna sent the Daimler storming through the wooded lanes with the indignity of a runaway hearse, and Ranklin would have imagined chickens fluttering out of their path if he could also imagine any chicken fast enough. He braced himself against the corner of the seat and said nothing to distract Corinna's attention. She was angry – at events, at the man O'Gilroy was following – and for the moment all life was on a par with a chicken's.

Then they turned onto a long straight beside Burwood Park, she changed up a gear and sat back from her jockey-like hunch.

"Would you mind if I smoked?" Ranklin asked shakily.

"Burst into flames. Was Senator Falcone dead?"

"Not then. I just don't know how bad." He lit a cigarette.

"Who was it? How did it *happen?*"

"Because I let it happen. I knew it could happen, but thought . . . They left a sort of note," he remembered and took it, limp with still-tacky blood, from his pocket. "It's just – *don't look!*" as the car swerved; "—it's just a drawing of a skull, knife, gun and bottle. Symbol of a Serbian secret society. Also known as the Black Hand, though I think that's getting mixed up with one of the Italian criminal gangs."

"What have they got against Falcone?"

"I don't know exactly. I'm sure he *could* have told us more . . ." His voice trailed off, then he said bitterly: "And I had a pistol in my pocket all the time . . ." He was wishing it had been in O'Gilroy's pocket quite as much as O'Gilroy did now.

O'Gilroy only remembered Waterloo as a big, sprawling station with more exits than a sieve. So he was off the train and walking briskly towards the ticket barrier – the one bottleneck he could count on – before it had stopped completely. Beyond it, there was a news-stand just to his right and he had almost reached it when he recognised Ranklin already there, buying a *Star* and muttering from the side of his mouth: "Have you still got him in sight?"

"Them. There's two of them. How'd ye get here?"

"Same train. Caught it at Esher. Got on the very front. Didn't want them to see me waiting, they might recog—"

"Fine." O'Gilroy hid his surprise that Ranklin had learnt so much. "They've jest come through . . . waiting under the clock . . . mebbe wondrin' what to do . . . or if they're followed . . ."

Ranklin opened his paper, apparently eager to see stock market prices or racing results. "I've got a revolver on me."

"Thank God for that."

"So we could just grab them."

"And what proof are we having of anything? I saw nothing worth saying in court; what about yeself?"

The stall's proprietor was looking suspiciously at them: two men not looking at each other but muttering like two old lags in the exercise yard. Ranklin didn't notice; he was realising how weak their situation was. He had merely been following O'Gilroy, now it seemed O'Gilroy had merely been following someone he *thought* was involved.

"They're moving," O'Gilroy said, apparently having been watching through his right ear. "Going for a cab, I'm thinking."

Ranklin risked a glance and frowned. "I know that one, the taller. He was outside the Ritz last week."

"Will he be knowing ye?"

"Probably." The confrontation in the taxi had been brief but vivid.

Still, they had to take the risk, strolling after the two towards the lines of motor-taxis and horse-drawn cabs waiting on the road that ran through the station, where the two chose a hansom. London was the most motor-conscious city in Europe, so perhaps it was not surprising that foreigners, and particularly unsophisticated ones, should feel happier behind a horse. And that left their followers with the flexibility of a far speedier motor-taxi.

Since taking up his new trade, Ranklin had often wondered what would happen if he asked a taxi-driver to "follow that cab". Now he learned that he got a surly up-and-down stare that made him wish his shoes were newer and less dusty. He was about to invent a complex tale about being a solicitor in a divorce case when O'Gilroy slapped a half-guinea into the driver's hand, said: "It's got a brother waiting at t'other end," and pushed Ranklin inside. So *that* was how it was done.

But almost immediately, the sheer speed of the taxi gave them a problem. To stay behind the cab, they had to crawl conspicuously, being passed by every other motor vehicle. So Ranklin told the driver to overtake and wait on the far side of Waterloo Bridge. There the traffic thickened and they could follow invisibly around the empty building site of Aldwych and into Kingsway. There they had to speed up and overtake again, stopping once more at the junction with High Holborn. The cab clopped past, keeping to the right for a turn ahead.

135

Ranklin was just thinking that this game of leapfrog couldn't go on much longer, when he realised what that turn implied: "Clerkenwell. They're heading for Little Italy."

"Where they'd be having plenty of friends?" O'Gilroy suggested. "I think I'll be taking yer pistol now, Captain."

Ranklin hesitated. But if the situation were going to need a pistol, it would also need O'Gilroy's rapid decisiveness. He passed it over, then leant forward to direct the driver. And decided to be – fairly – frank: "Where would you say the Italian quarter begins?"

"Yer mean past the police station?"

"Is there one?"

"Corner o' Gray's Inn. The wops live a bit furver, past Rosebery Avenue, but I'm not going dahn them hills."

"No—" the police station was tempting, but perhaps for later; "—no, just put us down past the Avenue."

They had time to pay off the taxi and cross to the "wrong" side of the road, to be less conspicuous. But the Clerkenwell Road was a main thoroughfare and tram route, where nobody looked out of place, something that would change a few yards into one of the side streets.

The two in the cab obviously hadn't given an exact address, just stopped the cab at the opposite pavement and stood chatting and glancing around until it had gone. Then they strolled, unhurried in the evening sun, further along the road before turning off down a narrow, steep side street.

Ranklin and O'Gilroy crossed the road again and, with Ranklin at least feeling that he was walking into a spotlight, passed the invisible frontier into Back Hill Street. It was some help that the two they were following, dressed to be inconspicuous at Brooklands, also showed up well in the grubbily colourful crowd that bustled around them. But they walked with confidence while Ranklin felt he was lurking. Then they vanished into an alley.

O'Gilroy took several sudden strides before Ranklin, less familiar with such terraced houses, had worked out that the alley must lead to a tiny courtyard and the back doors to houses on both sides. But which one? How O'Gilroy managed a glance into the alley while still looking straight ahead, Ranklin couldn't tell, but he had seen which way the men turned at the far end.

"The first house," he murmured, when Ranklin caught up. "On the right. Will we be grabbing them?"

But Ranklin was having doubts; they had pushed their luck a long way already. "We haven't really got grounds even for a citizen's arrest."

O'Gilroy glared. "If it makes ye happier, I'll swear I saw the little one stick the knife in. If'n we get them now, they'll be loaded wid evidence, tickets for Brooklands and the like."

"No. Let the police do it. We can have them round here in five minutes."

O'Gilroy's expression was pure exasperation, but when Ranklin turned back, he followed.

The police station stood isolated on the corner of Gray's Inn gardens, a red-brick fortress of law and order four storeys high with a semi-basement – probably the cells – beneath. They were shown into a small room, anonymous if that word included shiny, bilious green paintwork, while the desk sergeant called a uniformed inspector.

Ranklin presented his (genuine) calling card and began: "There was an attempted murder – it may be a murder by now – at Brooklands aerodrome this afternoon. I know that's for the Surrey police—" the Inspector's beefy face had begun to look resigned; "—but we've followed two men, suspects, from there to a house in Back Hill Street."

Now the expression was wariness. "Which house is that, sir?"

Ranklin gave the number and knew that the Inspector recognised it. He looked at the floor, the walls and the window, then said: "I'd best telephone to Surrey about this, sir. When you say 'suspects', you mean you didn't see them commit the act?"

"Saw it wid me own two eyes," O'Gilroy lied flatly.

"Did you, sir? I don't think I got your name . . ."

"Tom Gorman."

"Yes, well, that's certainly a help, sir. But I'd best confirm exactly what happened. It shouldn't take long."

Ranklin demanded: "Couldn't you at least put a guard on the house, send men to watch it, or—?"

"If they're in that house, they're not going anywhere else, sir. It's what you might call the end of the line. And – between us, sir – if they're what you think they are, what they're doing now is concocting an alibi with a dozen witnesses to say they've been there all day, nowhere near Brooklands."

137

Telepathically, Ranklin heard O'Gilroy saying "I told you so." But aloud, it was: "Ah, then I'll jest be stepping out for a smoke." And his voice was so understanding and reasonable that Ranklin looked at him sharply.

The Inspector frowned. "We'll need a statement from you, sir."

"But only when yez sure there's something to state about, isn't that right? I'll be back in a tick or so."

"That gentleman," the inspector nodded at the closing door, "would be a colleague of yours, sir?"

Ranklin managed to get his imagination onto a new tack. "He's an engineer – working on our aeronautical side. Very competent chap," he added, afraid that he was about to be proved right.

Ten minutes later the Inspector was saying: ". . . they've got the Senator to a hospital in Kingston, and he's still breathing, so . . . And no other eye-witnesses so far. It seems that everybody was busy staring at the aeroplanes – as perhaps you were yourself, sir."

"It's what we were there for. But by now, if what you said is correct, those two we followed will have a cast-iron alibi."

"These Italians do stick together. And we'd just be stirring up trouble if we went barging in . . ."

And let the Surrey police worry about their own unsolved cases, Ranklin realised.

O'Gilroy walked in. His dark hair stuck out untidily from under his cap, but he spoke quite calmly. "I think ye've reason enough for going in there now, Inspector. Feller took a shot at me." He laid an unfamiliar pistol on the table. "So I took a shot at him – ye know how one thing leads to t'other? Yer revolver, Captain."

"What happened to him?" the Inspector demanded.

"Ye'd best go see. He'll be waiting."

The Inspector grabbed the revolver, sniffed its barrel, then shook out the cartridges. Three were empty shells. He goggled at O'Gilroy. "Are you confessing to a *murder?*"

138

19

The police station had been ransacked for chairs, none of them comfortable, to crowd the little 'interview' room. O'Gilroy sat behind the small table, flanked by the Inspector, with Sir Basil Thomson on the opposite side and Ranklin, Dagner and Major Kell fitting in wherever they could. The rest of the space was taken up with tobacco smoke since even the Inspector, with direct permission from Sir Basil, had his pipe smouldering tentatively.

Exactly what Kell was doing there, nobody had said, but perhaps he saw himself as a bridge between the worlds of officialdom and secrecy. Which was fine unless those worlds started pulling apart.

Sir Basil was there because he was Scotland Yard's Assistant Commissioner for the Criminal Investigation Division and Special Branch. If this impressed O'Gilroy, there was no sign of it.

"I would appreciate it, Sir Basil," Dagner said, "that if Gorman makes any statement or answers any questions, it should be clearly understood that it is quite off any record." His voice was polite but firm – and with no hint that he knew 'Gorman' by any other name.

Sir Basil frowned. He wasn't a career policeman, of course. He had trained as a barrister and gone on to govern colonies and prisons before coming to the Yard only a few months earlier. Now in his early fifties, his face above the austere wing collar seemed as patchwork as his career: long and sleepy-eyed, it might belong to an undertaker, but the bulbous nose and full lips suggested he knew which coffin they kept the brandy in.

And nothing in face or career suggested he normally deferred to majors of the Indian Army.

"Or," Dagner added, "I should have, with respect, to advise Gorman to remain silent – as I believe a lawyer would."

Sir Basil decided to keep his authority in reserve and said cheerily:

"Fine. By all means let us get to the truth of the matter. We know what happened at Brooklands, and you trailed this fellow up to town . . . Start from the moment you left this station."

Dagner endorsed this with a tiny nod and O'Gilroy took the cigarette from his mouth and said: "They'd gone in round the back, so that's the way I went . . ."

. . . to his surprise, the little courtyard was crammed with large lumps of stone, a half-finished statuette of the Virgin, and a litter of stone chippings. Presumably the sculptor lived in the other house. He made a half-bow to the figure in half-admission of what might be going to happen.

"So you went to the back door." Sir Basil made a note. "And knocked?"

"Ye might say. 'Twas locked so I kicked it in." He paused – as he had once he was inside and half hidden in the shadow beside the staircase. It was a mean little house with cramped dimensions, patchily dark except for the lurid glow through a stained-glass panel in the front door. That lay straight ahead, at the bottom of the staircase whose top was right above him. And another door that must lead into a front room. He was familiar with houses of this size.

If there was anybody else in the place – and there had to be, since he could smell cooking – they must come and investigate the sound of the lock smashing. He kept his hand on the pistol in his pocket and waited.

Feet shuffled behind yet another door that led to the back of the house, and a small, fat man in an apron and large moustache peered out. He looked slowly from O'Gilroy to the broken door, and might have made a deduction if O'Gilroy had given him the time.

"Two fellers come in here ten minutes ago. Where'd they go?"

The fat face looked puzzled.

"Upstairs? Was they going upstairs?"

Perhaps the man didn't understand English: even in the shadowed light, he looked foreign, quite apart from that apron. Indeed, the whole interior was foreign, from the smell to the dingy ornateness of the wallpaper and pictures.

O'Gilroy moved away, partly to get a view through the bannisters up the stairs, but also to relax the threat he posed and give the man space to yell . . . and he went off like a liner's steam-whistle.

But whatever the yell included, it couldn't mention the pistol: he hadn't seen that.

A board creaked above and O'Gilroy flattened himself against the front-room door, feeling for the knob with his left hand, hiding his right hand with his body. Then a pair of feet showed at the top of the stairs, and he knew them.

"You knew his *boots*?" Sir Basil broke in.

"When yer shadowing a feller, ye take a good look at his boots. So when ye come close in a crowd, he don't catch ye looking at his face, but ye know it's him and which way he's going from his boots."

Dagner nodded approvingly. He might or might not know that boots trick, but he didn't mind Sir Basil being reminded that he didn't do his own legwork.

O'Gilroy went on: "If'n I can see his boots, I'm thinking he can see mine, so I got out me gun – the Captain's revolver – and he comes down a coupla more steps and I can see he's got a gun himself."

It was the smaller man, the one who'd done the stabbing, and O'Gilroy came close to opening fire right then. But some errant streak of lawfulness took over and instead he turned the door-knob behind him and said loudly: "Police! Brooklands!" – reckoning the man must know those English words if no other ones.

The feet took another step down, the gun swivelled, and O'Gilroy ducked as he threw himself back into the room behind. Two shots splintered through the door after him, close as two eyes and at head height, so the man fancied himself as a marksman.

O'Gilroy yanked the door open again while the man would be off balance coming down the rest of the stairs and shot him. Twice into the body, tumbling him the rest of the way to sprawl on the front-door mat. But instead of lying there and quite probably surviving, he had to raise his gun, still unbeaten, still trying. In a flare of fury at having to do it, O'Gilroy shot him in the face from no more than six feet. And then, swearing aloud, hurried over to snatch the pistol.

He thought of the second man, but he was deaf from the gunfire in that cramped passageway, so the odds were stacking against him. Anyway, he didn't have quite the same quarrel with that one. Waving a gun in each hand, he barged past the servant – who had his mouth open and might be yelling again, for all O'Gilroy could hear – and out of the back door . . .

". . . and back to the police station," he concluded. He took a drag at his cigarette.

And there you have it, Ranklin thought. Just another typical afternoon in the life of a typical Secret Service Bureau agent.

Only it wasn't over yet. There was a faint flush on Sir Basil's cheeks and a frown gathering above his eyes. He was, after all, supposed to be maintaining law and order in this capital of Empire.

Politely tentative, Dagner said: "That seems to me a fairly clear case of self-defence, since the other man fired first."

Sir Basil ignored him. "Only *you*," he looked at O'Gilroy, "were already, by your own admission, guilty of breaking and entering and the victim might – had he survived – have claimed he was simply defending his property."

Ranklin asked: "Has he been identified?"

Sir Basil glanced at the Inspector, who said: "Not yet, sir. Nothing on the body that tells us."

"Whoever he is – was – the fact remains that had you waited for my police to take the proper legal steps, none of this would have occurred."

Ranklin said: "Even after Gorman got back, it still took a while to persuade your chaps to go along and have a look at the house. By which time the place seemed rather underpopulated. And I could have identified the second man as one I'd seen trying to follow the Senator from his hotel last week."

Sir Basil checked with a report on the table. "All you found was a cook who speaks no English and an old man living upstairs – the householder?"

He looked again at the Inspector, who waggled his features and said: "It's difficult to be sure of things like that in those places, sir."

"Quite so . . . Who'd heard shots but says he's never seen the man before and so on . . . Is this usual with that community?"

"I'm afraid so, sir. Very close they stick, rather sort things out themselves."

"I understand." Then Sir Basil frowned. "But damn it, this is *London*, not the back streets of Naples. I will not have . . ." he gestured comprehensively but vaguely and finished: ". . . such things." And topped it off with a glare at O'Gilroy.

Now Ranklin saw what the local police had been waiting and hoping for: that the house would be empty not only of witnesses but that embarrassing corpse as well. Blood-stains and bullet-holes could be shrugged off as long as nobody made a complaint. But not a body.

After a moment, Dagner suggested gently: "I'm no lawyer, but it seems to me that, since Gorman began by seeing this man stab the Senator at Brooklands, and ended by giving himself up at this station, and there are no witnesses to what happened in between, why should we doubt his word? Particularly with the evidence of the bullet-holes and the man's pistol. Quite apart from any Other Factors."

But Sir Basil bristled at that last. "If I'm not having London turned into Naples, I'm not having your people turn it into a Wild West show, either . . . You say you've got the victim's pistol, Inspector?"

"Yes, sir. A bit of an odd one, that." He slipped into his witness-box manner. "A new type of Webley semi-automatic, which I understand has only been issued to the Navy. In which case it should have an Admiralty stamp as well as a number, only the stamp's been filed off."

Ranklin said: "May I ask the Inspector if the house in Back Hill Street has any sort of reputation?"

"Nothing for certain, sir."

"But—" looking at Sir Basil; "—since all this is unofficial and off the record anyway . . . ?"

Sir Basil nodded to the Inspector, who said: "It's said to be the headquarters of the local Mafia or Camorra, we don't know which – if they're different, in London. They're not that important, sir," he added quickly. "The Italian population isn't permanent enough for that sort of thing to have much of a hold."

"But still," Dagner took up the thread, "a place where a visiting assassin might find sanctuary?"

"Major—" and in Sir Basil's tone it wasn't much of a rank; "—we have only Gorman's testimony that the man *was* an assassin."

"Oh my Lord." Ranklin had suddenly remembered, and fumbled in his pocket. "There was a piece of paper stuck on the knife in the Senator's back. I'd quite forgotten." He handed the blood-stained and crumpled note to Sir Basil, who smoothed it on the table-top. Everybody craned to look.

"It appears to be the symbol," Sir Basil announced, "of the Ujedinjenje ili Smrt – a Serbian secret society." Ranklin was surprised he recognised it. Then he realised the head of Special Branch had to know about any conspiracy that might crop up in London – as most did, sooner or later. Sir Basil passed it to Kell, then swung around on Ranklin: "And why, may I ask, did you remove a vital piece of evidence?"

"I thought it might help us—"

"Us? Us? Your Bureau has absolutely no jurisdiction, no authority – you don't even have any statutory *existence*. Yet you interpret that as licence to suppress evidence and behave like a crowd of Buffalo Bills whenever the mood takes you!"

"I can assure you, Sir Basil," Dagner soothed, "that disciplinary action will most certainly be taken."

"Closing the stable door after a *herd* of wild horses has been unleashed on the community."

"Nevertheless . . ."

"No." Sir Basil was thinking. Finally he said: "Major, I'd like to co-operate with your Bureau. But if I agree to an unofficial resolution of this matter, I'd be behaving no better than your . . . your agents. Moreover, the Surrey Police are also entitled to expect the co-operation of Scotland Yard. At present, they have an unsolved case of attempted murder – highly unsatisfactory. If we leave it like that, they have to spend time and trouble demonstrating they're trying to resolve it whilst knowing, unofficially, that they never will – even more unsatisfactory."

Now he was looking straight at Dagner. "But if they can connect the dead man here with the stabbing at Brooklands, they can close their books. And the only way for them to do that is through Gorman. So by all means let him plead self-defence, and I'd be quite happy if the court accepted that. But court is where he's going. Lock him up again, Inspector."

* * *

It was well into the evening now. The public house on the opposite corner sounded busy, trams clattered and squealed at the junction, but there was little other traffic. A few yards south were the legal chambers of Gray's Inn itself, while hardly further to the north-east lay the tenements of Little Italy, and just south of that was Hatton Garden, the gemstone district. London was full of such anomalous neighbourhoods, each now becoming self-contained villages again for the night.

"Probably quite a quiet spot, later on," Dagner said, apparently inconsequentially.

"I have a motor-car," Kell offered. "If I can give you a lift . . . ?"

"I think I'll walk a little way . . . You feel there's nothing left to be done?"

Kell and Ranklin were forced to accompany him as he paced along Theobald's Road. Kell said: "He's only had the Scotland Yard job since June, so he probably feels a new broom should be seen to sweep clean – and within the letter of the law. He may even feel his authority has been . . . well, challenged. But by morning he'll probably decide you've learnt your lesson and drop the whole thing."

"Are you sure?" Dagner asked bluntly.

"Well, no, I can't be cert—"

"So in the morning Gorman may appear in the police court and from there things will be a good deal more difficult to untangle. I assume you feel there's nothing you can do yourself?"

It was clear that Kell felt there was nothing he *should* be doing, but he said politely: "The trouble is that, on the face of it, the picture is complete, no obvious loose ends to involve my service. I'm sorry," he added without overdoing the sincerity.

"The piece of paper stuck on the knife?" Ranklin suggested.

"Anybody can scrawl such a thing. It certainly doesn't prove Serbian involvement in one Italian stabbing another."

"But Falcone *is* an Italian senator, granted an interview by the Foreign Office—"

"And apparently up to something that interests your Bureau? However, you aren't inviting me to interfere in *that*, I presume. If the Italian embassy kicks up a fuss, I may get dragged in. But if we start digging up the Senator's private life, we could turn up all sorts of things that might embarrass his family – even his government. With the stabber dead, the embassy may not want to investigate his motive."

"So," Ranklin said, "a quiet vote of thanks to Gorman for

saving everyone embarrasment and let him face a murder charge on his own."

Kell smiled blandly. "That's up to you. You might even feel that, given his past connections, this is a good opportunity to be rid of him."

They were walking past Gray's Inn gardens, Dagner peering through the railings at the wide and empty stretch of turf. "You think so? But with his own freedom – even his neck – at stake, isn't he likely to mention the Bureau in open court?"

"If you chose the counsel to defend him – I don't imagine he can afford much for himself – then with you footing the bill, I think you'd find something could be worked out."

Dagner looked at Ranklin, who shook his head slowly and said: "*If* it's our counsel. But a few months ago, Gorman got slung in jail in Kiel. We happened to be there with Mrs Finn. The daughter of Reynard Sherring, if you know the name," he explained to Kell. "And before I could lift a finger, she'd hired the best advocate in town and a few minutes later, Gorman was back on the street. That was just suspicion of clouting a local policeman. She has a rather American view of personal rights."

There was a long silence. Then Kell said: "Is she likely to hear of this matter?"

"She reads newspapers."

Dagner had been staring around as if in a strange city. Now he started walking back towards the police station. When he spoke, it was as if he were dictating notes. "I've met Mrs Finn, Major; I don't think you have. And if she's paying for the defence, I doubt we'll have much influence on what gets said. Which leaves us relying on Gorman's loyalty and discretion. Do you agree, Captain R?"

Ranklin knew what Dagner felt about O'Gilroy's loyalty, so tried a different tack: "Skipping any loyalty we owe *him*, what defence can he put up that doesn't involve the Bureau? He only knew Falcone because of the Bureau, he felt responsible for him because of the Bureau's interest, and he used my pistol – what's my connection with him except through the Bureau?"

The lamplight showed Kell's knowing smile. He had, after all, had nearly four years of dealing with English police and justice, and these two were not just newcomers but, really, outsiders. "If one knows the ropes, there are ways that things can be arranged.

Say, a plea of guilty to manslaughter, the police not challenging his version of events—"

"That may satisfy Sir Basil, but what about Mrs Finn?" Dagner asked. "And I'm not sure that any version of events is going to satisfy me." He shook his head. "I don't like the Bureau's integrity depending on so many ifs and maybes . . . Can you see any alternative, Captain?"

"We could," Ranklin said as casually as possible, "always kill Gorman. It would need some arranging, but perhaps in the street as he arrives for the police court hearing . . . And the Italian community would probably get the blame."

Kell had stopped dead on the pavement, leaving the other two peering back at him in the lamplight. Pop-eyed by nature, he now looked as if he were about to fire both eyeballs across the street. "Do *what?*"

Dagner said mildly: "You must admit it would solve the problem of Gorman talking in open court. However—"

Kell stiffened where he stood. "I'm not being a party to anything like this! If you're seriously thinking of . . . then I don't want to hear any more."

But he hesitated. Dagner said: "I'm only thinking of the national interest, which the Bureau represents in a peculiarly pure form."

"*Pure?* You call that *pure?*"

Dagner affected a look of surprise. "Indeed. We certainly aren't concerned with concepts of Truth or Justice, just with what's best for the country and Empire. But if you don't want to hear . . ."

Kell strode away.

Dagner smiled. "Perhaps it's as well. Just as a matter of interest, how serious were you being, Captain?"

Ranklin didn't want to answer that, especially to himself. In battle, you sent men into *danger*, but only that. Or so you told yourself. But the murky half-lit world of spying had some sudden harsh lights . . .

Dagner didn't press for an answer; his zigzag mind seemed to have found a new topic. "When we talked about acting *alone*, I never thought of our whole service having to do so. We seem to be quite friendless. First the Foreign Office, now the police, even Major Kell and his people . . . But so be it." He didn't sound overly worried. "We were considering alternatives . . ."

Ranklin already was. If, next morning, they all turned up at

147

the police court in uniform and claimed O'Gilroy was a deserter and multiple military criminal, might the police . . . ? It seemed doubtful, but surely something along those lines . . .

But Dagner was looking up and down the street. "Really quite quiet, even this early. So in a few hours . . . You've got all their addresses at the office? We'd better get started."

Ranklin goggled. He hadn't been considering *that*.

20

The middle-aged constable had just stepped outside "to make sure things were quiet", which the desk sergeant understood meant having a quick smoke. London was never truly silent; if it did nothing else, it breathed, and stirred in its sleep. But a quarter to four was around the quietest time. The moon was down, leaving the Gray's Inn Road a broad corridor of darkness, patched with yellow-green light from the street lamps that were already fuzzed by the pre-dawn mist. And empty, save for one stocky figure in a long overcoat humming and mumbling towards him. As he shuffled into the light from the lamp over the station door, the shadow of his hat hid his downturned face, but not the broad red beard. Now that was peculiar: the beard looked false—

—but not the heavy pistol that suddenly poked into his face.

"Be brave," a stage-Irish accent whispered. "I love Englishmen bein' brave. Ut gives me a chanst to see de colour av deir brains. Now: how many more av ye's awake inside dere?"

"Th-th-three more." The constable was dimly aware of two other figures slipping past him into the station, but most of his attention was on the red-bearded man, who called softly: "Tree more av 'em. An' r'mimber more asleep upstairs.

"Now be turnin' around gentle and walkin' inside." The pistol vanished but the feel of it rammed into his spine. At the second try, his feet recalled how to climb the steps.

Inside, the desk was empty. He was hustled through the door beside it and almost stumbled over the sergeant, flat on the floor. For a moment he thought . . . then the sergeant snarled at his boots.

"Lie down yeself." And that wasn't difficult at all. He heard a gabble of awakened voices from the cells below, abruptly hushed. Then silence, and the constable found time to collect his thoughts. I am a London policeman with nearly ten years' service, he told himself. And no rotten Irish brigand can outwit—

"Be brave," the same voice whispered hungrily. "Ah, it's longin' I am for wan av yez to be brave and the blood spoutin' out an' drippin' av the walls . . . *English* blood."

But on the other hand, thought the constable . . .

Then more feet tramped through his line of sight and another voice commanded: "On yer feet. Up! Begorrah," it added. "And back inside." Along with the desk sergeant he was pushed along the corridor and downstairs into a dark cell. The door was closed gently – when he himself shut it on a prisoner, he liked to make a point with a chilling slam, but the quiet snap of the lock was convincing enough. Silence again.

Then the desk sergeant said: "We'd best call and try to wake the lads upstairs."

"Yes, Sarge," the constable agreed. There was more silence.

"So," the sergeant said eventually, "both together, right?" He coughed. "When I've cleared me throat."

Outside, another and younger constable returning westward along Clerkenwell Road noticed the big motor-car parked beyond the junction, beside the railed garden of Gray's Inn. It was a funny place to park, not outside any house, but its tail-light glowed, its engine rumbled faintly in the stillness, and a man was leaning against the hood, so perhaps it had some minor breakdown. The constable knew almost nothing about motor-cars but was ready to show willing on a quiet night, so marched forward. He made almost no noise, having slipped rings cut from motor tyres around his boots, a trick learnt from the older men.

He had almost reached the junction when two men came out of the police station and turned towards the car, not hurrying, but moving with purpose. A bit odd. The constable paused at the kerb. Two more men came from the station and walked quickly after the others. Definitely odd. And had that been a gleam of metal in one man's hand?

The constable stepped forward and called: "Wait a minute." The men started running, and so did he. By the time he had crossed the road he was going flat out but the men were scrambling into the car. Except for the one who had been leaning on the hood. He had straightened up to the rigid stance of a pistol duellist, arm and glinting metal pointing towards . . . There was a flash, smoke,

150

and what the constable afterwards remembered as a "boom" rather than "bang". He was so surprised he forgot to stop running. The man stayed quite still, there was another flash and boom and the constable's head was jerked back as his helmet tried to leap from his head. He stopped then, eyes watering from the jerk of the chin-strap. When he had blinked them clear again, the car was far down Theobald's Road.

Dagner had the car stopped in Horse Guards to let him and Ranklin walk the last two hundred yards while it delivered O'Gilroy back to Whitehall Court. A few lights burned in the War Office, but the wide streets were empty. This had become so much a self-sufficient government enclave that the police virtually ignored it at night. After a few slow paces, Dagner said: "I want O'Gilroy got back to Brooklands now, tonight. Use P's motor-car, don't go near railway stations. And tomorrow, abroad: make sure he takes enough kit with him now."

"You don't think our Irish act worked, then?"

"Of course not. Sir Basil may pretend to believe it, if he wants to concede the game to us and needs someone to blame, but if he decides to come after us . . . then God knows. But we'll find out soon enough." He paused, then went on in the same conversational tone: "I'm afraid I blame you for most of this evening's problem. You weren't alone – but you *were* in command."

Quite properly, he wasn't going to roast an officer in front of juniors. But also, Ranklin realised, he was making O'Gilroy Ranklin's subordinate rather than a member of the Bureau in his own right. But this was one of those never-explain-never-complain situations.

Dagner went on: "If you *must* behave as if you're abroad on a mission, and I'd far prefer that you didn't, then don't do things by halves. If you ever again decide to charge into some house ready to shoot somebody, then bloody well get on with it – and then be off like a scalded rabbit. Don't go near the police at all. As it is, you seem to have gone one way and let O'Gilroy go another – and all the rest followed from that. So now the shooting of one tu'penny Italian bandit threatens the secrecy, even the future, of our Bureau. And I will *not* have that. Do you follow me?"

"Yes, sir." The 'sir' was pure instinct.

"And do you agree?"

"Yes, sir." And I do, Ranklin thought miserably. I tried to be half secret agent, half solid citizen, and the two halves don't add up.

"On the other hand," Dagner said, "I think Certain Quarters may have got the message that the Secret Service Bureau, while perhaps not as legendary as legend has it, is still not to be trifled with."

But they'd only been rescuing O'Gilroy, hadn't they? Ranklin was about to say this, then didn't. It was his fault that any rescue had been needed.

21

"It isn't in the papers, and *may* never be," Major Kell said pointedly, "but did you hear that a group of Irish desperadoes stormed the Gray's Inn Road police station early this morning and freed one of their number who was being held on a murder charge? A man called Gorman."

Dagner pretended pretend interest. "Really? Should I have heard of him?"

"I just thought you'd be interested. Sir Basil Thomson certainly is. Indeed, I'd go as far as to say that he's in a mood to spit blood and would like it to be yours."

"Yes?" Dagner said, as if inviting him to get to the point.

"One of his policemen was shot." Kell paused to see if that brought any reaction. When it didn't, he continued: "Through the helmet. Sir Basil was talking of raiding this office and demanding that every one of you come up with an alibi for between three and four this morning."

"Most extraordinary." But Dagner still seemed only mildly interested. "However, I'm sure cooler counsels will prevail. I, for my part, would not permit him to know who is on the staff of this Bureau, let alone demand alibis of them. And I hope he bears in mind that any such raid will be upon a non-existent Bureau answerable only to the First Lord of the Admiralty."

Kell looked at him thoughtfully. "However, I think he might be assuaged if you just handed Gorman back."

Dagner seemed to consider this, but as if it were a strange and fanciful idea. "No, I don't think so."

Kell took a deep breath. "Major Dagner, do you really consider your service to be so far above the law that—"

"Yes, as a matter of fact, I do." Dagner leant back in his chair. "Because if it isn't there, it's nowhere. So there is no question of

153

my handing over one of our agents for judgment by that law – and that's quite apart from any questions of loyalty and morale. But I don't think it should harm your relationship with Scotland Yard if they realise you have no control over *this* service. Unless, of course, you'd led them to believe you had."

Kell clenched his face but said nothing. He took a paper from an inside pocket, and unfolded it on Dagner's table. It was a police 'wanted' poster for Thomas Gorman. There was no photograph, but the description was good – as it should have been, given that they'd had him in custody for several hours. Dagner read it with apparently mild interest.

"Those," Kell said, "will be distributed throughout the Home Counties unless I return either with your man or your promise to surrender him."

He had the feeling that Dagner was staring straight through him at some distant memory. "Most interesting – but it doesn't alter my position. May I keep this?"

*   *   *

Rich and lordly as the Naval Intelligence Division seemed from Whitehall Court, inside the Admiralty it ranked – to judge from its offices – on a par with bilge-scraping. Even the civilian stores clerk, to whom Ranklin's NID friend introduced him, lived in grander style. The Nelson touch, perhaps: Trafalgar had been won with stores, not spies.

The introduction was terse: "Here's the chap I was telling you about, the one asking about the missing pistol. He's Army, so fob him off with any old stuff."

The clerk greeted Ranklin with wary courtesy. "Are you *really* from the Secret Service?"

"I'm afraid so, yes."

"Gosh."

Ranklin added quickly: "But just the paper-shuffling side, not one of the stealing-the-Kaiser's-code boys."

"Ah." The clerk looked disappointed, then realised that a *real* spy obviously wouldn't admit it, so went back to wariness.

"Could we . . . ?" Ranklin suggested, gesturing at the nearest stack of paperwork.

"Of course." He shuffled through a pile of papers. "You were asking about a certain Webley pistol, serial number so-and-so . . . Here we are: a court of inquiry established that it was lost overboard from HMS *Gloucester* during a storm in the Adriatic last April. No disciplinary action, but the loss has been paid for. And everybody's living happily ever after." He looked up with a bright smile.

"I rather thought it would be something like that. However, for a heavy pistol, it seems to have floated remarkably well, and due to some oddity of tide and current which perhaps you'd understand better than I, it was washed up in Clerkenwell yesterday."

"*Oh* dear." A slow grin spread across the clerk's face and he consulted the report again before saying cheerfully: "Well, the paperwork's all in order. So if you want to take it any further, you'll have to talk to somebody in the Naval Branch—"

"No, no, I don't want to stir things up and get anyone into trouble," Ranklin assured him. "I'm not interested in the 'how' of it, just some idea of where it really went missing."

"Are you quite sure of that serial number?" Then the clerk reconsidered. "Sorry, that was rather a silly question: you've found a pistol and we've lost one . . ." He went back to the report. "How about the last port of call before the 'washing overboard'?"

"Where was that?"

"Trieste."

The atmosphere in the agents' office was like the last day of term. Lieutenant H waved the 'wanted' poster at Ranklin, grinning as if it were a report of how the school had just beaten Greyfriar's 60–nil. "Have you seen this?"

Ranklin said: "Oh Christ," and went straight to Dagner's door, leaving H standing bewildered.

"Exactly," Dagner said, seeing the poster in Ranklin's hand. "We have to get him abroad. Where the devil have you been? You'd better get down to Brooklands."

"Naval Intelligence. Right away."

Dagner strode to the door, pulled it open and called: "Somebody get Captain R a taxi-cab." He came back, muttering: "Like a bunch of . . . never mind. At least get him under cover—" he unlocked the safe against the wall and rummaged inside; "—and when you've done that, try and find out how Senator Falcone is. I can't go telephoning the hospital without some explanation." He spilled a small bag of sovereigns on to the table and began counting them swiftly.

"I should have told you," Ranklin said. "I talked to Mrs Finn on the telephone, earlier. He's not too serious at all. It was just the muscles in his back. It looked . . . you know how a little blood goes a long way, and he lost a lot. Apparently what saved him was he was wearing a medical corset, plaster and so on, after he'd hurt his back in an aeroplane smash."

"Is he conscious? – talking?"

"She didn't know about that, I'm afraid."

"We need to know if his plan's still going ahead. He was working with others, but we don't know who, nor if they can carry on without him."

This startled Ranklin. He had assumed the whole scheme was over or indefinitely postponed, but he said nothing. He still had some leeway of deference to make up.

"And," Dagner said, "am I right in thinking it hasn't been reported in the newspapers?"

"None I've seen have got it. He was awake enough to give a false name at the hospital – Vascotti. I don't know if they believe it, but as long as the bill gets paid . . . And it happened in a big crowd, at the height of the display, and most of the reporters there were aeronautical specialists. Oh, and another thing Mrs Finn told me: Signora Falcone's coming over. She'll be here this afternoon. She might know something."

"Getting here today?" Dagner wouldn't be familiar with Continental travel, but knew Italy was further away than that.

"Apparently she was already in Paris. Mrs Finn said she's going down to Weybridge to see the Signora herself – she was originally an Irish lady, I believe, so there won't be any language problem. And I expect Andrew Sherring will be anxious to know if the aeroplane deal's still on, too."

Dagner pondered, and Ranklin could guess at the unanswered questions. Did Signora Falcone know of her husband's plottings? – and if so, could they approach her instead? Or was she feeling anti-British-Government for letting her husband get stabbed? And how much of this dare they leave to Corinna to find out for them? Quite apart from Corinna's tactlessness in being born an American, Dagner must realise she was no helpless fly in their web.

He came to a decision: "Find out what you can from her, but

156

don't step outside your War Office persona. But first, get O'Gilroy somewhere safe. There's twenty-five sovereigns here—" he dropped the gold into Ranklin's hand; "—and those giggling schoolboys must have found you a cab by now."

Feeling he owed the 'schoolboys' some defence, Ranklin paused long enough to say: "I thought they worked very well as a team. Last night really brought them together—"

"Captain—" the unslept hours suddenly showed in Dagner's face; "—they've had years of that sort of thing in the Army. We're supposed to be teaching them to work *alone*."

*   *   *

The platform at Waterloo was surprisingly crowded, until Ranklin remembered that Pégoud was giving a second display that afternoon, puffed by ecstatic reports in the day's papers. He had also seen a couple of uniformed police in the booking hall who hadn't been there yesterday when they might have been some use, but more important were any plain-clothes ones that he couldn't identify.

It was a long, dusty trudge from Weybridge station to the aerodrome – any local taxis and cabs had been snapped up by the first off the train – and Ranklin's mood was very different from the cheery anticipation of the crowd around him. Then he had to use bluff and his calling card to get past the Aero Club officials to reach Andrew's shed. Frustrations apart, he was leaving a trail like an elephant stampede and could only hope the police didn't suspect him (not especially, anyway) or were moving at their 'proceeding' pace.

The sheds had no doors, just a row of shutters that could be taken down individually or, in Andrew's case, mostly left up to give the interior an air of dim, dusty, castor-oil-tinged privacy. And sharing that privacy was, thank God, O'Gilroy. He was helping Andrew fit the metal engine cowling back on to the Oriole.

"Hi there, Captain," Andrew greeted him. "If you're looking for Corrie, she's over at the hospital, but she said she'd come by before she goes back to town."

Since Ranklin hadn't remembered to think up an excuse for being there, he accepted the suitor role and propped himself against a work-bench.

"Trouble is," Andrew went on, juggling the flexible metal

carefully, "I don't know what the hell I'm supposed to be doing now. I wanted to get off today and maybe stop off a day at Rheims getting a look at the new racers. But with the Senator getting stabbed – have the police found out who did it yet? – what it was all about?" He glanced at Ranklin, who shook his head. "So now I don't know if I'm going at all. It's very sad," he added hastily, "but it's also a damn nuisance. Ah." The cowling had snapped into place and O'Gilroy was ready with the bolts to hold it down.

Andrew watched for a moment, then walked to the back of the shed, wiping his hands on a rag. O'Gilroy asked softly: "What's the news?"

"The police have got a flyer out for Thomas Gorman, probably at all stations and ports. Major X wants you out of the country or at least hidden under some bed."

"Does he now? Well, I've me private chariot waiting—" he patted the aeroplane; "—if anyone gives the word."

This was a completely new thought, and Ranklin gaped at it. "Will Andrew really take you?"

"Surely, only he don't know it yet. He thinks he's taking one of the fellers works here, and him having to choose between leaving his wife for a week and Mr Sherring promising him ten pounds gold, so if someone was to give him fifteen right now, it'd make up his mind something wonderful."

After a glance to make sure nobody was looking, Ranklin handed over fifteen sovereigns – and then the rest of the cash. "You'll need some working capital as well."

"I should've brought me passport, I'm thinking." Ranklin handed that over, too. "Yer a genius. So now we jest wait for Mrs Falcone to make up her mind."

"Is she here?"

"Mrs Finn said she'd be meeting her at the hospital."

"I could try telephoning her there, say Andrew's anxious to get moving."

O'Gilroy turned from the aeroplane and gave him a steady look. "And explain who ye are and why yer so concerned?"

Ranklin chewed his lip. His near-sleepless night was blurring his judgment and sharpening his agitation. O'Gilroy, if he knew him, would have slept like a babe in his cell until they came to rescue him.

"We'll know soon enough." O'Gilroy turned back to the aero-plane. "Nobody's coming looking for me in a place like this."

"I'm not so sure." Sir Basil knew 'Gorman' as an agent of the Bureau and probably thought Brooklands irrelevant, but Ranklin recalled saying at the police station that he was an aeronautical engineer and maybe somebody remembered that and thought it worth following up, so . . . oh, damn it! – he was worrying in useless circles. Angry and critical, he glared at O'Gilroy's clothing. "And if you're going abroad, you'd better change first."

O'Gilroy gave the cowling a final shake to make sure it was firm, then looked down at his grubby mechanic's apron. "Glad ye reminded me. Need me proper kit from the hotel."

"For God's sake, *no*. You've got to stay here until—"

"Ye worry too much, Captain." O'Gilroy stripped off the apron. "I'll be borrowing Dave's motor-bike and back before I'm gone."

And there was nothing Ranklin could do. Except wonder what made O'Gilroy so confident and then realise, with sick horror, that after yesterday's events he would certainly be carrying his own pistol today and see an unarmed policeman as no obstacle at all, at all . . .

22

"He has been drinking," the Padrone said.

"Is he drunk now?" Jankovic demanded.

"He has *been* drunk." The Padrone's hands made delicate but imprecise movements, trying to pass the message that Silvio would be as unpredictable as an unexploded shell. He didn't know what to make of Jankovic, who spoke a fluent if strange Italian but had a glowering low-browed face like a Slav farmer.

Jankovic growled to himself and asked: "What happened here last night?"

"Ah—" the Padrone was on surer ground here; "—first, the police arrested the man who broke into *my* house here and murdered Silvio's cousin. Then, in the night, a gang broke into the police station and rescued him. That is quite unheard-of. The police are most angry, yet they have not raided everywhere and arrested everyone, as one would expect. And there is also talk of the Irish. I think the house-breaker, and murderer, was Irish."

"Irish?" Jankovic was baffled. But it added another layer of bafflement for others, too, and he shrugged it off. "Take me to him, then."

The Padrone's dignity was already ruffled by the night's events, but expediency warned him not to get indignant at this brusqueness. Anyway, it would be wasted on a Slav. He led the way upstairs.

Silvio sat hunched on the unmade bed, red-eyed and fiddling with a pistol. The drink – mixed marsala and grappa, according to the empty bottles – was oozing out of him and he smelt like a pig farm.

Jankovic looked down and said: "You didn't kill him."

"Of course we killed him!" Silvio tried to spring up and got half way before toppling back.

"He's in hospital," Jankovic went on. "The nearest hospital to the flying field under an assumed but Italian name, so he hasn't learnt anything even from having your cousin scratch his back."

"Bozan *killed* him," Silvio insisted, waving the pistol. The Padrone moved a little more behind Jankovic, who didn't seem to care.

"I was there this morning. Also, Signora Falcone is coming, probably to take him home. What are you going to do about it?"

Silvio calmed down, or at least pointed the gun at the floor. "Go to the hospital and kill him."

"And his police guard?" Jankovic sneered. "We knew you came from a circus, but we thought we'd hired the lions, not the clowns."

"It was *you* who fouled things up in Brussels!" Silvio yelled. "We could have stabbed or shot him there easily. Bozan could. Oh, Mother of God." He began weeping and wiped his nose, mostly with the pistol. "I'm going to kill that Irish bravo, too. It was he who murdered poor Bozan."

"All right," Jankovic said, suddenly reasonable. "All right. If Falcone goes back to Italy, the bravo will probably go with him. So I'll tell you what we'll do: we'll go to Italy, too, and you can kill them both there. Yes, I know we aren't supposed to kill Falcone in Italy—" as Silvio's sodden memory churned up an objection; "—but if that's the only place left to us . . .

"And," he added sharply, "it would help if you were sober by then so you don't mistake your own arse for the Senator and shoot that instead."

*   *   *

Too tense to light a pipe, Ranklin puffed a cigarette as he paced the worn turf – baked almost to concrete by the long summer – outside the shed. It was past noon, and even hotter than yesterday, with a gently swirling crowd murmuring like a distant waterfall. He let his hand brush against his empty side pocket and felt a pang of anxiety as he remembered the police had kept his revolver as 'evidence'. He had to remind himself that crowds did not breed assassins as a natural process. But not feeling really safe in the sunny English countryside without a pistol in his pocket was, he thought gloomily, yet another milestone on his personal road.

He trod out his cigarette and, with nothing better to do, almost immediately lit another. He daren't get distracted by starting a conversation with anyone, he just had to wait and watch. And convince himself that O'Gilroy was merely caught up in the mob on the road and not . . .

Then, unmistakable above the heads of the crowd, came the black box-shape of the Sherring Daimler – and an unfamiliar man in a dark suit standing on the running-board and waving some official card. Ranklin first assumed that Corinna had borrowed a Club official to clear their path, but there was something too solemn about the man's face and demeanour. He didn't belong.

Corinna shot out of the car without waiting for anyone to open the door, and scurried across. "I don't know what in hell's going on," she muttered, "but we collected a policeman at the hospital who—"

Then the solemn man arrived at a fast lope, hand outstretched aggressively to clasp Ranklin's. "Captain Ranklin? I'm Inspector Jeffries, Surrey Police. *Thank* you, madam." He tipped his bowler hat at Corinna in a gesture one step short of saying "Scram".

Behind him, Ranklin was vaguely aware of a woman in a tweed suit stepping from the car and walking confidently towards the shed, as if she knew aerodromes. Corinna gave Inspector Jeffries a sharp look, then followed. Ranklin hadn't dared mention last night's shenanigans on the telephone, but she certainly knew something was going on.

"Glad to meet you, Inspector," Ranklin said, casually looking him over. He had prominent dark eyes in a thin face but the solemnity came mostly from the downturned moustache, and he held his head cocked forward in a deferential gesture that Ranklin didn't believe. A man content to dress so anonymously might be good at his job.

"I believe," Jeffries said, "you were a witness to the assault on Senator Falcone – or Mr Vascotti, as he seems to prefer at the moment – yesterday afternoon, sir."

"A sort of witness. But I made a statement to . . . in London."

"Yes, sir. Your name was sent to us by the Metropolitan Police. By Sir Basil Thomson of Scotland Yard."

"Really."

"May I ask what you're doing here today, sir?"

"War Office business."

"Of what nature is that, sir?"

162

"Just the usual confidential War Office business."

Jeffries seemed to hesitate. Perhaps he'd expected Ranklin to plead the secrecy of the Bureau, not put up the whole Army as an earlier line of defence.

He tried to outflank it with a confiding smile. "That wouldn't be, would it, sir, just an alias to hide your real job?"

Ranklin looked him quietly up and down, but Jeffries was used to that look from people who thought the police should use the servants' entrance. However, Ranklin then said: "You don't seem to have the current Army List on you – it's a bulky volume, I agree. So you can't look me up. In that case, all I can offer is my card, my driving licence, and what else would I have . . . ?"

"That's quite all right, sir, no need at all." Then casually but swiftly: "Where's Gorman?"

The frontal attack almost flustered Ranklin, but then he remembered the connection was undeniable, and that the more he concentrated on the name Gorman, the better for O'Gilroy. "I'm sorry, I really have no idea."

That became a lie as he said it. The motor-bike sputtered out of the crowd behind Jeffries' back, stopped beside the shed, and O'Gilroy began leisurely unstrapping a travelling bag from the pillion seat.

"Not even where he lives?"

"I'm afraid not. Inspector—" Ranklin had to say something to hold Jeffries' attention on himself; "—my connection with Gorman is entirely professional. Again, your best bet is to ask the War Office. No, I suppose the Yard will already have done that. Let me see, what else can I suggest . . . ?" He looked around as if seeking inspiration and saw that O'Gilroy had vanished into the shed. Would Corinna have the chance – and the sense – to warn him who Jeffries was?

Then she was walking quickly towards them, setting off a flare of a smile towards Jeffries and saying: "Hope I'm not interrupting, but the Signora's given the go-ahead and Andrew wants to be off right away."

Ranklin tried to make his smile meaningless. "Fine. Ah – is he going alone?"

"No, he's taking some new mechanic, one who's learning to fly."

Ranklin thought: I love you. Well, actually I don't know whether

163

I do or not, but right *now* I love you. He said: "Perhaps the Inspector already told you, but he's looking for a man called Gorman."

She knew the name as O'Gilroy's usual alias. "Who's he? What's he done?" Behind her, two of Andrew's mechanics began taking down the flimsy shutters and stacking them to one side.

Jeffries would rather be asking than answering, but Corinna tended to have first choice in these matters. And Jeffries couldn't turn his back on her, either. "He was in custody, madam, in London, charged with murder."

Corinna's eyes widened. "Gee! Of whom?"

"I'm not clear about that myself, madam, but the important thing is that he was in custody and he escaped. Aided by a group of men who stormed a police station in the early hours of this morning—" Jeffries turned his sombre look on Ranklin, not noticing, or perhaps caring, that the Oriole was being gently manhandled out of the shed; "—speaking in stage-Irish accents and who shot at and nearly killed a constable."

Suddenly Corinna was taking this seriously. "You mean really hurt him?"

"He wasn't actually hurt – by sheer good luck. The bullet went through his helmet."

The equally sudden bathos was too much for Corinna, who tried to stifle a giggle, and managed to choke out: "Yes, I guess that counts as pretty close."

"We don't regard it as a laughing matter, madam."

"No, no, of course not. And so you're looking for him. And for the whole gang, too, I guess?"

Jeffries hesitated, looking at Ranklin again. "We'd like to catch the whole gang, and we have some idea of who they are. But they regard themselves as untouchable."

"You mean they've got some political protection, just like our New York gangs? Didn't know you were so modern . . . Hold on a moment, I've got to see Andrew off." The Oriole was well onto the grass, with Andrew, in his calf-length leather jacket, superintending the preparations for start-up. There was already another figure in the cockpit, but under the shadow of the wing and wearing goggles, so even Ranklin couldn't tell who it was.

Corinna went up to hug Andrew and, judging by the resigned way he kept nodding his head, give him a sisterly lecture about keeping to the proper side of the sky and wrapping up warm.

Then he swung himself up into the cockpit, making the machine rock stiffly.

Jeffries asked: "Where's he off to?"

"I've no idea." Which was more or less true. As long as it was abroad . . .

The propeller was swung, the engine caught first time in a swirl of smoke, and settled down to the now-familiar buzz. Two mechanics seized the wing struts and helped steer it away across the grass, swung it into the light breeze and stepped aside. The buzz hurried a little, the aeroplane moved, its tail came up and, after a couple of long bounces, swayed into the air.

Ranklin should have felt a sag of relief, but the departure had been too casual to merit it. He reckoned himself well-travelled, but 'going abroad' always meant a fuss of steam-whistles, men shouting orders and crowds waving. He couldn't yet believe a little aeroplane scuttling across a hundred yards of grass in a few seconds had actually gone *abroad*. And neither, of course, could Jeffries. People didn't yet think of aeroplanes as going anywhere.

Perhaps there was a lesson for this island race in there somewhere, but it was too big to worry about now. He put on a bland expression. "You were saying, Inspector?"

Jeffries said reflectively: "Just that these people seem to think they can hide behind some cloak of national secrecy."

Ranklin nodded gently. "That's what they'll have been told to do, no doubt."

"And hide even their mistakes."

"*Especially* their mistakes. I imagine."

"I dare say you're right, sir." Jeffries looked pensive. "It's a real problem, that, when you've got two organisations, both on the same side, both doing their duty as they see it, and meeting head-on as you might say. Somebody really ought to sort it out – for the good of the nation."

Instinctively sympathetic, Ranklin might have grown confiding – which was probably just what Jeffries wanted; he was no simple flatfoot.

But then Corinna returned wearing a rather set grin. "Whoof! Always a strain watching your brother being a daring bird-man. Any more revelations about underworld London?"

Jeffries looked enquiringly at Ranklin, who smiled vaguely.

"It doesn't look like it, madam." He raised his hat to her. "I'll bid you good day."

She watched him well out of hearing, then turned to Ranklin. "Sounds like you had an exciting night after I dumped you at Esher. Who did Conall kill?"

"The man who stabbed Falcone."

"Ah. It's kind of tough, the way you give Conall all the dirty work."

"That's one way of looking at it. Is that Signora Falcone?"

"Come and say hello."

All Ranklin had seen, at a distance, was the tailored tweed suit in the soft grey-blue and green of Donegal's rain and meadow, and an elegance of movement. But closer . . . She must once have had a flawless, delicate beauty. But it had been a beauty that relied on perfect detail. Now, although she could hardly be fifty, the years had roughened the detail and Juliet hadn't grown into Cleopatra. Corinna had once said that "beyond a certain age, a woman needs either intelligence or cheekbones", knowing smugly that she had both. Ranklin found himself hoping the Signora wasn't intelligent, either: it must be terrible to know you looked as if you had once looked beautiful.

But she had kept her figure, and the elegance at least was ageless. She smiled, showing good teeth, and murmured: "Delighted to meet you, Captain."

"My pleasure, signora. May I ask how the Senator is?"

"Tired. He's lost a lot of blood. But he should make a full recovery. I believe you were there, yesterday?" Her voice had no trace of the Irish, but probably never had. Plenty of Dubliners saw themselves as 'West Britons' and Dublin as just down the road from London.

"I was. I'm sorry I couldn't do anything to stop . . ." Ranklin spread his hands helplessly.

"It wasn't your fault, he should have asked for police protection. He knew he was in danger." You wouldn't have realised her husband had nearly been knifed to death less than a day ago, but perhaps her control was part of the elegance. "And he wants . . . ah, things to go on as if nothing had happened." She glanced at a little gold wristwatch. "I need to send a cable saying the aeroplane's on its way . . . and get a ticket for Paris myself . . . It looks as if I shall be missing lunch."

"My office can fix your ticket," Corinna said. "And if you want to go to the hotel to do something about the Senator's things, you can cable from there and I can order some lunch while you do it. And take you back to town after."

Signora Falcone already had the grateful smile in place before she had decided to accept. "That's most kind of you, my dear. Then – do you mind if we . . . ?"

To the casual bystander, Corinna was just being helpful to a lady with problems. To Ranklin, she had her teeth into the Signora and wasn't going to let go until . . . he couldn't guess. As he handed them into the Daimler, already crowded with Signora Falcone's luggage, Corinna said casually: "Sorry we didn't have time to chat, Captain. *Do* call some time soon."

Dagner might not like it, but it looked as if the only way to Signora Falcone was now through Corinna. He'd better get back to Whitehall Court; this couldn't be explained on the telephone.

*　　*　　*

Oatlands Park, the hotel where Falcone had taken refuge, stood on the site of a royal hunting lodge and now looked like several yellow-brick-and-stone country houses run together. It was fronted by a wide lawn studded with huge old cedars and, on a day like this, a dozen small tables and clumps of chairs. Among the late lunchers and early tea-sippers, the two women twirled their parasols on their shoulders and picked over tiny sandwiches in an atmosphere as delicately rigid as china lacework. Neither knew quite what to make of the other or how she fitted in.

"So you're meeting Andrew at the aerodrome in Paris tomorrow," Corinna said, "to show off the airplane to a friend . . ."

"A most important Italian who's very interested in flying, although he isn't actually connected with it, and Giancarlo wanted him to see . . ." Signora Falcone had picked up the fluent Italian gestures; now her hand traced a graceful if rather fluttery flight. "In Italy it helps to have as many influential people on your side as possible, whether they know anything about machinery or not."

"I understand. And when Andy gets it to Turin next week, he'll demonstrate it to your military men?"

"And politicians and so forth, whoever we can get to come."

"And that's all he'll be asked to do?" Corinna persisted.

"Oh yes." She smiled. "What else were you thinking?"

"Oh, nothing, I guess."

And before Corinna could think of another approach, Signora Falcone asked smoothly: "Tell me, who is this Captain . . . Ranklin? . . . who seems to be always around?"

"A friend. And something to do with airplanes in the War Department here. I think he'd like to take up Andrew's airplane except for the British being stupid about monoplanes." She could always find time for a bit of saleswomanship where the family was concerned. "It's really a great machine. Very modern."

"I'm sure it is," Signora Falcone said. "That was why Giancarlo chose it, he saw its worth immediately." Then she looked casually around, a small smile loaded to fire if anyone caught her eye. But no one did and she turned quickly back to Corinna and lowered her voice. "I'd like to confide in you. As – if I can put it this way – you aren't English, either . . ." She let her voice fade. Like her movements, it was very controlled.

"Why, sure, go right ahead." Corinna tried to look open to confidences but closed to their repetition. It came out as a friendly grin.

"I hope this doesn't sound fanciful, but it does seem that Giancarlo, before he was attacked, was in touch with somebody from, well—" her smile was disarming; "—the British Secret Service. I do assure you I'm not romancing—"

"No, of course not."

"I'm sure I could find their address eventually, but if I'm catching the boat-train tonight, I'd rather like to have just a *little* word with them first. Just to make sure there's nothing . . ." The delicate gesture indicated those petty details one likes to sort out with the Secret Service before heading for Paris.

Corinna's grin stayed, but behind it she was thinking very quickly.

The pause prompted Signora Falcone to explain further: "Giancarlo meets *so* many influential—"

"As it happens," Corinna said slowly, "I do believe I know somebody . . ."

23

After the heat of Brooklands and the train, Ranklin called in at the flat to change his collar before reporting back to Dagner. He found half his clothes spread across the bed and Lieutenant J disapproving of his Norfolk jacket.

"What the devil's going on?"

"It might do for a weekend ramble with royalty, but one has to maintain higher standards among foreigners, don't you agree? *You're* going on: Trieste via Paris, and I'm helping you pack. It seems somebody got around to asking where a certain aeroplane was going, jumped to a certain conclusion (the right one, I trust? – it sounded a splendid scheme) and Sir Basil turned his wrath on you: helping a fugitive from justice, conspiracy in the original death of that Italian, general suspicion of being Jack the Ripper. So Major X wants you abroad before they've had time to send out 'wanted' posters like the one for O'G. One of the girls is getting you a ticket in the name of James Spencer – you've got a passport saying that, I believe."

"That's right." Ranklin sat down on the bed to think. "Trieste?"

"Yes. The Major doesn't think the Yard knows about this flat, but suggested you get over to the Charing Cross Hotel and wait there, just in case. I'll bring your luggage. I can't find a pistol – are you taking one?"

It wouldn't be suspicious to carry on the fringe of the Balkans, but a man with a pistol was a different man. Knowing he had it to fall back on, he might forget to use his wits.

"I don't think so. You too often end up shooting the wrong person."

"And which suits d'you want to take?"

"The ones with the James Spencer labels in them, of course."

"Of course," J murmured, impressed, and Ranklin felt cheered.

*

Although Charing Cross station had lost much of its Continental traffic to Victoria, it still had the raffish air of Paris-starts-here. It was too close (for some tastes) to the music halls of the Strand and had a reputation as a loitering-ground for unaccompanied young ladies. But its hotel rose above this with its bold Italian Renaissance interior and, of more interest to Ranklin, a virtual club of bar, billiards and smoking-rooms with a private balcony overlooking the remaining Continental platforms.

The french windows onto the balcony were open on the warm evening, blending the travel smell of steam with those of tobacco smoke, coffee and spirits, and bringing a background of whistles, clanks and babble to the peaceful click of billiard balls. Lieutenant J was, of course, an expert, but had politely just let Ranklin win a game when Dagner arrived.

"You take over, sir." J offered his cue. "I'll keep an eye on the trains." He strolled tactfully out of earshot onto the balcony.

Dagner took off his jacket and studied the table. "Hm. I hope there's no money on this. I don't want to lose young J his inheritance . . . You've got your ticket? And J's seen to your luggage? The police have been up at the office and they've got watchers in the street by now. We've been laying false trails to boat-trains at Liverpool Street and Waterloo, and had you paged at Euston and Paddington – anything to over-stretch their force."

He failed to hole the red and went on: "I'm here partly to brief you – there's not much I can say – but also to meet Signora Falcone. I got a telephone call from Mrs Finn, saying the Signora wanted to meet the same men the Senator met. She's also catching the boat-train, so we're meeting in the Conservatory in half an hour. That's all to the good – *but* I thought I conveyed to you my feelings about letting Mrs Finn become involved in the Bureau's affairs. Let alone arranging our affairs for—"

"You did, but she'd cornered the market in Signora Falcone, and there was nothing I could do while staying in character as a minor War Office wallah." Ranklin brought off a flukey cannon. "And Mrs Finn's worried that her brother's getting involved in something more than just demonstrating the aeroplane."

"I trust she didn't get that idea from anything you yourself said."

"I think—" Ranklin holed the red and then realised it made his next shot almost impossible; "—I think she just noticed the Bureau was interested in Falcone."

"Hm." Dagner metaphorically took a step back. "What a tangled web we weave . . . However, tangled webs are our business. And at least I should learn how much the Senator's told his wife."

Ranklin deliberately missed his shot to concentrate on what he had to say. A loyal subordinate had a duty to act as devil's advocate, pointing out risks and flaws. "It sounds like rather too much. We also know there's others involved but not how much they know, nor who they are. But we do know somebody in Trieste is suspicious enough to try and kill the Senator." He took a deep breath. "If Falcone really trusted us, he could have told us more about all that – so why are we trusting him? It seems to me that we're getting deeper into this than we planned but without learning anything more."

Unless, of course, Falcone had told Dagner more and he wasn't being told because he was about to go behind enemy lines, as it were. If that were so, he couldn't argue.

Dagner straightened up without taking his shot. "We mustn't lose sight of our own purpose: to change the whole naval situation in the Mediterranean. That seems worth a certain effort, even risk. You originally suggested we should look at Trieste for ourselves, and now you've placed O'Gilroy in Falcone's camp, more or less, I think we should cover both ends." He paused, then seemed to take a decision. "But . . . *but* if you uncover anything there that convinces you we should drop it, then get word to me and it'll be dropped. Does that reassure you?"

That really was as much as Ranklin could ask – provided Dagner really meant it. And he certainly couldn't ask *that*. He said formally: "Thank you, Major."

Dagner acknowledged that with a nod, then, staring straight at Ranklin but keeping his voice gentle, said: "But do remember one thing, Captain, if it should ever come to it: you're working for Britain, not for peace." He bent over the billiard table again.

Mostly to change the conversation but perhaps also because it nagged him, Ranklin asked casually: "Has your wife got home yet?"

Dagner abandoned his shot and straightened up to chalk his cue. "No. No, I'm afraid she hasn't yet."

"I was sorry to hear about your first wife—"

"What d'you mean?" Dagner spoke quite sharply. "I've only got one wife."

171

Confused, Ranklin stumbled over his own words. "I'm most frightfully sorry . . . chap I met . . . he said your wife had died in India . . ."

"She got ill, everybody gets ill in India. She recovered. Thank God."

"I'm sorry, I must have . . ."

With unconscious tact, J drifted back from the balcony, winced politely at Dagner's shot, and said: "There seems to be quite a gathering of policemen on the platform. And, I may be wrong, but I thought I saw Mrs Finn holding court down there."

Ranklin blinked. He hadn't thought J knew Corinna, but J seemed to know everybody. Perhaps she'd come to see Signora Falcone off. He went to the balcony.

It was dark now, the electric lights glowing coldly through drifts of steam, and although the train wouldn't leave for nearly an hour, the controlled panic of departure had already begun. Couples and families, wearing too many clothes because they were going Abroad, stood in islands of luggage, waving for porters or swapping papers with railway officials and Cook's agents. And right in the middle, more sensibly dressed but unquestionably for travelling, was Corinna.

'Holding court' was right, too. Jaded by travel, she usually tried to make an occasion of it with last-moment meetings and farewells on the platform. She was doing just that to a small crowd of flunkies – but around it moved pairs of uniformed policemen and men in dark suits without any luggage.

Ranklin stepped back, took out a James Spencer calling card and scribbled on the back: *Are you going to Paris? So am I. But prefer not be seen by Signora. Meet on boat?* He gave it to Lieutenant J. "D'you mind acting as messenger?"

"Delighted." J slipped on his jacket and vanished.

"*Is* Mrs Finn going, too?" Dagner asked.

"It looks like it." Then, seeing Dagner's expression, he added: "A House of Sherring connection isn't just a good alias, it helps open doors. She may be able to put me in touch with well-placed people over there."

"But at the cost of telling her where you're going."

"Banking is also a secretive profession." Ranklin made that as polite as he could.

"Very well, I'll leave you to handle it your own way. I'd better get off to meet the Signora. Good luck, Captain." They didn't shake hands.

J came back with one of Corinna's cards, her slanting handwriting sprawling over both sides: *Thought I'd better become Andrew's manager or agent or whatnot. They arrived Paris safe, I got a cable. Are you going on to Italy? Never mind, tell me later. I'll be in sleeping compartment 7 on the Calais–Paris train. Help yourself.*

Ranklin goggled. She'd given this to Lieutenant J? Was he too much of a gentleman to have read it, or too much of a spy not to have? His bland smile could belong to either. Ranklin put a match to the card and let it burn in an ashtray.

J coughed politely. "I hate to say it, but given the police infestation, it might be time for *this*. We found it in the Chief's safe."

This was a large blond false moustache. The Commander loved disguises.

"It's from Clarkson's," J said apologetically, "so the best quality. I've got the glue and I can make a reasonable job of it."

Ranklin handled the thing distastefully, then put off a decision by saying: "You know everybody, don't you?"

"Oh Lord, no. I just—"

"What d'you know about Major X's wife?"

"She died in India."

"Yes," Ranklin said, then more firmly: "Yes." But Army habit stopped him sharing his puzzlement with a junior.

He ignored J's polite curiosity and got his mind back to the more immediate problem. Perhaps Corinna . . . he scribbled on another card: *May I borrow your maid?*

Half an hour later a short, slightly tubby man with a large moustache strolled on to the platform arm in arm with a younger woman. She wore the self-conscious, giggly look of one heading for a naughty weekend in Paris and was such a familiar sight to the officials and station police that they ignored them both. As Dagner himself had said, the best disguise is always other people.

*   *   *

Feeling uncomfortably like a man who prowls the corridor of sleeper trains in search of an unchaperoned young lady, because that was just what he was doing, Ranklin tried reassuring himself by listing the crimes he was already wanted for in London. He had released Corinna's maid once they were on the boat – the Dover police hadn't given them a glance – and hidden himself in the saloon for the crossing.

Compartment 7 – she *had* said 7, hadn't she? He offered up a prayer and knocked tentatively. But he had misjudged the sway of the train and it became a thundering wallop. "Most masterful," Corinna said, wearing a Japanese robe, a wide smile and perhaps nothing else. "Thank the Lord you got rid of that moustache. I saw you on the platform and nearly had hysterics. And Kitty said you behaved like a perfect gentleman; I think she was a bit disappointed. Would you like a cognac?"

She poured him one out of a silver flask from what she insisted on calling a 'purse' and Ranklin would have called a travelling bag, and he sat at the foot of the bed and sipped. She sat with her arms wrapped round her knees and asked: "So where are you off to, one jump ahead of the police? And what's that all about?"

"Trieste. And the fuss is just Scotland Yard trying to balance its books. Why did you suddenly decide to go . . . well, where *are* you going?"

"Wherever Andrew does." She because serious. "I don't know what's going on and unless you tell me, I'm sticking to that boy like a leech."

He nodded. "I can't blame you. But I still don't think he's likely to get mixed up in anything, I think Falcone had several irons in the fire and we're only interested in one of them, but . . ."

"Is Trieste part of that? Like it's part of Austria that Italy covets?"

Ranklin studied his tiny cup of cognac. And with her lantern-slide change of expression to a broad grin, she said: "You poor darling, you really don't know what the hell's going on, do you? Come up this end and let Mama cuddle you and you tell her all your troubles."

Ranklin accepted half her invitation. "Is this how private banking conducts business?"

"Invariably. But at least take your damned overcoat off."

"Sorry." He laid his head tentatively on her breasts; she certainly had nothing supportive on beneath the kimono. After a while, he said in a rather muffled voice: "Something I don't understand . . . Do you remember Major Dagner talking about his wife?"

"His second wife, you said."

"I did, but just hours ago he told me his wife got ill but recovered. So the chap who told me she'd died must have got it wrong." But damn it, the Scots Guards major had been specific enough about Dagner's grief.

"I know," she said calmly. "Adelina was talking about him—"

"Who?"

"Lady Hovedene. She said, with his medal and that Tibet stuff, he was the most eligible widower in London. And believe me, she doesn't get those things wrong."

Ranklin raised his head, puzzled. "But he says his wife's on the way home."

"Sure. But I figured that was just his act – and you seemed to be backing him. Spy stuff. Or maybe he doesn't want people like Adelina trying to marry him off, so he pretends she's still alive. Like me being Mrs Finn only the other way around. You don't *have* to be a spy to be an out-and-out liar," she added. "But I guess it helps."

"But why put on the act with *me?*"

She went cross-eyed looking down at him. Then smiled as she stroked his silky hair. Men got so outraged at each other not being Pukka Sahibs.

"Maybe he pretends to himself," she said evenly. "He just can't bring himself to face it, so he believes she's forever on the next boat home. I find that rather romantic."

Ranklin obviously didn't find it so. She felt she was cuddling a plank. "Or maybe you could say he's a bit *eccentric*. Don't you have to be, to be a top spy? Anyhow, what can you do about it right now? Just relax."

And gradually, soothed by her and the rocking of the train, he did. Most of him.

24

They met again at ten that morning in the Sherring office on the Boulevard des Capucines. After – probably – a couple of hours' sleep in her own bed, a bath and a change of clothing, Corinna looked crisp and fresh. Ranklin didn't. On what was obviously going to be another hot day, he had spent three hours taxi-cabbing from café to café in his overcoat and burdened with his luggage.

She had a Baedeker *Austria-Hungary* open at the Trieste pages. "The Excelsior Palace sounds good enough for a Sherring representative. Shall I cable them to book a room? – I suppose there's no hope that you *aren't* going to pose as one of us?"

"Er, well, it . . . that is . . ."

"I thought not. But please try not to shoot anybody in our name, will you?" She scribbled on a form and gave it to a clerk.

"And since you mention it," Ranklin said hopefully, "can you give me any names in Trieste? – business acquaintances?"

She pulled a sour face. "Give an inch and . . . Oh well." She rummaged in her bag once more and found a small but bulky notebook. "Trieste . . . I've never been there myself, but . . . Here we are: there's Signor Pauluzzo on the Exchange there. He thinks he knows more than he does but he does know about shipping. He breeds orchids and has a son in Boston." The book obviously held more than just names and addresses and Ranklin longed to add it to the Bureau's "registry".

"I could," he suggested helpfully, "look them up myself, see who seems likely—"

"No you don't. This sort of stuff is our real family jewels. Your Bureau can buy its own notebook." She gave him a couple more names, complete with character sketches, then said hesitantly: "There's also a Conte di Chioggia listed. Apparently no good on business affairs, but knows everyone socially and is involved

176

in pro-Italian politics at a dilettante level. Spends every morning in the Café San Marco. Sounds good for a gossip, anyway. What time's your train?"

"One o'clock at the Gare de Lyons. Gets me into Trieste tomorrow night. What about you?"

"I'll get out to Issy to see about getting the airplane onto a train for Turin." She saw his surprise. "Andrew doesn't want to fly it all the way down, thank God, what with the Alps and saving wear and tear on the engine. Did you know those engines only last fifteen hours or so between overhauls? Crazy. The Signora's already there, some Italian she wants should see it . . ."

They chattered on, the gulf of parting gradually widening between them, until a cable came back from the Excelsior in Trieste confirming that Ranklin – James Spencer, that is – was booked in from Sunday night.

But as he was about to leave, she suddenly hugged him fiercely. "Take care of yourself," she whispered. "And I really mean that. I'll be at the Grand de Turin, cable me if there's any problem. *Any* problem."

"And you know where I am. It's not too far. And stick close to O'Gilroy: he's got a good sense of self-preservation."

She nodded. "Yes. That's why I wish he were going with you."

As Ranklin looked for yet another taxi, he reminded himself: I'm working for the *Bureau*. I think.

The Paris aerodrome, on an old drill-field in the suburb of Issy-les-Moulineaux, was surprisingly deserted for a fine Saturday afternoon until Corinna recalled Andrew talking of the Gordon Bennett air races at Rheims that weekend. They (she and the Sherring chauffeur) finally tracked down the Oriole behind the two vast airship sheds and found it already in pieces. Andrew and O'Gilroy, shirt-sleeved and oil-smudged, were directing a handful of French mechanics as they lashed the body onto a flat motor-truck. Much as she trusted her brother (she told herself) she was always cheered to see his aeroplanes in unflyable condition.

She greeted them, was assured that an unfledged sparrow could have made yesterday's Channel crossing safely, and asked: "What happened to Signora Falcone?"

"Went off with the wop poet," Andrew said, turning back to the loading.

177

"The who?" she asked O'Gilroy.

"Dannun-something. Seems he's a famous poet. Italian."

"D'Annunzio?"

"Ye know him, then?"

"I know *of* him, of course – is he the Italian she was talking about?"

O'Gilroy shrugged. "Best ask the Signora. But seems he's in it with Falcone, buying the Oriole for the Italian Army."

Corinna frowned. From what she'd read of Gabriele d'Annunzio, what he spent money on was himself – which included actresses – and the money wasn't usually his own. Indeed, wasn't he exiled in France by bankruptcy? But he was still popular in influential Italian circles, and while getting a poet-playwright to endorse an airplane would be pointless in America, in Italy things were different.

"Seems he's writing something," O'Gilroy went on. "A poem about the aeroplane, mebbe, and they'll be doing a stunt dropping copies of it from the air. Mr Sherring took him up jest an hour gone, and he was scattering bits of paper to the divil and back." He clearly disapproved of such snake-oil salesmanship in Serious Aeronautics.

Corinna grinned and relaxed. If they were merely concealing a sales stunt that might be spoiled by advance gossip, she'd been worrying unnecessarily. However, not about Ranklin in Trieste.

Andrew was busy yards away, overseeing as one of the wings was lifted on to the truck. She said: "Matt came across on the same boat, and he's gone on to Trieste. And with Scotland Yard close behind."

O'Gilroy frowned. "Was they now? I wasn't wanting to get him into trouble with—"

"He's not blaming you. Umm—" she wasn't sure how to tackle this; "—do you know anything about Major Dagner's marriage?"

"Never a thing." It was very prompt, like a door closing.

She knew that expression, and this time it annoyed her. So she put on a superior smile and changed the subject to: "Were you thinking of taking a pistol to Italy?"

O'Gilroy looked at her but said nothing.

"Because it's strictly against the law there. I suppose they have so many gang feuds. If you don't believe me, I'll show you in Baedeker's."

"And that law would mean yeself, too?" he growled, staring at her travelling bag.

"Don't be silly."

"So I'd best stick close to yeself for protection."

"That's right. Now, when you're ready, I'll ride you over to the freight yard."

*   *   *

The Simplon Express couldn't be called "Orient" because it terminated at Venice for political reasons. But it had the same carriages, staff, speed and luxury, so it was the train they took, although it meant a change at Milan to backtrack eighty miles to Turin. It also charged Orient Express prices, which was why Ranklin wasn't travelling it on Bureau expenses.

In Corinna's experience, taking maids to Italy was more trouble – in Rescuing their Honour – than it was worth in hairdressing. So with Kitty left behind, she had only Andrew and O'Gilroy to get to the Gare de Lyons on time and reasonably presentable. Andrew's luggage had come with her own, and O'Gilroy could pass as an eccentric Irish squire with the minimal luggage he had crammed into the Oriole. And at least she had made sure neither of them smelled of castor oil.

Having dumped them in the salon end of the dining car with a batch of French aviation magazines, she waited on the platform, exchanging greetings with the senior staff who remembered her (and most made sure they did) until Signora Falcone and d'Annunzio arrived.

Men who were supposed to be irresistible to women and were careless with other people's money were guaranteed Corinna's mistrust, and d'Annunzio gave her almost every excuse. He must have been about fifty, shorter than she and stocky, with a long fleshy nose and small moustache and beard. He wore a very fresh white linen suit and wide hat, and moved in a cloud of lavender water and greyhounds. The greyhounds frisked around, all paws and wet noses, rushing up to check passers-by then rushing back to nuzzle their Master. The lavender water didn't behave much better.

He bowed over her hand with perfect correctness. "I am delighted to meet you, Mrs Finn." His English was good but with a strong accent. "May I compliment you on having a

179

brother who is a superb aviator and most gifted designer of flying machines?"

Annoyed that she couldn't argue with that, she forced a smile.

"The flight was—" he hunched shoulders and hands, then spread them in an opening gesture; "—a rebirth! I have been given a new life! Now forgive me, I must say my farewells."

These were to a clutch of theatrical-looking hangers-on and, Corinna was relieved to see, the dogs. She left him to it and joined the men in the salon until Signora Falcone came through. They ordered coffee.

"I should have mentioned d'Annunzio," Signora Falcone said briskly, "only I wasn't sure we were going to meet him here. You can never tell with Gabri, he does tend to live on a different planet."

"He's – as it were – endorsing the airplane?"

"That sort of thing. He's a big name in Italy – and he's got a new opera opening at La Scala soon – he isn't coming to Turin immediately, he's stopping in Milan – so the publicity works both ways. He doesn't live *that* much on a different planet."

"Is he an old friend?"

"Yes. Did I tell you I was on the stage once myself? I played in a thing of his *ages* ago now." She smiled graciously. "I don't think I had Sarah Bernhardt worried. Nor Eleonora Duse or Donatella." There might have been a coded message there: those last two had certainly been d'Annunzio's mistresses.

"In fact," she went on, "we're rather letting Gabri hog the limelight, as if the whole aeroplane scheme is his inspiration and we're supporting him. The Senator has political enemies – every senator has, of course – and as long as he gets the manufacturing rights . . ."

Corinna nodded. Limelight didn't show on balance sheets. "Is the Senator thinking of starting up his own manufacturing plant?" she asked, casual as a hungry tigress.

At dinner, d'Annunzio proved an easy conversationalist, slipping unselfconsciously from English to French to Italian, then apologising to Corinna for the self-indulgence of speaking his native language again. Her own Italian was exam standard and rusty with it. Andrew and O'Gilroy sat at a separate table and she doubted the conversation there ever fell below a thousand feet.

*   *   *

The stillness woke Corinna. The train had stopped, and from the lack of human babble, not at a station. The only sounds were distant clankings and chuffings and a brief hoot of a shunting engine. She waited a few minutes, trying to sense the mood of the train, before deciding it had become as immovable as a fat, sleepy cat. She put on slippers and a robe and stepped into the corridor.

From the view through the window, they were stranded in the middle of a marshalling yard, too big to see what lay beyond in the darkness: mountains or forest or a sleeping town. This was a world of its own, dim-lit with lines of both bluish electric lights and yellower gas ones. Neither brought any colour to the rows of freight cars, dark carriages and lines of dull-glinting rails. It looked as still and cold as a morgue.

"'I am the way into the doleful city'," a voice said quietly. It was d'Annunzio, wearing a royal blue gown that reached to the floor and a white silk scarf thrown around his neck. "I think we have reached the gates of Dis."

"Does it inspire you?"

He shuddered. "I find it hateful. A graveyard, not even of men, but of their hopes. Machines built to rush about the world, now heaped in a common grave."

She smiled. "I find it rather romantic."

He turned to look – up – at her in the thin cold light. "Romantic? This is not an outpost on your great American prairies. Here was once forests and villages, perhaps even Hannibal's camp-fires."

"I still like it," she said cheerfully, pressing her nose to the cold glass.

"Do you then see it as romantic that each carriage and truck out there has a value?" Probably Signora Falcone had talked about Corinna's background.

Unruffled, she said: "In a way, maybe."

"You see so many stacks of money?"

"No. You can't see the sort of money that interests me. It's the muscles under the skin: you see the movement, not the muscle."

He shook his head firmly. "That, I do not understand. I like money you can—" He made a fingering gesture. "And you say movement? Here nothing is moving. It is all dead!"

181

"Just resting."

Smudges of steam, slow to dissolve in the cold air, drifted past. "Except," d'Annunzio said in a sonorous voice, "for the souls of unfinished journeys, turned to ghosts."

"I said it would inspire you."

"Pff, just description, sterile imaginings." A flick of his hand threw it away.

"A lot of—" But then the sleeping-car attendant noticed two of his charges were awake and came along the corridor to assure them that the train would move on at any moment. Meanwhile, could he bring them anything? D'Annunzio politely deflected the question to Corinna. She shook her head. "Not for me."

"Ni moi, merci – un moment: vous n'avez-pas des cigarettes?"

The attendant hadn't a stock, but happily gave d'Annunzio one of his own, lit it for him and said good-night. D'Annunzio took a cautious drag, stifled a cough, and murmured: "Horrible. Truly horrible. I smoke only weak cigarettes and not often, but tonight I am restless . . ."

Corinna eyed him cautiously, having a clear idea of what men got restless for on night trains. Women, too, she admitted, in view of last night. And as for ocean liners . . .

D'Annunzio took another careful puff. "You are saying?"

What had she been saying? Yes. "Just that a lot of good poetry is description and recollection."

"Most often by your English poets – if you also claim them as your own. But for me, I am tired of just describing. It is not enough." He paused, then went on thoughtfully: "To make people say 'I recognise' or 'I remember' no longer satisfies me. And even when my words are spoken by a great voice and spirit – I have heard Sarah Bernhardt and Eleonora Duse make audiences weep with my words . . . but I have doubts. Here, at this hour, in this ante-room to the Inferno, I doubt my own words. Was it those words – or those voices? Would the audience have wept if Duse had read a railway timetable?"

Curious, Corinna asked bluntly: "Are you jealous of actresses?"

"Envy, envy – it is the great Italian sin. In a world of riches and power, we have only beauty and envy." He dropped the unfinished cigarette on the floor and was about to stamp it out, then realised his slippers were too thin, and kicked it aside.

182

"A lot of countries have only got the envy," she said diplomatically.

He didn't take it as diplomacy, and snapped: "Italy is not a lot of countries! It is Italy – of Rome and Dante and Venice and Michelangelo . . . And one day I will speak words worthy of them, not in the theatre but in the world, that will rouse Italy again to her true glory. I *feel* it, that I am alive at this time to do this."

Startled by his sudden passion, Corinna looked away, through the window. A hunched figure swinging a lantern trudged up the track, going quietly about his job, probably with no idea of how it fitted into the complexity of the shunting yard. And probably content with that. "There's a lot of people around Europe, quite enough already, I'd think, giving speeches like that—"

"Then Italy deserves the finest and most rousing."

"D'you mean war?" she asked flatly.

"Yes." He stood four-square, facing and challenging her. She looked at him for a moment, then turned to the window again and began speaking quietly.

"I know a soldier – an artillery officer. He fought for the Greeks in Macedonia last year, and told me something about it. Mostly it was mud and cold and marching and being hungry and scared. Just moments of excitement, then the same thing only now with men dying of gangrene with no medical aid. And finally – not in his area, thank God – typhus, too, so the ones who lived to go home found they were kept out of their own villages. In the end, you got all the Four Horsemen. He believed it could happen all over Europe." She looked at him. "To your beautiful Italy, too."

D'Annunzio seemed unmoved, but nodded to show he had understood. "No. Your friend fought only in a peasant brawl. Serbians, Bulgarians, what do they know of modern war? Even the Greeks – and I love Greece – they cannot be Romans. True war, *our* war, will indeed be terrible, but it will be quick. Quick as an aeroplane, as a torpedo, as a bullet is quick. And the suffering will be terrible, worse than anyone can imagine. But true courage is to know this and still to go into the fire, seeking to be destroyed – or cleansed and made free and strong once more. Because only the strongest will survive, only a Dante may come back from the Inferno. That is the justice of war. It will be the . . . the . . . *crucible* that will create our new leaders, to sweep away the old feeble ones *elected* by bribes from the Camorra."

She couldn't argue about the length of any future war; a lot of people believed it would, must, be quickly over. But: "A lot of your bravest and best are going to be the first to get killed. And your crooked politicians and gang bosses aren't going to get anywhere near a bullet. Be careful they aren't the only ones left to be your leaders."

"The fire will destroy many, but it will make more strong those who live. And the people who have been through the fire also, they will never be led by any others."

His voice stumbled and strained against the barricade of a foreign language, but that only added to his sincerity. And she saw, bursting through the shell of self-indulgence and disrepute, the attraction of the man. Sure he loved himself, but mostly for what he believed he could do, in his art, in his patriotism. He was reaching outside himself, and not always for the nearest woman.

They just come with the mail, she thought, reining in her admiration. So she said in her mildest tone: "Forgive me asking, but had you any specific enemy in mind? – or just a good old war?"

He seemed about to reply, then clamped his mouth shut. And then he said: "Flying machines – such as your brother has made. You have seen the lion in the Piazza San Marco? You remember it has wings? I, Gabriele d'Annunzio, shall give him wings again. I vow it."

Corinna sat for a while on her bed, picking over their conversation as if summarising it for a report to her father. There was no doubting the sincerity of d'Annunzio's patriotism any more than its power. It was a smart move to harness that to selling the Oriole. But she had to remember the Falcones were up to something else, something that interested Ranklin and the Bureau. Something that had brought assassins to London. She could only pray they were separate deals – and keep an eagle eye open for a connection.

* * *

A couple of hundred miles ahead of them, Ranklin sat on the edge of his non-de luxe sleeper bed and lit a cigarette. He disapproved of smoking in bed, so sitting up was his compromise, despite the Alpine chill. The cigarette was to stop thoughts prowling restlessly through his head and it wasn't working.

He was glad to be heading out on a new task; such jobs were the core of his new trade. But he was also scared he would find Trieste as recent newspapers drew it: flourishing and prosperous rather than discontented and yearning to riot. And the idea of handing out revolutionary pamphlets at shipyard gates didn't fit with his image of Senator Falcone. It lacked flamboyance; something was missing.

Did Dagner know what that missing something was? Or had he got his teeth too firmly into his 'mission'? That wasn't a good position from which to see the whole picture. And the business of Dagner's wife . . . Spies are liars; they have to be. But not when they're so easily proven wrong, like whether their wives are alive or dead. So perhaps his superior hadn't so much been been lying as . . . as what? No answer he could think of promised him a good night's sleep.

25

The worried, sleepless hours on the train had caused Trieste to loom ominously. It would be strange and sinister, closed against him – and yet sucking him in. Ranklin felt it would want to trap him, be full of eyes, unseen but all-seeing, waiting to pounce on his slightest mistake.

But now, from the steps of the Excelsior Palace on a sunny morning, the nightmare faded with the sea haze. If Trieste was full of eyes, it was also full of ships, fat Italians, thin Greeks and screeching seagulls. And the most immediate thing likely to pounce on a mistake was the traffic, albeit most still horse- and even ox-drawn except for slow-chugging goods trains that ran along the dockside just across the road.

The long, busy waterfront stretched away on either side. To the right, the bigger ships nestled against the warehouses of the railway yard; to the left lay smaller steamers, trading schooners and fishing boats. And beyond them, somewhere round the point with its stubby lighthouse, were the warship slipways of Stabilimento Tecnico. He was *not* going to goggle at them, even if it were, physically possible.

Instead, he turned right and right again into the Piazza Grande with its trees, bandstand and cafés, heading vaguely for the Exchange but mostly trying to fit into the city's pace and mood. Just spending a few pfennigs on a packet of cigarettes helped convince him of some sort of rapport. Because what he was really looking for was the ordinary confidence of an honest man.

Half an hour later he was sitting in a dainty bright café with Signor Pauluzzo and two friends who were delighted to chatter to the House of Sherring. And since the name so impressed them, Ranklin lost nothing by explaining that he was both

186

new and junior (and thus didn't know any juicy high-level gossip).

"The troubles in the south Balkans affect us not at all," Pauluzzo was claiming. "They have their own ports for what little trade they do. What happens here does not matter to the Carso—" he waved a pudgy hand vaguely eastwards; "—for perhaps 200 kilometres inland. Trieste lives with Vienna, Budapest, Prague, Berlin even. Since the new railway five years ago, each year is a new record in trade. In manufactured goods alone . . ."

It is always difficult to guess the age of foreigners, but Ranklin made Pauluzzo over sixty, with his aura of comfortable worth in black suit, wing collar and a white moustache that disdained the dashing upturned ends favoured by the Austrians. And the other two about his own age or younger; one even wore a turned-down collar like his own, which probably counted as rather flash on the Exchange. So far they had done little but nod and smile.

"And local industries?" Ranklin prompted.

"Again, new records – especially in shipbuilding. This year, Stab Tec will build over twenty warships and eighty other vessels."

"Perhaps over one hundred," ventured one of the others.

"It sounds as if there is no problem with strikes," Ranklin ventured, "as at Fiume?" It was pure luck that the yard down the coast, building the fourth of the dreadnoughts, was strike-bound at the moment. He had no idea why, but it made it a reasonable topic for an outsider.

That brought confident chuckles and some unkind murmurs about managers and workers down there. Pauluzzo held up a hand. "No, we must be fair," he said solemnly, and the expressions on the younger faces warned: Joke Coming. "It is not easy to build a battleship from the keel downwards, in the Hungarian manner."

They all duly guffawed. But before he could work around to another rib-tickler, Pauluzzo was called away by a messenger and the atmosphere relaxed in the international camaraderie of the same age group.

Ranklin put his pipe in his mouth. "And no hint of political – nationalist – problems?"

They swapped glances, then the one with the turned-down collar and a long Venetian nose shrugged and said: "I only speak of the Italians. The Slovenes, in the city there are not so many, and I do not know what they think. Probably they hate both Austrians and

v

Italians. But the Italian worker, he thinks of himself as Italian, so when he gets drunk he says he is oppressed by the Austrians. But all around are Italians also getting drunk and agreeing with him, eating Italian food, reading newspapers in Italian, in the city where their fathers and grandfathers got drunk and complained also. And when he is sober in the morning, when he goes to work in the shipyard, he looks at the colour of his money before the colour of the flag. He loves Italy, but does he want Italian poverty and politics?"

The other had been nodding gently. Now he said: "Also, they listen to the Church which tells them to be good citizens and loyal to the Emperor, who is a good Catholic himself and not like Italian politicians who have robbed the Church of land and power."

The first one said: "If there came an avenging angel, a new Garibaldi, even Oberdan, then perhaps – who knows? But until then—" He lifted a couple of coins set aside as a tip and chinked them. "This is the music of Trieste. It is so since Roman times."

If this is true, or even half true, Ranklin thought, how does Falcone reckon to get the workers to rise and wreck their own livelihood? He steered the conversation into the innocent waters of capital shortages before it ended.

The trouble, he told himself as he paced slowly around the Piazza, is that I don't know even how British civilian workers think and feel. Oh, I know the Army's view of civilians, but since I left off the cocoon of uniform, life has looked a lot more complex.

Still, I've only heard one view. Perhaps I'll find another one in the Café San Marco.

He knew the place immediately: he had, he felt, sat there in every Central European city he had visited, among the same almost democratically diverse clientele. Intellectuals gathered there because no-one objected to their loud argument, ladies came in because the coffee was good, businessmen might meet there because it was centrally placed, and students because they were left alone to read. And the café didn't mind if you only popped in to view such diversity, particularly such flamboyant and slightly scandalous characters as the Conte di Chioggia.

There was no mistaking him; he clearly didn't want there to be. He was elderly, slim, aristocratic, wearing a light suit, a wide floppy hat and holding a silver-knobbed cane like a staff of office; on a cooler day he would surely have worn a cloak. Ranklin sat and watched as a stream of visitors arrived at his table, drank a coffee, said a few words, listened and went about their business. They were a well-mixed bunch, but that didn't mean that a complete stranger would be welcome.

Past noon the waiters started clattering cutlery and serving lunch, and the turnover at the Count's table dried up to one man who was obviously going to stay and eat. But first, he had to greet a lady on the far side of the room and Ranklin acted on an impulse.

Carrying a menu and frowning at it, he moved to the Count's table. "Beg pardon, Excellence, but do you speak English?"

The Count showed no sign of surprise at being recognised by a total stranger. "I retain a modest competence in that language. How may I be of assistance?"

"If you could explain what this dish here is . . . I was recommended to this café by Senator Falcone." The Count's face showed only polite interest. "Or perhaps it was Signor Vascotti."

"Ah yes." The Count smiled. "How is he?"

"Recovering." That was commitment.

"Good." No questions, just "good". *That* was commitment, too, Ranklin exulted.

The Count took his time putting on a pair of gold pince-nez that were tied to him by a scarlet cord and peering at the menu. "And who are you, pray?" he murmured.

"An English businessman with connections to the House of Sherring."

"That sounds as if it could easily be verified – or disproven."

"Yes."

"Hmm . . . I seem to be taking a long time to explain this dish, which is no more than rice and vegetables. Perhaps I should wave my hands in culinary gestures. I think we should meet more privately, most of the waiters here are police spies . . . Do you know the Galleria di Montuzza, the tunnel under the Castello?"

"I can find it. You could suggest other dishes instead."

"An excellent idea. If you are just inside the tunnel at the Piazza Goldoni end at four this afternoon, my carriage will pick you up and nobody will see. More seriously, I recommend this dish: the *scaloppa*."

"You're most kind."

"*Prego*."

189

Ranklin stayed and ate his *scaloppa* without another glance at the Count's table. He seemed to have found the right man, and been invited to a Secret Meeting. He would rather it had been a mere secret meeting, but the Count's flamboyance wouldn't allow that. With contacts, too, you had to work with what you'd got.

* * *

Putting the Oriole together again at Veneria aerodrome was a much longer job than dismantling it had been. It was covered in smoke-smuts and with a couple of small rips in the wing fabric. These weren't serious – such things happened all the time – but Andrew insisted on doing the patching himself, trimming the ripped area, sealing on a new patch with cellulose dope, then weather-proofing it with varnish. O'Gilroy was permitted to wash off the smuts.

After lunch they began the re-assembly. In principle this was straightforward; in practice it was a cautious procedure of re-attaching wires, both for control and rigging, then tightening or loosening each one on turnbuckles to achieve what Andrew saw as just the right tension. Two experienced pilots could disagree on the last touches of rigging, preferring marginally different wing incidence or stiffness. As yet, O'Gilroy had no views; he hadn't even touched the Oriole's controls, since they were all on Andrew's side. His job had been map-reading, keeping the engine log, and passing sandwiches.

But when he wasn't doing any of these, he had studied Andrew's hands as they coped with the ripples and bumps he could himself feel in the air.

Around what would have been tea-time if Italy had such a time, O'Gilroy primed each cylinder with petrol, spun the propeller, and saw Andrew off on a short test flight. As he watched the aeroplane bobbing and weaving around the local sky, a large cream-and-red tourer drove onto the field and the chauffeur released Signora Falcone.

"Is that our aeroplane?" she asked, looking up.

"It is, ma'am."

"And is all well?"

"Seems to be."

"Good. But it's most annoying. I've just had a telegram—" she

flourished it unnecessarily; "—from Gabri. D'Annunzio. It seems
. . . No, I'll explain to Mr Sherring when he gets down."

She treated O'Gilroy with polite reserve, obviously puzzled by
the way he seemed to crop up, first as her husband's bodyguard,
then as Andrew's assistant. And perhaps the Irish accent reminded
her of her own social climb. She must have been better born than
O'Gilroy, but true Dublin society didn't let its daughters go on
the stage.

The Oriole drifted down to a smooth landing and O'Gilroy joined
the mechanics in man-handling it over to the usual sheds. Andrew
climbed down. "A *little* tightening up on the underside wires, they
always work a bit loose after re-rigging. And I've put another twenty
minutes on the engine, don't forget that." He turned to Signora
Falcone. "All ready to go, Signora. When's the—"

"I have just had news: that vexing man d'Annunzio now wants
us to do the first demonstration in *Venice* – of all places. Some
people there he wants to impress, and we're really in his hands.
So I'm going to have to ask you if you can fly there tomorrow, I
think it's only just over two hundred miles . . ."

"Fine, whatever you say." Andrew was untroubled. "All we need
is a map. Maybe we can make it part of the demonstration, a
timed trial?"

"As you like. But luckily our main home is near Venice and
Giancarlo did much of his flying from one of our fields, so you can
land there. I don't suppose Mrs Finn will want to come, it's a dreary
journey by train, and Turin's much more a centre of things."

I wish I dared ask her to bet on that, O'Gilroy thought.

*   *   *

After lunch, Ranklin sat in the hotel lobby and wrote out a
cable that started "First impression" and included the phrase
"apparently stable workforce with no inclination to strike and good
economic reasons not to", then had it sent to one of the Bureau's
accommodation addresses in London. He wasn't yet ready to advise
Dagner to back out of what might prove a fiasco (though possibly,
thank God, an unnoticed one) but he could sound a warning. He
still hoped to learn more from the Count.

So at four o'clock, he was loitering just inside the tunnel
entrance, which was framed by operatic flights of stairs leading

to the Castello, and feeling as obvious as an anarchist with a sizzling bomb.

A closed four-wheeler drew up beside him, the door swung open and he stepped up and in, rocking the little carriage like a dinghy.

"Excellently contrived," the Count said from the companionable darkness beside him, and rapped on the front with his cane. The driver whipped the horse into a sedate plod. "Perhaps you have more complete news of matters in England? – I received only a guarded cable."

"You know the Senator was attacked: it was by two Italian thugs, one of whom was killed that evening in London by certain new friends of the Senator. The other escaped. The Senator lost a lot of blood but otherwise it wasn't serious, he'll return to Turin as soon as he can travel. Signora Falcone arrived from Paris, so everything continues as planned. All right so far?"

He left the implication that there was more hanging and kept his voice unemotional, but his inner self pleaded for the Count to give him a lead.

And quite calmly the Count said: "I understand. And the aeroplane?"

My God, it *is* involved. But how? – how do you start a shipyard strike with a flying machine?

"It left for France the day I left London. I know nothing more, but it should be in Turin by now."

"Ah, excellent." Gas lamps stuck out on ornate arms from the walls of the tunnel and in their intermittent flares, he saw the Count's head bowed as if brooding. One window of the carriage was open, letting in the echoing clip-clop of their own and other horses, along with a concentrated horse smell.

The Count raised his head and peered at him. "Are you permitted to tell me whom, apart from the House of Sherring, you represent? – so ably, if I may say so."

"You recall that I said the Senator had certain new friends in London. Our assistance is entirely unofficial, you understand."

"Ah, when was England's interest in anything ever official?" the Count chuckled. "And you are here to report – unofficially – on the outcome, I presume?"

Ranklin made a noise that (unofficially) could have been agreement. "But I was talking this morning with some dealers on the Exchange ... They had the impression that the shipyard workers were very content with their lot. At the moment."

"Indeed. That has always been the problem, the selfishness of the working man."

The Count would have been right at home in an Army mess. Ranklin said: "But you're happy that this can be overcome?"

"Oh yes ..."

Ranklin tried again. "I may be called home soon, going back through Italy. So if you have any message for the Senator – or perhaps the Signora ..."

"That is most kind, but I must consider. If I do not see you again, where do you stay, may I ask?"

"The Excelsior."

The tunnel was only a quarter-mile long and growing lightness showed they were coming to its south end.

"I will not detain you with effusive thanks, however much you deserve them," the Count effused. "Save only to wish you a pleasant – and safe – stay in Venezia Giulia."

'Julian Venice', the Italian name – and claim – to the region. And that gave Ranklin an opening. "Is there anybody in particular I should beware of?"

"Ah ... I think only Police Captain Novak. A suspicious man. And unscrupulous on behalf of his Slovene brothers. But *how* to beware of him is by no means so easy."

Ranklin stepped down just inside the south entrance and had to stop himself peering suspiciously around. God save him from people who loved deviousness and darkness; they shone like lighthouses in the world of drab, unnoticed skulduggery.

*   *   *

Corinna swept into their hotel suite without knocking. "Are you going through with this Venice business?" she demanded.

"Sure. Why not?" Andrew was surprised. "It's only two hundred and twenty-seven miles and all over land—"

"I don't mean that. I mean ... all this chopping and changing. First it's going to be Turin, then—"

"If you've tied yourself into a publicity stunt with a nutty poet like d'Annunzio, you got to expect some flim-flam."

"Sure, and it's just *lucky* they happen to have a villa near Venice—"

"Corrie," Andrew said firmly and (perhaps he thought) soothingly, "you've been too much tied up with the finance end of things. When it comes to selling hardware out in the real world—"

"The *real world?* – you blinkered bird-man—"

O'Gilroy had been trying to merge into the furniture; not easy, since it tended to mock Louis XVI rather than oil-stained tweed. But he felt there were limits to what even a spy should overhear. "I think I'll be having a jar downstairs," he said.

Corinna glared from one to the other of them. "I'll come with you," she decided. "*And* to Venice besides."

She had dropped below boiling-point by the time they were seated in the lounge and had ordered drinks.

"We came more'n two hundred miles jest getting to Paris," O'Gilroy said reassuringly.

"Only this time it's two hundred miles nearer Trieste, where Matt's up to some Bureau shenanigans," she said grimly. "Let me tell you, if you're trying to involve young Andrew in any of *that*, I am going to set up a scream. And when I scream, factories in the next county think it's quitting time. Is that clear?"

"Surely. But like ye said—" The waiter put down two small glasses of what looked like red wine and O'Gilroy sipped cautiously. "What'd ye say this was?"

"Sweet vermouth. D'you like it?"

"It's new. Funny, the flavours people think up . . . But ye'll be there yeself, and if they're wanting anything 'cept a demonstration of the aeroplane, ye can scream then."

"Only," she said grimly, "the boy so much wants to make this airplane a success he could get talked into *anything*."

"But with yer own screaming 'gainst their talking, I know which me money's on."

*   *   *

Ranklin got back to the hotel feeling more tired than the efforts of the day warranted. He thought of sending a second cable, but what could he say? All he'd learned from the Count was that the aeroplane was involved – but not how – and that they seemed confident that the workers *could* be roused. By the sight of an aeroplane? By something it would bring? And how could that pass in a cable for economic chit-chat?

He was still worrying about this when he let himself into his room – and found it had been searched.

26

Ranklin didn't rush to check if the intruder(s) had found this or that; by now he was experienced enough not to have a this or that. He sat down on the bed to think.

To report it or not? The search had been thorough, but not blatant; his things weren't strewn about. A careless man might not have noticed it had happened – but only a guilty man could notice and *not* report it. That was the deciding fact. He sighed at the prospect of official entanglement ahead, but perhaps that had happened already.

The office had been carved out of one corner of a bigger room, partition walls chopping off the once-elaborate cornice moulding at two places and making it awkwardly high-ceilinged for its size. Too awkward to reach the cobwebs on the electric fan up there, anyway. After he had waited alone for some minutes Ranklin wondered if this were a test to see if he went snooping on the cluttered desk. After another few minutes, he did go snooping, but only for an ashtray. Perhaps that did the trick, because almost immediately a man in uniform bustled in.

Police Captain Novak was barely taller than Ranklin but built like a bear, with a deep chest, sloping shoulders and very quick, powerful movements. His squarish face would have been stolid if it, too, wasn't always moving in small expressions and chewing or lip-pursing. He wore a neat middle-ranking moustache, neither too grand nor too humble. And he spoke no English.

But he had to speak German, the language of his Austrian masters, and they got along slowly in that. Their very different accents excused the slowness, but weren't the real cause: Ranklin was thinking carefully before he spoke and he suspected that, despite his apparent impetuousness, so was Novak.

He started off with much shuffling of blank forms, then decided there was none that suited this occasion and carefully wrote down James Spencer's details on a writing pad. "And you say nothing was taken? Most curious. In fact, an insult. To be robbed is shocking, terrible, but in a city full of Italians, quite normal. But to be robbed yet robbed of nothing is a trampling of your honour. Did you have anything worth taking?"

Ranklin shrugged. "A pair of gold cuff-links, not much more."

Novak threw up his hands. "Not even taking gold cuff-links! Italian thieves are getting so rich! Or poor – perhaps he didn't have any cuffs. Are you sure he didn't steal any cuffs?"

"I didn't really count them."

"But then he would have taken the cuff-links as well, so we deduce that he most likely did not." He smiled very quickly. "We progress . . . What have you been doing since you arrived in Trieste?"

Ranklin blinked. "Ah . . . talking to some gentlemen at the Exchange, lunching – alone – and wandering around the city."

"And where did you have lunch?"

"At the Café San Marco. What does this have to do with my room being ransacked?"

"Ah!" Novak said explosively. "I am trying to establish a pattern. Men are creatures of routine, police work is mostly routine. If a thief should know that every lunchtime you are at the Café San Marco—"

"But I've been in Trieste less than a day. How can I have established any routines?"

"Ach, then my theory fails. No matter. Did you meet the Conte di Chioggia at the Café?"

"Is he an elderly gentleman? Dressed a little . . . artistically?"

"A most charming man and a truly great conspirator."

Ranklin raised his eyebrows. "Is that so? What does he conspire?"

Captain Novak shrugged violently. "Just conspiracies. He has been conspiring for twenty years, and one day he will go too far. Perhaps tomorrow." He glared fiercely at the pad. "We have not made much progress. You will not be in Trieste for long?"

Ranklin hadn't said how long, but perhaps he was now being told.

"Probably not long. A few days."

"Then, as you have already been robbed but nothing taken, the word will be passed that you have nothing of which to be robbed and you will be safe for the rest of your stay." Then, with casual abruptness: "How is Senator Falcone?"

It was probably a trap, but the change of subject struck Ranklin dumb. "Huh? I beg your pardon?"

"The Italian Senator. You must know him."

"I don't think I've heard of him."

"He was attacked and stabbed. In England."

"No! Killed, you mean?"

Novak made a vague gesture. "Almost – perhaps." He already seemed bored by the topic.

Ranklin put on a heavy frown. "Very distressing. And rare, for Britain."

Novak had gone silent. So at last Ranklin said: "Is that all, then?"

"I could show you some photographs of criminals, to see if you recognised one."

"But I didn't see anyone, just my room, ransacked."

"Of course. It would not help anyway, they all look the same: hideously ugly. It is nonsense to say there is no criminal type: just to see those photographs proves it. SO!" He sprang to his feet. "Thank you for coming in, I apologise that I can be of no more help, enjoy your short stay in Trieste, good day."

He sat down again and Ranklin found his own way out.

You Have Been Warned, he thought. And by now he was pretty sure Novak himself had organised the room-searching. Trieste's eyes were back.

He sent another cable before dinner. It was mostly facts and figures about Triestine trade, but included the phrase "feeling a bit ill" to tell the Bureau he was under suspicion. They had progressed that far in developing a cable code – if anybody remembered, that is.

*   *   *

He devoted the next morning to behaving like a loyal and industrious Sherring employee. He called on the British consul and both the other names Corinna had given him and – apart, he hoped, from persuading any police watchers that he wasn't a spy – only

198

reinforced the impression that Trieste's Italian workforce was not about to go on strike. He didn't fool himself that he "understood" the city after a bare twenty-four hours, just that he had seen no sign of the unrest they hoped for and plenty of signs pointing the opposite way.

He asked at the hotel desk if there were any cablegrams for him, but got only an odd, stiff smile. Damn it, had that policeman Novak been snooping round, staining his reputation? He stumped off towards the lift – but didn't get there.

Police Captain Novak was guarding a large potted palm beside the lift gate, and in case the plant turned nasty, he'd brought two policemen to help out.

He took Ranklin's arm and urged him towards the front door; he had a grip like a lobster. "When I arrest people like you," he confided, "I am allowed the expense of a carriage. You may also ride in it, or you can be carried through the streets by my men. It makes no difference to me. Either way, *I* still get to ride in the carriage."

27

Turin to Venice was 365 kilometres in a straight line, which was 227 miles, which was 3 hours 46 minutes at a steady 60 m.p.h. in a dead calm. Only it wasn't going to be a dead calm, it was impossible to maintain a steady 60 m.p.h. and certainly not a straight line. But O'Gilroy had learnt that the original perfection of measurement and calculation was still vital. Then, when you spotted an unquestionable landmark, you could work out just how far off your perfect plan you were, in time or distance, and correct accordingly.

That left only the problems of identifying unquestionable landmarks you had never seen before in an unknown countryside and hazy weather – and getting some sense out of the compass. O'Gilroy had had no dealings with compasses before: they went with officers, and a rare old mess that combination usually made. Now, watching the needle swing unprovoked a good ten degrees either side of north, he had some sympathy with the lieutenants and captains of his Army past.

Andrew had been unworried. "Venice is on the sea, we can't miss that. If you've any doubts, err to the south, so we'll know which way to turn when we find the coast."

But O'Gilroy was determined to do better than that. Flying was a matter of precision, and unless you started with that, there came a point when all you believed in vanished. He had experienced it even within a few miles of Brooklands aerodrome: a sudden sense of being utterly lost in an alien world. A familiar landmark, popping out from under the Boxkite's wing, had saved him then. He remembered the sense of relief as everything clicked back into place, putting him just a few minutes from home. But he remembered also the sense of utter loss.

At least the haze meant that the wind was light, perhaps 10

m.p.h. at 2,000 feet where Andrew chose to fly. Their course headed just north of east, down the wide and ever-widening valley of the Po. It looked good agricultural land below, studded with farms that were like miniature fortresses – and maybe had been, in wilder days. O'Gilroy knew nothing of Italian history, but enough about mankind to assume that any flat rich land had been well fought over.

An hour and a quarter after Turin they were supposed to pass just north of Piave and south of Milan, which should give a reasonably accurate check on progress. But while Milan was obvious enough as a long sprawl of red roofs under a smoky haze, it was too obvious, too big. Towns and cities weren't as neat as on the map: they straggled away into suburbs and half-absorbed villages, and he wasn't sure about Piave at all. But the railway joining the two saved him with a near-precise position.

"We're running late," he called to Andrew, "and being pushed north. Head due east a while."

Andrew nodded and nudged the Oriole slightly to the right, glancing down at the compass and then, probably, finding some landmark on the horizon and steering for it. O'Gilroy began re-calculating on the basis of a stronger south-east wind than they'd assumed.

There weren't, or shouldn't be, any more cities until they passed Verona, an hour and a half ahead, and O'Gilroy tried to relax. He had never foreseen that so much flying would be like this: as dull as marching across the South African veldt. The engine droned steadily, a fine mist of castor oil condensed on the little glass windshield – it was really more an oil-shield; they both wore goggles against the wind – and Andrew corrected the little joggles in the air with minute movements of the stick. Getting rid of the bulky control wheel of earlier aircraft was one of the Oriole's modern touches. And the stick was topped by a "blip" switch to cut off the ignition momentarily, so Andrew could leave the petrol and air levers alone once he had achieved the delicate balance needed. True, the switch worked (he said) by transferring the current from the ignition to his thumb, but it did work.

O'Gilroy looked at his wristwatch, checked the revised timetable scrawled on the edge of the folded map, and began looking ahead for a useful conjunction of river and railway that should pinpoint them at Pontevico. They trudged on across the wide veldt of sky.

*   *   *

This wasn't the normal town jail for drunks and pick-pockets. That might be modern, light and airy, built according to the latest humanitarian theories of penal reformers. Ranklin doubted that, but it was still possible. Any theories about this Castello dungeon came from four centuries ago.

And at first glance in the dim light, so had the other occupant. Ranklin seemed to have strayed into popular romance, where jails always had a gaunt, bearded prisoner who had been there since forever. But as the man got up from one of the three army-style iron cots, Ranklin saw this one was merely dirty, ragged, tousle-haired – no beard – and possibly younger than himself. His smile showed even but stained teeth, and he said something in a crackling language that was probably Slovenian.

Ranklin dumped the armful of thin blankets and barely thicker mattress on a cot and said politely: "*Buon giorno*," but that didn't help. He tried German, French, and finally English without success. The man just smiled agreeably, then pointed to himself: "Pero."

So Ranklin did the same: "James. Or Jim."

"Jee-eem." Pero smiled; he did a lot of smiling, and Ranklin wondered if he were simple-minded or just making the best of a bad job. Then Pero began a mime show: he had been painting on walls – slogans, presumably – had been arrested, slapped around, finally thrown in here. Meanwhile, his wife (kissing and cuddling the air) and child didn't know where he was, would be weeping and starving . . . It was, Ranklin had to admit, very well explained and he was sorry he couldn't reply in kind while staying in character. Private banking didn't come across well in mime.

So communication languished, and Ranklin sat down and looked around. The dungeon itself was reasonably big, around twenty feet square, with a barrel-vaulted ceiling, and made of roughly-dressed but close-fitting stonework that had been whitewashed not so long ago. The one window, sealed with glass and an iron grille, was in a tunnel at head height, showing the outer wall to be at least five feet thick, so he wasn't going to scratch his way to freedom with a toothpick.

Apart from the cots, there was a wooden table, two chairs and a chipped, enamelled bucket. The uneven floor was felt-covered and slightly damp, but the atmosphere was muggy rather than chill. And that was it, apart from some old iron rings set into the walls, presumably from some penal theory that Ranklin hoped was long forgotten.

Putting suspected spies in a fortress was normal in many countries. Perhaps espionage was felt to be contagious, and nobody wanted to infect common criminals, or perhaps spies might be officers and thus deserve special treatment – though there were two ways of looking at that idea. But the police could have no automatic power to slap someone into a military prison – the Castello was an army HQ and the guards were soldiers – so Novak had at least the tacit approval of the Austrian authorities. Which would make it that much more difficult for anyone to get him out. The Bureau would miss him – eventually – but have to act discreetly.

He was, he reckoned, on his own. Well, that was spying for you.

Indeed, Novak might be trying a simple test: shove a man in jail, and if nobody complains, then you know you've caught a spy. He fished out his cigarette case – that, matches and his watch were all he had been left with – and wondered whether jail etiquette meant he had to offer Pero one. In the end he did, but luckily it was refused politely, so he lit one of the nine he had left and settled down to feel the seconds limp by.

* * *

They were lost, and it was O'Gilroy's fault. He had made the mistake, which could be fatal, of warping what he saw to fit what he wanted to see: a distinctive bend and island in the Adige river followed soon by a railway crossing a smaller river. Oh, he had *seen* them all right – but the Adige had many bends and islands, and the country below was veined with small rivers and canals, half of them not on the map. If he'd been right, they would now be slap over the middle of Padua, and there was no sign of the place.

Moreover, the haze was thickening from a whitish blur that made the sky overlap the landscape to a grey-brown stain that subtly distorted what it didn't hide.

He yelled his confession to Andrew, who nodded philosophically and called back: "Wind's probably changed, we're getting towards the coast. We know that much. D'you think we're north or south?"

"Jest don't know," O'Gilroy had to admit.

"Don't worry, we've got plenty of gas. But best to know . . . There's a railway line: I'll do a bit of Bradshawing." And he tipped the Oriole into a gentle spiralling descent.

To 'Bradshaw', from the name of the British railway timetable, simply meant going down to read the name off a railway station. Hardly scientific, but very precise.

Andrew headed north along the line, down-sun where the visibility was better, then swerved and banked around a small village.

"Did you get it?" he shouted, curling away.

"No!" They'd banked towards Andrew's side.

"Damned oil on the goggles." Andrew pushed them up onto his forehead and wheeled the Oriole round and down for a second look.

O'Gilroy tensed: hadn't he been told that if you frightened up birds on the first swoop, you might hit them on a second pass? But it was his fault they were having to do this anyway. He kept quiet as they straightened and flattened close to the ground – then black shapes flickered for an instant, there was a thump and bang and Andrew screamed.

He must instinctively have jerked on the stick, because the aeroplane leapt upwards. Then he hunched forward, blood masking his face. "Take it! Take it!" And O'Gilroy reached around him to seize the stick, suddenly conscious of a new wind in his face, a wind that was slackening . . .

He pushed the rocking, swaying aeroplane forward, down away from a near-stall, looking ahead and trying to position himself in the sky. Horizon level – blast it! there was almost no horizon in that haze – just as level as possible . . . can't reach the engine controls; doesn't matter, the engine's running, God bless it; what had caused the *thump*, then? The windscreen's gone . . . They'd hit a bird and Andrew had got a face full of broken glass.

He was making grunting, gasping noises, pawing at his face with now-bloodied hands.

"Best leave it alone!" O'Gilroy shouted. "I've got her safe!" But he wasn't at all sure of that. They were crawling and rocking up in a wide and unintentional circle, because Andrew's feet were still on the rudder bar. "Push right rudder!" O'Gilroy ordered.

Andrew heard and pushed.

"A bit less . . . fine. Hold that."

"Can't see a damned thing!"

"Then leave it, ye'll make it worse. I think we hit a bird."

"Damn. Stupid of me." Andrew was leaning back as far as a big man could in that cockpit, speaking in gasps against the blasting wind. "Damn, damn, *damn*. How's it look?"

O'Gilroy snatched a look at his face. It was streaked with blood like crazy warpaint, but barely flowing. "Not much blood. Keep yer eyes shut. Ye'll be fine." Certainly the bleeding wouldn't kill Andrew; he himself might.

Suddenly that made him angry. So they expected him, the new boy, the bog-Irish amateur, to make a balls of it, did they? So he'd bloody well show them. Just knowing that he couldn't do worse than expected buoyed him up. He began a cautious, gradual turn towards the east again.

"Are you landing?" Andrew croaked.

"Not yet."

Perhaps he should, though. The land below was flat enough, the fields big enough – for an experienced pilot. But how near was any hospital?

Yet would he recognise the proper landing-field when he saw it? Andrew had had the instructions, he himself had concentrated on the navigation. Hadn't someone said there was an aerodrome at Venice itself? At an aerodrome they were used to injuries, and in getting there he might learn to fly this thing.

He took a deep oil-laden breath. All the precision, the time-keeping, were gone. Now it was step by simple step, and the first step was to reach the coast. If they really were north of Padua, he should aim south of east. He tried another turn. The Oriole was both more sensitive than the Boxkite and yet, he began to feel, more predictable. And he skidded outwards on the turn, but they'd taught him to do that rather than risk a spin by over-ruddering (though Andrew had kept his turns perfectly balanced). When – judging more by the sun than the lazily-spinning compass – he reckoned he was on course, he flattened out of the turn. Then, leaning against Andrew's shoulder to get a glimpse of the airspeed indicator and reaching left-handed across Andrew's thigh to clutch the stick, he tried simply to fly straight.

Instead, the Oriole gradually developed a rocking, switchback movement. *It was taking over.* Maybe that bird *had* done more damage, maybe half the tail was fluttering loose – he daren't look round – but then he realised he was over-controlling. He clamped the stick still and let the aeroplane sort itself out – in a slight downward turn – then corrected that. Moment by moment, it got easier.

"Not far now," he said aloud. But perhaps he was talking to himself.

28

Time in the dungeon was very exact, no "abouts" or "nearlys"; there was nothing else to do but note exactly when anything happened. Fifty-three minutes after Ranklin had been locked up, a guard came in with a metal jug of water and a worn but clean towel. Pero thoughtfully gestured for Ranklin to have first go, then muddied the towel without making too much difference to his face and hands.

One hour and seven minutes later, the door opened and Captain Novak came in. "I must apologise for the overcrowding, but this is the high season," he smirked in German. Then he reached behind him and effortlessly hauled the Conte di Chioggia past. "*Auf wiedersehn.*"

As the heavy wooden door slammed shut, the Count got his breath back, and spent nearly two minutes being outraged in alternate Italian and German. He promised to report everybody concerned to the Comandante (when he returned), the Chief of Police, and the Governor of Trieste. He was starting to list his connections in Vienna when a guard came back and shoved an armful of bedding at him. The Count dropped it, kicked it, but then seemed exhausted; he glared around.

"James Spencer," Ranklin said. "We met – briefly – in the Café San Marco."

"Ah? Then you know who I am. My humblest apologies for not recognising you immediately, but I had not expected . . . And our friend here?"

"His name's Pero. He seems to speak only Slovenian."

"My God! This is the final insult!" He swung round to tell the door, in German: "Police Captain Novak will be walking a beat in the sewers next week!"

Pero had been gazing at the Count with a loose smile. Now he

207

got off the bed and stuck out a welcoming hand, along with a quick burst of Slovenian. The Count stared at the hand as he would at a plague rat, spat some insult that rocked Pero back on his heels, and sat firmly on a chair.

Then all the firmness vanished, and he was suddenly old and frail. Ranklin sat up, expecting him to slide to the floor, but the Count raised a thin, trembling hand. "Please, I am just a little tired. Do you have a cigarette? Ah, thank you, thank you . . ." Ranklin lit it for him. Now he had only five left. He mentally shrugged and took one for himself.

*　　*　　*

Abruptly, the way things seemed to happen from the air, the city was *there*. An unmistakable terracotta-coloured shape, split by the bold S of the Grand Canal, had magicked itself out of the haze. And this was one city that didn't sprawl: where it ended, the sea began in swirled blue and green streaks of channels and mudbanks.

"I got Venice!" O'Gilroy shouted triumphantly. "Ye say there's an aerodrome here? *No* – don't try to look! Jest tell me!"

Andrew stopped struggling upright and, presumably, was trying to imagine the city below (actually, off their left wing). "On the Lido . . . big, long island . . . just east, out to sea, runs north–south . . . can you see that?"

The Oriole rocked as O'Gilroy craned to look. The blasted place was a spillage of islands . . . Then he realised the Lido was bigger than he'd thought, already stretching out on both sides of them.

"Got it. Bang over it."

"Right at the northern end . . . Should be there."

O'Gilroy began a cautious circle over the sea, peering down past Andrew. It must be there . . . yes . . . was it? *That* thing? Just a few sheds, a low line of what seemed to be fortification, and in the middle a patch of sun-baked mud.

"I've got the aerodrome," he said more soberly.

"Does it look okay?"

No, it didn't. But it was all he was going to get. "I'm going down for a look."

"Try to touch down at forty."

"Forty. Right." Only he wouldn't know, because when he was down on the edge of the stall he'd have no time to lean over and

consult the indicator. And he still couldn't reach the engine levers
... "Can ye reduce the power a bit? By the sound of the engine?"

Andrew's blind but experienced hand fell immediately on the
levers and the engine buzz slowed fractionally. The Oriole sagged
and O'Gilroy lifted her back. And a little more – the engine
stuttered and so did O'Gilroy's heart, but it caught again.

"Best I can do," Andrew panted. "Should be around a thousand revs."

As the Oriole slowed, her grip on the air became less firm. "It'll
do," O'Gilroy called, and let the nose drift down. Chimney smoke
showed the wind as coming from almost due south, so he came in
a gentle swoop from the north, over the sea, blipping the engine
to keep in a shallow dive. But each time the engine restarted, the
nose came up unless he synchronised it with a downward push. And
the wings rocked more in the uneven low-level currents, and she
pulled right as she slowed ...

"Left rudder!" he yelled, then, as the Oriole swerved wildly, had
a better idea. "Get yer right foot off!" And managed to kick his
left foot onto the rudder bar. Now he had more control, but was
using his wrong foot – would he remember *that* in a moment of
decision?

Suddenly his anger flared again. They'd expect him to get this
right, think because he'd flown the thing for half an hour without
crashing, he should at least be able to land safely ... And then
he shook his head, splattering sweat and oil. Self-pity was no help
now. Who were *they*? Fuck *they*. *He* was a pilot, and he had a
problem – just like any pilot. And whatever happened, pilots would
understand. And that was what mattered.

But he was going to land off this attempt. Andrew would never
get the engine revved up in time to drag them around for a second
chance.

"Keep yer foot pushing steady," he ordered. So, in effect,
Andrew's foot spring-loaded the rudder into a left turn which
O'Gilroy could override with his own foot.

"If we're over the sea," Andrew warned, "you'll get an up-draught
coming over the land."

"Right." He should have thought of that himself, but at least he
was ready with a forward push and a final blip to cut the engine
when the Oriole tried to rear. They rushed over a brief beach, a
very solid line of wall and then floated, floated, a foot or two above

the landing-field. Then fell with a thump and a swerve, rocking as O'Gilroy rammed his foot on the bar. And couldn't relax in time when the swerve reversed. He heard the bang as a tyre blew, but then they were still. And upright.

"Beautiful," Andrew croaked. "Just beautiful." He sounded very loud in the silence, and O'Gilroy realised the engine had stopped. He reached across to pull back the levers and turn off the petrol and ignition. It took all the strength he had left. And he still had to try and explain to the running men . . .

*   *   *

The cell darkened gently in the silence, the tiny semicircle of sky beyond the window turned yellow, then quickly russet and slowly grey. At 5.05 a bugle sounded, then at 5.35 a guard came in with a lit paraffin lamp and hung it on a bracket on the wall, warning that if they fiddled with it and burned themselves to death, no pension would be paid to their relatives.

"So now we know a little history," the Count observed. "Once such a thing happened and now it is in the regulations that such a warning must be given. Is there another cigarette?"

Ranklin noted that "is there"; the Count was truly democratic with other people's property. "There's two left. We'll save them for after dinner."

"Dinner?" The Count thought about it. "Yes. I imagine we will need a cigarette." He looked sideways at Pero – they were all three lying on their cots – who seemed to be asleep. "I am sure he will find it a banquet. Do you know why he is here?"

"He play-acted writing slogans on walls. But you could ask him yourself."

The Count chose to ignore his own grasp of Slovenian. "I am not sure of the etiquette of prison life. It is a long time since I was locked up and then for young matters like drunkenness and duelling, but is one permitted to ask what you are accused of?"

"I think Police Captain Novak believes I'm a spy."

"Truly? How very exciting."

"Perhaps. But I doubt that being in jail can be the most exciting part."

"Probably not. One thinks more of dark, mysterious women, secret treaties, rushing about Europe in the finest trains . . . No, I understand that sitting in damp dungeons would not be mentioned by the recruiting officer."

Ranklin was watching the shadows in the barrel vaulting above. Their edges moved, infinitesimally, with the tiny wavering of the lamp flame. "And yourself?" On the curve of the vaulting above the lamp, a smear of soot was forming on the whitewash.

The Count sighed. "I do believe these imbeciles place me in the same class as this fellow here – although, I trust, on a rather higher level. Accused of painting words on minds, not walls. But mostly, I think, it is the time of the year."

"I beg your pardon?"

"Do you know of Oberdan?"

"I've heard of him."

"He believed that Trieste was truly Italian and was executed thirty-one years ago for plotting against the Emperor's life. To be honest, I do not think he was a danger to anyone but himself. He only wished to be a martyr. And this is the time of year when he is remembered so, as the most notable Italian of the city, Captain Novak wishes me to be in prison until the time is passed. The man is a presumptuous moron even for a Slovenian policeman, and can do this only because the Comandante of the garrison is away. But when he returns . . . And possibly it is the same for you: you are just locked up until for the time of Oberdan."

Ranklin reckoned he was locked up for more specific reasons, but since Novak hadn't even interrogated him, couldn't be sure. "How long's that?"

"He was executed on the eighteenth of December."

Ranklin calculated. "Damn it, that's a good six weeks."

"True. But it will all be changed long before that. And once my distinguished friends and my lawyers know where I am, I will be free anyway, and then . . ." He paused, glanced at Pero, and turned stiffly on his side to face Ranklin. "I can ask my lawyer to work for you also," he whispered hoarsely, "but perhaps you do not wish to make our connection so public?"

This was the first time the Count had acknowledged any "connection", and it cheered Ranklin up. The Count knew things that he didn't, and had no-one else to talk to. But this couldn't be hurried, so he said: "That's very thoughtful of you. But I certainly don't want to incriminate you, so may we wait and see?"

The Count was silent for a while, then said in the same whisper:

"I hear some employers now pay a man his wages when he is sick. Most extraordinary. Do they – I mean, I wonder if they pay spies when they are in jail?"

*   *   *

The train reached Mestre after dark. Corinna took her time, letting the joyously tearful reunions that were so much part of the Italian railway system erupt before she stepped down. Anyway, this was Signora Falcone's territory; she was in charge. So she was startled when she came face to face on the platform with a figure as scruffy as any railway ganger and reeking of castor oil: O'Gilroy, alone.

"What are you doing here? Is Andrew . . . ?" It flashed through her mind that O'Gilroy couldn't have got there without Andrew, yet . . .

"He's in hospital but all right. We ran into a bird and he got bits of glass in his face, near his eye, but seems he'll be all right."

"My God! Did you crash? Which hospital? – where?"

"In Venice." He consulted a bit of paper. "Called the . . . the . . . here." He gave her the paper rather than try to pronounce Giudecca. "No, we didn't crash."

Corinna swung round to find Signora Falcone coming up behind her. "Did you hear?"

"Yes. Terrible – only Mr O'Gilroy seems to have saved the day." She was reappraising him with a wary smile.

"Where's the hospital? How do I get there?"

Signora Falcone hesitated, then realised it was pointless to do anything but smooth Corinna's path. "I'll see to it."

Corinna may have gone as far as stamping her foot with impatience, but knew it was pointless to interfere. Then, frowning in thought, she tried to imagine the accident, and . . . "Did he manage to land here, then?"

"Had to do it meself. Went and burst a tyre. But they say—"

"Hold on: that airplane's only got one set of controls. On his side. My God! – you must've . . . You saved his life!"

"Me own was there with him."

Her face suddenly bloomed into a radiant grin. "You're quite a guy, Mr O'Gilroy. Thank God you were there."

"Ah, 'twas nothing special . . ." He lapsed into a mumble and was clearly going to stay there.

"All right, I won't gush. And the airplane's all right?"

"Like I said, I burst a tyre, only they reckon they'll have one to fit or mebbe find two whole new wheels – if somebody'll pay for them."

"Heavens, don't worry about that."

Then Signora Falcone came back with a man who was probably one of her staff. "It's best to catch the mail steamer from Fusina. Matteo will drive you and see that you get back. Do you want to go, too, Mr O'Gilroy?"

O'Gilroy hesitated and Corinna chipped in: "There's no need. You must be done in, Conall. Get some sleep – and thanks again."

The Falcone family seemed well endowed with motor-cars; whatever the Signora and O'Gilroy climbed into wasn't a taxi-cab, and nor was the racier affair Corinna and Matteo had zoomed away in. This one went off at a pace consistent with the tasselled pelmets at the windows, but was soon beyond the lights of the town and rolling on through flat, dark countryside. Sinking back into deep leather, O'Gilroy found himself yawning; as always, it wasn't life's incidents that were wearing, but the long aftermath of explanation, clearing up – and waiting.

After a time, Signora Falcone said: "I hadn't realised you were a proper pilot yourself, Mr O'Gilroy."

"I'm new to it."

"But you must have been very competent. Have you flown that particular machine much?"

"Not much at all."

That kept her quiet for a while. Then: "When do you think Mr Sherring will be fit to fly again?"

"I'd guess a while yet. They'd bandaged over his eyes and was talking about keeping him quiet and dark."

Another silence. "If you could practise tomorrow, would you feel up to a demonstration flight on the next day?"

The Oriole wasn't built for Pégoud-style stunts: all it did was take off, fly and land. And after an hour or two's practice . . . "Surely. Mind, I couldn't be telling all the figures of its range and fuel consumption—"

"That won't matter."

"—and they'll need to be fixing that wheel."

"That will be done." It was the positive statement of someone used to having her orders obeyed. "You're quite happy about it, then?"

O'Gilroy was happy, all right, both at getting to fly the Oriole again and being in the middle of events. But he was also wary because he wasn't sure what event was planned. Still, if they were relying on him as a pilot, they were handing him control.

"Surely," he said confidently. "That'll be jest fine."

29

The distant bugle call that began the day came as a relief. Night in jail was not fun. When there was light, you could think of the reasons why you would soon be out, but the darkness crushed all reason and hope. *They* had won, had forgotten you, and were sleeping peacefully. And you were alone with dozing thoughts, not even the exotic terrors of nightmares, just coldly logical and gloomy. Ranklin loved that bugle call.

He sat up and realised he must at least have lain still a long time, since he was horribly stiff. The Count, a good twenty years older, must feel like a corpse.

Perhaps he *was* a corpse, Ranklin thought in a sudden panic. Died before I've found out what's really going on. But when he leaned over to peer through the gloom, the old man was blinking and mumbling under the thin blankets. Only then did it occur to Ranklin that it had been a rather selfish thought. So he got all the way up, shook his shoes to make sure nothing had crawled into them, then went to piss in the enamel bucket and splatter his face with dusty water.

Pero sat up quickly, his smile as bright as ever, and made pantomime gestures of how the Count must feel. It was intended as sympathy, but the Count caught a glimpse and husked: "Please do me a favour and kill that damned Slovene."

* * *

O'Gilroy was woken by a manservant with a tray of coffee. He lay for a minute or two wondering where he was before remembering he didn't know. The ride in the dark last night had shown him very little, and the conversation had been either in Italian or about more important things.

At least he had no problems about what to wear: it was still the tweed suit he had left Brooklands in, the cleaner of two shirts and (he hoped) a fresh collar. He'd meant to buy more in Paris or Turin, but there hadn't been time. He got shaved and dressed and found his way downstairs.

The house was grand but, he discovered, a simple square block. Bedrooms and bathrooms led off a wooden gallery that formed a hollow square, while below was a large living space surrounded by dining-rooms, drawing-rooms and God-knows-what rooms. Kitchens and staff quarters must be below that, half buried in a semi-basement.

Corinna didn't wake for another hour, but had a better idea of where she was: in Senator Falcone's villa. If it wasn't by Palladio himself – and he couldn't have designed every one of the hundreds of such villas in the Veneto region – it was in his style: symmetrical and classical. Her window, once she'd pushed open the shutters, looked out past a colonnaded portico to the formal garden, maybe a quarter of a mile of it before the River Brenta. A steam-launch was just chugging off from a landing-stage and heading downstream, probably to the lagoon and Venice, which she reckoned was a dozen miles away.

Downstairs, she was served coffee, toast (of leavened bread, thank goodness or Signora Falcone's Irish background) and even offered a boiled egg. Then she began asking questions, and learnt that the Signora and O'Gilroy had already gone to the Lido in the launch, she to make sure the aeroplane was repaired, him to fly it, while Matteo would again get her to the hospital when she was ready. And – this from the major-domo, who had rather more power over the household than the grandest of English butlers – would she inform them if she wished to move to a hotel in Venice so as to be nearer her brother? She was, of course, welcome to stay, but the Signora would quite understand if . . .

Corinna said she'd decide when she'd seen how Andrew was. Did the telephone work?

But of course the telephone worked. Probably.

*　　*　　*

Ranklin had eaten far worse breakfasts than the Castello dungeons provided, and paid good money for some of them, too. It wasn't elaborate: coffee, bread and a few slices of spicy sausage, but it was all fresh. And come to think of it, it might be more trouble to store things until they'd gone stale than just send down a helping of whatever the Castello guard was getting – particularly since they might well be the only prisoners. He didn't believe Novak about the dungeons being crowded. The way the lamp-smoke had stained the wall showed this one hadn't been used since it was whitewashed, and that was weeks ago. You couldn't be in the Army and not be an expert on whitewash.

"Tell me," the Count said, "that I only dreamt we had smoked our last cigarettes."

"No dream, I'm afraid." Ranklin displayed his empty case.

"Ah me," the Count sighed. "How can we continue the fine old tradition of bribing prison guards if we do not meet them? Never mind. Soon my friends will know where I am, and then . . . I will send in cigarettes to you if they allow it. English ones may not be possible, but . . ."

"Have you really got friends in high places?" Ranklin asked innocently.

The Count seemed pained. "I have friends everywhere; you must not think I am blinded by my noble birth. But, as I am sure you already know, the title of a Venetian count is quite equivalent to marquis from anywhere else. And I admit that I find my best friends are those who understand that simple fact. So yes, indeed I have friends in what you call 'high places'." He glanced at Pero, apparently asleep on his cot, but by now seemed to have accepted him at face value. Still, he lowered his voice. "I may also tell you, in the greatest confidence, that I have taken trouble to impress those friends with my loyalty to the Emperor. I even applied for Austrian nationality. Probably they will not grant it, no matter what they say their policy is, but that is of no consequence. What greater proof of loyalty can they ask?"

Ranklin grunted. He couldn't see the point of such a move. But at least he had the Count talking in confidence. The trick now was not to rush, let the man take his time. He suggested: "Possibly they assumed it *was* only to cause them embarrassment."

"Perhaps – but they could not help being flattered that a man of my birth should ask to become an Austrian citizen. I mean," he added quickly, "not a citizen in the French meaning. I would, of course, retain my title. It has a most splendid history. My

217

great-grandfather . . ." And Ranklin had to smile and nod his way through a personalised *Almanac de Gotha*. But, he told himself, there's still time. One thing you weren't short of in jail was time.

*   *   *

Signora Falcone's crisp instructions and the chink of gold coin got a new set of wheels – they hadn't a suitable tyre, or so they said once they smelled the gold – on the Oriole by lunchtime. That left the afternoon for O'Gilroy to get in an hour's practice, refuel, and fly the aeroplane over to the pasture across the road from the villa. Signora Falcone was very insistent that the demonstration flight should start from there. It all seemed a bit odd – or foreign – and O'Gilroy's suspicions were showing healthy growth. But his mind was a pretty suspicious place at any time, and he concentrated on learning the Oriole.

He had been left a picnic of bread, cheese and something called 'salami', since the nearest restaurant on the Lido was nearly a mile away and probably thought more of its reputation than of his suit. Then the local mechanics helped him start up the Oriole, turn her into wind – and he was on his own.

After half an hour of weaving and banking at three thousand feet he felt confident enough to start practising landings. With its high wing, there was little tendency to "float" – scoot along just above the ground with the far wall getting closer. She just sat down firmly and stayed down. But coming in for the last one, he felt a flood of stickiness over his left foot, saw there was no drip showing in the oil-feed glass, and just scraped over the near wall with a dead engine.

They pushed the aeroplane into the half-shade of a shed and he smoked a cigarette while waiting for the engine to cool. There was no doubt about the problem – his shoe squelched with castor oil (the oil tank was just above the rudder bar) – only the solution. The mechanics were fascinated by the short length of fractured pipe, once he had got it unscrewed; they just didn't have any ideas about mending or replacing it.

*   *   *

The dungeon lunch confirmed Ranklin's view that they were

getting straight soldiers' fare: some sort of stew with rice and a plate of figs, with a flask of wine. And again not stale; the wine tasted only a few days old. He and the Count exchanged horrified glances at the first sip, then watched Pero lap it up, and flop back on his cot snoring.

But by now, the Count was getting agitated. He consulted his watch every ten minutes – Ranklin had given up on that, lapsing back to timing himself by the bugle calls – and muttered: "But my friends, *one* of my friends, must have asked where I am by now? Come, I must walk."

So they paced solemnly around the perimeter of the cell, just as if it were the Piazza Grande except for a detour past the latrine bucket.

"What does that peasant of a police captain achieve in keeping us here?" the Count fretted.

"Last night, you said it could be until the Oberdan 'season' is over – another six weeks or so."

"For you, yes. But why me? And he does not even question me. Why not? If I am arrested I have a right to be questioned, to explain. Not, of course, that I have to explain myself to that uniformed monkey."

"Maybe he's afraid of you."

That brought a spring to the Count's slow pace. "Yes, yes. Well may he be afraid of me. And soon he will have even better reason."

Ranklin seized the opportunity and put on a carefully worried voice. "Perhaps it's this place that's getting me down, but I can't help worrying about the aeroplane, whether it's truly capable of the job . . ."

The Count glanced at him sharply. "Giancarlo has seen it, he has flown in it. And he is an expert. Why should it not be capable?"

"Oh, I don't know . . . I know very little about aeroplanes, but flying all the way from Turin . . ."

"Not from Turin. They take it to Giancarlo's house by Venice. They did not tell you?"

"Oh good, they *did* decide on Venice," Ranklin said hastily. He gave a satisfied nod as if a minor detail had been cleared up and they strolled on, round and round.

But now he was beginning to fret, too. He'd thought of having plenty of time, but it was passing. And perhaps he'd subconsciously been thinking that as he'd been first in, he must be first out – and that was nonsense. At any moment, one of the Count's friends might whisk him away, ending any revelations.

It was time to stir things up. "And I hope," he said, "there's enough ammunition for the Lewis guns?"

The Count stopped dead. "The Lewis guns?" He sounded surprised but, significantly, didn't need to ask what they were.

"The two Falcone got from Britain."

"He told you?" The surprise in the Count's voice was almost horror.

"Oh—" Ranklin waved his hand and smiled; "— we, my people, *are* in the business of knowing things."

"Yes . . . yes . . ." The Count was obviously thinking quickly. "He has many interests, the Senator. I believe he bought the machine-guns for the Italian Army. To test, to see if they will buy them."

"Really? That wasn't what I heard."

"Then you heard wrong! Now, I have had my exercise, I must rest." And he laid himself, limb by aged limb, on his cot.

Rather than just stand there, Ranklin sat down himself, turned so that nobody could see his face. I wrecked it, he thought. I ran it into a wall.

But perhaps the wall had always been there. So much he was expected to know, but other things he wasn't. And the Lewis guns were on the far side of the wall. He had expected a touch of flamboyance in this plot; now he smelt a Borgian twist as well.

But just what plot? Nobody had said it was actually *impossible* to mount a Lewis gun on Andrew's aeroplane. What did seem impossible was getting Andrew himself to pilot a flight intended to spray a city with machine-gun fire. But if Falcone had another pilot standing by, and the firing wasn't supposed to be accurate but just a dramatic gesture, the whole thing became possible. Insane, but possible.

Damn it, it would be an act of war! And put Italy so far in the wrong that they'd hang Falcone for it, no matter what happened next. The Count might dream up such a plot, but Falcone was a practising politician . . .

I'm missing something, he thought. And just how much is Dagner missing? – or rather, how much does he know?

*   *   *

At five o'clock the Falcone launch arrived at the northernmost of the Lido's jetties with Corinna already on board, a loose white dress fluttering in the breeze, clutching on a wide straw hat. "Hi. Signora Falcone's having the vapours about where you'd got to and thinking you'd broken your neck. You *haven't* broken your neck, have you?"

"Jest this." O'Gilroy gloomily held up a few inches of oily copper pipe. "Oil feed. And seems nobody on the island can braze it, or don't know what the devil I'm talking about."

"Poor you," she soothed. "D' you want me to try my Italian?"

But by now the launch helmsman had taken a look. He said something to Corinna, who asked him to repeat more slowly, then she grinned at O'Gilroy. "Seems one of the chauffeurs back home can do it in a trice. Always doing something like it to the automobiles, he says. You'd better bring it aboard."

O'Gilroy hesitated, then stepped into the boat. "They'll have to bring me back to fix it and I want to do a plug change while I'm at it . . . Won't be getting the Oriole across today, I'm thinking."

"Then it'll have to be tomorrow. How is it, flying it from the proper side?"

O'Gilroy's gloom vanished. "Ah, it's like . . . like I don't know the words for it. Riding a winner at the Curragh, mebbe."

She grinned back. "Little brother knows his stuff, then?"

"Surely – and how's he doing?"

"Not so bad at all. Mostly bored, with the bandages still on and not able to read. I talked myself hoarse until I found a priest who speaks English and accepts donations to the Church. Then this boat arrived and I learned you'd gone missing – why didn't you telephone them?"

"In Italian, and not knowing the number besides?" And also, though he wouldn't admit it, because he wasn't yet used to the world of telephones and simply hadn't thought of it.

Once clear of the gondola routes and little islets, the helmsman started showing off like any chauffeur when the owner isn't on board: they streaked across the lagoon like a torpedo boat. Corinna thought of telling him to behave, decided it would be improper and simply threw her hat on to the bottom boards and let her black hair

221

stream in the wind; perhaps the Signora would lend her a maid to untangle it.

"Have you learnt any more about tomorrow's demonstration?" she called.

"Never a word."

She tried again: "Well, whatever it is, Andrew's out of it."

"Sounds like that's what ye wanted."

"Let's say I've got my doubts."

O'Gilroy considered. "Like what?"

She'd rather have said this with quiet significance, not bellowed it against the wind and rumble of the engine, but: "That it won't be a demonstration but dropping inflammatory leaflets written by d'Annunzio over Trieste."

He stared at her. "Where d'ye get that from?"

"From that practice flight you told me about in Paris. And listening to d'Annunzio on the train. And because Pop Sherring didn't raise his little girl to believe everything she hears from big men with fifty-dollar suits and hundred-dollar smiles. Though," she admitted, "he may have slipped up with his little boy."

"Ye worked that out yeself, then . . ."

"They'll have to tell you pretty soon."

O'Gilroy thought a while. "I wish the Captain was here."

"D'you think Matt knows it and didn't tell you?"

"Mebbe . . ." Ranklin wasn't a naturally devious man, but over the past nine months he had been learning. O'Gilroy had helped teach him. "It's not his way, though, not with me."

"Perhaps he doesn't know everything himself."

O'Gilroy nodded vaguely and went back to his own thoughts. Ranklin trusted her – up to a careful point defined by their relationship, but he himself was right outside that. (To tell the truth, which he didn't like to do even to himself, he disapproved of the affair. Such behaviour was normal for Ranklin, an Army officer, and he had no illusions about the morals of upper-class British women, not after being in service at a Big House. But he had expected better of an American lady.)

Finally he said: "Ye really wouldn't want to be letting down the Captain?"

Corinna was about say something witty or withering, then thought again and just called: "No. I really wouldn't. And," she added, "I wish he was here, too."

"They're wanting to start a strike in the shipyard there."

She frowned over this, then: "Just that?"

"How d'ye mean?"

"These things can get out of hand, God knows they do in the States. In Trieste it could set Italians against Austrians. Or maybe that's what they want . . . Except that Falcone's a senator; he daren't get mixed up in . . ." She reflected for a moment. "Only he's doing a pretty good job of unmixing himself, letting d'Annunzio take the credit, and a foreign airplane flown by a foreign pilot . . ."

The launch slowed suddenly, curving skilfully, or so the helmsman wanted them to think, to avoid the milling boats at the mouth of the Brenta.

Meanwhile, O'Gilroy had become an intellectually rigorous Intelligence agent. "Jest how much of this do ye *know*, or would it all be guessing?"

Corinna almost pouted, but kept her voice low, now the engine noise had dimmed. "Guessing? It's logic. Deduction."

"So where's d'Annunzio? And the leaflets?"

"I bet he – they – both will be here tonight." She saw his look and hissed: "Suppose Matt had come up with the same idea, would you have believed *him*?"

With rash honesty, O'Gilroy said: "More like."

"Oh would you? Just because he's a *man*."

He seemed surprised. "No. Because he's a spy."

She sat back, stunned by the logic. Yes. Quite. What *was* the answer to that? "You don't *have* to be a spy to figure out other people for crooks," she growled.

They scurried the first few yards from the landing-stage to escape the cloud of insects, but could then stroll up the long garden. It was designed to frame the house: lines of cypresses and flowerbeds and stone walls all leading to it or at right angles from it. The villa itself, pink in the sunset, stood four-square on a slight rise, its 'ground' floor raised further so as to need impressive flights of steps on either side of the portico.

Seeing it without distractions for the first time, O'Gilroy broke the long silence. "Nice enough little place."

"Needs more gardeners," Corinna said succinctly. And correctly, because the formality was blurred by overgrowth, moss and crumbled stone. But it hardly mattered, since nobody could make decay as elegant as the Italians. "I must ask if it's genuine Palladio." She was quite sure O'Gilroy had never heard of him.

But O'Gilroy didn't ask. He was noticing other villas, half hidden by trees, a quarter of a mile away on either side. In Ireland and England, such houses would have been miles apart, each the dominating Big House of its area. But here, on a vast scale, they had built a Renaissance garden suburb.

It was like words, he was coming to realise. They didn't translate exactly, and nor did the patterns of life.

As they came near the house, O'Gilroy pitched his cigarette-butt into the dampest bit of undergrowth he could see and got a sharp look from Corinna. But at the last moment she relented as far as saying: "I don't know what orders you're following, but for what it's worth, I'll back you if you want to abandon ship. And I'll tell Matt that."

But he just muttered something gruff, and they walked up the cracked, mossy but still elegant steps.

*   *   *

With its thick walls, the dungeon was out of phase with the day. It was late afternoon when it had realised it was a warm day outside, but it took to the idea enthusiastically. Already bad-tempered, Ranklin had sweated on the itchy blankets long enough. He grabbed the water-jug, found it was empty, walked to the door and stab-kicked it several times. He heard the guard come scurrying down the corridor to peer through the Judas window.

"*Wasser, bitte, und schnell!*" Ranklin bawled, waving the jug at the guard's startled eyes. Looking back, he was a bit surprised the guard hadn't told him where to stuff the jug, but instead called a mate to stand guard while he hurried away to fill it.

The Count watched and said cynically: "The word of an Englishman – when shouted loudly enough."

So Ranklin tried again when the guard returned, demanding the window be opened. That, however, was definitely *verboten*.

224

"Perhaps," the Count observed, "you did not shout loudly enough that time."

Ranklin finished washing his hands and face and left them to dry by evaporation. "And perhaps," he said nastily, "you haven't as many friends in high places as you thought. Looks like you're spending another night here."

The Count sat up. "That is impossible. I cannot be here tomorrow."

"Hard luck," Ranklin said callously. Then that "tomorrow" echoed in his mind. "Why tomorrow? – because you don't want to be here, in the Castello, in their hands, when they realise just what you've been plotting? *Is it happening tomorrow?*" He grabbed the Count by his coat and hauled him up, shaking him like the frail old man he was, and Pero leaping up to intervene . . . But the Count's frightened nod had got through to Ranklin and he let go.

They all just stood for a moment, the Count trembling, Pero tensed to jump, Ranklin panting – but thinking. And deciding to play the cards he had; it was too late to hope for more. He looked at Pero. "Right: go and tell Novak I want to make a full confession. Go *on*, man, can't you see it's over? Get on with it."

Pero hesitated a moment longer, then smiled. "Almost I thank you, it was so very tiring." He went to the door, thumped on it, and called out in fluent German.

The Count had caught up with events and now his trembling was rage. "You, sir, are an English hound of extreme obscenity! You are . . . *without honour!*"

Ranklin considered this briefly, then nodded. "Yes, I do seem to be growing out of that."

*   *   *

Signora Falcone was having first-night nerves but the house servants must be used to it, because they tiptoed around her as they would around sweating dynamite.

"Just plain bad British workmanship!" she flared at the oil-feed pipe.

"Happens all the time," O'Gilroy said stolidly. "And mebbe I shook it up on yesterday's landing, along with the wheel. Thing is to get it brazed."

225

Signora Falcone controlled herself and called for Matteo. He took one look, started explaining the problem and its solution, but then saw her expression and vanished to the garage.

She turned to Corinna, smiling professionally. "And you, my dear, perhaps you'd care to bathe before dinner? I want to go over a few details of tomorrow's demonstration with Mr O'Gilroy."

There wasn't much Corinna could do but accept graciously. But she dawdled her way and managed to hear Signora Falcone saying: "Giancarlo – the Senator – will be back on the sleeper early tomorrow morning, so he will tell . . ."

Well, Corinna reflected, now Conall's finding out whether I, *a mere woman*, had deduced the truth about tomorrow's 'demonstration'. And as she turned along the gallery to her room, she ran into a distinct whiff of lavender water. So d'Annunzio *had* arrived, she'd been right about that, and walked slower until her nose and the sound of movement identified his room – next to hers. Probably that corner was all guest bedrooms; still, she'd remember to lock her door.

She took her time with bathing, dressing, and sorting out her hair – she now didn't want a strange maid distracting her – and thinking. With Andrew safely out of any plot, it really wasn't any longer her business. Conall could look after himself, might even be acting under orders – though he'd seemed genuinely worried – and Ranklin wouldn't thank her for interfering in British policy, if that were involved. It might be wiser to think of the House of Sherring's good name, since London had a way of having a quiet word with itself that could leave you suddenly out in the cold. But those schemers downstairs had still, she believed, planned to talk Andrew into something dirty. He'd probably have let them, too. She wasn't in a hurry to forgive that.

She came out of her bedroom wearing a royal blue evening dress and carrying just a small purse. The scent of lavender was still there, perhaps renewed. She paused, standing back from the balustrade of the gallery, and listened. There was a gentle babble of conversation in Italian from the big hall below. That was the hub of the house, onto which all the ground-floor doors opened and where both staircases began. People naturally gathered there and it had little Italian formality: chairs and small tables scattered in a way that would have been cosy if you couldn't have thrown a party for a hundred people in the space. D'Annunzio would be down there by now, and if she couldn't see anybody, nobody could see her. She stayed back by the wall and sidled towards his room, trying to remember just what a New York detective had told her about how a skilled burglar worked.

30

Probably Novak wasn't even in the Castello; certainly he would want to hear Pero report first and alone. Meanwhile, Ranklin was kept waiting in a room that was only slightly more office than cell, watched by two large soldiers. They regarded him with some awe, but also as if they could overcome that if he gave them an excuse. So he sat quietly, at first wondering if he were really betraying the Count and deciding, a little surprised, that the question was a waste of thought. What mattered now was working out just what Novak would believe.

At last he was called through into a slightly larger, military-style office with sheaves of printed orders and a couple of maps hung on the walls. Novak had placed himself behind someone else's table, Pero on a chair at one side.

"So." Novak glowered heavily and launched into his own brand of German; it was a good language for climactic speeches. "So we have an agent of the famous English Secret Service. Odd, but you look like any other slimy little spy to me. And Pero here has told me everything, *everything*, that you and the Count plotted together – see?" He flourished two pages of notes. "So your pitiful denials will be useless, quite useless. Your one hope – and it's a thin one, I warn you – is to make a complete confession. Because even more than wanting to watch you rot into fungus in some forgotten cell, I want to see the Count on the gallows. *Twenty years* he's spent plotting treasons at his café table, and now I have him in my hand. So: make your confession complete enough to hang the Count for treason and I might perjure my immortal soul to let you off lightly. Begin."

"Yes, that's fine, but it isn't what I wanted to see you about." Ranklin helped himself to a cigarette from the packet on the desk. "Actually, I need your help—"

Novak leaped to his feet, roaring: "I did not say you could smoke!

228

Especially not *my* cigarettes! *You want my help?* Dear God, for that I'll testify that you called the Emperor a fornicating old fossil and hang both of you for treason." He sat down and his tone made a chameleon change. "What made you think Pero here was an informer?"

"He was good," Ranklin lied, "but his teeth were too good for the rest of him. Just staining them isn't enough."

Pero smiled, then hastily shut his mouth and worked his tongue at the stains. "It feels horrible," he murmured.

"Was that all?" Novak demanded.

The honest answer was that Pero *had* to be an informer. There was no point in bringing himself and the Count together without someone to overhear. After that, everything about Pero, from the excessively greedy way he ate to the impersonal raggedness of his clothes, had seemed stagey, convincing from the back row of the stalls but not close to.

But honesty would only help them improve the act for the next British agent they nabbed. Ranklin shrugged and conceded: "His feet, too. Down-and-outs let their feet rot."

"Ach!" Novak's act became one of melodramatic delight. "You betray yourself! Such careful observation confirms you are a snivelling spy." He jerked his head at Pero. "All right, you can go and clean yourself up. Also, you might be sickened to watch what I may do to this disgusting maggot. You did well enough."

Pero clicked his heels at Novak, gave Ranklin a sympathetic grin, and vanished. Novak lit a cigarette and slumped in his chair. "Go on, say something. I'm beyond surprise. *Help*, Dear God." Behaving like an erratic fuse was obviously intended to keep Novak's victims off balance, worrying that he might explode. But behind it, Ranklin guessed, was a shrewd, nasty, and committed mind. But committed to what?

He took a cautious drag on his own cigarette, which tasted of perfume-soaked hay. "I assume you know that Senator Falcone has bought an aeroplane in Britain and plans to provoke a violent strike in the shipyards here. Naturally, the British Government dislikes having such plots hatched on its territory, so I came here to discover more. And, since you were kind enough to lock me up with the Count, I did discover more – but unfortunately not everything. Perhaps together, we can work out what's missing."

"Together?" Novak made a wild gesture of despair. "Now I'm

expected to collaborate with a loathsome creeping spy . . . But go on, go on."

"Tomorrow, they're going to fly—"

"Are you sure about tomorrow? Pero reports that you were trying to beat that out of the Count, but—"

"It's tomorrow: I could see the Count's face, Pero couldn't. Is it some anniversary of Oberdan?"

"This whole damned time is the anniversary of Oberdan," Novak grumbled, "but tomorrow has no special meaning. Continue."

"Tomorrow they'll fly over in the aeroplane and do something to try and stir up the strike – or worse, possibly. And I'd guess they're planning to spray the city with machine-gun fire."

"Guessing? You're *guessing*? You can't *guess* with me, you vile cockroach. You may cheat your English masters with your idleness, but with me you're pleading for your *life*! Remember that."

"Sorry," Ranklin said calmly, "but that's the best I can do."

"For the love of God," Novak grumbled. "Is this what the famous English Secret Service employs? I should have left you there another year or— Come in!"

But the officer of the Austrian Landwehr who had knocked so perfunctorily hadn't waited to be asked. "Ah, this is where you're hiding yourself. I've been looking everywhere." He sat down. "Remember to make sure this office is properly tidied before you go."

Although Ranklin had never seen him before, he already knew him well. Every army has its plump, fussy staff officers who go unerringly for the least important detail and stick to it. The Captain's stars on his collar were superfluous; the bunch of papers in his hand was his rank, his whole purpose.

He seemed to become aware of Ranklin and asked: "Who's this?"

Stone-faced, Novak said: "This, Hauptmannn Knebel, is an English spy."

Knebel didn't seem impressed. He looked at Ranklin again, but only as if estimating his value in paperwork. "Then hadn't you better get rid of him while we talk?"

"Ach—" Novak waved airily; "—I'm sure he already knows everything that's going on here."

"Then perhaps I should borrow him until this damned relief is done with."

Novak acknowledged the quip by baring his teeth, then said: "He has been conspiring with the Conte di Chioggia."

"Ah yes, it was about the Count." Knebel shuffled his papers. "I have just spoken to the Kommandant, in person, on the telephone. He orders you to release the Count immediately."

With Knebel, Novak had tried to curb his histrionics. But not now. "*Release* him? Just when I've *proved* he's a traitor? – after all these years?"

Secure behind his papers, his spectacles and an upturned but still non-belligerent moustache, Knebel seemed unconcerned. "Possibly, possibly, but your orders are still to release him. You can keep that one," he added, indicating Ranklin.

"But they're in it together! Listen, please listen to how I trapped them. Yesterday they met both at the Café San Marco and, more suspiciously, in the Galleria di Montuzza. So observe—" he held up a thick forefinger; "—that implicates this worm in whatever the Count is doing, but does not yet implicate the Count with this worm. You understand? But then, early yesterday, I get proof that this verminous—"

"Verminous?" That had been a mistake; vermin were something Knebel took seriously. "He didn't pick up anything in our dungeons. I've had those dungeons inspected every—"

"No, no." Novak waved his head in agitation. "It was just a way of talking. Poetic, you might say. Please let me continue. So – the proof implicates this . . . this man, and so each now implicates the other – you see? So I arrest them, put them together, and trap them into revealing more of their plots. And that is what has happened. Each proves the other is guilty!"

"Quite so," Knebel said indifferently. "But your orders are to release the Count."

"But," Novak wailed, "if one is not guilty, neither is the other!"

"Possibly, but the Count is not regarded as an enemy of the Emperor. You may not know this, but—"

"He's applied for Austrian nationality. Yes, of course I know about that nonsense."

"Hardly nonsense, as you would see if you gave it some thought. Whether nationality is granted or not, just applying will ruin his name in the Italian community. He's thrown away all his influence with them."

"And doesn't *that* tell you he's up to something worse than usual?

231

He wants to fool you into thinking he's given up plotting, just when—"

"Ah, but it isn't just the nationality, it goes further than that." Knebel smiled confidently. "However, I cannot discuss such matters."

"He *has* fooled you! He's got you playing his game!"

"*I* don't play games," Knebel corrected him. "I just obey orders. Whether you do the same is between you and the Kommandant – and, of course, your career."

Novak said something explosive in Slovenian, then controlled himself. "Then let me tell you what they're plotting. They've got an aeroplane, probably at Venice by now. No." He turned to Ranklin. "You tell him. Confess again."

Ranklin felt he was losing track of whose side he was on, but it was too late now. "It's expected to fly over Trieste tomorrow and perhaps fire a machine-gun—"

Knebel was shaking his head gently, and Novak snatched back the narrative. "They want to stir up the shipyard workers, delay the battleships, fill the streets with whizzing bullets – perhaps even *assassinate the Kommandant!*" That was desperation.

But it was no use: machine-guns are soldiers' business, and nobody is more relentlessly soldierly than a fusspot staff officer. Knebel shook his head again. "I can assure you that there's only one type of machine-gun light enough to be carried in an aeroplane and that isn't even in production yet."

Novak glared at Ranklin, who said nothing, then scrabbled through Pero's report. "Yes, here, my own informer heard them talk of machine-guns—"

"Hauptmann, I appreciate your enthusiasm, but it is leading you beyond your depth."

"But they've certainly got an aeroplane," Novak growled mutinously. "And if that flies over tomorrow—"

"It would indeed be a violation of our laws. But answer me truly: do you really believe our Italian workers are going to start strikes and riots because they've seen an Italian aeroplane fly over? – with or without machine-guns?"

It was like asking Novak to pull out one of his own teeth. His big body writhed in the chair. But it came out at last: "No. But—"

"Then stop acting like an old lady whose candle's blown out. And if an aeroplane comes, let us soldiers worry about it. So." He stood up. "I've passed on the Kommandant's orders: you're to release the Count. And if you still want to charge this one, complete the proper forms and we'll take him over. Now I've got the relief to worry about. Remember what I said about tidying the office – and open a window to get rid of this cigarette smoke. Good evening."

Novak watched the door close, then raged morosely: "Someone's trying to pull down his Empire on his head and he pisses his pants about *cigarette smoke!*"

But Ranklin was thinking about the gulf in attitude between the Slovenian policeman and the Austrian soldier. Perhaps here was Novak's commitment. And perhaps that gulf was wide enough for him to slip through. "So what now?"

Novak clamped his jaw and said through his teeth: "At least I still have you. If I can do nothing else, I can see you rot your life out in a dungeon. A truly verminous one, this time. And if there aren't enough vermin, I'll bring you more on visiting day!"

Ranklin nodded. "Yes, but that won't help tomorrow. What was he saying about a relief?"

Novak scowled. "For a spy, you don't like working at your job, do you?" Then he whacked his hands on the table-top, spilling an ashtray. "Dear God! – that's it! The changeover of regiments at the Caserma barracks. The old regiment gone and the new one wandering around looking for the piss-house and nobody with the key to the ammunition cupboard when the trouble starts! Only the Castle Guard here. *That's* why your friends chose tomorrow. Nothing to do with Oberdan – not much, anyway." He forced himself to calm down. "They've thought this out."

"Only you don't believe there'll be any trouble."

"They've planned so much, there must be more . . . And there's still those machine-guns – unless that was one of the Count's damned fantasies?"

"Oh no, Falcone got a couple in Britain, light enough to go in aeroplanes." And Knebel had heard of the Lewis gun, too, he was remembering.

"Then what are they going to do with them?" Novak urged. "Come on, you're supposed to be the spy."

"I'm not supposed to be spying for you," Ranklin pointed out. "However, if you let me go—"

"Ah! Yes! I *knew* it would come to that! Let a crawling, snivelling, contemptible wretch of a spy go free? Why should I? What could you do?"

"Get to Venice and try and stop it. Whatever it is."

Novak opened his mouth, then closed it and looked what was probably, for him, reflective. Finally he sighed and shook his head. "No – perhaps the time for cleverness has gone by. After all these years, I've got the Count where I want him. And I can still keep both of you: if I hide you away as two drunk-and-disorderlies, d'you think the Commandante's going to search every police station in the city? Then tomorrow, when your aeroplane does whatever it does, I'll be the hero. The Count will hang, you'll rot, and I'll be promoted. Piss on the Empire and politics, it's time for me to be a policeman again."

"You could keep the Count and still let me go," Ranklin suggested diffidently.

"Why?"

"Hauptmann Knebel heard me warning you about the plot."

"You were confessing. That *makes* you a spy, it doesn't let you off."

"But to defend myself in court I shall have to drag in every silly detail . . . Now, *I* don't blame you for sending assassins after Falcone, pretending to be from the Ujedinjenje. What else could you do? Mind," he said reflectively, "I do think it was a mistake to give them that Royal Navy pistol, so easily traced back to Trieste. Still, I expect there's no record of you taking it off the criminal who stole it."

Novak was pop-eyed with astonishment. "You're trying to *blackmail* me!"

"Blackmail?" Ranklin managed to look offended, but mostly because Novak had so easily seen what he was doing. "I'm trying to *help* you. We both want this thing stopped. And I'm even prepared to deny that you mentioned Falcone getting stabbed. It wasn't in the newspapers, you see." He smiled apologetically.

Novak thought briefly, then shrugged. "Policemen are supposed to know things."

"I'm just defending myself, I don't really want the Austrians suspecting a Slovene policeman's been poking into international politics, assassinating Italian senators and so on."

Novak sat back and sighed loudly. "I'm almost happy: my faith in your loathsomeness is restored. You really do want to see my career swimming in piss. But just remember one thing." His forefinger stabbed the air. "I *caught* you. Whatever else you do with your despicable life, always remember *I caught you.*"

He opened a folder and took out a creased slip of paper. "But I had help, and that isn't *sporting*, is it?" He held up an international cablegram.

It was actually sent *from* Trieste and addressed to Senator Falcone, c/o the Italian embassy, London. And in Italian, of course; Ranklin wrinkled his brow trying to read it.

"Perhaps your Italian is not so good as your German? I would be most happy to assist you." Grinning broadly, Novak whisked the cablegram back and read: "'Have met man calling self James Spencer who claims to have joined our syndicate' – ach, how delicately he puts that! And you were telling me you had never heard of the Senator! 'Is short, fat and fair' – such poetry! – 'Please confirm he is genuine.' Oh, this confirms you're genuine, all right: a genuine spy. Who foolishly trusted an amateur. Did he really think we would not read his cables because he is equivalent to a marquis? – or applied for Austrian citizenship? As another professional, I sympathise with you – just a little. This stays on your file."

He tucked the cablegram away, then tossed a cloth bag across. It held Ranklin's passport, wallet, pipe and so forth. "And should you ever think of coming back to Trieste, remember that file. It isn't under Herr Spencer, *but—*" he leant suddenly across the desk and leered into Ranklin's face; "—under Short and Fat. You can't change that."

*   *   *

The launch had already taken O'Gilroy back to the Lido (after an early dinner, Corinna hoped) so there were only three of them, d'Annunzio in full white tie and tails, to eat in the 'small' dining room. They dined by candlelight and Corinna reflected how quickly a display of electric lighting had become vulgar ostentation; even at her age, she could recall dining tables lit like a photographer's studio. They were served sea bass and duck, and d'Annunzio dug in heartily but drank only water.

Corinna waited for the conversation to come round to tomorrow's 'demonstration', then realised Signora Falcone was preventing that. It wasn't difficult, since d'Annunzio had two stage productions due to open in December – *Parisina* at La Scala and *Le Chèvrefeuille* in Paris – and was very willing to expand on his problems and hint at the triumphs to come. This went on until they were back in the central hall sipping coffee.

"But perhaps," he added with a smile, "history will say they are not the most important work of d'Annunzio in this year."

Signora Falcone gave him a warning frown but Corinna had her opening. "Ah yes, tomorrow's proclamation to Trieste," she said with feigned innocence.

D'Annunzio shot a startled look at Signora Falcone, who offered only a well-drilled smile. "What *can* you mean, my dear?"

"The leaflets Signor d'Annunzio's written. The ones to start the shipyard strike."

There was an offer of escape there, but also a trap, and in her haste to patch things over, Signora Falcone took the one without noticing the other. "Ah, you've been told about that. Our European politics must seem frightfully complicated and devious to you, but it's all part of the game. Over the centuries, nations have come to expect interference in each other's affairs . . ."

D'Annunzio was trying to suppress bewilderment. Perhaps he hadn't been told he was only starting a strike.

"Mind you," Corinna said when the Signora had finished, "though my Italian isn't all that good, it does come across rather strong for a strike call." And she unfolded a leaflet from her purse.

Manners forgotten, d'Annunzio leapt up to snatch it away. "You have stolen this!" he shouted. "You have robbed my bedroom!"

"Dear me, a woman in your bedroom? We can't have that, can we? I'd like to hear Signora Falcone read it. I never heard you on the stage, and I'm sure I missed a treat."

It was a tense moment. But Corinna would learn nothing more, and d'Annunzio was never loath to hear his own words spoken aloud. He took a sudden decision and thrust the leaflet at Signora Falcone.

She took it reluctantly, scanned it quickly since she wouldn't just be reading but translating, then stood up. She began stiffly, perhaps trying to play it down, but then the power of the words took over, and she relaxed, gestured, declaimed. And she was good.

"*From Gabriele d'Annunzio: To my brothers of Trieste, most Italian of cities, Courage! Courage and constancy! There is no enemy which*

236

cannot be destroyed by our courage!, no lie which cannot be deflated by your constancy! The end of your martyrdom is at hand! The dawn of your joy is imminent! The lions of St Mark will roar again at the sacred entry. The Carso will be ours by force of arms. I tell you, I swear to you, my Brothers, our victory is certain! The flag of Italy will be planted on your Great Arsenal. From the heights of heaven, on the wings of Italy, I throw you this pledge, this message from my heart . . ."

D'Annunzio leant forward, listening intently, nodding, mouthing with the words. And when she had finished, smiling proudly. "Bravo! Bravo! How I wish those words should not be thrown from a machine, but spoken by you from a great stage!"

Corinna said: "But like I say, no mention of a strike. To a simple American like me, it sounds like a call to arms. Declaration of war, even."

D'Annunzio frowned. "What is this strike?"

Back in her seat, Signora Falcone said calmly: "I do hope, my dear, that until the demonstration is concluded, you'll go on regarding yourself as our guest?"

Keep me shut up here? Corinna boiled. But I asked for it: they were never going to cry: "Alack! – all is revealed! We must flee." They'd invested far too much in this plot to let her louse it up that easily.

She began to feel frightened. And because of that, she hit back instead of stopping to think. "Okay, if that's what the British Secret Service wants you to do, who am I—"

And that really tore it. D'Annunzio's demand of: "Secret service? What is this secret service?" collided with Signora Falcone's yell of: "You stupid Yankee bitch!" There was a moment of loud confusion, then Signora Falcone won.

She stood up again. "Gabri, be quiet. This silly child is just trying to cause trouble, saying anything to get you angry. Don't let her. Giancarlo will explain everything when he gets here."

D'Annunzio gave Corinna a sullen glare. She said brightly: "But *I* know, don't I? D'you think the British Secret Service knows less?"

D'Annunzio's look swivelled to Signora Falcone, who said icily: "If you can't remember your manners as a guest, Mrs Finn—"

"You'll lock me in my room? I'm just making conversation, as a good guest should. About how the British Secret Service helped you get that airplane, lent you the pilot, approved the idea of recruiting d'Annunzio as a *secret agent*—"

237

"It's lies! She's making it up!"

Well, yes, she was, of course. But d'Annunzio had already detonated. "I do not work for the English! You have sold yourself *come una puttana* to the Secret Service, but I, d'Annunzio, *mi rifiuto!* I tear up my tracts! *Non parto più!*"

There were shadows behind the pillars beneath the gallery, the major-domo and Matteo, drawn by the shouting. Perfect poise recovered, Signora Falcone turned to them: "*Per favore accompagna il Signor d'Annunzio nella sua stanza e chiudilo dentro.*"

D'Annunzio stared at her. But whatever their past had been, it was long dead now. She was in total, icy command, ordering him locked away like a soldier with dirty boots. He had sense enough not to challenge her on her own stage, and let himself be escorted up the stairs and presumably to his room.

Signora Falcone remembered the threat to the leaflets and called after them: "*E porta giù un pacco di volanti.*" She turned back to Corinna. "I know Gabri: he will feel differently in the morning, with Giancarlo to reassure him." She sat down again. "Or if he does not, it is his words, not some figure in mask and goggles throwing them out, which matters. As long as he is not free to spoil the event, all will be well."

Could a woman *use* a man so coldly unless there were some great hatred, and consequently love, in their past? Corinna shivered.

"And that also applies to yourself," Signora Falcone smiled. "Now, I think we need some fresh coffee."

31

Novak came with Ranklin in the carriage, first to the hotel, where he threw his baggage together and picked up a cablegram from 'Finn', then to the Meridionale station. He didn't bother to read the cablegram: he didn't want to remind Novak of the Sherring connection.

"Do you know Venice?" he asked as they rolled along the lamplit waterfront.

"Do you not?"

"I haven't been there for years and I certainly don't recall any aerodrome."

"Ah, yes. They have made one at the north end of the Lido, on the old San Niccolò fort drill ground."

Ranklin paused to visualise this and the problem of getting there. He would need to find a steam-launch still in business in the early hours. But some were sure to meet any arriving train.

Novak said: "You will go first to the aeroplane, then?"

"Give me thirty seconds with a hammer and all bets for tomorrow are off."

"Most direct," Novak approved. He stayed with Ranklin at the station, saw him into his seat and was obviously going to wait until the train left. The uniform made it look as if Ranklin were being deported, but perhaps Novak didn't mind that.

"Tell me," Ranklin asked on an impulse, "are you in touch with the other assassin?"

Novak said nothing.

"I mean, if Falcone's fit enough to go back to Italy, is your bandit likely to turn up, too? He'll probably remember me."

Novak examined the glowing end of his cigar carefully. "Do you really think I am close to a man like that? I light his fuse – then I throw him far away. But for me, he is another chance to stop this

239

madness. So if, for some reason I cannot predict, you should fail
. . ." He shrugged, and then smiled widely.

When the train was moving, Ranklin took out Corinna's
cablegram. Now thirty-six hours old, it simply said she was going
to Venice and gave Falcone's address there.

The train rolled on at its own . . . well, you couldn't say "speed";
perhaps "pace". It was 140 rail miles and a frontier crossing to
Venice, but he had time. Surely nobody was fool enough to try
to fly in the dark.

*   *   *

Long after midnight, Corinna still sat in the hall. There was nothing
stopping her going to bed, save lack of tiredness and knowing that
if she went to her room she'd be locked in. "You can, if you want,
jump from the window," Signora Falcone had pointed out. "It's over
thirty feet down to a stone terrace, and quite frankly, I don't care if
you do."

Corinna now believed that. "Then what are you going to do with
me? – and d'Annunzio?"

"Giancarlo may have other ideas, but as far as I'm concerned,
you stay as guests until – say – noon, and then you can go where
you will and say what you like."

"Because by then Trieste should be in flames and it'll be too late
to care why?"

Signora Falcone may have given the faintest shrug.

"But why?" Corinna demanded. "Why rock the whole international boat? You must know—"

"Did you think Gabri's leaflet was just fine words? Oh no, my
dear, he's a spoilt child, but he speaks with the true voice of Italy.
An Italy that deserves to be great again, not living in shame. Not
hawking our favours in the streets of Europe, as that pimp of a
prime minister Giolitti's been doing. As he'll go on doing, if he
wins the November election. Giancarlo has been saying this in
the Senate for years. Now—" She broke off, shaking her head.
"You don't understand a word I'm saying, do you? No American
can understand what Italy's been through."

"I understand what a full-blown riot in Trieste could start. But
why? – you weren't born an Italian yourself, come to that."

"No, my dear, I was born Irish. And watched my parents and

their friends jostling to kiss the nearest pure English boot – does *that* tell you anything?"

Corinna was silent for a while, then tried to rally her old anger. "But you were going to involve my brother Andrew."

"He'd have known what he was doing." Signora Falcone dismissed the matter. "He could have refused. *Si?*" Matteo had come up beside her chair and begun talking quickly and quietly. Signora Falcone glanced at her gold wristwatch, gave a nodding reply, and Matteo headed for the front door.

"It's early," she explained, "but we need to make sure they stop the sleeper at Mestre to let Giancarlo off. In his condition, I don't want him rolling around in boats from Venice."

Corinna wasn't really listening. She was thinking about O'Gilroy piloting the flight and Matt being in Trieste – did *he* know what was going on? Or was he just obeying orders? And would Major Dagner give such orders? From her brief conversation with him, yes, he might well . . .

The doorbell rang, bringing Signora Falcone to her feet in surprise. "Surely not Giancarlo already, he may need help—"

From where she sat, Corinna could see the big front door, and the servant hurrying to open it. And then take several quick paces backwards as two men with guns pushed their way in.

* * *

Soon after four o'clock, Ranklin found himself a dark empty mile from where the aerodrome should be. It was a clear, moonless night and Venice itself was a low shape on the horizon sparked with random lights whose reflections wavered in the wakes of an occasional slow-moving ship. A big port never sleeps, just retreats into havens of lamplit privacy.

Getting a place on a steam-launch had been no problem; getting it to drop him at the northern jetty of the Lido, well away from the big hotels, had taken time and money. Maybe he should have got off at the main quay and found a cab . . . but what he was planning must be illegal. No witnesses. He tramped on alone.

He couldn't even be sure he'd found the aerodrome. What he had was a wall, obviously military, and not much higher than himself. The road led off to the right, but he reckoned that any gate must be locked and it was easier to climb the wall, which was sloped so

241

cannon-balls would bounce off. Getting down the far side, unsloped, took longer.

But now what? He was on the edge of what could be a drill-ground-turned-aerodrome, but beyond that all he could see was vague dark shapes against a dark sky. Certainly nothing that looked like an aeroplane. Perhaps it was locked in a shed, that seemed the norm at Brooklands. The only solution seemed to be to walk around the edge of the ground, investigating anywhere that an aeroplane might be pushed off it. He began trudging again.

Ten minutes later he had an extra idea, and lay down to peer from ground level, hoping the distinctive shape would show up against the sky. Still nothing. He started to get up – and a torch flared in his face, dazzling him.

"Try standing up quick and ye'll go down a sight quicker – Arseholes! What ye doing here, Captain?"

Fright, relief and sheer blindness kept Ranklin where he was. He rolled on his back. "Turn that blasted light off. What are *you*— Is the aeroplane here?"

"Sure it is, I was working on it 'til past midnight. Now, what was ye doing, sneaking around like . . . like a spy?" He hauled Ranklin to his feet.

"Looking for the damn thing." In the darkness, he didn't notice O'Gilroy's wince at hearing the Oriole called that. "But thank God I found you, too. Look, I've learnt in Trieste just what – roughly what – it's supposed to do today—"

"Sure and I know that. I'm flying it over to the Senator's house at first light. He'll be back by then."

"*You're* flying it?"

"Surely. Mr Sherring got himself banged about, we hit a bird . . . Anyways, I've been practising and—"

"You're actually going to fly the thing to Trieste?"

O'Gilroy winced again but said patiently: "That's the plan, isn't it? Ye mean ye weren't knowing about it?"

"Of course I bloody well didn't. Did you think I'd let you – *anybody* – go firing machine-guns over the—"

"Hold on, now. Machine-guns? Where are ye getting machine-guns from?"

Ranklin peered at him through the starlit gloom. Was it possible O'Gilroy didn't know? But if he was doing the piloting . . .

"All right," Ranklin said, "all right. Let's get this sorted out, Have you got a real cigarette?"

O'Gilroy lit both of them. Ranklin breathed deeply, got a violent coughing fit, and said in a strangled voice: "Now: just tell me what the plan is."

"Me and the poet feller, d'Annunzio, we fly ov—"

"*D'Annunzio?* The poet-playwright chap? – he's mixed up in this?"

"Surely. He's written the pamphlets. He throws 'em out over Trieste, then we fly back. Only Mrs Falcone, she didn't want us to start from here, but a field back near the house."

"Then where the devil do the machine-guns, the Lewis guns, fit in?"

"Jayzus, don't be asking *me*. They're yer own idea entirely. And anyway," he added, "ye'd need a mounting on the aeroplane – not that I'd be letting that feller fire a catapult from any aeroplane I'm flying."

Baffled, Ranklin regrouped himself on a known point. "But any dropping of leaflets is off, too. Have you seen the things?"

"No, and they'll be in Italian, anyways."

"Well, I bet they're urging more than a shipyard strike. They've picked a day when the main garrison's changing over, the best time for a real riot. Nobody seems to think that'll actually happen, but we don't want to be involved in either a riot or a fiasco."

O'Gilroy said nothing. In the sudden glow of his cigarette, Ranklin saw the lean face looking puzzled, undecided.

"Tell me this, then," he said quietly, "has Major Dagner been in touch, has he ordered you to be part of this?"

"No-o. I'm thinking he doesn't know 'bout me doing the flying at all."

"Then *I'm* ordering you not to."

He could almost hear the snap as O'Gilroy came to a decision. "Fine. Mind, I'd've liked the flight, but . . . whatever ye say. What are we doing now, then?"

Get out of it all, was Ranklin's thought. "You say you're expected over there at first light? Say six o'clock . . ." By then, they could be at Venice station instead, maybe leaving the Oriole disabled – but also leaving Corinna behind. The Falcones could hardly do her any harm, but for all that . . . "Can we telephone the house from anywhere here?"

"Surely. In the office yonder, I've got a key. I called to say the aeroplane was fixed and all jest a while back."

O'Gilroy had the number and what to say to the operator written out in careful phonetics, but Ranklin took over. He decided to be somebody from Sherring's wanting to talk to Corinna.

The telephone was answered remarkably quickly for a household that should have been asleep. A man's voice said simply: "*Si?*"

"Do you speak English?"

Then, from the background, a woman's voice yelling: "Giancarlo! Ne—" The telephone was cut off.

Ranklin looked at O'Gilroy; he had heard the yell. "Mrs Falcone, most like. Something funny, d'ye think?"

Ranklin called the operator to get the number again, waited, then put the instrument down. "He says the telephone's disconnected. Broken."

O'Gilroy took it very calmly. "Sounds bad."

Novak's second assassin.

"Someone could be waiting for Falcone himself, holding the women as hostages – how quickly can we get there?"

O'Gilroy shrugged and glanced out at the sky. "Twenty minutes. If ye don't mind a broken neck."

32

The takeoff, as O'Gilroy had promised, was only normally terrifying. The engine pulled well in the cool night air and they climbed in a wide circle over the sea and headed for the mouth of the Brenta. Perhaps awakened officials below were thumbing their law-books, but Ranklin was feeling the aeronaut's heady and dangerous detachment from earthly regulation.

"Will you know the house?" he called.

"Mebbe. But 'tis the field that matters."

Ranklin looked around at the landscape and it wasn't frightening, just totally unfamiliar. The dark shape of Venice was sparked with lights like diamonds on a dung-heap, then inland a spatter of sparks that must be Mestre, but beyond it lay nothing. For the first time he thought of night as something tangible, a black flood that had settled on the land.

But at least he could see the coastline and river banks as the water dutifully reflected even the thin starlight. Just follow the river and they should wind up close to the house. Fairly close anyway.

On his side of the cockpit, O'Gilroy was sweating. He'd managed to sound confident about flying at night, and the takeoff had fooled him into thinking he might be right. But the step from two dimensions into the freedom of three was never tricky. Now the glib conviction that he'd be able to see enough was dimmed; darkness made everything not only dark but fuzzy, like a thick coating of soot. The instruments didn't matter; he could feel the speed and hear the engine revs. But he had to *see* the faint line of the horizon, and occasionally he lost it behind the wing and the aeroplane wavered as he fought a dreadful dizziness. If you couldn't see which way up you were, you died. That was the law, as simple as gravity.

And when it came to landing, to shedding that extra dimension

... He'd made Ranklin carry a length of rag, soaked in both oil and petrol and wrapped around a stone, to light and throw out as a landing flare. And the man had trustingly accepted that that made everything all right, that now O'Gilroy could cope. Officers could be so gullible.

Only now O'Gilroy *had* to cope ... Officers could be so crafty.

Quite unaware of all this, Ranklin called: "Have you got a pistol with you?"

"No. Mrs Finn said 'twas a jailing matter in Italy. Have ye one yeself?"

"No. A marvellous pair of secret agents we are." He thought about the possibilities. "Did Corinna leave hers behind?"

"Not her." No, Corinna believed laws applied only to others. It was infuriating how often she was right.

"It should be in her room, then. She may be asleep there ... Can we sneak in?"

"Not so easy. And we're not there yet ..."

The villas were strung along the north bank of the Brenta, and O'Gilroy was keeping well to the south so that he could see the river to the right without leaning over. At that range, only a line of occasional lights – wondrously sharp and unsooty – showed there were any houses at all. But the distance meant, he hoped, that nobody at the villa would hear the engine, particularly if they were in the central hall, where the telephone was.

Trying to recognise the outlines of the landing-stages on the river was no help: they all had landing-stages. But now the white villas themselves showed as faint blurs of not-quite-darkness contrasting with the extra-darkness of tall trees around them. The Falcone villa had no tall trees.

Ranklin was also staring. He turned to ask: "D'you think we're there yet?"

"Hope we've passed it." O'Gilroy curved right, edging across the Brenta and then the line of villas, to reverse his course out on the far side of them. Now he looked for the pasture where he should land, but without losing sight of the villa that *might* be the one—

Ranklin said: "If they're expecting Falcone back, there should be outside lights on."

Bless the man. Only two villas showed such lights. Which meant that *that* must be Falcone's, and *that* the landing-field ahead. Now that he was heading east, the horizon was more distinct with just the slightest paleness of the new day. But real light was half an hour away, and twilight a treacherous time when you imagined more than you saw. This landing was going to be real, not imagined.

"Right, Captain: light the flare."

He felt, more than saw, Ranklin lean down to strike a match. He himself kept his head turned away to save his eyesight, but turning the aeroplane to lean Ranklin towards the ground. He heard a curse as one match failed, then the cockpit exploded with light and he shut his eyes.

Ranklin said: "Christ!" Then: "It's gone."

O'Gilroy reversed the turn and saw the fluttering spark getting smaller against the dark pasture. Then stop, almost vanish, and flare up again.

"Right." He snapped off the ignition and tilted the aeroplane down, keeping the speed – the tune from the wires – high, and weaving gently, like a man moving his head to judge the distance, watching the angle between the flame and the horizon close and close . . . Back on the stick, and the wires hummed lower, too much, stick forward again, and back, forward—

"Brace yeself," he warned. "May not be me best—"

They hit.

*   *   *

The wrought-iron gates of the villa had been left open, and they slipped through, past a small old car that O'Gilroy didn't recognise, and through shrubs and dwarf cypresses around to the back of the house, away from the lights. By then, Ranklin appreciated the problem: Palladio had believed in high, airy ground-floor rooms, so the bedrooms were a long way up. And up plain stucco'd walls with no foot- and hand-holds, except the drainpipes added in later years. These were tucked within the corners where the portico joined the main wall, and from the portico roof you could reach small windows on either side.

"Tis me own bedroom up there," O'Gilroy whispered. "Almost legal, ye might say."

"Can you do it?"

"Like enough." He grasped the pipe: it was fat and solid. "Surely."

They went softly across the terrace to the french windows. Inside was a short, doorless corridor into the main hall; at the opposite side of the villa, a similar corridor led to the front door. The hall was lit, and there was occasional movement.

After a couple of minutes, O'Gilroy whispered: "I see two of them."

"Yes." Ranklin thought he recognised the man from the taxi at the Ritz, Silvio. He didn't know the second man, actually Jankovic, but wasn't surprised that there were two. You could hardly hold captive a house full of servants single-handed. "I can't see either of the women."

"Be sitting down ... That's Mrs Finn, to the right, wearing blue."

"Thank God." They backed away along the terrace.

"Captain," O'Gilroy said, "if'n no harm's come to Mrs Finn yet, I'm thinking she's safe until Falcone gets back anyhow. So why'nt we stop him on the road? – he'll mebbe have a gun. And now we know there's two of them ..."

"All right." They started back around the house. "Will you know his car?"

"Seems he's got dozens. Won't be small, anyhow."

"Then we'll stop everything."

But there was nothing to stop. A farm cart plodded past, going the other way, then they just stood and began to shiver in the pre-dawn air.

After a while, Ranklin said: "I want to be quite clear what we're doing. We're going into that house *only* because Corinna's there, no other reason. And I think we can get her out more safely than the Carabiniere – the police."

"Surely we can."

"And if you go inside, you'll be closest to her."

"I will that," O'Gilroy said evenly.

"I just wanted to be sure." After another while, he said: "I'd rather like to take one of those men alive and confessing who sent them. It was a police captain in Trieste and I'd like to see him disgraced, dismissed – for purely professional reasons."

Far down the road, headlights flickered between the trees. O'Gilroy said: "Jest professional reasons."

"That's right. So that I can go back there some day."

Now they could hear the hum of a powerful motor moving at a decorous speed. "Even with two guns, it'll be trouble enough taking these fellers dead, never mind alive. Which d'ye want most, Captain: the women safe or taking prisoners?"

There was a pause. Then Ranklin nodded. "All right. We forget about prisoners." They stepped out and waved their hands.

The car was the high Pullman-bodied one with tasselled curtains that had brought O'Gilroy from the station, and Matteo was driving it. He drew up gently, recognising O'Gilroy – and then a rear door opened and Dagner stepped out.

Ranklin was astounded. And so must Dagner have been, only he had recognised them in the car's headlights and had time to choose his expression and voice. He was brisk: "Captain – I thought you'd still be in Trieste. And O'Gilroy. Does this mean a problem?"

Ranklin, still dazed, just managed to be polite. "Major . . . What on earth are you doing here?"

"Travelling as the Senator's personal physician." Behind him, Ranklin could see the bulky shape of Falcone sitting very upright on the back seat. Matteo took the opportunity to get in and fuss, re-arranging the rug and making soothing comments. Dagner lowered his voice. "And taking an excuse to get out into the field again, making sure this operation goes ahead smoothly. What do you have to report?"

Ranklin had quite a choice, including the question of the Bureau being left leaderless eight hundred miles away, but restrained himself to: "There's a fair selection, but most immediately, a couple of assassins are waiting for the Senator at his villa, with his wife and Mrs Finn as hostages. Have you got a gun with you?"

Dagner paused. Then: "No. No, I'm afraid . . . I gather it's unlawful in Italy."

But Falcone had been overhearing. "Signora Falcone, is she safe?"

"I wouldn't say safe, but I think she's unharmed. Have *you* got—?"

"Yes, yes, it is in my luggage. But you must be very careful . . ."

It was the Browning Ranklin had seen before, just like O'Gilroy's, and he instinctively passed it to him. Falcone added: "There are many guns in the villa, but . . ."

Ranklin could guess at a whole cabinet of shotguns and hunting rifles, but in a downstairs room they couldn't reach. "Well, it's a start. Back to plan A."

"What's that?" Dagner asked.

"We think we can get hold of another pistol and do a bit of outflanking if O'Gilroy can get up to a bedroom window."

"Sounds rather complicated." He was taking charge now. "We ought to think this out—"

"Major, we've been thinking it out, and reconnoitring the house, for half an hour. We *must* get somebody inside before we do anything else, or the women . . ." He shrugged. "The ground-floor rooms all open onto the hall, that means O'Gilroy getting in through the bedroom floor, so he may as well look for a second gun while he's at it. Or just call the Carabinieri and let them handle it all."

He risked nothing by suggesting that; he knew Falcone wouldn't want it, or the explanations it would lead to.

And turn it down he did, but added: "But you must be sure you save Signora Falcone."

Ranklin didn't answer him. "Then we'd better get going while it's still dark enough."

"Fine," Dagner said. "I'd like to see how you two work. If you can fit me into your plan, fine. If not, I'll keep out of your way."

Ranklin made a face he was glad Dagner couldn't see. He knew senior officers who promised to do just what they were told. Then he started rethinking.

Despite his height, once they were inside the gates Dagner showed all his Khyber cunning, moving like the shadow of a snake through the tangled garden and up onto the back terrace. Artillery training didn't involve creepy-crawling and Ranklin felt distinctly bovine, lumbering behind him.

Then, with the eastern sky definitely turning grey, they watched O'Gilroy, barefoot and coatless, clamber up the drainpipe. He climbed without haste or scrabbling, sometimes walking his feet up the walls on either side, sometimes using joints on the pipe. A few flakes of white paint fluttered down.

"Has he done this before?" Dagner whispered.

"Shouldn't wonder."

O'Gilroy vanished over the portico roof, and there was a slight creak as a shutter was eased back. A minute or so later, a faint glimmer showed behind the shutters of the next room along, Corinna's, and Ranklin could visualise what O'Gilroy was facing:

without a maid, Corinna's bedroom would look like an anarchist outrage in a dress shop.

That was indeed how it struck O'Gilroy. He tried one handbag – too light – another that was empty, then started shuffling under heaps of clothing, some of which embarrassed him and some he just didn't understand. And then, in plain sight on a chest of drawers, he saw a third bag. It felt heavy enough, but he still had to sift its contents before coming up with a Colt Navy-calibre pocket pistol. He thumbed it to half-cock, spun the cylinder, and saw all five were loaded.

This might, he thought, be going to work.

He packed the gun back into the bag, well wrapped in clothing, then opened a window and shutter – they all seemed to creak – and dropped it into Ranklin's arms, then saw him and Dagner move back around the corner.

In no hurry now, he waited, looking at the greying sky, at the steely glint on the river. It would, he thought wistfully, have been a fine day for a flight to Trieste, and he might never get to handle an aeroplane like the Oriole again. He took a breath of morning air, checked the Browning and moved towards the light switch and the door. This, after all, was the work he knew best.

The gallery itself was dark, but light seeped up from the below. O'Gilroy crawled to the balustrade and peeked cautiously through. Corinna, sprawled but tense, was on a chaise-longue, and when he moved a little further along, he could see Signora Falcone in an armchair next to her. Grouped together, easy to watch. He saw one man immediately, wearing a black suit and pacing slowly, puffing on a cigarette. A pistol dangled from his other hand. But that was all.

O'Gilroy tried to estimate the distance. The gallery itself was a good twenty-five feet high, and the slant made that a range of up to forty feet. Long for a pistol, and the light from table and standing lamps was very blotchy, but he could use the balustrade as a rest when the time came.

Then the man stopped pacing and spoke to someone out of sight beneath that side of the gallery. O'Gilroy waited, then moved round a corner of the gallery to his right, almost in line with the front door and bringing the second man into sight. He was sitting in a hard-backed chair with a shotgun across his knees. If *that* thing went off . . . But O'Gilroy couldn't choose his target; he was to cope with whoever didn't go to the front door.

It was silly how your mouth got dry, waiting for action. Every time.

As at the back, the front of the villa was a terrace under the high portico reached by flights of steps at either end. Only these were well lit from electric lamps on the house walls. Staying against the wall, Ranklin sidled along and stationed himself to the right of the tall double front doors, still against the wall. Dagner came up from the opposite end. They waited.

Ranklin tried to concentrate on what was about to happen yet have no preconception about what the enemy might do. It was best to think of them that way, as the anonymous 'enemy' of his soldiering days, just targets without feelings or loved ones. And they might want Falcone to get inside the house, or rush out to kill him before he could escape. Or – most likely of all – do something Ranklin hadn't thought of.

He cocked the hammer of Corinna's Colt, wishing he'd thought to unload it and test the trigger-pull earlier. Given a choice, he wouldn't have picked a gun that caused so much smoke and had only five shots, but O'Gilroy needed the better weapon. Ranklin just hoped that, if they forced a servant to open the door, he was dressed as one and wouldn't cause the waste of surprise, time and a bullet. And bad luck for himself, of course.

He waited on, feeling his mouth dry up.

Then, with a growl and crunching of gravel, the car swung in through the gates and Matteo tooted the horn as instructed. Then he scuttled out of the far side to leave the car between himself and the house. That was his own idea, and Ranklin didn't blame him for it. The front doors clicked and began to open, and Dagner, following orders perfectly, stepped forward to show himself in the light, hands visible and empty.

Ranklin couldn't see who opened the doors, but heard a quavering voice ask: "*Che cosa volete, signore?*"

But before Dagner could answer, there was a shout from inside the house, a gunshot sounded followed by the boom of the shotgun, and another shot.

O'Gilroy had heard the car as soon as those below did. It prompted a flurry of Italian and arm-waving which suggested an uncertainty about which of the gunmen was in charge. But the one with the pistol – Silvio – seemed to win. He strode towards the front door while the one with the shotgun went to guard the seated women. Signora Falcone made a move to stand, but the shotgun waved her down, and the three of them stabilised into a tableau. O'Gilroy rested the pistol on the balustrade, wrapped his left hand around his right, and aimed at the foreshortened figure below. One squeeze and it – Jankovic had become an 'it' – would fold like a puppet, backbone cut through. But not quite yet.

An elderly servant appeared from the service stairs, buttoning a livery jacket. Silvio herded him towards the front door, out of sight, and there was a long-stretched moment of silence. Perhaps Signora Falcone heard something O'Gilroy couldn't, or perhaps she just snapped: she jumped up, screamed, and ran for the front. Jankovic took a step but didn't fire, perhaps fearing he would scare Falcone away.

She might have counted on that, but O'Gilroy couldn't. He fired as Jankovic moved, and missed. Jankovic whirled round and jerked a trigger at the likeliest source of the shot, the french windows. O'Gilroy heard glass crash as he steadied and fired again.

The shots seemed to blow the servant out of the front door like a cork, but it was Silvio charging out from behind to reach Falcone. Instead of jumping aside, Dagner tried to grab him. Silvio slashed at him with the pistol but they hung together, grappling. Ranklin yelled, Silvio half turned to see and Ranklin took a stride forward and fired from no more than a couple of feet. He saw Silvio jerk backwards before the black-powder smoke blotted him out. Ranklin ducked as he recocked, seeing Silvio's feet and firing somewhere above them, vaguely hoping he wouldn't hit Dagner. The feet vanished.

Blundering through the smoke, Ranklin rammed one of the columns at the edge of the terrace and realised Silvio had gone over. He lay sprawled on the lamplit gravel below, winded, wounded and empty-handed, but squirming slowly.

"Get down there and . . ." Ranklin ordered, but Dagner was on his knees, looking surprised and fingering his head where Silvio had hit him. "Oh *blast* it!" – because Silvio's pistol was down there, too, and he might recover enough to find it and – "Oh *damn*!"

So he carefully shot the enemy dead as he would a twitching wounded rabbit. Then rushed for the house and Corinna. He still had two shots left.

O'Gilroy's pistol had jammed after the second shot. He knew he had hit Jankovic, seen him stagger, but he still had the shotgun and one unfired barrel. As O'Gilroy wrenched at the pistol's slide, Corinna swung to her feet.

"Stay still ye stupid—!" O'Gilroy screamed. She probably didn't even hear; people don't hear things at such moments. But Jankovic heard, raised his head and the gun – as Corinna smashed a table lamp on his head.

Then she seemed to freeze in place, just stood there watching Jankovic pitch forward and skid on the polished floor, piling up a fur rug with his head. The slide of the automatic slammed free, Corinna was clear of the line and O'Gilroy had an easy target.

Ranklin had been delayed by colliding with Signora Falcone in the doorway. He never knew that when he appeared, just a running figure in the patchy light, O'Gilroy had switched aim to him and taken the first pressure on the trigger. Then he switched back to Jankovic and shot him dead.

The sound of the shot faded, leaving just the smell of gunfire. Ranklin reached Corinna and grabbed her arm; it was like trying to pivot a statue.

"Are you all right?"

"I guess so . . ." She seemed dazed. Then suddenly she sagged. "Sit down."

"Hell, I've been sitting all night . . ." But then she slumped onto a sofa. "Is it really all right? Really?"

He sat beside her, clutching her hands. "Yes, yes, all right."

"I knew you'd come . . . No, I didn't see how you could, but I *believed* you would. You and Conall, you're the only ones in the world who could . . ." She freed a hand to gesture at the room, its broken glass, bullet scars, its corpse. "Are they both . . . ?"

"Both dead, yes."

She gave a shiver and was silent for a few moments, then: "I *wanted* them dead, but . . . We made you kill them, didn't we?" She stared at him as if they'd never met before. "How can you stand it? All this killing people? You don't *show* anything!" She looked up at

254

O'Gilroy, who was making a slow business of counting his unfired cartridges. "Neither of you!"

"You're not supposed to show it," Ranklin said.

"But you must – Oh *God*!" She jumped up and fled up the stairs. Ranklin stood, looking after her hesitantly. There was a burst of chatter by the front door; servants were bringing in Falcone in a wheelchair.

O'Gilroy replaced the automatic's magazine with a loud snap.

"You don't show anything," Ranklin said, "and you don't feel anything."

O'Gilroy smiled faintly. "Is that an order, Captain?"

"I suppose it is."

33

The rising sun threw long shadows from the pillars of the back portico and the cypresses beyond, there was coffee on the terrace table and the air was fresh but with an underlying warmth. In all, a perfect Italian autumn day if you could ignore the shattered french windows, a few bullet-holes and two bodies stowed somewhere back in the house. And Ranklin had no trouble ignoring them; they were strictly Falcone's problem. He took another gulp of coffee.

Signora Falcone was also back there, placating the servants, who had been shut up in their basement rooms, and sending out breakfast in dribs and drabs. D'Annunzio had been locked in his room and probably asleep until the shooting started. They had caught a glimpse of him in a vivid bathrobe, demanding explanations; now, presumably, he was getting properly dressed. Falcone himself sat at the table in his wheelchair, still with a rug over his knees, looking pale and serious. But then, he had problems. Ranklin put some smoked ham on a piece of bread.

"The last meal I had," he recalled, "was in jail."

O'Gilroy smiled. "That's the first time for ye, isn't it, Captain? How did ye take to it?"

Ranklin reflected. "Slow. And mostly quiet."

"And how did ye get out?"

"Talked my way, I suppose."

O'Gilroy nodded approvingly. "Always best, that."

Dagner had been sitting quietly. The bang on his head hadn't been serious, and Ranklin suspected the real pain had been to his pride. You reach an age when you should only get into fights when armed – and then shoot first.

Now Dagner said: "I'd like to hear all about your doings in Trieste,

Captain, but time's getting on." He looked at Falcone. "When do you think the aeroplane should take off?"

Ranklin felt he'd been told Sorry, the doctor was wrong, you *have* got cancer. He forced himself to sit upright, trying to make his mind do the same, and managed it in time to hush O'Gilroy with a gesture and say: "Major, may I have a private word with you?"

Dagner gestured gracefully at Falcone. "I don't think we have any secrets by now . . ."

"Major, I'm your second-in-command! Can we please talk?"

"Very well." Dagner followed him to the other side of the terrace, past the french windows. Ranklin was about to start when he realised a dutiful servant had followed, carrying their coffee cups. But he put them down on another table and went back.

They didn't sit. Ranklin said: "Surely the whole thing's off. D'Annunzio was going to drop wild rabble-rousing pamphlets from the aeroplane – or did you know about the aeroplane, and him, from the start?"

"I'm afraid I did," Dagner smiled gravely. "But I thought it best to conceal that. You seemed to have rather fixed ideas about the risk of war."

Ranklin was a bit surprised to find he didn't mind that so much; after all, the man in the field often shouldn't know the whole picture. But: "Didn't you get my cable saying nobody in Trieste believes the Italian workers are going to strike or riot or whatever? Or was I sent there just to get me out of the way?"

Dagner didn't answer that directly. "Falcone knows his own people better than we do and he has no doubts."

"No, he doesn't, does he?" That suddenly struck Ranklin as odd. "He must be very sure . . . Could there be something he hasn't told *you*? Something to do with those Lewis guns you helped him get?"

"For the Italian Army—"

"He pretended that about the aeroplane, too."

"Perhaps the guns were a blind, to help hide the aeroplane in an arms-buying mission."

"I think it's more. The Count—"

"Captain, I know how you've always felt about this affair." Dagner's voice had become stern. "It may be part of how you feel about the Bureau. When it started, I can well believe the Chief

257

had to take whom he could get, and get them any way he could. Like you and O'Gilroy. I'm afraid I know exactly how he got you. You did good work in your time, and did well together in the fracas just now, but the Bureau's future demands more than what we used to call 'Khyber Pass' stuff, like that and the events in Clerkenwell. We're working on a much larger canvas now. And we're getting a new generation, young men who've *volunteered* and can be trained up with the vision to make this service what it deserves to be."

"So O'Gilroy and I are yesterday's newspapers, just to wrap the fish and chips."

"Time passes for all of us." Dagner's tone was calm but urgent. "This could be the first vital step to the service living up to its legend, getting away from its pennyweight antics. If we can make this big a change in the Mediterranean situation, we can do anything. I don't think I'm being overly romantic in foreseeing the day when every statesman in every country will have to take the British Secret Service into account in all he does or proposes. He'll spend half his time wondering if we're dogging his footsteps or already ahead of him. We've learnt the Navy can no longer do everything for us, and certainly the Army can't, not in Europe. But now our service itself could hold the balance of power, become itself one of the Great Powers of Europe.

"Can you and O'Gilroy really share that vision with us, Captain?"

The answer must have been written in Ranklin's expression, because Dagner said sympathetically: "Times change, Captain."

"You've got far more experience," Ranklin said doggedly, "but the secret service I know is grubby and demeaning and frightening, and can involve shooting people who . . . well, you just hope they deserve it—"

"All that and worse," Dagner agreed. "But also *more*. And all the more reason to need a vision, a clear sight of what one is working for."

"Do you trust Falcone, then?"

The change of tack didn't bother Dagner. "Trust him? Not what he says, of course not. But what he *wants*, yes. A political triumph, showing up the Prime Minister as hesitant and feeble by forcing a squabble between Italy and Austria. And we're using that ambition for our own ends."

"But where do the Lewis guns fit in?" Ranklin persisted. "The Count—"

"You mentioned him before. What Count?"

"Falcone's crony in Trieste, he was in jail with me."

"Why should he know anything about them?"

Ranklin stopped, wondering why he hadn't asked that question himself. If the guns weren't going on the aeroplane, why had the Count heard of them? – let alone be so worried that Ranklin had? And, come to that, why should that paper-pushing Austrian Captain Knebel know of such guns?

And then he knew the answer.

Dagner had waited briefly to see if Ranklin had more to say, then turned and strode back to the breakfast table to ask O'Gilroy: "Is the aeroplane ready?"

O'Gilroy glanced past him at Ranklin, coming slowly and thoughtfully up behind, and said carefully: "'Tis in the field, far side of the road. How about Mr d'Annunzio?"

Corinna suddenly appeared and sat down. "I don't think he likes working for the British Secret Service."

Dagner looked at her sternly. "Madam, I'd be grateful if you could exercise a little more discretion—"

"That went out the window when you tried to recruit my brother. We're all family now. Go right ahead." She smiled decorously at Ranklin, seeming quite composed again. She now wore a plain white dress with an apple-green bolero jacket and a wide straw hat. And with both elbows planted firmly on the table, looked very permanent. Catching O'Gilroy's eye, she said: "So I was right, wasn't I? – despite being a weak and feeble woman."

"Never said ye was wrong. Jest that ye wasn't . . . sure."

A bit reluctantly, in front of Corinna, Dagner went on: "Senator, will you have a word with Signore d'Annunzio? But if that doesn't work, anybody can pretend to be him, throwing out the leaflets."

"Would you do it?" Ranklin asked quickly.

"Certainly I'll go. Perhaps better me than you."

"Ah." That seemed to mean something to Ranklin. "But just suppose—" he looked from Dagner to Falcone; "—it fails? – the Austrians laugh it off as a silly prank?"

There was something about Ranklin's tone that made both Corinna and O'Gilroy glance sharply at him, then each other. Dagner, not knowing him so well, just looked impatient, but let Falcone answer. "I know Triestine Italians, Captain Ranklin. The sight of the great patriot flying over – as they will believe – and reading his trumpet words, it will stir them as you do not believe possible."

"Umm . . ." Ranklin looked thoughtful. "I wonder if you believed that, to start with. And then decided it would be even better if they saw the Austrians blow d'Annunzio out of the sky, martyr him with those Lewis guns you sent them. Sorry, Major," he said to Dagner, "but we've all been working for the Senator's vision of Europe."

Everyone was briefly still and silent. Then they all began at once. Ranklin leant over to whisper to O'Gilroy and get a reply.

He overrode the hubbub. "O'Gilroy says he'd been told to drop the leaflets over the old town, around the Castle. So the Lewis guns'll be on the battlements there, manned by the Castle guard, not the coming-and-going garrison."

Dagner said: "Captain Ranklin, these are fantasies. But they come very close to that *sabotage* you spoke of."

"No, Major, I *know* this. First I thought those guns must be for the aeroplane, really they're for shooting it down. Falcone sent them to the Count who presented them to the Austrian Commander."

Falcone waved the idea away. "Ridiculous! Quite impossible! Would I arrange for such a popular patriot as Gabriele d'Annunzio to be—"

"That's just what makes him a good sacrifice. And I was in jail with the Count yesterday. I heard all about him sucking up to the Austrians so they'd think the gift of the guns was just part of that, not its purpose. But when he thought of being in their hands when they realised they'd been tricked into publicly slaughtering a great Italian, he was going berserk, and he talked . . ." He delicately left the sentence open.

"Hold hard," O'Gilroy said. "Ye say the aeroplane was going to be shot down by machine-guns?" He turned on Falcone. "*And what about the pilot?*"

Falcone licked his lips but said nothing, watching Dagner. Very deliberately, O'Gilroy took a pistol from his pocket and laid it beside his cup. "Seems like a feller needs some protection around here."

Corinna suddenly caught on, but turned her fury on Dagner. "D'you mean it would have been *Andrew?*"

She pitched her coffee at his waistcoat, and at that moment d'Annunzio, freshly lavendered and in an uncreased cream linen suit, came onto the terrace. He stopped and spread his arms delightedly. "Ah, such drama! And so early! Are these—" he gestured at Ranklin and Dagner; "—yet more English secret agents?"

"Yes they are," Corinna snapped, "and since the plot was to get you bumped off, you'd better sit down and listen."

Ranklin reassured her: "I'm afraid Major Dagner didn't know, or he wouldn't have volunteered to go. He – all of us – were being used by Falcone and the Count."

Perhaps Dagner winced at that. Corinna switched her glare to Falcone, and asked O'Gilroy: "Are you thinking of shooting him?"

"Oh, I'm thinking of it, all right," he said softly, and picked up the pistol – though perhaps to stop her grabbing it.

Falcone still didn't say anything. And unless we shoot him, Ranklin thought, there's really nothing we can do to him. Except leave him here with the wreckage. And bodies.

D'Annunzio had been enjoying himself without in the least understanding. "Now please, someone explain to me."

Ranklin stood up. "They planned to have you killed over Trieste, made a martyr like Oberdan, that's all. Don't fret about it." He patted d'Annunzio's shoulder, leaving a smudge of powder-smoke and oil on the fresh suit. "Come on, let's get away from here. Major?"

Corinna pushed back her chair so firmly that it fell over. Dagner got to his feet slowly, dreamily, making no move to mop the coffee off his front. "Then he was *using* me . . . I let him use the whole service . . ."

Ranklin gripped his arm and he let himself be led away from the table. "In Europe things are . . . well, perhaps different."

"I thought we had a chance to . . . Was I really so wrong, Captain? Was my whole vision wrong?"

"No, no, of course not," Ranklin reassured him desperately. "Let's just get *away*."

A spark of life seemed to re-enter Dagner. He smiled wryly. "And then what? Do you leave me alone in the library with a pistol on the desk?"

"For God's sake!" Ranklin felt everything was sliding out of control.

Then Corinna said gently: "Why don't you just get back home to your wife, Major Dagner?"

He smiled with relief at the thought. "Yes. Yes, of course. She'll understand. . ." And he seemed to relax.

Corinna must have packed like an impatient burglar; less than ten minutes later, servants were carrying her bags downstairs and out into the garden, where threads of smoke were rising from the steam-launch.

Signora Falcone met them in the hall still wearing last night's evening dress. But although it looked as limp as yesterday's bouquet, she herself was very poised, even imperious. "I have told Matteo not to load your bags. I have learned what you were saying, but I said you must not leave before noon and that still holds good." Matteo stepped out behind her, squat and solid, sort-of-casually holding a shotgun.

"Oh *no*," Ranklin said wearily. "It's all over. Go and ask your husband."

"He's a sick man, easily depressed. But we still have the aeroplane—"

"Ye don't, ye know," O'Gilroy said. "On account I smashed it up, landing in the dark. Only the wheels and propeller and a strut and the cowling, but a week's work, mebbe."

Corinna and Signora Falcone spoke at once; the consensus was: "You mean all this time . . . ?"

"The Captain said to keep quiet, he wanted to hear the rest of the plan out. And we *was* dashing to yer rescue."

For the first time, they saw Signora Falcone lose her elegance. She sagged, hunched as if she suddenly wore a rucksack of rocks, staring at the floor. Then in a tired, soft voice she spoke to Matteo and he laid the shotgun aside.

O'Gilroy took his hand out of his pocket.

"And now," Signora Falcone whimpered, "you're leaving me with all . . . this." A gesture scooped in the whole night's happenings.

"I'm sure you'll manage," Corinna said crisply. "And I shall watch your husband's political career with great interest."

Then slapped her hard enough to spin her round.

The baggage was already loaded into the launch. Ranklin peered under the canvas canopy. "Where's Major Dagner?"

O'Gilroy shrugged and indicated his own small bag. "I was packing. Thought he came down ahead of us."

Corinna turned her exam Italian on the servants. After a bit of gesticulation, she reported: "They saw him going down the garden ten minutes ago. Towards the river."

The three of them instinctively looked down into the slow, placid, deep Brenta.

Ranklin said: "Oh Christ."

O'Gilroy said: "He's an expert. If he don't want to be found . . ." He shrugged.

Corinna said softly: "Maybe he did go home to his wife."

34

The Commander still had the curled moustache he had grown for his curtailed Bavarian holiday, and a new mannerism of stroking it every few seconds – either from pride or to make sure it hadn't escaped.

"Why the devil have you written all this down?" he grumbled, waving Ranklin's report. "Did you expect me to leave *this* lurking in the files?"

"No, sir. I expect you'll burn it. But it helped clarify my thoughts, getting it all onto paper."

"And at the end of it all – making the Bureau a legend and a Great Power and believing his wife was still alive and storming a police station – you don't conclude the man was *mad*?"

"No, sir. I think perhaps he'd been a sp— an agent too long. Living in a make-believe world . . . And he talked about us having a mission—"

"Dangerous," the Commander grunted.

"—and the loneliness of the job . . . Perhaps pretending to himself his wife was still alive made it less lonely." It sounded pretentious as he said it, so he added a shrug to water it down.

But the Commander had his own thoughts. "I should have been more suspicious when Indian Army Intelligence handed him over so easily. You don't let your best men go. And I shouldn't have left him alone so soon. Hoped you and your blasted paperwork would keep him busy."

"He *was* doing it all for the Bureau."

"For his idea of the Bureau," the Commander said sharply. "There's only one idea of the Bureau that counts, and that's mine. I suppose he never thought *I* might have an idea of what we might some day become? And how to get there?" Then he calmed down. "Would you have called him a decent upright English gentleman?"

"Yes." Ranklin was surprised. "Of course."

The Commander sighed. "Without thinking how difficult it would be to turn decent, upright Englishmen into useful agents? – around Europe, anyway. Goes against everything they've ever been taught. Maybe it's easier on the frontier, dealing with tribesmen, fuzzy-wuzzies, whatever-they-call-'em. Cheating *them* don't count. But then he comes home, not on the frontier now, but where the real troubles are, and the real crooks. But he sees it as a chance to have world visions, start a crusade . . ."

"I think he trusted Senator Falcone too much, I mean trusted his own idea of what Falcone was up to, and never believed he might risk, even want, a war . . . But he was a good example to the new chaps."

The Commander gave him a fierce stare and then an explosive grunt. "If any one of those new chaps of ours had stayed where he was a few weeks longer, he'd've been drummed out. Or court-martialled. Of course it didn't show on their reports," he answered Ranklin's expression. "If it had got that far they'd have been out of my reach. But each one of 'em had his hand in some shady financial affair or up the skirt of the colonel's daughter."

After a few moments of rather stunned re-appraisal, Ranklin ventured: "Then you didn't tell Major Dagner any of this, sir?"

"Up to him to spot it, if he'd been more open-minded – and less taken with Italian senators. Anyway, not the done thing to talk about, what? We'd given them a fresh start in the Bureau, chance to put it all behind them, forget the past . . . and all that balls. I picked 'em for bounders, even cads, and they'd better stay that way."

"But you're telling me . . ."

The Commander smiled sunnily. "Thought you'd have spotted it by now. After all, you're one of 'em. Two, if you include your bandit chum O'Gilroy. Why did you think I came after you?"

Because you got the wrong end of the stick, Ranklin's whirling thoughts protested. My bankruptcy was all my brother's doing, I *am* a decent upright English gentleman . . .

. . . well, of course, I've learnt to be a bit suspicious and devious and a little bit unscrupulous, just to survive in this business, but—

"It's all in your report, you know." The Commander waved it. "Have another look, if you've any doubts about who you really are. Oh, I'm sure you've got your self-justifications, we all need 'em, long as we keep 'em quiet and just do the damn job. Have you thought what you did at the end? – when you'd worked out what those Lewis guns were really for? You *could* have tried persuading Major Dagner quietly and privately. I don't say you'd have succeeded, but you chose instead to humiliate him in front of the others, destroy him."

There was a long silence. The Commander struck a match, lit the report and dropped it into his big glass ashtray. "Frankly, I'm very glad you did; it got rid of him, and I don't know how I'd have done it otherwise." He struck another match, put it to his pipe and said between puffs: "But who knows? – perhaps he was right, and we're wrong. But then, spying's wrong, ain't it? So probably it's best done by us wrong 'uns."